orig. 5.95

P9-CAG-201

THE GOD
OF THE
LABYRINTH
Colin Wilson

Copyright © 1970 by Colin Wilson
Originally published by Rupert Hart-Davis, London.

Cover photomicrograph by Karl Mills, copyright © 1982
Cover design by Michael Patrick Cronan
Wingbow Press books are published and distributed
by Bookpeople, 2940 Seventh Street, Berkeley, California
94710

Standard Book Number 0-914728-39-3
Library of Congress Catalog Card Number 82-050968

First America edition September 1982

No, I want sky not sea, prefer the larks to shrimps,
And never dive so deep but that I get a glimpse
O' the blue above, breath of the air around. Elvire,
I seize—by catching at the melted beryl here,
The tawny hair that has just trickled off—Fifine.

BROWNING

'God keep from hurt', said he, 'the good fellow whose great codpiece has just saved his life. God keep from harm the one whose long codpiece has been worth to him, in one day, one hundred and sixty thousand and nine crowns. God keep from hurt the one who, by his long codpiece, has saved a whole city from dying of famine. And by God, I'm going to make a book *On the Advantages of Long Codpieces* as soon as I have time'.

In fact, he did compose a large book, and a very good one, complete with diagrams; but it has not been published yet, as far as I know.

RABELAIS, Bk II, Ch. 15

Esmond Donelly died in December 1832, at the age of eighty-four. Towards the end of his life, he became fascinated by numbers, and corresponded with the great mathematician Gauss, who quotes him in the preface to the fifth edition of the *Disquisitiones Arithmeticae*. It is in one of his letters to Gauss that Esmond speaks about the 'magical' properties of the number 137—which is, of course, a prime. Coming across a copy of this letter the other day in the archives of Mr Xalide Nuri, I was thrilled to realise that this book will be published exactly 137 years after Esmond's death. I take it as an auspicious sign.

The story of my 'quest for Esmond Donelly' begins on April 10 of this year. In January, I had flown to New York to begin a lecture tour that took me from Florida to Maine, from New Mexico to Seattle. I had taken my family with me—my wife Diana and my daughter Maureen (Mopsy), aged three, but since it was impractical for them to travel with me, they stayed with friends in New Haven, and I spent weekends with them whenever I was on the east coast. After two months or so of one-night-stands, the strain was beginning to tell, and I struggled to preserve a degree of detachment by writing every day in a journal notebook. On re-reading these entries recently, it struck me that there could be no simpler way of beginning this account than quoting them exactly as I wrote them.

It is eight thirty in the morning, eastern time—five thirty for me, since I flew in from Portland, Oregon, yesterday. I am propped up on my bed in the campus guest room, drinking tea and eating buttered whole-wheat biscuits; at nine thirty I have to address convocation. They tell me Dylan Thomas slept in this room, and caused a scandal by allowing the football team from Koyukuk, the male university on the other side of town, to sleep on the floor and vomit in the washbasin. That man's energy must have been fantastic. After nine weeks of lecturing around America, I'm in a state of glassy-eyed exhaustion. I always know when I'm getting run-down because objects suddenly take on a curious, intense quality. Diana packed me a cake of ordinary green kitchen soap—motels provide tiny cakes that slip out of your hand in the shower—and when I went to pick it up this morning I had to stop and stare. It's hard to explain the sensation. It wasn't simply that it seemed as green as a piece of malachite; it also seemed soft, almost fuzzy, as if it was trying to expand. Seen in these moments, objects seem to have another dimension or sense : hardness, colour, smell, taste...and *something else*, quite distinct from these. In a human being you might call it personality, or even soul.

I walk around the room in this dream-like state, feeling like a new-born baby; oddly helpless, yet strangely happy. When I poured hot water on this tea—sent to us from Findlater's in Dublin—I had a momentary sensation of dissolving in the rising steam, and the smell of the tea became exotic, almost frightening.

These tours are killing. My agent wants me to do another one next year, but the idea revolts me. The best moments are sitting alone on airports, eating hamburgers and drinking fresh orange juice. Occasionally in these moments, I achieve a beautiful detachment, a sense of the sheer size of this country, and feel suddenly contented. It also happened two nights ago, sitting in the motel bar in Portland, watching cars and buses slashing through the black rain, tearing the reflection of the neon sign into red shrapnel. And I never fail to experience a certain delight as I approach an airport bookstall, even if I only have five minutes between changing planes, and I already have more paperbacks than I can

7

carry. At O'Hare yesterday, I bought Apollinaire's *Debauched Hospodar*, a surrealistic piece of pornography, and I read about the poor devil's miserable life while waiting for the plane. And then it came to me with great clarity : my business and the business of all writers : to refuse to be a part of everyday life, to stand aside, even if this demands a pose of brutality or nihilism. We must not be absorbed. There is a perfectly simple relation between the mind and its environment. The environment carries us along like a stream, and the mind is like a small engine that can carry the boat upstream—or at least enable it to stay in the same place. While the engine works, man is fundamentally healthy; if it stops, he is no better than a piece of driftwood.

Convocation went well enough—I talked about the nature of poetry and mysticism. Afterwards, half a dozen girls dragged me along to the Coffee Shop and asked me questions. They'd all read my Diary (which the American publisher issued under the sickening title *The Sex Diary of Gerard Sorme*—a court case about it in Boston cost me every bloody penny of the royalties), and they were full of questions about Cunningham. Strange— that even through the unflattering medium of my pages, Cunningham's personality can still exercise its fascination over girls. I'd love to see him turned loose in an American girls' college— I think he would have met his match. The most aggressive sexual impulse in the world would drown in this sea of unripe American girlhood. At the University of Portland, I gave a seminar with the girls sitting around in a circle—a marvellous panorama of long legs and mini-skirts. But when a group of them took me out to lunch, I realised that the American girl hasn't changed since James's Daisy Miller. The apples look appetising enough, but they turn out to be made of wood.

A curious coincidence. I had lunch with Mervyn Dillard, head of the English department here, and he asked me if I knew anything about Esmond Donelly. Apparently Donelly was a famous Irish rake, contemporary of Sheridan, who spent his life begetting bastards in the area of Galway. Some of his correspondence with Rousseau was published in Berne around 1800 under the title *Of the Deflowering of Maids*, although apparently his family declared the work to be a forgery. Now Grove Press are issuing the book in America, with an Introduction by Mervyn Dillard. I told Dillard that I've lived in Galway for seven years and never heard of Donelly. Either he's been totally forgotten, or his memory has been suppressed.

When I got back to the guest room, there was an envelope from my agent full of mail, including a letter from some people called Linden Press, which I insert here:

Linden Press, 565 Fifth Avenue, New York, N.Y. 10016
April 6, 1969

Dear Mr Sorme,

I gather from the interview in the *New York Times* Book Review that you are lecturing over here. The interview mentioned that you were returning shortly, so I hope this letter reaches you quickly.

I've been an admirer of your *Sex Diary* ever since its publication. The other day, I remembered that you'd dated the Introduction from Moycullen. In *Memoirs of An Irish Rake*, which we are publishing in the fall, Esmond Donelly describes seducing both illegitimate daughters of the priest at Moycullen, Father Riordan.

In view of your local knowledge, I wonder if you would be interested in writing an Introduction to our edition? I might also add that we would be happy to commission a book about Donelly, if you should feel any inclination to undertake such a work.

In the event of your receiving this letter before leaving the country, I wonder if you would call me collect at this number, so we might discuss a meeting?

Looking forward to hearing from you, I am

Yours sincerely
Howard Fleisher

Having an hour to spare before the car would take me to the airport, I phoned the number he gave me. He sounded amiable enough—wasn't disappointed that I'd never heard of Donelly before today. I explained that I don't get into New York until

9

late next Friday, and he'll meet me at Kennedy and take me out to his home on Long Island. This coincidence about Donelly impresses me. Such things happen with absurd frequency. The other day, I heard the name of the Russian poet Lomonosov on the car radio; a few hours later, I saw it in an encyclopedia when I was looking up something else. The coincidence made me wonder, so the next time I went into a campus book store, I asked the manageress if she'd got anything by Lomonosov. ' It's funny you should ask—a book of his poems came in yesterday.' I bought it, read the Introduction, and immediately decided I have a magnificent character for a novel. Ten years ago, I would have regarded such a procedure as superstition. Now I eagerly follow the lead of coincidence.

April 11, Wilkes-Barre airport

Ten minutes before my lecture this morning, the head of the English department handed me my correspondence. There was a letter from Jim Smyth in San Francisco telling me that Helga Neisse has committed suicide—she jumped from the Berkeley tower, somehow climbing over the protective wire they've put there to prevent such things. I was feeling tired, rather bored, when the letter reached me; as soon as I read it, I seemed to wake up, and the fatigue became an illusion.

I also feel guilt, although it is a pointless guilt. I met Helga Neisse through Jim, who attends nude parties where everyone takes psychedelics and the girls paint their bodies. She was tall, dark-haired, rather listless; she had spent the previous night with Jim. We spent a couple of hours eating fish and chips and drinking pints of Youngers in the Edinburgh Castle while Jim talked astrology. He said the war in Vietnam would go on for at least another year because the stars were in conflict. And she suddenly said : Why did the stars bother to influence human existence when it was basically meaningless anyway? Wouldn't it be better to leave everything to chance? When I mentioned I was lecturing at Berkeley at midday the next day, she offered to drive me out there.

She came to the hotel the next morning, and said she'd spent the night reading my *Methods and Techniques of Self Delusion.*

10

She certainly looked as if she'd been up all night. I hate discussing my books, but I got the feeling she was on the edge of a breakdown and I ought to try to help. What amazed—and baffled—me was that she took it *absolutely for granted* that life is meaningless. She said this to me as if she was saying that water was wet. When I tried to explain that I didn't think so, she said that this was the message she'd got from my book: human beings are incapable of being honest with themselves, so they turn their lives into little plays in which they are the central character; they invent the fantasies called religions, philosophies, and so on. I tried to explain that, up to this point, her interpretation was accurate enough; but that I was being destructive only to clear the ground for real thinking. What the mystics experience is not religion or philosophy, but reality. She asked in a hopeless—almost annoyed—tone : ' What is reality? ' I said she didn't have to ask that, because she already knew. If you are thirsty, and you take a long cool drink, the feeling of the drink going down your throat is reality. It is quite different from talking about a drink, or thinking about one. Human beings also have an odd capacity for experiencing a kind of emotional reality (as distinguished from physical). It was what I experienced the other day with the bar of soap, or what I experience at least once a year when I first smell the spring. The senses seem to go very calm, and you get the sense of really seeing things, as Wordsworth saw the Thames from Westminster Bridge. And there is a feeling exactly like the real taste of cool water against your throat. I told her that her feeling of futility was a kind of reality-starvation, which produces the same kind of exhaustion and misery as real starvation or thirst.

I lectured at Berkeley, and a students' committee took me out to lunch; Helga came too. Afterwards, they took us to the top of the clock tower, and our host told us that there had been several suicides in the past year or so—one more than from the similar tower at Stanford. I suppose this gave her the idea.

We drove back to town and she talked all the way. Then she said she wanted to do some shopping, and asked me to go with her. I said firmly that I wanted to rest—too many hours of talking and lecturing leave me exhausted. But I invited her out to a meal in Chinatown. I read Hölderlin and then slept until seven. She came to the hotel at eight; we had some wine in my room, then walked to Chinatown. She told me she'd spent the afternoon walking around the docks. I began to understand why she seemed so exhausted. We drank Californian wine with the meal, and she seemed to relax. She talked about her problems—her marriage to a homosexual whom she'd failed to 'reform', affairs with various phonies—she couldn't resist anything that sounded like a poet, painter or philosopher. And I began to see the real trouble : laziness, weakness, desire for something to *happen* to her, for some Avatar to appear and give her the Answer. When we were into the second bottle of Almedan, she suddenly became very complimentary—explained that she had been trying to meet me since I was here in January. She explained she wasn't asking anything of me except that I should be a friend, write to her now and then, and so on. I said I'd do my best. ' It's not that I want to sleep with you. I sleep around too much.' My feeling was that there was nothing I wanted less than to sleep with her. On the previous evening, I'd thought her attractive, and rather envied Jim his night with her. And ten years ago I'd have slept with her anyway, without thinking about the consequences. Now I was clearly aware that she was trying to bargain with me, offering me something *in exchange* for something I could give her. I didn't want to be her debtor.

We spent an hour in the City Lights Bookshop, met some friends of hers, and moved to a café across the road for more wine. At midnight, I said I had to get back—I had to be up the next morning to lecture at Palo Alto. She said she'd walk down to Sutter with me because she needed the fresh air. At the corner of Sutter, I tried to persuade her to get into a taxi, and she said she needed coffee to sober up. So, very reluctantly, I let her come to my room. (The night clerk is a friend of mine, and only winked.) I didn't think she had seduction in mind—she seemed to be just lonely—but I was determined it wouldn't happen anyway. She spent ten minutes in the bathroom while I made coffee. I went in the bathroom, leaving her to pour the coffee, and it reeked of perfume—I still can't imagine what she had been doing with it, for she wasn't wearing any. When I came out, she was lying on one of the twin beds with her eyes closed, looking very pale. I asked her if she felt all right and she said no, but she'd be ok in a moment. I put the coffee on the table at the side of the bed, and she reached out and groped for my hand. Then she said : 'Would you kiss me please, just once?' I was still being paternal; I patted her on the head, said, 'Yes, yes, all right', and bent over her. She had a soft and attractive mouth, even though the lower lip was slightly chapped. Kissing her was a shock—like what I'd been saying to her earlier about swallowing a cool drink and merely thinking about it. She gave a kind of moan, and lay there passively; when I tried to pull back, she made the same noise in her throat. It was an uncomfortable position—my neck was aching—so I put one knee on the bed. She suddenly began breathing deeply and regularly, as if immensely relieved, and her hand brushed against my trousers, as if by accident, and rested there. The inevitable response occurred. I had been curious all day whether she was wearing stockings or tights. I knew this was my last chance. If they were tights, or if she was wearing a panty girdle, I could linger a moment politely, then tell her to drink her coffee, while my expectations subsided. If not...Her thighs opened as my hand touched her knee; then I reached the bare flesh above the stocking. A moment later, my hand reached the crossroads, and I found she was wearing no pants. She must have removed them in the bathroom. By this time she'd unzipped my fly and was holding me. Even at this point, I knew we could stop, even though I was like a battering ram and she was already moving herself against my hand. But it would have seemed pointless. Within seconds, I was inside her. I must admit there was a terrific surge of sheer delight; it was pure male and female coupling, without personalities. Her warmth, as she closed around me, seemed predestined. It lasted only a short time. We were both so excited that we reached a climax within seconds. I lay inside her for a moment, looking at her face; she looked very peaceful. Then she said : 'Let's take our clothes off and get into bed.' It was a reasonable suggestion, and we followed it. But the rest of the night wasn't the same. She had got what she wanted; I had got what I had been determined to avoid. What bothered me most was that she didn't seem capable of

13

affection. She enjoyed the sex with a physical abandon I haven't seen very often—proving again that promiscuous women are not necessarily frigid. But in between, she wanted to talk about her problems, about men, about psychology, about my lecture...We had to talk in whispers, so as not to disturb the people in the next rooms.

On the train to Palo Alto the next morning, I cursed myself for not bringing my journal notebook, for I suddenly saw that I had important material. I hadn't wanted to go to bed with Helga because I knew in advance that it would leave nothing behind. Then why do I get such physical pleasure from Diana, although I've been married to her for seven years? For years now, I've been trying to define the basis of the sexual impulse. Why *should* a man want to thrust his erect penis into a woman? There must be a reason; to say it's an instinct is no answer. When Mopsy was a baby, I used to wonder why she sucked her thumb and held her ear with the other hand; then I noticed other babies doing it. I wonder if this is connected with breast feeding— whether a baby automatically reaches out for the other nipple as it sucks, and treats its ear as a nipple? There ought to be an analogous answer to the sexual impulse.

Helga told me a strange story. When she first went to college, she was a very repressed young lady from the middle west who held strong views on sex before marriage, especially as her mother had told her that a husband can always tell if his wife is not a virgin, and would probably desert her on the spot. For six months or so, she went out with various boys, permitted a little petting, but stopped them short if they tried to remove her pants. At the beginning of her junior year, she moved in with another girl, who told her that she had solved the problem by means of an artificial vagina. This object fitted around the loins by means of a belt; it was little more than a kind of rubber tube that lay on the pubis, and the opening slit had to be moistened with olive oil. Helga said she didn't think it would work; her boyfriend had already told her he would break with her if she didn't come across. But she tried it, borrowing her friend's artifice. To her surprise, the boyfriend didn't mind in the least. They slept together in motels at weekends; she insisted on wearing panties, in case the boy got carried away. But she said he didn't even try to perform normal intercourse; he brought on her climax by caressing her after he'd had his own. She subsequently used the same thing with two more boyfriends, believing that she was being marvellously virtuous, until one night *she* got carried away and asked the boyfriend to make love normally.

I remembered that Diana had told me the same sort of thing about her earliest sexual experiences. She once quarrelled with her boyfriend, and went to bed with a man she'd met only that afternoon, to spite him. Before they even went to his room, she explained that she was a virgin and wanted to remain one. He agreed immediately, and they spent the night petting without actual intercourse.

Now I suddenly saw that this is an important clue. *Of course* he hadn't demurred. There was Diana, a pretty, middle-class girl with a slim figure and demure manners. He wants to *know* her. She is like something in a museum case with the label ' Do not touch '. There is a story in Maupassant of a criminal on the run who poses as a lady's maid, and helps a beautiful woman to dress and undress for months. *This* is how a man wants to know a woman who sits opposite him on the Underground, or stands at the perfume counter in an expensive store. The actual penetration of her vagina is the least important part of it; merely the final symbol of surrender. He can look at her and think : ' I've had her.' But he has had her almost as completely once he has spent a night in her room, watched her take off her clothes, let his hands wander all over her body and felt hers on his, watched her dressing and combing her hair, seen the way she applies cosmetics, the kind of toothpaste she uses. The hunger of the male for the female is the hunger for her *female-ness*, her alien femininity, for *everything about her*.

Again, I was always fascinated by Kleist's story of the Marquise Von O——, in which Russian soldiers invade a town and drag off the young countess to rape her. She is rescued by a Russian officer, and faints from her ordeal. A few months later, to her amazement, she discovers that she is pregnant, and is so certain of her innocence that she puts an advertisement into the newspapers asking the father to come forward. Eventually, the father does so—it is the young officer who rescued her. Kleist had the sense to make the story end happily; most of the romantics would have had her committing suicide out of shame and the officer becoming a monk out of remorse. Goethe apparently said harsh things about Kleist's story, declaring that it was too absurd to be true to life. Which demonstrates that Kleist knew more about human nature than Goethe—or at least, about sex. There is no need to postulate that the officer is a rake. He rescues her in the spirit of a knight of the round table. When she faints, he places her tenderly on a divan. She lies as still as if asleep; he feels curiosity about what her lower half would look like unclothed, for he knows he has only to raise her skirt to her waist to see her naked—these were the days before pants. He does it cautiously, afraid she will wake up, slips his hand between the thighs to open the legs. And then it doesn't matter if she wakes; suddenly all that matters is to get his tight trousers off and bring their nakedness into contact. He does it and finds her easy to enter; he has an orgasm immediately. Ashamed, he withdraws, expecting to see her stirring; but she lies still. He adjusts her clothes, then his own (he would do it in that order); then he goes away for water. When he returns, she is sitting up, and regards him with gratitude. This is the moment; will she know that a stranger has visited her darkest recess? But she is so bruised and shaken that she notices nothing…Yes, Kleist understood that raging male curiosity that thirsts for knowledge of the female as dry ground thirsts for water. Goethe must have understood something of it too. What else was it that made Faust seduce Margaret? She is an ordinary peasant girl, not particularly bright, and if he was her doctor, he would simply feel paternal about her. But she is alien, strange; he is not even sure what a peasant girl wears under her Sunday frock; he badly wants to know.

Which explained my relative indifference to Helga the morning after. She had already laid herself bare to me; her defeat, her laziness, her longing for attention and reassurance. There was only one more thing to find out : was she wearing tights or pants? That first time of entering her was natural sex, the kind of sex that animals must have when they couple. After that, our minds were back to dilute it…

She has written to me twice since then: the first time to describe her involvement with a middle-aged company director, the second to announce her engagement to a student at San Francisco State. I hadn't replied to her second letter when I heard of her death.

And the news of her death brought a shock of reality. I realised that the fatigue of this lecture tour is false. It is the result of the same lack of contact with reality that led to her suicide. The last time I saw her—I left San Francisco on the night plane the same day—was at Jim Smyth's apartment. He had put a record on his gramophone and lowered the needle on to it. Nothing happened —silence. He checked the loudspeakers by putting his ear against them, and peered at the needle to see if it was coated with fluff. He lowered the pick-up arm again. Nothing. Then I noticed that the arm was lowered by a pneumatic device designed to prevent scratching, and I suggested that it wasn't lowering the needle completely on to the record. He got down on all fours and peered at it; no, he said, the needle was touching the record all right. Nevertheless, he made some adjustment to the pneumatic device; immediately, the room filled with music. It had lowered the needle to within a hundredth of an inch of the record—so close that the gap could not be seen with the naked eye. Yet the gap was enough to make the difference between silence and music.

What fascinates me is the gap between the mind and reality. Extreme boredom widens the gap; so does fatigue. But the gap can be so slight that to all intents and purposes we are in contact with reality. Then a sudden shock fills the inner-being with music, and you know that there was no contact. You were deceived. You were in your private vacuum, slowly suffocating to death.

Later—en route New York

I owe a debt of gratitude to Helga: her death has snapped me out of the state of will-lessness I was letting myself drift into. Human beings are like car tyres; to get the best results, you need to keep them inflated. If your tyre is flat, and you drive it a couple of miles, you've destroyed it. The same when the will is flat. I've been allowing my will to get steadily flatter over the past week or so, and wondering why I get so exhausted.

17

De Sade argues that all men are sadists, because even the most virtuous get a certain odd satisfaction from contemplating the misfortunes of others. He's right, but it's nothing to do with sadism. For some strange reason, boredom makes us lose all sense of reality. You might think, for example, that a man who has been rescued from a tent at the South Pole would be incapable of boredom for the rest of his life, because every time he began to take things for granted, he'd simply recall how close he'd been to death, and see his present circumstances as entirely delightful, no matter how dull they are. In fact, such a man would be as easily bored as a man who has spent his whole life working on the same farm; perhaps more so. The misfortune of others sometimes awakens us from our strange sleep.

I am fascinated by this flaw in human nature—implied by the existence of boredom. Eradicate it, and you would have the superman.

Saturday, April 12, Great Neck, Long Island

Fatigue makes good resolutions difficult to keep. I arrived at Kennedy late last night, and was met by Howard Fleisher—small, Italianate, full of bounce and enthusiasm, who drove me out to this place—fine house on a cliff-top, which he says he bought from the widow of a famous Mafioso who was killed by Murder Incorporated. Fleisher is one of these people whose manner implies that you've *got* to like him, because you and he have so much in common...I kept expecting him to put one arm round my shoulders and call me ' kid '. He's obviously in a great many businesses besides publishing—in fact, I suspect Linden Press is a sideline acquired for tax purposes. As we drove back, he told me solemnly that he knew immediately that the *Sex Diary* wasn't straight pornography, that I'm a sincere person with ideas I want to express...I cringed. We got back to his place at 11.30, and the door was opened by a strikingly beautiful negress whom he introduced as his secretary. There was also a younger girl, Beverley, who seemed dowdy by comparison; she shares a flat with Sarah (the secretary) and is studying at secretarial school. The girls had laid on an excellent cold supper, including crab and lobster. By the time I'd eaten, and drunk two

18

beers, I was feeling less hostile to my host, but so tired I could hardly keep my eyes open. But Howard (he insisted on Christian names immediately) actually got bouncier and more enthusiastic after midnight. He talked about the new freedom in literature, the revolt on the campuses, and said there was a new generation to cater for, a generation hungering for ideas, for freedom of expression, for straight, honest talking. I tried to find out what he meant by ideas and freedom of expression, but as far as I could discover, he meant freedom to express aggressive impulses without restraint and uninhibited pornography.

He described the play he means to finance in an off-Broadway production. A young girl brings home a drunken football player after a college game, and he forces her on the bed and rapes her. The rape is supposed to go on throughout the play, and this is symbolised by projecting her face, as she lies on her back, on to a screen at the back of the stage. She imagines all the men she would have preferred to take her virginity, beginning with her father, and the play is a series of fantasy scenes in which she becomes increasingly abandoned. As each seduction scene comes to an end, the face on the screen convulses with ecstasy. Each scene begins with the seducer as he is in real life—polite, re-pressed, etc—and then her imagination transforms the situation until it ends in bed. At the end of the play, the football player staggers off her, gasping, and says : ' Sorry, I just can't go on ', and she gets up, smooths down her underskirt, and says : ' Weak-ling.'

The two girls thought it a marvellous plot, and I had to pre-tend to be enthusiastic too. Finally, at about 3 a.m., he showed me to my room and, as he left, winked and pointed to the room next door. 'Beverley's in there, if you want her.' I muttered something about it being very kind of him, and fell into a coma-tose slumber. Just before I fell asleep I remembered that I'd forgotten to call Diana in New Haven.

This morning, Beverley woke me up at about nine with break-fast, and asked me if I slept well. I thought I caught a satirical inflection, and wondered if she's as demure as she looks. I was feeling depressed. Listening to Howard for three hours last night had got me into a state where all I wanted to do was get out.

19

I wanted to shout : ' Let me alone. I hate every damn thing you stand for.' I don't think he'd have been offended. He'd have said : 'No you don't. You only think you do...', and talked faster than ever.

He came in while I was eating my breakfast—an English breakfast of eggs, bacon and marmalade—and handed me the manuscript of Donelly's book. It was only about sixty typescript pages long. I asked what had happened to the rest, and he said : ' Yes. Well...er...that's the problem.' After another half-hour of voluble explanations and assurances that he always stands by his friends, I began to gather what I should have realised last night. He's jealous of Grove Press for publishing de Sade and *My Secret Life* before anyone else thought of it. But he doesn't see why he shouldn't go one better and produce every volume mentioned in Ashbee's *Bibliography of Prohibited Books*. He is starting with a translation of the confessions of Brother Achazius of Düren, a Capuchin monk who ran a society in which he flagellated and screwed his female followers. Howard lent me the typescript—it was definitely one of those ' books you read with one hand '. He has also commissioned a book called *Scandalous Priests*, although he did not explain where he got the material.

Finally, we got to the point. He will pay me $5,000 to do research around Moycullen and Ballycahane (Donelly's birth-place), which will cover the cost of an Introduction. If I can produce more ' material ' for the book itself—i.e. if I can unearth more manuscript by Donelly, or forge it myself—he will pay me a further $10,000. He obviously doesn't really mind whether I find more of Donelly or write it myself. He points out that Alex Trocchi wrote most of the fifth volume of Frank Harris's *My Life and Loves*, and has since published it under his own name. The main thing is that I should be prepared to take the blame, if any arises.

The prospect of that much money is tempting. We shall be lucky if we have $500 left of the money I've made on this tour. I told Fleisher I'd think about it, and he left me with the type-script.

I spent the rest of the morning in bed, getting increasingly depressed as I read Donelly. I don't understand how he managed to keep the friendship of people like Sheridan and Rousseau. He seems to be just a dirty-minded ruffian. Worse still, I suspect he is simply a liar. The women he seduces—starting with his sister and the maidservant—all sound like versions of the same wish-fulfilment fantasy. They all begin by resisting virtuously and saying : 'Fie, for shame.' Then, when he gets his finger into the 'coral slit', they gasp, and their thighs 'part as if involuntarily '. From then on, it's straightforward progress until they moan with ecstasy in bed. Either Fleisher is a bigger fool than he looks, or he knows damn well he's been swindled and doesn't care.

He came in and told me we were expecting guests to lunch. This was about the last straw—I felt anything but sociable. I went into the bathroom, and turned on the shower. Suddenly, I felt dizzy, and had to cling on to the curtain rail. I sat down on the lavatory seat and stared at the flowered bath-mat, feeling the waves of depression trickling over me. I thought of Helga —that last morning, as she had sat on the edge of the bed, pulling on her stockings. She said : 'I'm glad we slept together. We may as well take what pleasure we can get.' She said no more, but I understood her. She meant that life is meaningless. We had climbed into bed together, fucked like two animals, slept and got up again; but we were strangers, too honest to have illusions about love or tenderness—alienated from one another and the universe. And suddenly I wanted to explain to her. I wanted to tell her that the world seems meaningless because her subconscious has gone to sleep. When we're happy, bubbles of pleasure keep rising up from the subconscious—memories, smells, places. When you're exhausted, the subconscious goes off duty, and the result is the state Sartre calls 'nausea '. You see things without the penumbra of meaning supplied by the lower depths of the mind. St Augustine says : 'What is time? When I do not ask myself the question, I know the answer.' Quite. Isolating a thing in consciousness robs it of its meaning. The fact that *consciousness* sees the world as meaningless is neither here nor there. Consciousness isn't supposed to perceive meaning; it's supposed to perceive *objects*. But how could I explain this to a girl who is firmly jammed in a state of total nervous exhaustion? To get her out of it, she would have to be persuaded to make an effort.

21

And she won't make an effort because she says all effort is pointless. She's trapped in a vicious circle.

I was determined that I wouldn't make the same mistake. I snapped myself out of it, stepped into the hot shower, and thought about seeing Diana tomorrow and flying home in ten days' time...

But lunch was as bad as I'd thought it would be. The guests were obviously rich neighbours, and Fleisher had invited them solely because they *were* rich neighbours. It came to me how much of this kind of thing goes on in America—people drinking and talking together when they have nothing in common—and I plunged back into a state of irritable depression. I felt that Fleisher had no *right* to inflict these damn bores on me—fat businessmen and their silly wives, and their chatter about the holiday villa they've just bought in Florida or on the Carmel peninsula. Beverley was on the far side of the room with a fat young executive type whose wife was away for the weekend, and this irritated me more than ever because I felt she was there to entertain me—even if I didn't want to sleep with her. I wanted it to be *my* choice.

I went out on to the terrace, by the heated swimming pool, and looked across the sound to Connecticut. The air was warm and mild. Suddenly I decided I'd tell Fleisher I didn't want anything to do with his damn book. I couldn't even undertake the Introduction without dishonesty, because Donelly struck me as a vicious bore. I'd leave right after lunch and catch the afternoon bus to New Haven...

I was just about to go in and tell Fleisher when Beverley came out bringing me a plate of smoked salmon and a beer. She said : 'You look bored.' And I said—rather angrily, as if I blamed her —' I am. I'm sick of this whole bloody thing.' I said I intended to leave immediately after lunch. Her concern surprised me. She said : ' No, you don't have to do that. Wait until after the others have gone.' Her attention flattered me, and I promised. Five minutes later, Howard came out and asked me how I felt. I said I was fine but that I was thinking of leaving later in the day. He also got very concerned, and hurried off into the house.

I ate the salmon and some cold meat, and went up to my

room. I was sitting on the bed reading the Donelly typescript when Beverley came in. She looked very unsure of herself. 'I've brought you some cranberry pie.' I said thankyou, and she sat on the bed. She said : 'Howard says I'm to persuade you not to go.' 'Why?' She hesitated, then said : 'It means a lot to me. I want you to stay.' I said 'Why?', more surprised than ever. She rambled on vaguely about only having another year of study before she could take a well-paid job, and it gradually dawned on me that Fleisher was paying for her studies, and that, in return, she was expected to 'entertain' guests like myself. I suppose it all fitted in. Sarah was Fleisher's secretary and his mistress; Beverley shared a flat with Sarah...Then I gathered that Fleisher had been angry with her for not spending the night with me. I said : 'But didn't you explain that I was fast asleep?' She said : 'Yes, I know you were. I came in to see.'

I was eating my cranberries—although I didn't want them —out of embarrassment. It was one of those awkward, stupid stituations. I couldn't say : 'All right, take off your clothes, and we'll make up for lost time.' I said : 'But I explained to Howard that my wife and daughter are waiting for me in New Haven.' She said miserably : 'Yes, I know.' I said : 'But what difference does it make whether I spent the night with you or not?' But in fact, I could guess. Fleisher was one of those men who are determined to have their own way. He had read my book and decided that I was the person he needed to supply his Donelly book with a respectable image. And if I'd spent the weekend in his house, with a girl he'd imported for me, then I'd be under some sort of obligation to him.

I said : 'Look, I don't think I can accept this commission. This book is just a stupid piece of pornography. It's not even well-written pornography. It doesn't convince.' I read her the scene where he gets into bed with his sister when she is menstruating, and she allows him to take her virginity. 'An Irish girl in the 1780s wouldn't even have allowed her brother to know she was menstruating.' I found nevertheless that reading it aloud produced a stirring of the loins that made walking uncomfortable, so I sat down on the window-sill—a deep one. She objected that manners were more free in the eighteenth century, and that

23

perhaps Donelly was simply a careless writer who left out important steps in the seduction. I said : 'All right. How about this, then.' I turned to the scene where he describes seducing his sister's schoolfriend. Beverley moved to my shoulder, and let her breast press against it. The scene describes how she is standing with him, watching a parade go past; he unlaces her bodice and sucks her nipples, then inserts his finger in the 'coral slit'. They end by having intercourse with her sitting down on him, her legs astride his. I said I thought it was preposterous, but I was aware that my voice sounded strained. The combination of the pornography, and her breast leaning hard against my shoulder, had me in a state of tension that would have been obvious if I hadn't been holding the typescript in my lap. She was wearing an off-the-shoulder blouse of fluffy pink wool that went well with her golden skin. As I finished reading, she wet her right index finger, reached around my head, and placed it gently in my ear. I don't know where she learned the trick, but the effect was shattering. Suddenly, this was *her* situation, and she knew it; the awkwardness had gone. I reached up and pulled the blouse right off the shoulders, then pulled down the cups of her brassiere, a small thing that was little more than a band of lacy material. Both her nipples were erect and very pink; I took them in my mouth in turn, and worried them with my tongue. She slid on to my knee, pushed the manuscript on to the floor, and unzipped my trousers. We sat there in that position, both breathing very heavily. I wondered whether she wanted to move over to the bed, but her fingers caressed with a sort of skill that made me want to sit quite still, letting her go on. I could see past her shoulder, out of the window, the black outlines of trees against the sea, their branches only just covered with green shoots. They looked magnificently hard, as if they were made of some black and silver metal. Then my climax came, and the trees lurched, and something inside me went very hard, so that everything I looked at was hard, hard and very beautiful, beautiful as only the hard and clean can be. She bent over me, and inserted her tongue in my mouth, holding it there until I gradually subsided in her hand. I gave her my handkerchief, and she wiped her fingers. She pulled my hand, and we moved to the bed, and

24

simply lay there, fully clothed. I was beginning to fall asleep when some slight sound made me look up. In the mirror, I saw the reflection of the door opening. Fleisher peeped in, saw us, and instantly withdrew again. Beverley was asleep, her lips open. I suddenly felt pity, and an upsurge of a feeling that was basically love. Fleisher had told her to come and give herself. She had done her best; she had set out to give me pleasure without thinking about her own, and my handkerchief held the result. I kissed her parted lips; then, when she stirred, her forehead.

When I got downstairs, I told Fleisher that I wanted to leave immediately, but that I would accept his contract. He said : ' Sure, man, that's ma boy ', and punched me on the shoulder.

Later

I began the last entry at Great Neck and finished it in the bus station at Kennedy. Now, travelling back to New Haven, I recall that Bergson stumbled upon the answer to Helga's sense of meaninglessness. In one of his essays, he described how a stage magician (Houdin, I think) trained his five-year-old son to instantaneous observation. The boy was shown a domino, *but not allowed to count the dots*. Later, he was asked to recall how many dots there were; i.e. he had to count them ' in imagination '. Then he was shown two dominoes, and told not to count the dots; again, he had to ' imagine ' them when they had been taken away and recall how many dots there were. He was being trained to take visual photographs with his memory. Later, he was taken past toyshop windows, allowed to glance in for a second, then asked to write down all he could remember. Within a short time, he could write down forty or fifty items from memory. Houdin was training the boy to pretend he possessed second sight. The boy would go on stage, and glance at the audience for a minute or so while his father introduced him. In that time, he would ' photograph ' all the visible objects—watch-chains, etc. Then he would be blindfolded, and some signal from his father would enable him to identify the object roughly. He would, of course, hear the voice of the man who handed it over and be able to judge where he was sitting.

Bergson points out that the essence of this method was *not* allowing the boy to count the dots. Instead of *interpreting* what he saw, as we all do in everyday perception, he was asked merely to let the upper level of his mind photograph it. The upper level became dissociated from his feelings, intuitions, judgements, etc, and could move much quicker; it was ' travelling light '.

Clever young people soon learn this trick—particularly if they are cramming for exams. They learn to dissociate the levels of the mind. But observe what this means. You teach yourself to photograph ' facts ' *without their meaning*. If I was asked to memorise the contents of a toyshop window, I should say : ' That's a fire engine in the middle, and a doll in that corner, and a teddy bear in that one...', and I wouldn't memorise more than two or three objects in several seconds.

This easily becomes a habit : grasping things without their meaning. It becomes difficult to re-connect your upper levels with your instincts and feelings. The horse refuses to be harnessed to the cart, as it were. You go around merely 'seeing ' things without their meanings. And you say : ' The world is meaningless.'

Monday, April 14, Charleston, S.C.

A Sunday with Diana and Mopsy has me feeling more sane. I spent yesterday toying with the idea of scrapping the Donelly fragment and writing Fleisher a complete book of Donelly memoirs. But this morning, just before I left New Haven, Fleisher rang me. He had just remembered that I was going to Baton Rouge, and he wanted to tell me that a descendant of Donelly's—Colonel Monroe Donelly—is living at a place called Denham Springs. I shall be there for thirty-six hours, and try to call on him.

I keep thinking about Beverley. Not just about her, but about what happened to the trees as I stared at them. I keep trying to put it into words. Just as, when you're feeling miserable, everything you look at seems tinged with your misery—becomes a kind of *symbol* of your misery, like grey skies or falling autumn leaves—so in the moment when the orgasm convulses the whole body, everything becomes a symbol of the sense of power. This explains why I detest Donelly. His insipid little orgasms led nowhere; he never tried to pursue them to their source in himself.

[Entries for the following week are omitted]

Monday, April 21

What has happened over the past twenty-four hours is so amazing that I must describe it in detail.

On Saturday morning, and again on Saturday evening, I lectured at Louisiana State University—good lectures, in spite of this blanket of tiredness that I can't shake off. (But I don't much enjoy lecturing. I keep remembering that comment of the Marquis of Halifax: 'The vanity of teaching doth often tempt a man to forget that he is a blockhead.') Early Sunday morning, I ate breakfast at the motel, and hired a taxi to take me out to Denham Springs, some ten miles away. (Fleisher offered to pay all such expenses.) I purposely hired the taxi from Denham Springs. It was driven by a middle-aged negro. I asked him if he knew where Colonel Donelly lived. Oh yeah, he said, he knew the Colonel all right. He lived a mile outside town. He asked me if I was a friend of the Colonel's, and I said I'd never met him, but was hoping to find him at home. He said: 'Well, maybe he'll see you and maybe he won't. With the Colonel, you can never tell what he'll do.' He proved to be as talkative as most American taxi drivers, and in twenty minutes he'd told me a great deal about Donelly. There wasn't much that I liked. He moved to Louisiana from Mexico shortly after the war, and bought land outside the town. He got it cheaply because it was swampy and full of snakes. He hired heavy equipment and had the land drained and cleared; then began to farm, growing rice, sugar and oranges. He paid well, but he became known as a man who drove himself and his hired labour. The hands—mostly negroes—lived in wooden barrack-like buildings. Donelly was a complete tyrant, although he had a reputation for fanatical fairness. He settled disputes himself, and even ordered whippings, which he occasionally carried out himself. Anyone who wished to leave could do so. He lived alone, and was never known to sleep with a woman. His only servant was a huge, morose Mexican he

27

brought with him. There were rumours that he beat the man—the sound of blows and curses was sometimes heard from inside the farm building—but the servant never complained. He died of typhoid a few years later.

In 1962, the Standard Oil Company—which has a big refinery at Baton Rouge—discovered oil on his land and offered him a large price for it. Donelly finally rented part of the land to them. And although he had plenty of farming land left, he gave up farming, dismissed his labourers, and lived a hermit existence. He had been living alone ever since, growing thinner and more taciturn. Several times a year he vanished—it was believed he went to New Orleans. A resident of Denham Springs claimed to have seen him in a brothel there, but it was not widely believed.

We were within a few miles of Denham Springs, and the driver advised me to roll up my window. He explained we were about to pass a chicken factory that had recently burned down, and the bodies of the dead birds had not yet been removed. We passed the place on the right—little more than a large wooden shed, as far as I could judge from the burnt remains. Even with the windows closed, the sickening smell came in. The driver told me they had many fires in the area. The labourers' quarters on Donelly's farm had been burnt down, as had a barn full of hay.

This didn't surprise me. The only thing that surprises me about the south part of America is that the whole thing doesn't burst into flame in midsummer. Although it was not yet eleven in the morning, the air was like a furnace.

We drove through the sleepy little town, where everything looked very empty and quiet on a Sunday morning, then turned to the right, down a steep, narrow track that wound below the town. Half an hour's cautious driving—to conserve the springs of the taxi—brought us to straggling wooden farm buildings that looked deserted. I paid him and got out. He said : ' I'd better jus' wait 'n' see if he's gonna let you in. He might just decide he's not.' So I crossed the dusty yard, past rusting farm equipment, towards the main building. A mangy yellow-coloured dog growled at me, but made no attempt to get up.

Before I reached the door it opened, and Donelly stood there. I knew it must be Donelly—he looked too European to be anybody else; the kind of man one used to see on old advertisements for Planter's Tea and Camp Coffee : thin, sunburned, with a face in which all the muscles showed through. He watched me approach without speaking, then said : 'You're Mr Somme?' It was a relief. I expected him to say : 'Who the hell are you?' I said I was. He nodded, very briefly, and held open the door for me to go in.

The room was bare and tidy, like an officer's billet. Donelly hadn't smiled or shaken hands. But I turned as he came in the door—he stood there to watch the taxi drive away—and thought he was watching me with an odd expression—speculative, like a cat watching a hedgehog. He said : 'Can I offer you tea?', and I said yes with enthusiasm. He went out, and left me alone. It was clear he lived in this one room. There was a camp bed, an uncomfortable armchair and an ordinary wooden chair, and a small folding table. The floor was bare and clean. There was an old green safe in the corner of the room. Half a dozen prints on the wall—of bare-fist boxers squaring up to one another, and fine horses. No books.

Donelly came back with the tea, and a plate of buttered cream crackers. I got the feeling that he wanted to unbend, to say something friendly, and had forgotten how. As he poured the tea he asked me if I'd had a good trip. I said yes. I resisted the temptation to talk to try to fill the silence. As I sipped my tea— which was well made—I recalled Heine's definition of silence as the conversation of Englishmen, and found it hard not to smile. Finally, I stopped trying. Donelly looked at me at that moment, and I turned my smile into a friendly grin, and said : 'Well, it's really a pleasure to find an Englishman living in this weird spot.' He said stiffly : 'I'm Irish.' 'Same thing at this distance', I said, wondering if he'd throw something at me. But he gave a kind of frozen smile and said : 'Yes, I suppose so.' For some curious reason, the ice was broken. He said : 'So you live in Moycullen? Where abouts?', and I described the cottage we'd rented, and the house we'd moved into. Then he asked me if I knew anything of the Domenech murder case—the girl who was found at the bottom of the cliffs of Moher two years ago. I knew all about it, and described it in detail. She was an American girl whose lover killed her for her traveller's cheques. I knew the fisherman who found the body, and the member of the local gardai who was called to view it. The face was apparently unrecognisable, but the murderer had made the mistake of leaving one item of clothing on the body—a pair of black lace panties. These contained the name tag of an American manufacturer, and eventually led to her identification. I had also spoken to the detective inspector from Dublin who took charge of the case, and he told me something of the methods he used. All this first-hand information fascinated Donelly, and I began to hope he might feel co-operative on the subject of his ancestor.

Towards midday, the heat was becoming oppressive. Donelly removed his pullover, and sat at the table wearing only a shirt—open to the waist—and his trousers. I also removed my jacket. He suggested that we might have a drink, and I agreed. Donelly produced a bottle of black rum. I knew I had no more lecturing until Tuesday, so I accepted without misgiving. Donelly produced more buttered crackers, and opened tins of sardines. After we had said 'Cheers', he brought up the subject of Esmond Donelly. He said :

'I suppose this publisher chap told you I told him to go to hell?'

'No, he didn't.' That was typical of Fleisher—suggest I call on Donelly without explaining that he'd already met a hostile reception. Perhaps it was just as well; I wouldn't have called if he had.

He asked : 'Have you seen this manuscript?'

'Yes. I've got it with me.' I took it from the inside pocket of my jacket. He took it eagerly. After reading half a page, he threw it down on the table with a gesture of disgust.

'Just as I thought. A forgery. Just a stupid bloody forgery.'

'Are you sure?' I was astounded.

'Of course I'm sure. Haven't you read Esmond's Diary?'

'I'm afraid I haven't. I didn't even know it existed. Is it published?'

'Of course it is. Published in Dublin in 1817.'

He went out of the room. A few minutes later he returned and tossed a small leather-bound volume on the bed. The title was *The Diary of Esmond Donelly, Gent.* It was published by Telford's, Dublin. The Epistle Dedicatory was addressed to Lord Chesterfield :

'My Lord, I have often had cause to remember your saying that the worst bred man in Europe, if a lady let fall her fan, would certainly take it up and give it to her; the best bred man in Europe could do no more. It was this reflection upon the similarity of talents of the great and humble within limited spheres of activity that hath nerved me to offer this unpretending volume to your Lordship...'

There was no need to read further. The man who could write this graceful, well-turned prose could not be the gloating moron who wrote : 'Within seconds my lucky doodle was in her virgin niche, my sperm sticking my balls to her arse.' This last quotation catches the essence of the style of Fleisher's manuscript. I would not argue that the same man could *not* have written the Epistle Dedicatory to Chesterfield *and* the above sentence; but an intuition that amounted to a certainy made me feel that it was not so. I said :

'I see what you mean. You don't think it's possible that the style of a private journal might differ from that of a travel diary?'

'It differs from his unpublished diaries too.'

'Have you seen them, then?' I tried not to sound too eager.

'Oh yes.' He said it casually, and poured himself more rum. I wolfed half a dozen sardines and a buttered biscuit before drinking more, and reflected that I could spend the afternoon and evening asleep in my motel room.

I then told Donelly about my meeting with Fleisher, explaining that I had never heard of his ancestor before this time. He agreed that that was not surprising. Donelly's journal had no more merit than a dozen others of the period, Thomas Turner, Mary Cowper, the Earl of Egmont; and was simply not in the same class as Fanny Burney. Esmond Donelly was known to students of Irish literature; but he is not even mentioned in the *Cambridge History of English Literature.*

By way of extenuating Fleisher's motives, I pointed out that there is seldom smoke without fire, and that if there is a rumour

that Donelly kept 'sex diaries', it might well have some foundation. He stared at me with his cold eyes, his face expressionless,
then said finally:

'Assuming it might have some foundation, do you suppose his
descendants are eager to see such things published? You know
Ireland.'

I saw his point. The Irish are not precisely bigoted about
matters of morals; they have a certain flexibility. But the southern
Irish are Catholics; there is much banning of books, and the
Index is still a matter to be reckoned with. I could understand
that the Donellys of Ballycahane might well find sudden notoriety
embarrassing, even if profitable.

Towards one o'clock, I was distinctly drunk, and I said I ought
to leave. To my surprise, he objected. 'No, no. You can have
food here. I'll cook eggs and bacon. Or there's sweet corn.' He
went off to the kitchen, and I read a few pages of Esmond
Donelly describing Venice. The heat was making me drowsy.
In fact, I was almost asleep when Donelly woke me up as he
brought in an enormous saucepan that was full of corncobs. He
poured half a dozen of these into a deep oval plate, stuck a huge
slab of butter on them, and told me to eat. I have never eaten
so much sweet corn in my life; but it was superb. Donelly, to my
astonishment, washed down his food with rum. I was impressed
by the quantity he could hold. Between us, we had emptied the
best part of a bottle, and I had only taken two glasses. But I
could see no sign that he was drunk; his speech remained slow
and precise; the voice kept the acid, slightly sarcastic tone. The
only change was in the subject matter of his conversation. He
began to talk about sex. He held up a corncob—from which he
had chewed the seeds—and said that he had heard of a book in
which a girl's virginity is taken with a corncob. I told him it was
Faulkner. Donelly said Faulkner had not invented the episode:
that a corncob is a well-known expedient if a girl's hymen proves
too tough to be penetrated by the more usual method. Then he
went on to tell me an anecdote of one of his negro farm workers
who had found his daughter masturbating with a corncob. He
described how the man had tied her hands to a hook on the wall
and lashed her with a leather belt; then ended by inserting a far

larger cob into the girl by way of driving home the lesson. He told me this story coolly and reflectively, as he ate another corncob; but he did not look at me as he talked. He went on to tell me more anecdotes—all involving floggings. He opened another bottle of rum as he talked. Logic told me that this succession of anecdotes about flogging and incest could not really spring from a disinterested desire to give me a picture of life in the deep south; but his manner certainly betrayed no sadistic intention. It struck me that he had lived alone for a long time; he was sex-starved and lonely, and enjoyed having a fellow-countryman to talk to. There was nothing very abnormal about that.

But I began to wish that I'd timed my visit for later in the day. It began to look as if he intended keeping me here all afternoon and evening. I could leave, of course, But Donelly was my only source of information about his ancestor, and I had taken five thousand dollars to write about this man. Guilt alone would have kept me sitting there as long as I was welcome.

As the afternoon wore on, I began to yawn every minute or so; but Donelly appeared not to notice. He had brought in a deck chair, and sat in this, with his feet on the wooden chair. He insisted that I take the uncomfortable armchair, and put my feet on the bed. We were now drinking beer—Budweiser from the tin—and he was smoking cheroots. Periodically, I tried to bring the conversation back to Donelly, but he evaded the subject. Finally, at about four o'clock, he asked me if I felt like a walk. I said all right—anything to break the hypnotic daze. I was beginning to feel rather irritable with him. He could see I was sleepy; he might at least have suggested that I doze for half an hour, or left me to read Esmond Donelly's journal. But he wanted to talk, and he obviously didn't care whether I was sleepy or not.

In spite of the heat, Donelly put on a clean shirt and tie, and a sports jacket. I carried my own jacket slung over my shoulder. He looked as if he was on his way to his London club for a midday drink; I felt crumpled, sweaty and will-less. Aware by now that he was talking from some compulsion, I scarcely paid attention to what he said, walking along beside him over the rutted fields. The great yellow hound followed us; its legs were so long that it seemed to be moving in slow motion. Donelly walked with long strides, pointing out various objects of interest with his cane. 'That's known as the lynching tree. The Klan hanged three negroes there a few years back.' 'What had they been doing?' 'Setting fire to hayricks.' Some of the areas of woodland we strolled through were pretty, but I was amazed by the quantity of rusty tins and Coca Cola bottles lying in the undergrowth. We leaned on a fence to watch the oil derricks, and I suddenly noticed that Donelly was wearing a revolver in a holster underneath his jacket. 'What's that for?' 'In case of snakes', he said. He evidently felt that the noise of the derricks interfered with conversation, for he hurried me on. I noticed that he kept glancing at his watch. 'Are we going anywhere in particular?' I asked. The flow of talk stopped for a moment. 'No.' He looked blank. I was beginning to feel thirsty, and his tension was communicating itself to me. 'Where *are* we going?' 'Oh, I thought we'd just stroll along for a mile or so, then make our way home.' The word 'stroll' was so inappropriate that I smiled. 'I ought to think about getting back.' He ignored the remark. But he consulted his watch again. The great yellow dog was growling and barking at a clump of grass in a ditch. I peered down, and saw a black snake coiled there, hissing. As it saw me, it slithered off. I expected Donelly to shoot at it, but he only said : 'Come on.'

We clambered over a fence and on to a dirt road. There were farm buildings a few hundred yards away, and a mail box indicated that we were now on somebody else's land.

Donelly said suddenly :

'Hello, that looks like a fire.'

'Where?'

He pointed across a field next to the farm, but all I could see was a faint wisp of smoke rising from an open barn full of straw. But a few minutes later, flames were shooting high into the air, and the black smoke billowed and twisted like a materialising genie. Donelly was suddenly running, his gun banging against his buttock, and the great dog loping alongside like a small pony. We scrambled over a fence and crossed a field with pigs rooting

34

in the black mud. Men were also running from the direction of the farm buildings.

I could see no point in running. There was obviously nothing we could do, and the fire would certainly not burn itself out before we arrived. So I walked across the field, my hands in my pockets. Five minutes later, I joined Donelly. It was certainly an impressive blaze; the flames were so powerful they carried up fragments of burning straw that slowly rained on us or drifted in grey wisps. It was impossible to approach closer than fifty yards; the heat was tremendous. Something exploded—a barrel perhaps—and a part of the roof fell in. Showers of sparks rose like fireworks. I said something to Donelly, but he ignored me. I looked at his face, and looked away quickly. His jaw was set and rigid, and his eyes were staring as if they were made of blue glass. It was as if he was drinking in the noise and smoke. Even when smoke blew towards us, and made my eyes water, he went on staring. His fists were clenched in his trouser pockets. There was something about the set of his face that made me realise that he was experiencing a weird exaltation. To some extent, I could understand it. The fire was majestic; there was something symphonic about the crackling and the heat and the shower of sparks.

I felt that some of the other spectators were looking at us with a certain resentment, as if we had no right there; so I retired to the fence and sat on it. Half an hour later, when nothing remained of the barn but the metal uprights, the fire engine arrived.

Someone behind me said : ' Mind tellin' me your name? ', and I found a burly policeman looking at me with an expression of sour disapproval. Two men were standing behind him, holding guns; they looked like farm labourers. I gave my name, and said that I was with Colonel Donelly. At this, the elder of the two men said : ' Oh, you're with Donelly, are you? ', and I wondered why his tone was so hostile. The cop frowned at him, then said to me : 'Do you mind tellin' me how long you been here? ' ' Since just after the fire started. We were taking a walk.' The questions puzzled me, but it seemed easier to answer. ' Who are you? ' When I explained that I was lecturing at Baton Rouge, his tone became more civil. I had the lecture contract in my pocket, and an I.D. that I always carry in America. I was on the point of asking if it was against the law to stop and watch a fire, but it hardly seemed worth while. The cop examined my papers, said thankyou politely, then strode over to Donelly, followed by the two men. The great yellow dog stood by Donelly's side, and as the men approached, it growled and started to crouch, as if for a spring. Donelly held its collar. The conversation was brief; I saw him pointing towards me. Then he came across to me, yawned, and said : 'Well, I think we may as well get back.' The fire engine had finally got water spraying on to the smouldering ashes, and clouds of steam came up, carrying ash and fragments of charred wood.

'What was that all about?'

'Oh, they're very suspicious of strangers in this area.'

'But they couldn't have suspected us of starting the fire.'

He shrugged, then began to whistle an Irish jig. He walked back with the same long strides, but it struck me that he had ceased to be tense. During the earlier part of our walk, he had talked and walked like an automaton—or a man with his mind rigidly fixed on something else. Now he was human, relaxed. As we entered the house, he even placed his hand on my shoulder and said : 'Well, I think we both deserve a long cool drink.'

He produced bottles of English ale—Worthingtons. As I watched him pouring, and humming to himself, something silly came into my head. Exhaustion had given me a feeling of recklessness; I obeyed the impulse and said it.

'I don't suppose you had anything to do with it, did you?'

For a moment I wondered if I had gone too far. But he held out the beer with the happy, innocent smile of a schoolboy.

'What an odd question. How could I?'

And suddenly, with a certainty I cannot explain, I knew that he had. Perhaps it was the way he said it, or the immediate way he had understood the question. An innocent man would have hesitated, wondered if he had understood me correctly. I sat in the armchair and drank deeply. When I looked at him again, the certainty had vanished. He had been with me all day...

'Here's to Esmond Donelly.'

I drank. It seemed irrelevant.

He went into the kitchen, and I heard sounds of food being prepared. He had switched on a radio—another sign of relaxation. A cool breeze blew through the open window. The more I thought about it, the more I was inclined to believe that he had some fore-knowledge of the fire. It all fitted in : the attempts to persuade me to stay; the obsessive, mechanical conversation; the absurdly long walk on a hot afternoon; the gun he carried and the great dog; the increased pace as we came close to the haystack and the glances at his watch. The man was a pyromaniac. Probably he had set his own out-buildings on fire. Perhaps he had fired the chicken factory too. Perhaps—I suddenly felt a cold shock—perhaps he had caused the fire for which the negroes were lynched. But how had he done it? An accomplice who started the fire as we approached? Too dangerous, surely? Some timing device? That must be the answer.

I finished my ale and began to doze. I woke up when he brought in the food—yams, french fries and sausages. He poured more beer; I ate from a tray on my knee. He was obviously very hungry; I watched him furtively as we ate in silence. He didn't look like a Count Dracula, guarding his terrible secret. He looked like a tired, worn-out man of fifty who habitually drove himself too hard and could not be bothered to eat proper meals. I knew it was my duty to mention my suspicions to someone—perhaps to the head of the English department at the University of Louisiana. But I knew I wouldn't. He was my host. I could only hope he got caught soon.

It was nearly nine o'clock when I finished eating. I said :

'You've been very kind, but I really ought to think about getting back...'

He was piling the dishes on a tray. He said casually :

'What, before you've seen the Donelly manuscript?'

I was unable to believe I had heard correctly.

'Manuscript?'

'That's what you came for, isn't it?'

'Do *you* have some of his manuscript?'

He nodded as he carried the tray out. When he came back, he took a key from his pocket, and opened the green safe in the corner. He said :

'These are not for publication, of course.'

There was a wooden box in the top part of the safe and, on the lower shelf, a number of buff envelopes. He took out one of these and handed it to me. There was a great wad of papers that had been sewn together with waxed twine. The handwriting was distinctive and idiosyncratic, but easy enough to read :

Falmouth, March 6, 1787

The glass is sinking; the west wind gently breathing upon the water, the smoke softly descending into the room, and the sailors yawning dismally at the door of every ale house. Beckford has left me to go in search of his lady love on the hill; I remain here, lulled into a state of drowsy tranquillity, watching two young girls, beautifully shaped, and dressed with a kind of provincial elegance, walking by the edge of the sea. Ah, these delicious, glorious creatures! Who would question the assertion of Zozimus the Panopolitan that woman did not spring from the same root as man, but was created to people some other star, and allowed to stay in our male world as an afterthought! Are they not the supreme mystery of creation, the visible presence of magic in this draffish and Boeotian world?

Godwin said the illustrious Bishop of Cambrai was of more worth than his chambermaid, but I would not exchange ten bishops for the pretty minx who shared my bed last night. The wench—whose name is Clara—served us at supper yester-eve, and Beckford, whose tastes lie not in that direction, said the girl had a behind like a boy. I said I thought it too shapely for a lad, at least, to judge by the little bosoms I could see when she bent over the table to pour melted butter on my lobster. When she came close to me, I whispered that I would give her a crown for a kiss, and she laughed and blushed. Until Beckford spoke of her, I had paid her but small attention; but now my notions had become fixed upon her, the little god of pleasing anguish entered my breast and made a pincushion of my heart. Each time she came into the room I looked upon her as if I had newly fallen in love; indeed, for a moment it would have seemed no great price to marry her for the sake of a closer investigation of her charms. Although I believe I have less of the feminine in me than Beckford, I own to the consuming curiosity of a Pandora, that is capable of dismissing all other considerations. When she came close to me to refill my glass, I passed my arm about her and allowed my hand to rest upon her thigh, knowing that if she objected to this, we would get no further. But she stood quietly, like a well-trained horse; then the landlord came in with more negus, and I withdrew my hand. I had no further opportunity to caress her during the meal; but when I left the room, I slipped a guinea into her hand and whispered : ' This is for you, my dear. There's five more waiting if you'll come to my room when everyone is abed.' She said nothing, lowering her eyes, but took the money. Later, Beckford told me that he had discovered that she was married to a fisherman, and that I had probably wasted my money. I replied that money given to a pretty girl is never wasted, if she be virtuous, for it must be regarded as a votive offering to Aphrodite, who will acknowledge the compliment in her own good time.

On this occasion, Beckford proved to be wrong, for the nymph slipped between my sheets at three in the morning, after I had given up all hope, and thereafter denied me nothing. I asked her in a whisper what had become of her husband; she said he was out with the fishing fleet. She was wearing a coarse linen shift, which I soon had about her throat. I kissed her and called her many soft words, for I have never had patience with the fellows who rob a girl of her virtue and then treat her as if the robbery hath deprived her of all right to consideration or tenderness. Added to which, I was aware that the girl was a gift of the foam-born goddess, and deserved a part of the worship due to her donor. So I caressed her ears with soft words and the tip of my tongue, and then allowed its eloquence to speak to her breasts, and even to the velvet walls of the temple itself. By this time, the stirrings of her buttocks betokened excitement, whereupon I transferred my tongue to its proper resting place in her own mouth, and entered her as softly as a man slipping into bed. We fucked quietly and gently, barely moving the mattress, until her knees gripped me suddenly, and she spent with a shudder that was like the silver explosion of a sky-rocket. I lay there within her for a long time, kissing her lips as if to make up for a lifetime of abstention, hardly able to believe that this milk-white priestess was the same Clara who poured the gravy on my roast beef and gave me a glimpse of nipples that looked newly formed. Although her buttocks were now still—those buttocks that were too round to be a boy's—my steed quivered within her, as if unable to believe itself in so delicious a stable. I resolved to lie there unmoving and see how long I could hold the starry fluid; but she undid me by slipping her hand between our bodies and caressing my balls with her fingertips; the seed gushed, and the earth drank the rain. We continued the sport until daylight, when she left me. I lay there and meditated upon the argument I had with Beckford in the coach yesterday : that the Greek manner of love is more spiritual and exalted than that known between men and women. In my overflow of felicity I could have wished Beckford the company of Clara's fish-spouse in his four poster; but could the mating have been other than hairy and lusty, as befits knights jousting with lances of flesh? Such a union partakes of the bemuscled bounty of the sun, not of the green water-magic of Artemis.

I read on, forgetting Donelly's presence. His remark that this was not for publication kept my excitement within bounds of restraint; but I had the feeling that I've experienced at other crucial moments in my life—for example, when I met Austin at the Diaghileff exhibition; almost a sense of repeating a scene you have already rehearsed.

Donelly was back at the rum bottle. I refused a glass, but accepted a Budweiser. When I reached the end of the section, I put the manuscript volume down.

'Are you quite sure you wouldn't be willing to have this published?'

' I think so.'

I said : ' It rather makes nonsense of the whole project. I see now what you mean about Fleisher's version being a forgery. But I don't see how I can recommend Fleisher to publish his version. It would be absurd.'

' I agree.'

' Is there no chance of a compromise? '

He lit a cheroot.

' The family would be most upset if the papers were published.'

' But you said you weren't on good terms with the family.'

' Neither am I. That's no reason for spiting them.'

From a man who had just burned down someone's haystack, this struck me as a little over-scrupulous. I changed my line of approach and asked him how the papers had come into his hands. He seemed to think about this for a moment.

' Yes, I suppose there's no harm in telling you that. When Donelly visited Rousseau at Neuchâtel in 1765—Donelly was about seventeen at the time—he presented him with an essay, written in French, refuting Hume and d'Alembert. This is mentioned by John Morley in his Life of Rousseau. Donelly and Rousseau became friends, in spite of the age gap. But Rousseau was having a hard time of it. The clergy in Neuchâtel were all preaching against him, and he was accused of bewitching a man who'd died of colic. One morning, Donelly found that someone had balanced a huge stone outside Rousseau's door so that it would fall on him when he came out—it would certainly have killed him. Esmond removed the stone, and the next night he set up the booby trap outside the house of the blacksmith—who was a particular enemy of Jean-Jacques, and who was also the only man strong enough to lift the stone without help. It broke the blacksmith's arm and collar bone. But it didn't help poor Rousseau, who had to leave town anyway—the people got to the point of stoning him in the streets. Two years later, when Rousseau was staying in London as the guest of David Hume, Donelly asked him what had become of the manuscript, and Rousseau said he'd left it behind in Paris, and would return it when he went back. He never did.

41

'Shortly after the war, I was staying at Lausanne and I was introduced to a bookseller named Clouzot, who had a business in Neuchâtel. I told him the story of Donely's manuscript and he said he might be able to help me. Six months later, he wrote and offered it to me for sale—at a fairly reasonable price, I might add. I think he found it at the house of the man from whom Rousseau had rented his house, in a trunk of odds and ends. He also found pages of a travel journal by Donelly.

'A few years later, Clouzot wrote to ask me if I was still interested in Donelly manuscripts. He'd come across another in Geneva. I knew that Esmond had rented a house in Geneva and spent most of the last twenty years of his life there. But he moved back to Ireland a year before he died in 1830, and took most of his possessions. I've no idea how this particular manuscript got left behind, although I do have a rather interesting theory. Byron visited Esmond at Geneva—he'd met him through Sheridan. A few weeks later, Byron was writing to Hobhouse from Pisa that he was reading a "most bawdily diverting manuscript by old Esmond". I presume Esmond was Donelly—in which case, it's possible that Byron borrowed the manuscript and forgot to return it.'

I had to admire the lucid way Donelly told the story; well into his second bottle of rum, he discoursed as soberly as a clergyman arguing about transubstantiation.

The odd thing was that I was suddenly feeling indifferent about the whole business. I rather resented Donelly having this much power over me. I had already decided to return Fleisher's $5,000 and forget the whole thing. So I didn't give a damn whether Donelly could be persuaded to change his mind. And as soon as I decided that I didn't care, I felt free and indifferent. I decided that, whatever happened, I would leave in half an hour and get back to the motel. I asked Donelly how he had become interested in his ancestor. He said he'd discovered the published travel diary in the family home in Ballycahane. I asked him how much of his life he had spent there.

'Very little. We moved to Dublin when I was five, and to Malaya when I was nine.'

'Did you ever think of keeping travel diaries?' I asked the

question without real interest, to fill in time, as it were. The result was an incredible flood of self-revelation. He said heavily :

' I have never kept a diary because there are too many things I'd never dare to record.'

' That didn't deter Esmond.'

He gave an odd, twisted smile.

' Esmond's sex life was the kind he could write about. Mine isn't.'

I thought he was referring to the burning of the hayrick. I nodded sympathetically and said I understood. He said, with a kind of weary self-mockery :

' I doubt whether you do. When I was eight, we had a governess who spanked us and played with our penises.'

' We? '

' My brother Esmond and I. Esmond was a year my senior. This girl was a Scot from Glasgow—one of those big, healthy wenches. We both adored her from the moment we saw her. We followed her around like lap dogs. One day, we were chasing one another round a table with a porcelain bowl on it, and the bowl fell off and smashed. Our parents were out, and we begged Bridget not to tell them. She agreed to hide the broken fragments, but said she'd have to punish us both. We were both delighted at the idea. She told us to go up to our room and get our trousers off. When she came up with the cane, we were both naked. She sat on the bed and made each of us bend over her knee, then gave us ten strokes each.'

' Did it excite you? '

' Not really—at least, the punishment didn't. What excited me was being naked and pressing against her legs.'

I won't try to give the rest of the story in his own words, because he went into all kinds of minor detail that wasn't important. What he said was that he and his brother both agreed they enjoyed being punished by Bridget. The next time they were alone in the house with her, they deliberately broke something, and went through the whole performance again. This was in 1928—the era of short dresses. He was able to press his penis against her knee as she spanked him, and said that the sensation was so exquisite it almost made him faint. This time, she saw that he had an erection as he backed away, and reached down to touch it. Donelly's parents had believed in never trying to force back the foreskin, so the glans of his penis was hidden by it. The girl said this was unhealthy, and began gently pulling the skin back. He said that, from that moment on, he and his brother thought of nothing but how they could persuade her to spank them again. After a week or so, they no longer had to smash things to obtain their spankings. As soon as they were alone in the house with the girl, they would propose to play at schools. She was the schoolmarm. They would give the wrong answers or cheek the teacher; after a while, she would order them to their room. There they'd undress, and then they'd go through the whole charade, ending with her pushing back their foreskins ' for medical reasons '. One night when their parents were away, she allowed them to climb into her bed, and removed her nightdress. Donelly said this was oddly disappointing, even though she went through the usual sex play. They needed this image of her fully dressed, inflicting just punishment, in order to feel excited.

It came to an end when he was nine; they went to Malaya, where his father was manager of a tin mine. While they were away, they heard that Bridget had married, and were plunged into despair; each had bet the other that he would marry her when he grew up.

Two years later, they had almost forgotten her. Then one day, their mother asked them how they would like Bridget to come to take care of them again. Her husband had left her, and she wanted to get away from Scotland. She joined them when they were on holiday in London, and returned with them to Malaya. Donelly said she had become bigger and heavier, and that they both found her more attractive than ever. As soon as they were left alone with her, his brother said : ' Will you spank us if we're naughty? ', and she said : ' Of course.' Donelly said they both shuddered with delight.

For the first few weeks after their return, nothing happened. They had native servants, and she was afraid of compromising herself. But the hot climate and lack of sexual outlet soon began to erode her caution. The natives wandered around almost naked ; she claimed that her upbringing had been strictly religious and

44

that she found this shocking. The boys took pleasure in teasing her and sometimes pinching her, and she would slap them. They could tell from the increased hardness of the smacks that they were an outlet for something else besides annoyance. She saw them naked after a bath one night, and remarked on the development of Donelly's sexual member. Esmond was jealous; that night, he and his brother had a bitter fight which ended with black eyes and cut lips.

One day, she caught them hiding in a shed and smoking, and told them she would punish them on the spot. This was what they had been waiting for. It was impractical to remove all their clothes; they only lowered their trousers, and pressed against her. He said that when it was over, all three of them were very red and breathing heavily; he was sure she had had an orgasm (although, of course, he did not understand this at the time).

A few days later, his mother had taken Esmond into the nearby town to buy him clothes; Donelly was alone in the house. He went up to Bridget's room and found it empty. He opened her wardrobe, and found the dress that she used to wear when she beat them in Dublin—a brown dress of some stiff material. He placed it on the bed, undressed, and lay on it, smelling its distinctive smell. Suddenly, he heard the door slam. He recognised Bridget's step. She went through the house to the kitchen. He wanted her to see him lying on her dress, so he knocked something over. She called : ' Who is it? ' and came upstairs. He pretended to be asleep, and opened his eyes with a start as she stood over him. She appeared to be genuinely annoyed that he had looked in her wardrobe, and said : ' I shall have to punish you—get up.' Even before he bent over her, he had an erection, but she pretended not to notice it. She picked up a hairbrush and made him bend over her. This time, he noticed that her knees were farther apart than usual, and that by cautiously pressing on her dress, he could make it slide up her thigh. He tried to peer up her legs, but they were facing the door, and there was not enough light. Suddenly, she said : ' This place isn't high enough. Move around the other side ', and moved to the side of the bed that faced the window. He bent over her again, and inadvertently pushed her dress higher. She opened her knees wider, raising one of them to place it on a footstool, and he could see to the tops of her thighs. She was wearing very loose knickers with wide legs and, with her knees apart, the crotch hid nothing. He began moving his erect member against her knee as she beat him. She changed her position, and her other hand brushed against it, then slowly closed round it. Suddenly, she began to beat him with fury, striking as hard as she could, and at the same time he felt a sharp pleasure in his loins that made him feel faint. He half fell across her, and she went on beating him; then she shuddered, and dropped the brush. She said : ' Oh, you've made me feel ill ', and lay back across the bed, closing her eyes. He also lay on the bed. He said they were both exhausted. Nothing further happened that day. When they heard his mother returning half an hour later, he hurried to his own room. He told his brother later : ' I'm going to marry Bridget and have her beat me every day.'

This situation continued for three years, and during that time Bridget became engaged to a mining engineer, and had normal sexual intercourse with him. She kept putting off marrying him because she said Mrs Donelly could not do without her help in the house; the real reason was that she wanted to stay close to the brothers and continue the beatings. Finally, the engineer won; she married him and they moved to South America.

For a week or so, the brothers were desolated. Then one day, Esmond said : ' Pretend you're Bridget.' He lay down on the bed, while his brother beat him with a leather strap. Esmond had an orgasm. Afterwards, Esmond wielded the strap; Donelly imagined it was Bridget, and also had an orgasm.

Back in England, at the age of fourteen, Donelly and his brother were sent to a minor public school. Donelly was made a fag; Esmond, a year older, was not. Donelly was such an unsatisfactory fag that he had the pleasure of being beaten once a week. And one day, after beating him, the prefect removed his trousers and sodomised him. Since his behind was still painful, the experience was doubly excruciating, and Donelly enjoyed it more than any experience so far. But he discovered that sodomy without the preliminary beating gave him no pleasure.

It is unnecessary to say that I did not leave at the end of half an hour. I even accepted more rum. Donelly talked on and on, detailing his experiences in the brothels of the world. The man had so many fixations and perversions that it would take another twenty pages to detail them—women's hair, patent leather shoes (women's), tennis shirts, rubber boots and raincoats, guns, whips, canes, razor blades...Towards midnight, he showed me his collection of guns, of obscene photographs, and of whips and canes. He handed me a cat-o'-nine-tails and asked me to try it. I swished it through the air, and he closed his eyes as if he was listening to delightful music. Then he said dreamily: 'Would you like to use it?'

'On you?' I had guessed this was what he was leading up to.
'Yes.'
'No. I'd feel silly.'
He gripped my arm.
'Not even in exchange for the manuscript?'
'You'd let me take it?'
'You could copy it and return it.'
'All right.'
His voice became a croak.
'Come in here.'
We went into the next room. There was nothing in it but an enormous, old-fashioned double bed with a mattress that looked as comfortable as a wooden board. Attached to each of the four corners there were leather straps culminating in handcuffs.

He undressed slowly, without embarrassment. I noticed that the curtains on the windows were very heavy. Now I knew why Donelly had been glad to get rid of his farm labourers. In a wooden building of this sort, the sound of blows was bound to carry for some distance, particularly in the still southern nights, where a cicada can be heard a mile away.

He lay down naked, face downwards, and I looked at him squarely for the first time since we had been in the room. His back, buttocks and thighs were little more than welted scar tissue. It looked like a snow-covered road after half a dozen vehicles have driven back and forth over it. It was amazing that he could feel anything.

I had to snap the handcuffs on his wrists, then on his ankles,

47

and tighten the straps until he was stretched out. I left them rather slack at first, but he said impatiently : 'Tighter.' Then, with his face turned towards me, his eyes closed, he breathed : 'Now.' I knew there was no point in holding back. What I wondered was whether I could go too far and make him ask me to stop. So I raised the thing above my head—it had a vicious swing—and brought it down as hard as I could. It hissed like a skyrocket. I was astounded to see the deep red mark it made. I hesitated for a moment, and he said between clenched teeth : 'Go on, keep on, don't stop.' So, remembering my part of the bargain, I laid in as hard as I could. If I'd been hurting him, it would have been impossible; but it was obvious that he was gaining the most ecstatic delight from it. I became worried when the blood began to trickle, and to hit my face in spots as I struck; but if I stopped, he groaned : 'Please.' At one point, he said 'Stop', and I thought he'd had enough; but he only said : 'Now the cane', and I had to fetch a vicious officer's cane covered with leather, and beat his buttocks and thighs with it. To begin with, I tried to make it snap by hitting him as hard as I could—my arm was getting tired—but it made no difference. It only bent. After ten minutes, I sank on to a wooden chair and said : 'It's no good, I shall have to rest.' He lay still, and I realised he was unconscious. I tried shaking him by the shoulder, but his eyelids didn't even stir. I was glad he was still breathing. If he'd died, it might have been difficult to explain that I was doing this in the cause of literature.

I went back to the other room and poured myself a beer. Then I went and got the safe key out of his trouser pocket, and opened the safe. The other envelopes proved to contain letters and other papers. There was nothing more relating to Donelly in it. I took the box from the upper compartment and looked into it. A red cross on its side indicated that it was a medical chest, and at a first glance the contents confirmed this—rolls of bandages, a tin of adhesive plasters, bottles of antiseptic. It struck me that if Donelly got himself beaten only once a year, he would need a good stock of bandages and antiseptic. On closer inspection, I saw there were certain items whose purpose was not immediately apparent—a number of green tubes, sealed at either end, small round caps with wires attached which even I recognised as detonators, a bottle of a coarse brown-coloured powder. I examined one of the tubes. It was made of plastic, and there was a removable plastic cap at either end. I took out both caps, and tried to peer through it like a telescope; but there was a blockage halfway down; the tube was divided into two compartments. Under the ceiling light, the dividing wall looked like metal.

I opened the bottle of powder and sniffed it. It had a distinctive smell, but nothing I recognised. I picked up a bottle of a yellow liquid, and removed its glass stopper. I recognised this smell from my schooldays: concentrated acid, either hydrochloric or nitric. I found a saucer in the kitchen—peeping in at Donelly as I went past—and poured a small quantity of the brown powder in it. Then I cautiously poured a drop of the acid into the other side of the saucer, so that it formed a small pool. I tilted the saucer so the acid flowed across it. As soon as it met the powder, there was a fierce crackling, and I jumped backwards. Something spattered on my face in drops, and burned; I rushed to the kitchen and rubbed my face with a damp cloth. Smoke was already billowing out of the other room and into the corridor. The powder in the saucer was crackling and hissing, throwing off sparks. I opened the front door, and then reached out cautiously for the saucer; as I did so, it split in two. But the crackling had stopped—I had used a very small quantity of the powder. I raked the two halves on to a newspaper, and took them outside; they were still so hot that the paper was scorched. It took ten minutes or so for the room to empty of smoke.

So the problem of the haystack fire was solved. The method was simple and foolproof. The brown powder would be sealed in one half of the tube. The acid would be carried to the scene of the fire in a small bottle—there were several in the box. It would be carefully emptied into the second half, and a hole would be made in the cap to allow the hydrogen to escape. Then the tube would be set carefully on end, with the acid half uppermost, in the barn or haystack. Donelly presumably knew exactly how long it would take for the acid to eat through the metal dividing the two compartments; if the acid was diluted, it could possibly take twenty-four hours. Probably he had placed the miniature firebomb in the haystack in the dark hours of Sunday morning. No wonder he looked pleased as he stood watching the fire. It was a triumph of exact timing.

I replaced the box in the safe, together with the other papers, and locked it. Then I returned the key to Donelly's trousers. I was even tempted to solve the moral problem of Donelly's pyromania by fusing one of his time-bombs and leaving it in the safe among the papers, so that his arson kit would be destroyed. But it might burn down the house with Donelly in it. That would be poetic justice, but unnecessarily cruel. (Or would he enjoy it?)

I covered Donelly with blankets, but left him attached to the bedposts. If I was going to sleep in the house, I would prefer to feel safe; his set of guns and razors made me nervous. Then I locked the door and climbed into the single bed. Early this morning, I went into Donelly's room, and found him asleep. His breathing was regular. I unlocked the handcuffs, and he stirred and groaned. By half past six, I was walking down towards the town. I found a roadside café open and ate fried eggs, ham and grits, then rang the taxi driver who brought me. By eight o'clock I was back at the motel, and I wrote most of this account before I left to catch my afternoon plane. I have posted the Esmond Donelly manuscript back to Diana, so she can type it before we fly back to Shannon on Thursday. Considering how much I've drunk in the past twenty-four hours, I feel remarkably well.

April 22, Dallas, Texas

I found myself wondering this morning why I had gained a certain pleasure from beating Donelly. Is there a hidden sadistic component in me, a touch of Austin? And then, after my lecture this morning, the answer struck me. In an odd sort of way, Donelly's perversions are a proof of the freedom of the human spirit. All animals shrink from pain. Donelly had deliberately *acquired* the opposite attitude. He had chosen that pain should be a value, and he made it a value—something he enjoyed. I know the explanation lies in association of ideas and so on— Bridget, sex, pain—but that makes no difference. If a man can choose to experience pleasure from a beating, he can also choose to experience mystical ecstasy at the sight of a tree or a leaf. He

50

is not necessarily a victim of his changing emotions and physical needs. *That* is why I couldn't betray him. In a distorted way, there is a touch of the saint about him. A saint without a purpose.

On Friday, April 25, we flew back to London, and I had no more time for long journal entries, for reasons that will become clear.

We had intended to return by sea; but the literary puzzle represented by Esmond Donelly made me impatient to return; I was afraid that some other researcher might get to Ballycahane first. But I wanted to spend a day in the British Museum, finding out anything I could about Donelly. Before we left New Haven (where Diana had been staying with friends), the Donelly manuscript was sent back to Denham Springs by registered mail; Diana had made two typed copies. The plane trip from Kennedy to London was my first opportunity to study the typescript.

It was tantalisingly short. I had not realised, when Colonel Donelly showed it to me, that the manuscript included Esmond's *Refutation of the Theories of Dr Hume, with some reference to the Discours Preliminaire of d'Alembert*. I had supposed that Donelly had bought the manuscript already sewn together, but evidently this was not so. The *Refutation* was thirty or so pages long; Donelly's journals were less than twenty (of which I have already quoted three).

What most impressed me about Esmond Donelly was the modernness of his mind. The language is the language of Walpole or Gray; the thought was often closer to Goethe, or even William Blake. The central point of his argument against Hume and d'Alembert is very simple: that when man outgrows religious authority, he usually becomes the victim of his own triviality. When does man most frequently experience the sensation of freedom? he asks, and answers: When he is bored. 'Boredom is to be free, but to experience no particular impulse to make use of the freedom.' And he invents a Swiftian parable to illustrate his point. In the midst of the high mountains of Tartary, he says, there is a valley in which dwells a race of small but sturdy and healthy people. From the earliest times, it has been part of the religious observance of these people to carry two heavy weights, in the shape of a water-bottle, on either side of the waist. They

51

would no more think of walking abroad without their weights than an Englishman would think of walking naked along White-hall. They wear them from birth to death, and there are strict penalties for removing them. But the greatest pleasure of this race is the exercise of walking, and a small band of rebels declare that the weights are intended to make walking uncomfortable. Then even bolder spirits declare that man should be able to fly like a bird or float like a balloon, and that the weights are intended to prevent them from enjoying the freedom for which they were created. There is a revolution; the king is executed (a remarkable anticipation of the execution of Louis XVI), and the people tear off their weights. To their amazement, nothing happens, except that they find it hard to maintain balance without them. The more timid spirits resume their weights; the bolder ones practise walking without them, and soon declare that it is merely a matter of habit. They are so delighted with this new accomplishment that at first they walk day and night, striding from one end of the valley to the other, and even attempting to climb the mountains. They soon discover that the mountains are sheer walls of rock that cannot be scaled. And now some of the weightless ones fall into a frenzy and rush frantically from one end of the valley to the other until they collapse with exhaustion. Others attempt to scale the steep walls out of the valley, and either fall down when they are exhausted, or cast themselves down out of terror or despair. But by far the larger number of the weightless ones simply sit at home, utterly bored, since they know every inch of the valley. They jeer at the people who still wear weights, calling them superstitious hogs. But after a few generations these weightless ones are dead, for their lack of exercise makes them grow immensely fat and die at an early age. Finally, only those who wear weights continue to survive; they elect a king, and for many generations the Great Revolt is only a terrifying memory. Until a sect arises that declares that man was created to fly like a bird...

The story sounds utterly pessimistic, an allegory of original sin. But I am inclined to reject this view. For Donelly says : ' There were some of those climbers who were never seen again; yet certain shepherds whose flocks fed under the shadow of the great walls affirmed that they heard voices hallooing from far above their heads, where the slopes of the mountain vanished into the clouds.' In other words, perhaps a few of the climbers got beyond the cliffs and over the top of the mountains.

What Donelly is saying—and it is a remarkable perception for a seventeen-year-old boy—is not that 'Men need weights', but that the men *of the valley* need weights. They are healthy, sturdy and adventurous (i.e. love walking), and the only way in which to maintain these qualities in their tiny valley is to wear heavy weights. But a few among them, a very few, are born climbers...

Donelly was a born climber—that was obvious. And this was what baffled me. This man had lived to be eighty-four (according to Colonel Donelly); he was a talented writer, an original thinker, a friend of Rousseau and Wilkes. Why, then, had he left so little mark on history? If the *Refutation of Hume* and the published travel diary were all I had to go on, I might have concluded that here was a talent that spent itself early, like Rimbaud or Wolf. But the unpublished journal could leave no possible doubt that his talent remained unimpaired. So what had happened?

I should add, in parenthesis, that the purely philosophical part of the *Refutation* contains some of its most interesting pages, characterised by a psychological subtlety that was at least a century before its time—I could think of nothing like it before F. H. Bradley. He cites Hume's *Abstract of a Treatise of Human Nature*, in which Hume argues that the notion of cause and effect is derived from our habits, and is not a 'necessary connection'. Hume says: 'Supposing a man such as Adam were created in the full vigour of understanding, but without experience', would it not be impossible for him to see the necessary connection between cause and effect? If, for example, he were watching two billard balls striking one another, he could not possibly infer, by the use of his intelligence, that they would click and then career off in opposite directions. For all he knows they might coalesce, or leap up into the air, or simply stand still side by side.

Donelly plunges quickly on that phrase ' in the full vigour of his understanding ' and points out that it is a sleight of hand.

53

'Hume implies that Adam's perception of the billiard balls will be innocent and unprejudiced, when, in fact, a completely innocent perception, like that of a newly born baby, would not perceive the balls at all, or rather, would perceive them without taking them in, as I might peruse a letter written in an unknown tongue. If Adam is to be allowed the full vigour of understanding, enough to watch the balls with interest, then he must also be allowed some knowledge of cause and effect. He may not know whether the balls will spring apart or combine together like two drops of water, but he knows that *something* will happen, which is to say that he knows an effect must follow the cause.'

No, a man as perceptive as this *must* make some mark on his age. How, then, is it possible that I had never heard of him? Even if he wrote very little himself, others would mention him —Boswell, for example, or even Crabb Robinson. Total obscurity for such a man is inconceivable.

I had written to a friend in the British Museum from Dallas, asking if he would find me any available material on Donelly; I hurried there promptly at nine o'clock on the Saturday morning after my arrival in London. Tim Morrison—of the Department of Printed Books—invited me down to the staff canteen for coffee. I had told him all about Fleisher—even about the suggestion that I might forge some Donelly manuscript. Tim's approach to life is grave and cautious—he often gives me the impression of a man peering cautiously over a hedge as he approaches a subject in his precise, hesitant manner.

'I suppose you know what you're doing. I mean, you don't want to land in gaol for fraudulent misrepresentation...'

I assured him there was no danger of that, and produced the typescript of the *Refutation of Hume*. He read it carefully for ten minutes, while I drank my coffee and glanced at the headlines of the *Guardian*. He said:

'I agree this seems genuine. There's only one thing that bothers me. Why did he give it to Rousseau? With views like this, he must have thought Rousseau a complete fool.'

'I'm not sure. There's an element of optimism in Donelly that probably responded to Rousseau. Besides, Rousseau isn't as simple-minded as most people seem to think. He never really suggested that people ought to go back to nature.'

'No. No.' He seemed abstracted. I asked him if he'd found me any books on Donelly. He frowned into his coffee cup, then said : 'You'd better come and look.'

We walked back to his office, which is approached through a labyrinth of corridors and spiral stairways. It was immaculately tidy. On the desk there were half a dozen volumes with slips of paper stuck in them. He told me to sit at the desk. Then he sat in the armchair opposite, lit a cigarette, and returned to the *Refutation of Hume*.

The books were disappointing. There was an edition of the travel diary that I had already seen, printed in London in 1821 by John Murray, Byron's publisher, with a brief preface (by the publisher) describing Donelly as 'an Irish gentleman and scholar', but offering no other biographical information—not even whether Donelly was still alive. (He was, though; he was seventy-two in 1820.) There was a brief reference to him in Gilpin's *English Diaries in the Seventeenth and Eighteenth Centuries* (1876), and a quotation from his diary in a book on Venice by an author whose name I have forgotten. The only interesting reference to Donelly occurs in a letter of Byron to Francis Hodgson in June 1811 (*Collected Works*, edited by Prothero and Coleridge, Vol. 9, p. 420) : 'Sherry [Sheridan] told me that he never knew a wilder character than my father ['Mad Jack' Byron], although he had known Wilkes and Donelly in their younger days.' And in another letter to William Gifford (Vol. 13, p. 193) he remarks : 'I was much struck by Esmond Donelly's assertion, that it was the comparative insignificance of ourselves and our world, when placed in competition with the mighty whole, of which it is an atom, that first led him to imagine that our pretensions to eternity might be overrated.'

While I was making a note of the various items—I had to pad out my Introduction somehow—Tim was looking through some papers in a cupboard. When I had finished, he placed a single sheet in front of me. It was a photostat of a page of manuscript. The handwriting was not difficult to read, although there were a few *ʃ*s instead of *s*s. It read :

...was satisfied he meant to fulful his engagement.

The custom of eating dogs at Otaheite being mentioned, Goldsmith observed that this was also a custom in China : that a dog butcher is as common there as any other butcher; and that when he walks abroad, all the dogs fall on him. JOHNSON : 'That is not owing to his killing dogs, Sir. I remember a butcher at Lichfield, whom a dog that was in the house where I lived, always attacked. It is the smell of carnage which provokes this, let the animals he has killed be what they may.' GOLDSMITH : 'Yes, there is a general abhorrence in animals at the sign of massacre. If you put a tub full of blood into a stable, the horses are like to go mad.' JOHNSON : 'I doubt that.' GOLDSMITH : 'Nay, Sir, it is a fact well authenticated.'

This passage is followed by several lines that have been blacked out very thoroughly. Then it goes on :

THRALE : 'You had better prove it before you put it into your book on natural history. You may...'

I looked up at Tim with a feeling of bafflement, suspecting he had given me the wrong page. He placed another photostat in front of me, this time of a typed sheet. It read :

GOLDSMITH (contd) : 'I was told as much by Esmond Donelly, who assured me he had tried the experiment.' JOHNSON (rising into warmth) : 'Ay, Sir, I don't doubt that such a man would be capable of that and worse.' GOLD-SMITH : 'He does not lack convivial qualities.' JOHNSON : 'Indeed, I believe he is a phoenix of convivial malice. The same might be said of the Devil.' GOLDSMITH : 'Yet he knows horses.' THRALE : 'You had better prove it...'

Tim said :

'Boswell usually blanked out the passages he wanted to cancel so they couldn't be read. That's a page of the manuscript of the *Life of Johnson*—Yale let us have photostats of most of the Isham collection. They've deciphered most of the cancelled passages.'

' Amazing. How did you find it? '

' I didn't. I mentioned your interest in Donelly to the man who's cataloguing the photostats. By complete chance, he'd seen Donelly's name the day before.'

' So there may be other references to Donelly in the manuscript of Boswell? '

' It's possible. If we find any, I'll let you know.'

I spent the rest of the day in the Reading Room, but found nothing else of interest. Back at Kensington Square (where we were staying with Jeremy Worthington, one of the directors of the John Jamieson whiskey firm), I discussed my day's work with Diana and Sue Worthington. We agreed that it was clear that Johnson disliked Donelly, which seemed to indicate that he knew of Donelly's reputation as a rake. But why should he flare up so quickly at the mention of his name? Boswell was a rake too; so was Wilkes, with whom Johnson came to terms. Why pick on Donelly? What did he mean : ' he'd be capable of that *and worse* '?

Sue thought that it probably meant nothing at all except that Johnson was irritated at Goldsmith's gullibility. I was inclined to agree. Then Sue said :

' You ought to ask Jeremy about Boswell. He knows someone who discovered some Boswell manuscript.'

This was interesting news. I had spent part of the day reading Boswell's journals, and the story of their discovery, which is fascinating reading. Since it has some relevance to this narrative, I will outline it briefly. Boswell died in 1795 in his mid-fifties, probably of cirrhosis of the liver. Three of his friends were appointed his literary executors—the Reverend William Temple, Sir William Forbes and Edmund Malone. Boswell's instructions were that these friends should read his private journals and papers and publish whatever they thought interesting. They read the papers, but apparently decided that the stuff was either too boring or too shocking to be worth publishing. After Macaulay's murderous essay on Boswell (1843), the latter's stock sank so low that he was virtually forgotten. The Victorian ladies of his family who occasionally glanced into the papers were so shocked by what they saw that they felt justified in circulating a rumour that the Boswell diaries had been destroyed. One can understand the effect of a passage like the following (for November 25, 1762):

> I picked up a girl in the Strand; went into a court with intention to enjoy her in armour [contraceptive]. But she had none. I toyed with her. She wondered at my size, and said if I ever took a girl's maidenhead, I would make her squeak. I gave her a shilling and had command of myself to go without touching her.

In the mid-1870s, Birkbeck Hill, editor of Boswell's *Johnson*, was practically thrown out when he went to Auchinleck—the seat of the Boswells—and asked to see the Journals.

In 1905, the last of the Boswell line died, and the estate passed to Lord Talbot of Malahide, near Dublin, including the ebony cabinet containing papers that Boswell had mentioned in his will. An American professor, Chauncey Tinker, became interested in Boswell and advertised in the Irish Press for material on him. He received an anonymous letter suggesting that he try Malahide Castle. A letter to Malahide produced no effect, so Tinker finally decided to call there. This time he was in luck. Lord Talbot allowed him to see a small part of the collection of Boswell papers. Subsequently, an American lieutenant-colonel, Ralph Isham, heard of the papers, and succeeded in buying them from Lord Talbot in 1927. Professor Geoffrey Scott, and then Professor Frederick Pottle, set about the task of publishing this vast body of material—more than a million words. And from then on, new Boswell manuscripts continued to turn up. A croquet box at Malahide Castle proved to contain more Boswell letters and the manuscript of the *Tour to the Hebrides with Dr Johnson*. In 1930, Professor Abbott of Aberdeen was going through the papers of Sir William Forbes—one of Boswell's executors—and discovered another rich cache of letters and manuscripts. Forbes had obviously borrowed some of the papers to examine them, in accordance with the will, and then forgotten to return them to Auchinleck. And in 1940, still more Boswell papers were found in an old cow barn on the Malahide estate, including the manuscript of the *Life of Johnson*; the page I had seen in the Museum came from this manuscript. No one has ever explained quite how Boswell's papers got into a cow barn.

Obviously, the Boswell manuscripts were thoroughly dispersed. In fact, the earliest discovery was made in 1850 by a Major Stone in Boulogne, who bought something in a grocer's shop and found it wrapped in a letter signed ' James Boswell '. Stone was able to buy a whole pile of letters written by Boswell to the Reverend William Temple—a clergyman to whom he confessed the filthier episodes of his life—and he later published them, suitably bowdlerised. Those had apparently got to Boulogne through Temple's daughter, whose clergyman husband moved there in 1825. When they died, their papers were sold—or given—to a pedlar of wrapping paper, who passed them on to the grocer.

Tracing the complicated history of the Boswell papers had made me aware of the difficulties I might face in the quest for Esmond Donelly. Obviously, no amount of patience and diligence would be of any avail unless luck was on my side. Oddly enough, I had a curious feeling of confidence, which may simply have been the outcome of my intense interest in Donelly and the literature of his period—for, apart from Blake and Goethe, I have always found the writers of the eighteenth century a pretty disappointing bunch, and therefore never taken the trouble to study them.

From what Sue Worthington had told me, I assumed that Jeremy was acquainted with some member of the Talbot family, or perhaps with whoever had discovered the papers in the cow barn. As soon as he came in the door, I asked him :

' What's the name of your friend who found some of Boswell's papers? '

' Oh, he didn't actually find them. They were found by a chap called O'Rourke in Portmarnock."

' Not Malahide? '

' No, not Malahide, although it's pretty certain they came from Malahide. As far as I can make out, some of the Boswell papers were borrowed by a retired clergyman named O'Rourke during the first world war, and they never got returned. His son found them after his death.'

' What happened to them? '

' Well, they're in the hands of a strange old maniac called Isaac Jenkinson Bates, who lives in Dublin. His nephew's one of our testers in the distillery and he told me about them one day.'

' Have you ever seen them? '

' No. The old boy's pretty cagey about them. Obviously, they really belong to the Malahide estate—or perhaps to this American university that bought the papers.'

' But do you know anything about them? '

' Nothing much, except that some of the stuff's pretty pornographic.'

' That sounds odd. I mean, what would a clergyman be doing with it? '

' He was probably a dirty-minded old man.'

' Do you know the address of this Jenkinson character? '

' Not offhand, but I've got to ring Dublin on Monday—I'll ask Hurd—that's the nephew.'

And there the matter stood for the weekend. I knew that my chances of getting to see the old boy were limited, if he was as cagey as Jeremy said; but there was just a hope that his nephew might be able to apply pressure.

On Monday, Jeremy rang me from his office. He had just spoken to the old man's nephew. Hurd had verified that Jenkinson Bates was extremely cautious about showing his material. But in the course of the conversation, he had mentioned something that sounded promising. Bates was extremely interested in murder. So it was not impossible that he had read my book *The Sociology of Violent Crime*. Jeremy suggested that I write to him on the subject of Irish murder in the eighteenth century, and try to make his acquaintance that way. Jeremy gave me Bates's address at Baggot Street in Dublin.

There was not a great deal more to do in London. I spent two more days there, seeing friends, lunching with publishers and drinking cocktails. Under normal circumstances I would have enjoyed the total change from lecturing; but now I thought about nothing but Donelly. I wrote a letter to *The Times Literary Supplement* about my interest in Donelly, and another to the *Irish Times*. And I spent a futile afternoon in the British

Museum, trying to discover if Isaac Jenkinson Bates had ever written a book on murder; if he had, it was not in the Museum. On Wednesday morning, Sue Worthington drove us to London Airport to catch the plane for Shannon. Just before we left the house, Jeremy rang, and asked to speak to me.

'I've just been talking to Jim Hurd again. He mentioned something that might help you in your approach to old Bates. Apparently the old man believes that the Ireland's Eye murderer was innocent. Do you know anything about the case?'

'I remember a little. Man called Kirwan.'

This was a valuable piece of information. At midday we caught our plane, landing in Shannon just over an hour later. Tom Kenny, our local garage man, had driven our old car down to the airport to meet us. Two hours later, we were back in Moycullen.

There is an immense feeling of relief in returning home from a long journey. I love Ireland : the narrow roads, the shabby small towns, the incredible green of the fields, the low clouds, the peaty lakes. I began to feel something like resentment of Donelly, for preventing me from relaxing completely for a week or so.

Our house stands half a mile outside Moycullen, up a narrow, rocky lane that becomes a torrent in the rainy season. It is an eighteenth-century vicarage, built of grey limestone, the walls covered with lichen and ivy. We bought it in 1963, on the proceeds of the 'Sex Diary'. In our absence, Diana's former husband, Robert Kirsten, had been looking after the house for us. Since 1960 he has been Composer in Residence at a series of American universities, and has been enormously successful. Last autumn he decided he needed a long period of solitude to compose, so we invited him to stay with us. He'd been in the house since January; Mrs Healy, the wife of the shepherd down below us, cooked his meals. Kirsten had left for Dublin three days before we returned—two of his chamber operas were being performed there, and he was to conduct. The house was empty and peaceful. Mrs Healy had lit fires in the dining room and our bedroom, giving them a cheerful brightness. Our house tends to be dark, since it is surrounded on three sides by trees, and some of the rooms are panelled in mahogany; except for the electric

61

lights, it could be the setting for one of Le Fanu's novels.

I stood at our bedroom window—Mopsy was jumping up and down on the bed and making its springs creak—and looked out over Lough Corrib. There was a slight drizzle that was little more than mist. The trees, with their spring buds, looked black and wet. There is a hypnotic quality about our part of Ireland; visitors to our house find themselves sleeping for twelve hours at a stretch, and still yawning at four in the afternoon. As I stood there, the firelight flickering on the walls, I experienced an enormous relaxation that made me realise how much my lecture trip had tired me. My emotions seemed to sink into a deep feather bed; a great peace and detachment came over me. And it struck me suddenly that Esmond Donelly might have looked out on this scene, nearly two centuries ago, and seen very much what I now saw. Then I remembered Fleisher's assertion that Donelly had seduced both illegitimate daughters of the local priest, Father Riordan, and I felt jarred. If it had been one daughter, it would have been understandable; some pretty, innocent country girl, probably brought up by a neighbouring farmer or shepherd (perhaps an ancestor of Sean Healy), who might have seen Donelly as he paused at the local grocer one day for a glass of whiskey or porter, and been fascinated by the well-dressed, cultured gentleman. And Donelly would look at the healthy cheeks, and think how pleasant it would be to remove the coarse linen dress and run his hand over the shapely body as if she was a thoroughbred horse. This would be natural and pleasant; but the seduction of two girls indicated a gloating sensuality, an obsession with conquest.

Mopsy said: 'Daddy, can I have a bath now?', and broke my train of thought. I undressed her, put her into the bath, then went downstairs to open the bottle of Californian burgundy I had stood near the fire—I had brought it all the way back for the pleasure of drinking it in my own sitting room. I put a record on the gramophone—Delius's violin concerto—and allowed myself to sink into a state of blurry and soft-edged melancholy. The wine was very slightly warm. Most of the wine authorities say that one should never expose it to direct heat, but I find that ten minutes in front of a fire never does a vin ordinaire any harm. I poured myself a large glass-full, and drank half of it straight down—the way I like to drink the first glass of wine of the evening. It quenches the thirst, gives the best of its flavour to the palate, and produces an immediate warm glow. Our cases stood by the door, still unpacked; but I wanted to enjoy the savour of being back in my own home. Our sitting room has a distinctive, not unpleasant smell—resembling somewhat the smell of old books. Most of our furniture was bought by Diana at local auctions—she has a passion for jumble sales and auctions—and there is not an item that could be described as modern. Looking around, it struck me that Esmond Donelly might have sat in a room such as this; for all I know, he had sat in this very room. I reached out for one of the shopping bags Diana had carried on the plane, and found the typescript of Donelly's *Refutation of Hume*, and opened it casually.

> ...I am not criticising Mr Hume's logic, which is invariably cogent. But I am suggesting that his temperament is such as to blind him to certain varieties of feeling. His logic may demolish the aspirations of the alchymists; but what does he know of their visions?

I stopped to think about this. It was obviously worth a critical footnote, pointing out the similarity of the idea to Blake's:

> How do you know but ev'ry bird that cuts the airy way
> Is an immense world of delight, closed to your senses five?

And again I wondered: How could such a man be a boasting Casanova, pursuing women out of some absurd obsession for mere quantity? And what had Johnson called him: 'a phoenix of convivial malice'? Somehow, this was the last phrase I would think of applying to the author of the *Refutation of Hume*.

The record finished; I went to turn it over, and looked for a moment out of the window that faces west. The clouds were low on the hills of Iar Connaught, but the sky behind them was bright. On the opposite hillside, a row of poplars stood against the skyline. For a moment, I was back in the bedroom at Long Island, tasting the faintly smoky taste of Beverley's small nipples, then feeling the exploding warmth of loins as I looked past her

63

shoulder at the trees on the cliff top. I pushed away the blurry melancholy, grasped at the flavour of hardness that came over the poplars, and knew again with sudden total insight that human beings must *never* accept the ingredients of present-consciousness, that greater horizons always lie beyond the bounds of immediacy judgements. For a moment, I was Esmond Donelly, asking what Hume knew of the alchemist's vision. The contradictions vanished; suddenly, I understood Donelly. For him, the alchemist was not a transmuter of metals, *but a transmuter of consciousness; and sex was the philosopher's stone that could transmute the base metals of ordinary consciousness into vision.*

Mopsy yelled: 'Daddy, I want to get out.' I got Diana out of her kitchen and sent her upstairs. I wanted to fix this insight and explore it. Because there was still an obvious problem. No one would deny that sex has this power to raise consciousness to a higher intensity; since Lawrence, it has become a commonplace of the twentieth century. But Lawrence also knew another secret of the sexual impulse: 'What many women cannot give, one woman can.' Ever since I had been with Diana, my own interest in seduction had waned to a mere curiosity. I could look at a pretty girl and wonder what kind of bra and panties she was wearing under her clothes or whether she lay passively in bed or moved violently, but the curiosity was not strong enough to lead to pursuit. In recent years, I had even been surprised to discover an increasing tendency to reject those harmless forms of mutual satisfaction that are offered with ' no strings attached '. A girl at a party once said to me frankly: ' Why don't we share a bed afterwards? It's better than masturbating in separate beds.' I agreed and we spent the night together, with ' no strings attached '. But in the morning, I realised that it wasn't entirely true that there were no strings. Two bodies had interpenetrated; so had two worlds. I didn't particularly like her world; it was too vague and futile. Like planets that have approached too close, we had caused seismic disturbances in one another. I can no longer remember what she was like in bed; but I can clearly remember certain anecdotes she told me about the failure of her marriage, that still disturb me. I would have done better to leave her spinning in her own orbit.

This is why I suspect Casanova's veracity. He was neither stupid nor insensitive—that much is clear. Yet there is little evidence in the *Memoirs* that these mutual disturbances took place. A girl is young and 'amiable'; she begins by rejecting the liberties he tries to take, until his blandishments 'change anger to a softer passion', after making him promise not to despise her afterwards, she allows him to undo her corset strings. Even if the girl is a seventeen-year-old virgin just out of a convent, there is never any suggestion of the usual difficulties, physical or psychological; only vague references to spending 'several delicious hours' or 'giving ourselves up to an ecstasy of pleasure until daybreak'. There is a dream-like air about it all.

Donelly was no Signeur Jacques Casanova de Seingalt, that was clear. And the necessity of finding out more about him became an almost physical discomfort. I went into the dining room, where I keep my books on law and criminology, and searched until I found an account of the Ireland's Eye murder case. It was commonplace enough. William Bourke Kirwan was an artist who lived at Howth with his wife in the year 1852. One afternoon in September, they hired a boatman to row them out to Ireland's Eye, the attractive little island that lies a mile outside Howth harbour—and within sight of Malahide. It was a still day, and at seven o'clock, screams were heard from the island. At eight, the boatman arrived and found Kirwan still sketching—a suspicious circumstance, since it was dark. Kirwan said he wasn't sure where his wife had gone—he presumed she was somewhere on the other side of the island, still swimming. They found her in a shallow rock pool, her face badly bruised, her lungs full of water. Although a verdict of accidental death was returned, the circumstances were so suspicious that the body was exhumed. Kirwan was sentenced on circumstantial evidence; he claimed not to have heard the screams which could be heard on shore; he had a mistress with a baby in Dublin. Many people believed him to be innocent, and the death sentence was subsequently commuted to penal servitude. He later married his mistress, and emigrated to America.

I went to my study, switched on the electric fire, and typed out a letter to Isaac Jenkinson Bates, saying that I intended writing about the Ireland's Eye case in a book on murder, and wondered if he would mind explaining to me why he believed Kirwan innocent. Then I walked down the hill and posted it. After that, I felt relaxed enough to read Mopsy a story about Peter Rabbit.

I was up early the next morning, and took a stroll around Ross Lake. When I came back, Diana said : ' Miss Donelly of Croom rang up. She wants you to ring her back.'

' Did she sound friendly? '

' More or less. She says she's written you a letter.'

There were two large cardboard boxes full of the correspondence that had arrived while we were in the States; so far, I had not worked up the energy to go through them. Now, while Diana cooked me egg and bacon, I emptied them on the floor of the study. I told Mopsy to sort out all those that had been redirected from my publisher—these could wait. I opened two parcels of records, and several books from publishers who hoped for a favourable quote they could use in advertising. (Regrettably, they never send the books I would like to get free; only the ones that are likely to get bad reviews.) Finally, I found the letter with a Limerick postmark, addressed in a neat, round hand.

I must confess that I had not been entirely frank with her in the letter I had written from New Haven. I saw no point in getting doors slammed in my face from the beginning. So I had simply told her that I had heard about Esmond Donelly during my lecture tour—leaving her to infer that someone in my lecture audiences had raised the name—and wanted to write an essay on him for a future book. I took the risk of adding that I had spoken to Colonel Donelly and seen a copy of Donelly's *Travel Diary*.

Her reply made me feel ashamed of myself. Dignified but friendly, she said that she was happy to hear that her ancestor was not entirely forgotten, and that she had spent years trying to persuade an English publisher to reissue the Diary. She and her sister would be delighted to see me any time I cared to call. In the meantime, they would write to the solicitor who was holding the Donelly papers in safe-keeping and get him to bring them to the house...

Again I had pangs of conscience, and felt inclined to drop the whole thing. Then I fortified myself with a glance at the manuscript I had already uncovered, and decided it would be absurd to drop a venture whose beginnings had been so auspicious. I rang the exchange and got put through to Miss Donelly's number. A brisk, rather English voice answered.

'Ah, Mr Sorme, it was kind of you to ring back. Your wife tells me you only got back from America late yesterday. You must be quite exhausted.'

I said I was feeling fine, and enquired when they expected to get the papers from the solicitor.

'Oh, they're here now. He was very prompt. We've been reading them through. It's simply fascinating material. How do you propose to travel? By train?'

When I said by car, she asked me why I didn't drive over immediately and have lunch with them. I looked at my watch, and said I could be there by mid-afternoon. Before I hung up, she said:

'I hope you won't be offended if I ask you one question.' My heart sank. 'I hope you're not interested in any of the nasty stories about him?'

'Nasty stories?' I saw myself entangled in a web of evasions and half-truths. But she said:

'My sister saw one of your books in the library, a book about murder. I hope you're not interested in the silly rumours about Esmond and Lady Mary Glenney?'

I was able to say, with an enormous sense of relief, that I had never heard such rumours. She said in a business-like voice:

'Good, I'm delighted to hear it.' There was a click, and she suddenly snapped:

'Tina, are you listening on the other line?'

A timid voice said:

'Yes, dear.'

'I wish you wouldn't. It's a most annoying habit.' The line suddenly went dead. I stared at the phone for a moment, then hung up.

Before leaving the house, I rang an old friend at the University of Galway, Professor Kevin Roche. His assistant said he was at home. I rang him there.

'Do you know anything about Esmond Donelly?'

'The fellow who wrote a book about deflowering virgins?'

'Do you think he really wrote it?'

'I don't see why not. My copy has his name on the title page.'

'Do you have it there? Could I come and see it?'

'Certainly. When would you like to come?'

'Now', I said. And within forty-five minutes I was in Kevin's study, overlooking Galway Bay, and with a fine view of Inishmaan and Inishmore.

I had already decided to pursue my policy of discretion, for news travels fast in Ireland. So after we had exchanged civilities, and I had accepted a small glass of Bushmill's, I handed Kevin the manuscript of the *Refutation of Hume*, and told him that I had been asked to edit it for publication.

'Rather short, isn't it?'

'I'm hoping to find other things—letters and journals. I'm just going to see the Misses Donelly at Ballycahane.'

He handed me the paperback book that lay on his desk; it had been printed by the Obelisk Press in Paris. *Of the Deflowering of Maids*, by Esmond Donelly. A short introductory note signed Henry V. Miller repeated the facts I already knew about Donelly —his date and place of birth, his travel diaries; the fact that the present volume was published in German by Brockhaus of Leipzig (who was also the publisher of Casanova's *Memoirs*) in 1835, and by an anonymous Dutch printer—obviously translated from the German edition—in English in 1863. I opened it to a chapter called: 'Of the Fallacy that all Women are Alike in the Dark'.

ROBIN. Pray, sir, continue with your instruction, for I hang upon your words.

LORD COBALD. You flatter me, my dear boy. But I find it highly gratifying that you agree with me about the importance of acquiring this tender knowledge. We must next consider the fallacy, propagated by Claude de Crebillon and Mr Cleland, that has been expressed in the words 'All cats are grey in the dark '. You may take my word for it that, when I look back over a lifetime of women, I can remember no two who were alike when their thighs were apart. I am not now speaking merely of the formation of the nether regions of delight, which may be plump or boney, fleshy or firm, downy or bristly, but of what I might call the soul that dwells in the cunt. No man of breeding would confuse the dark wine of Burgundy with the clairet of Bordeaux, and even a child can tell the difference between an apple and a pear, though one be soft and juicy and the other hard and astringent. So it is with women. And just as the taste of a wine is judged by the first mouthfull, so the individual flavour of a girl may be most clearly grasped in the first movement of encunting, as the velvet head is received by the coral lips. I have known wenches that were sharp and fresh, like an apple eaten by moonlight, others that were syrupy and soft, like a pear or a peach; others who were hard and round in the arms, but sweet within, like a melon.

ROBIN. Indeed, sir, I understand you well, for my two sisters, who were born within an hour of one another, are as different as could be in bed.

LORD COBALD. Your penetration delights me [a Freudian pun, this]. Pray acquaint me with your own view of the difference between them. For I myself have never succeeded in telling one from the other by appearance alone.

ROBIN. As to that, sir, my mother herself often calls one by the other's name. Yet between the sheets they are as unlike as could be. Agatha is such as you describe, syrupy and soft like a peach. When I enter her, her cunt welcomes me with warm and tender embrace, as is appropriate from a sister who loves her brother. And then, sir, I feel as if I have become my own prick, and am tenderly engulfed from head to foot. The sensation is not unlike immersing in a warm bath, as I do every Candlemass. Now Christina, on the other hand, produces a most lewd and lustful sensation as I slip within her, for she seems to experience surprise that a man should perform so strange an operation, or even that she should be lying there naked. In consequence, I find myself

69

imagining her fully clothed, in the brown velvet dress with silver buttons she wears when pouring tea, or the green gown she wears for riding in the park, and the shock of finding her cunt defenseless makes me drive into her like a stallion, so 'tis wonder that her belly has not swelled before this.

LORD COBALD. Your gift of expression is remarkable, my dear boy. That is precisely the difference I have observed between them. You are lucky to have such gifted sisters. My own sister, when I finally succeeded in overcoming her modesty, was pleasing enough, but as tasteless and fuzzy as an apple that has been left in the bowl too long.

I put down the book, and looked across at Kevin, who was still absorbed in the *Refutation of Hume.* If he had looked up, I would have said : This is another forgery. The first page might have been written by Donelly, for it has the kind of psychological penetration I have come to expect of him. But the paragraph about the sisters has more than a touch of de Sade's *Philosophy in the Bedroom,* while the last sentence has a touch of cruelty that is not justified even by its psychological insight.

But by the time Kevin looked up from the typescript, I had changed my mind about speaking. If I explained why I was certain it was a forgery, I would have to admit that I knew more of Donelly's work in this manner. So, instead, I made remarks about it being fascinating stuff. Kevin himself was delighted with the *Refutation,* and asked me if he might get it copied, to write an article on the development of Donelly's style. I promised to let him have it when I had shown it to the Misses Donelly, and left him. It was after midday, and I wanted to get to Limerick. It was only after I had gone through Oranmore that I remembered I had forgotten to ask him if he knew anything of a scandal involving Lady Mary Glenney.

I dropped off Diana and Mopsy in Limerick, where they could do a few hours' shopping, then drove south on the Cork road, through flat, drowsy, pastoral country that looked almost feverishly green in the April sunlight. I stopped in Ballycahane to enquire for Castle Donelly, and was told that I had come too far and would have to go back towards Adare and turn off the road. With these instructions, I managed to draw up at the front door of Castle Donelly at about three o'clock.

It is not, of course, a castle, but a Queen Anne house, built of silvery brick with red brick Corinthian pilasters; the walls are covered with ivy, and the house has an atmosphere of neglect that is so common to great Irish houses, particularly in Connaught and Munster. A fine flight of water-lily steps—which are curved—ran up to the front door. Their surface was so irregular that I wondered how anyone could get up and down without twisting an ankle. The River Meigh runs beside the house, and the ruins of Adare Abbey stand against the skyline. It came as a shock to realise that this house looked new and smart when Donelly was born in it—for it was built around 1700—and that the walls were probably free of ivy even when he died here. It was like taking a leap back into the past, and it brought a disturbing sense of passing time.

Before I had reached the top of the steps, the door was opened by a vigorous lady in riding clothes; she had cropped iron-grey hair, and stood with her legs astride, like one of Rowlandson's country squires. The handshake was as hard and firm as a man's.

' I'm Eileen Donelly. Delighted to meet you.' Her accent was English upper class, with a touch of Irish in the vowels. ' I'm glad you made it.'

The place was impressive and cold, with a huge flight of stairs running to murky upper regions; there was a great deal of marble, which contrasted oddly with peeling Victorian wallpaper. But the library she led me into had a large fire. Another lady, also in male attire, was knitting by the fire. She was introduced to me as Miss Tina; she was small and sweet-faced, and female clothes would have suited her better. I suspected that the riding breeches were to keep out the cold. They offered me tea, and Miss Tina went off to make it. Miss Eileen stood in front of the fire, her legs apart, hands behind her back, and made general conversation about the weather, the countryside, and so on. Then we talked about America. She seemed to be very curious about America, and after ten minutes or so, remarked casually that she had heard that Americans would offer large sums for houses such as this. I said this was probably so. How much? she asked. I took a very quick guess, and said that the right person would probably pay twenty-five thousand for it. 'Pounds or dollars?' she asked quickly. I said pounds. At this she looked very thoughtful. And as Miss Tina poured the tea, using a beautiful eighteenth-century tea-service that might have been the one Robin's sister Christina used, I realised suddenly why they were so interested in this revival of Esmond Donelly's reputation. These two had no children; why should they not sell this huge and uncomfortable house, and buy themselves a pleasant flat in London? I began to feel less guilty about my quest. The publication of *Memoirs of An Irish Rake* would certainly increase their ancestor's reputation more than that of the travel diary or the *Refutation of Hume.*

Miss Tina asked me about Colonel Donelly, and I told her a little about his career in recent years. She looked very sad.

'Poor man. We really ought to write to him, Eileen.'

'Maybe. I seem to remember there was something a bit rum about him. Did you find him odd, Mr Sorme?'

'No, not in the least', I said.

'Of course, he's only a second cousin', said Miss Eileen thoughtfully. I could see she was thinking of marriage—probably to Tina. It struck me that Colonel Donelly would probably like Eileen; she looked as if she might be a skilful hand with a riding crop. I made a mental note to drop Donelly a line.

Miss Eileen said : 'Well, if your wife's in Limerick, you don't want to spend all afternoon here, I suppose. Dreadful place, Limerick. Lot of damn fanatics. They burned one of my ancestors back in 1540. Bishop Donelly, known as Holy Joe. Didn't like his politics.' She led me into a small room adjoining the library. A single-bar electric fire was burning, so that it was not too cold; it also caught something of the western sun. On a small table there were two large folders, the kind made to look like books. She opened one of them, and my heart raced to recognise the handwriting on the topmost sheet of yellow foolscap. She said :

'I've stuck bits of paper in the places I thought might interest you. He's rather good at descriptions—there's a rather splendid one of Pisa. Well, I'll leave you to it. Tina'll be in the library if you want anything.'

She left me alone, and I began to read avidly:

Rue de Grande Chaumière. Sept 11, 1766
[when Donelly would be eighteen]

My dear Papa,

The letter of recommendation to M. Baizeau proved extremely useful, and I dined with his family last night. He sends you his kindest best wishes. His business has suffered reverses in recent years, but he still lives very stylishly. He excused himself early on account of his gout, and Mme Blaizeau and her two amiable daughters accompanied me on a stroll along the Promenade du Jardin Turc, whose coffee houses present singular and astonishing spectacles. They are not only crowded within, but other expectant crowds are at the windows, listening with *à gorge deployé* to certain orators who harangue their audience from chairs...

I glanced quickly through the rest of the letter. It was all pleasant, informative stuff of the kind one might expect from Horace Walpole or Arthur Young—obviously, the letter of a young man who is anxious to assure his parents that he is not wasting his life or substance. I glanced quickly through the rest of the letters, reading one here and there at random. As I read, my sense of disappointment deepened. There was nothing here of the kind that I could not find in the *Travel Diaries*; in fact, there could be little doubt that parts of these letters had been used in the *Travel Diaries*.

The two folders contained an enormous number of papers: letters, legal documents, a fragment of a novel that reminded me, in style, of Fanny Burney's *Evelina*, household accounts, letters of introduction—the kind of thing that would delight an academic biographer. I took notes—for the sake of appearances, in case Miss Eileen looked in on me—rather than out of interest. There was something very frustrating about all this stuff, most of which dated from the 1760s to 1785. I wanted to know the names of the Mesdemoiselles Blaizeau, and whether Donelly had been attracted to either of them. There were several references to them over the next few months; but not a word to indicate whether they were plain or pretty, let alone whether Donelly was romantically inclined towards them.

I tried to cheer myself with the thought that I would be a fool to expect that his family papers would contain revelations. Anything of the sort would have been destroyed during the Victorian era, or perhaps even by the Donelly sisters who were my hostesses. Somehow, I doubted that the sisters had removed anything from these family papers; they were too innocent, too open-faced about their ancestor.

Miss Tina peeped in the door and asked me if I would like more tea. I declined with thanks. She asked how I was getting on. I said politely that I found it all most interesting. Then I drew from my pocket the copy of the quotation from Boswell, and showed it to her. I said:

'Have you any idea why Dr Johnson should have disliked Donelly?'

She shook her head. 'No. Except...didn't he dislike the Irish anyway?'

I said I didn't think so.

'There's nothing in these papers to indicate that Donelly was a " phoenix of convivial malice " either. He emerges as a rather respectable, sober sort of person.'

She said: 'Oh, I don't think he was terribly respectable.'

'Why not?'

'Oh, I don't know. There were stories—rumours. Nothing very definite. He spent a lot of time in Switzerland and Italy, didn't he? I believe people were rather wicked in those days.'

She said this wistfully, looking out at the river, in which the tall forms of the ashes were reflected. After a moment, she said:

'Of course, Dr Johnson may have been making a sort of pun. Esmond's journals had a picture of a phoenix on the cover.'

I thought about this for a moment.

'No, that's impossible. Johnson made the remark in 1773. The earliest edition of the travel diary is 1791.'

'I don't think that's true. I'm sure we have an earlier one. Would you like to come and look? My eyes are not very good.'

We went into the library, and she said vaguely:

'I seem to remember it's on one of those shelves up there.'

The books stretched up to a height of about ten feet. I took a library ladder that rested against the wall, and climbed up to the shelf she indicated. It took me about five minutes of searching before I came upon a number of leather-bound volumes with Donelly's name on the spine. Some of them were the small, pocket-size edition of the Journal I had seen at Colonel Donelly's. This was an edition of the travel diary in four volumes, printed in London in 1793, with the note '3rd edition'. There was also a larger volume, beautifully bound in a leather that showed little sign of wear even after two centuries. It was entitled: *Observations upon France and Switzerland*, by Esmond Donelly, Gent, printed for J. J. Johnson (and a great list of other names), London, 1771. The front cover and the title page bore the image of a phoenix rising from its flames, the stylised kind of emblem to be found in heraldry. As I stared at it, it struck me that the feathers on its breast would be taken by a modern psychologist for phallic symbols. After all, the feathers of a bird point downwards, and taper towards the end; these pointed upward, and were shaped like sausages. I said:

'It's strange that no one has mentioned this earlier. Colonel Donelly didn't seem to know about it.'

'Probably not. I believe the whole edition was destroyed.'

'Why?'

'There was a fire. You'll find it mentioned in one of the letters. I saw it only the other day.'

I climbed down, bringing the book with me. Miss Tina went into the other room; after a five-minute search, she handed me the last sheet of a letter. The postscript read:

Calamity! Tooke has just told me that Johnson's warehouse in the Strand has burnt down, and every copy of my book with it. It is fortunate that the accident has cost me nothing.

The letter was dated September 11, 1771. This, then, explained why the *Observations upon France and Switzerland* had never been heard of. And, as I could see, even this copy had not been read from beginning to end, for many of its pages were still uncut. I turned over its pages, until my eye was arrested by the word 'phoenix'; I turned back to the previous page and read the whole passage. In Heidelberg, the carriage in which Donelly proposed to take an excursion broke down. The innkeeper told him that no other was available, but that the local pastor, the Reverend Kries, had a carriage which he occasionally hired out to distinguished visitors. Donelly found Kries in his garden overlooking the Neckar, and was taken to see the carriage, in a nearby barn; the pastor remarked that it had not been used all winter, and would be dusty and damp. Donelly looked at it and decided that it could be made presentable with a few minutes' work; the pastor declined to take money for its hire. On the way out of the barn, Donelly noticed the wooden image of a phoenix lying half-covered by straw. He asked the pastor what it was doing there, and was told that it had been included in a lot of furniture he had bought at auction a year before. Feeling that it was unsuitable for a vicarage, he had thrown it into the barn. Donelly, rather surprised, enquired why it should not be suitable for a vicarage.

He seemed surprised at my ignorance, and asked me if I was not aware that the bird was the symbol of a sect of heretics, sometimes known as the Brethren of the Free Spirit, sometimes as the Sect of the Phoenix. I replied that I only knew that the phoenix was sometimes used as a sign outside the shops of apothecaries, and that I presumed it had some alchemical significance. Whereupon the learned man discoursed to me upon the history of the Sect of the Phoenix. It arose in Europe at the time of the Black Death, when it became widely believed that venereal lasciviousness was a remedy against the disease. The basic argument ran thus : there can be no true spirituality without inwardness; man can never know the truth while he casts around outside of his soul, entangling himself in outward things. In the crisis of sexual pleasure, the spirit is more concentrated than at any other time. The Brethren of the Free Spirit believed that God is everywhere and in everything; every stirring of delight is a revelation from God. In the name of this belief, all manner of lewd excesses were performed, sometimes upon the very altar. The Inquisition uprooted these doctrines with cruel severity, but the Sect of the Phoenix proved to share the nature of its symbolic bird, and arose ever and again from the ashes of the stake and the funeral pyre. And since, according to Herodotus, the lifetime of the phoenix is five hundred years, we may confidently affirm that the sect will continue to flourish for at least another century.

I replied that I had read in the Epistle to the Corinthians of St Clement of Rome that the phoenix is a symbol of Christian resurrection, but the good man replied that this is Popish bedevilment, and that everyone knew that St Clement had been tied to an anchor and thrown into the sea as a punishment for his enormities. I thereupon offered to relieve him of this symbol of Popish degeneracy, and we settled upon the sum of three thalers.

This was the end of the passage—no mention of what became of the carved phoenix. I copied out the whole section in longhand. Then I went into the library and asked Miss Tina if she knew of a carved phoenix in the house—it seemed to me that it would be an appropriate symbol to place on the cover of the projected volume of Donelly's Memoirs. She said she had never heard of it, but that she would ask her sister. Before I could stop her, she had left the room. I sat on the arm of a chair, and idly glanced through the *Observations*. It slipped off my knee and fell on the floor, standing on end with its pages open. As I picked it up, it struck me that its back cover was thicker than the front one. Moreover, the flyleaf did not appear to be properly attached; unlike the front flyleaf, it was not glued to the last page of the book. I bent the cover slightly, to see why it was loose, and realised that there was a pocket between the cardboard cover and the flyleaf, which had been made by glueing only the edges of the flyleaf to the cardboard. Inside this pocket there was a folded sheet of paper. I drew it out and opened it. The paper was of excellent quality, very white and very thin. It contained only a fine drawing of a phoenix, rising from its nest of flame, and the inscription : *Felix qui potuit rerum cognoscere causas*, which I recognised to be a tag from Virgil meaning ' Happy the man who has been able to discover the causes of things '. What impressed me was the bird itself; the wings and tail feathers were of gold, as were the flames rising from the nest; the rest of it was as exquisitely tinted as a Blake drawing. In the lower right-hand corner, in the unmistakable writing of Esmond Donelly, was the sentence : ' Received, September 1, 1771 '. If it had not been for this date, I would have found it difficult to believe that the drawing was not far more recent, for the paper was whiter and finer than any I had previously seen from this period, and showed no sign of ageing.

I heard Miss Tina coming back, and I slipped the paper into the book. She told me that there was definitely no wooden phoenix in the house, unless it was hidden in one of the attics. I thanked her, and apologised for giving her trouble. Then I returned the *Observations* to its place on the shelf. Miss Eileen came in and asked me how I was getting on, and was obviously disappointed when I said I would have to leave. I assured her that I had found a great deal of valuable information among the papers, and showed her my notebook to prove it. The two sisters both accompanied me to the door, and told me to come back any time.

I drove back to Limerick in a very thoughtful mood. It might be said that the afternoon had been wasted; but this was not entirely true. I had learned that Esmond had two sides to his personality : the dutiful son and writer of travel diaries, and ' the erotic traveller ', to borrow a phrase of Sir Richard Burton's. And no scholar, studying the material at Castle Donelly, would have suspected the existence of the erotic traveller.

And then there was the minor puzzle of the phoenix. I talked to Diana about it as we drove back to Galway. The letters established that the *Observations upon France and Switzerland* had been printed in July 1771. The Heidelberg episode—when he had bought the phoenix—took place in August of the previous year. For some reason, Donelly had used the phoenix as a symbol on the cover of his book—perhaps an exact copy of the one he had bought from the Reverend Kries. On September 1, he had *received* the beautiful drawing of the phoenix I had seen, with its Latin tag about discovering the causes of things. Presumably, this meant received in the post. Diana objected that he might have ordered it to be engraved and received it from whoever had tinted it. I disagreed. If that was true, why had he bothered to write 'Received, September 1'? If I receive through the mail a book I have ordered, I may well write my name and the date inside it; I do not write 'Received', because it is obvious that I have received it. We use the word 'received' to acknowledge payment of bills, or in speaking of a letter or parcel. My own theory was that Esmond had received the drawing of the phoenix unexpectedly, and that it came anonymously—otherwise, he would surely have written 'Received from So-and-so', or even enclosed the covering letter with the drawing?

Then who could have sent the drawing? Someone interested in the phoenix as a symbol? Or—I suppose it is just conceivable —some member of the 'Sect of the Phoenix' mentioned by Kries? The latter was an exciting possibility, although only remotely conceivable. Diana thought it far more likely that some lady had sent him the drawing as a souvenir, perhaps with a billet doux. I wished I had examined it more closely. The paper might have had a watermark that would give some notion of its origin; a paper so expensive would surely have the symbol of its manufacturer embossed on it? I should also, of course, have compared the drawing closely with the phoenix on the cover of the book. If they were identical, then it would certainly argue that Esmond had commissioned someone to make a drawing of the bird he had bought from the Reverend Kries.

There was also the curious fact that Esmond reported that the whole edition of the *Observations* had been destroyed less than two weeks after receiving the phoenix. And it may or may not have significance that he never again used the symbol of the phoenix on his books—at least, it was not on the edition of the travel diary I had seen in Louisiana, or the one at Castle Donelly.

I had no idea how one could check whether such a fire had occurred; presumably it would mean finding out what had become of the firm of J. J. Johnson, and trying to trace their records. I found this notion discouraging; I have no particular

79

talent for this kind of detective work. Boswell, unfortunately, was in Edinburgh practising law from 1769 to 1772, or he might well have mentioned the fire—since J. J. Johnson was also Dr Johnson's publisher.

This explains why the days following my visit to Castle Donelly were completely uninteresting as far as this narrative is concerned. The Donelly letters had been my chief hope; now I was not sure what I should do next. I phoned or visited every public library between Cork and Sligo. Some of them had a copy of the Travel Diary; none of them had anything else. Kevin Roche tried to be helpful, suggesting various acquaintances in the academic world who might know something about Donelly; none of these leads came to anything. I wrote to Tim Morrison in the British Museum, and to every antiquarian bookseller I knew. And although Tim was unable to unearth any more references to Donelly, he was able to add one more item to my file on the Sect of the Phoenix. What he wrote was as follows:

> I've spoken to Ted Malory, who is our expert on the mediaeval church, about your Sect of the Phoenix, and he has some useful bits of information. He tells me that there is no evidence that the Sect of the Phoenix and the Brethren of the Free Spirit are the same thing. The latter were a heretical sect, founded by Almeric of Bena, who was expelled from the University of Paris in 1204, and died in 1209. Their doctrine, apparently, was that man becomes united with God through love, and that when this has happened, man is incapable of sin. So they practised a great deal of sexual licence, and a lot of them were burnt at the stake, including Marguerite of Hainault, a beguine nun, who seems to have been also a nymphomaniac.
>
> The only reference Ted can find to the Sect of the Phoenix occurs in St Nilus Sorsky (1433–1508), at the end of his third tract on spiritual prayer. My translation (from the German edition of 1903) is a very rough one:
>
> ' It is often believed that heretical notions are a danger only to those who hold them, and to others who come into

contact and are contaminated through them. But St Theo-
dosius tells us that they are hateful to God for their own
sake, and may result in suffering (or punishment) for the
innocent. The case of the Sect of the Phoenix in the pro-
vince of Semiriechinsk provides the most terrible example
of this. They believed that men and women may grasp the
divine revelation through carnal delight rather than prayer,
and their village (settlement) near Lake Issikoul was full
of abomination and harlotry. Then the Lord God sent a
disease that destroyed them all, and subsequently spread
through the country of the hyperborean Scythians, and subsequently to all the world. This was in the year of our Lord
1338.'

Incidentally, you may be interested to know that the
Russian archaeologist Chvolson believes that the Black Death
may have started in a Nestorian settlement near Lake Issyk-
Koul in Semiriechinsk—which is Kirghiz territory, near the
borders of China and India. This view is supported by
Professor R. Pollitzer, *Plague*, World Health Organisation
Publication, Geneva 1954, p. 13.

All this was fascinating, of course; but it raised so many un-
answerable questions that it was also very frustrating. Who had
founded the Sect of the Phoenix, and why? What were its doctrines? The eleventh and twelfth centuries were a time in which
many heretical sects were founded: the Waldenses, the Albi-
genses, the Khlysty—the latter have often been accused of holding frenzied religious ceremonies that turned into sexual orgies.
If the Sect of the Phoenix was regarded as sufficiently dangerous
to be responsible for the Black Death, why was it not better
documented?

This was not as irrelevant as it sounds. If I could not find out
much more about Esmond Donelly, then I might at least pad
out my Introduction with such material. As to the text itself, it
could consist of excerpts from *Of the Deflowering of Maids* and
Fleisher's spurious MS, as well as the undoubtedly genuine manuscript I had obtained from Colonel Donelly, together with the
Refutation of Hume. This meant that my main problem was still

to find more material for my Introduction.

On the Saturday after our return from America one of those coincidences occurred that I have learned to take for granted in matters involving any kind of obsession. Diana and our daily help, Mary, were sorting through an old box of letters, with a view to burning as many as possible. Mopsy picked up a letter with a rather elaborate woodcut across the top, showing the serpent twined around an apple tree, whispering to Eve. In the way that children have when they feel they are not getting enough attention, Mopsy came across to the study where I was writing, and said : ' Look what I've brought you, Daddy.' Thinking Diana had sent it, I glanced at the signature : Klaus Dunkelman, then at the letter. It was dated 1960, and was a ' fan letter ' about the Sex Diary, which had been published early that year. The writer asked me if I was familiar with the work of Wilhelm Reich, and went on to quote the titles of books I ought to read. It was a familiar kind of letter, even to the suggestion that the writer might have a great deal to teach me if I cared to listen, and that we ought to inaugurate a long correspondence. Diana had scrawled on it: ' Answered, 9/11/60 '. I presume I had thanked him for his suggestions, and promised to read the books he mentioned. I was now about to drop the letter into my wastepaper basket when my eye caught the name ' E. Donelly '. The sentence read : ' Körner's ideas have, of course, been anticipated by several other thinkers : de Sade, Crowley, E. Donelly, Quérard, Edward Sellon, etc.' Körner was apparently a disciple of Reich's, who believed that the orgasm held the secret of psychological health.

The address on the letter was Compayne Gardens, West Hampstead. It seemed unlikely that the writer would still be there after nine years, but it was worth trying; so I dropped him a line, mentioning my interest in Donelly.

On the following Monday, I had to reconsider the embarrassing problem of the Misses Donelly of Castle Donelly. A letter arrived, signed by them both, but presumably written by Miss Eileen. She said how pleasant it had been to meet me, and how she had been able to see at a glance that I was trustworthy and that Esmond's reputation would be safe in my hands. I groaned with embarrassment as I read it. She was glad that a writer of my reputation had at last become interested in Esmond, and felt that I would be the right person to do the standard biography... I dropped the letter on the bed and drank my tea; my first inclination was to throw it in the waste-paper basket and forget it. I thought she was a damned nuisance and ought to let me alone; I had better things to do than writing a standard biography. Of course, a revival of interest in Esmond would be greatly to her advantage; she might sell his papers to some American university at a comfortable figure.

But the problem nagged me. I had intended simply not to contact them again. After all, I had not made use of any of their materials; I owed them nothing. Now I had to plunge further into deception, or commit a breach of good manners by ignoring her letter. Suddenly, I decided that there was only one simple course : to tell her the whole truth. I slipped on a dressing-gown and hurried into my study, anxious to get it over with. It was a long letter—it was bound to be, since I was determined to unburden myself. I began by pointing out that she must be aware that the book *Of the Deflowering of Maids* was attributed to Esmond—that I had even seen a copy in the home of a professor in Galway. I told her about the New York publisher, and explained that he was determined to go ahead anyway, whether I co-operated or not. I explained that Fleisher's manuscript was a fake, and that, in my own opinion, the only way of vindicating Esmond, under the circumstances, would be to publish as much of his genuine work as possible. I also told her frankly that there was nothing in her Donelly papers that could be of the least use to me, since his letters home were as blameless as one might expect.

On my way down to the post box, I told myself that this was probably a stupid thing to do; I had not mentioned it to Diana, since she was sure to try to dissuade me. Miss Donelly might even write a letter to the *T.L.S.* denouncing my project and drying up all sources of information. But it was a risk I had to take. I dropped the letter into the box with the feeling of a man pointing a gun at his own head.

The next morning, I was still dozing when the telephone rang.

Diana picked up the bedside extension, then said : 'Miss Eileen Donelly for you.' I groaned. I was tempted to tell her to say I was out; but my conscience won through. If she quarrelled with me, at least I could go ahead without hating myself.

Her voice barked : 'Hello, Mr Sorme? '

' Speaking.'

' I've just had your letter. I'm jolly glad you've been so frank with me. Most decent of you. I rang you up to say I quite see your point.'

'You do? ' I was breathless, and wondered what she was leading up to.

' Look here, from what you say, there's nothing much we can do about this publisher chap.'

' I'm afraid that's so.'

' Right. Then the next best thing is to make sure things don't get out of hand. We've got to keep a close eye on him. Tina and I agree that we ought to give any help we can.'

I said that I was delighted, of course. In fact, I didn't know what to think. I needed time to collect my thoughts. But she gave me no time.

' We'd like to talk this over with you. When could you come over here? '

' Any time that's convenient.'

' How about later today? '

I said all right, and felt a wave of relief as the line went dead.

By the time Diana had made tea, I had begun to understand what had happened. The Donelly sisters had nothing to lose by the publication of Esmond's 'sex diaries', particularly if they managed to sell the house. I had assured them that the diaries were not mere pornography; that they would cause a steep rise in Esmond's reputation; that in these days of sexual frankness, no one would bat an eyelid. I had cited Boswell's journals and so on. Miss Eileen had decided they might as well be on the bandwagon. And full access to her papers would indeed be useful in writing the biographical part of the Introduction. But if she was hoping to persuade Fleisher to disgorge another fifteen thousand dollars for the use of her material on Esmond, she was due for a disappointment.

I was feeling pretty gloomy as I drove to Limerick shortly after midday. I had called on Kevin Roche and borrowed *Of the Deflowering of Maids*, and I now had the other fragments of the ' sex diary ' with me, including Fleisher's original typescript. But it was a beautiful day; the air smelt fresh, and everything looked so green that it was impossible not to enjoy it. And as soon as I relaxed and decided to forget the Donelly sisters, I experienced a great sense of warmth and richness, of the immense potentialities of the world that are obscured by our tendency to remain jammed in our petty motives. It crystallised further as I sat drinking a beer outside a grocer-tavern a few miles south of Gort, listening to the rippling of water as it flowed under a bridge and ran towards Lough Cutra. It was suddenly unimportant whether I drove on to Limerick, or sat here. The stream would go on flowing; that tree with its lime-coloured leaves, that overlooked the stream, would remain itself. And it struck me that here is one of the strangest and most important things about human existence : this capacity of the mind to detach itself from people and events, to stop identifying with human emotions, and to identify instead with the timeless, the world of Nature. What happens? I stood on the parapet of the bridge and watched the water reflecting the sunlight, and it seemed that something in me followed the flow of the water, ran away towards the lake. When I returned to the car and drove on, I had the odd sensation that my soul was free of my body and was flying alongside like a bird, taking occasional swoops and dives. When my mind came back to the Donelly sisters, I had ceased to feel foreboding.

I experienced a momentary apprehension as I saw Miss Eileen coming down the steps to meet me; but she dispelled it by taking my hand in her mannish grip and saying : ' Well, well, it's pleasant to see you again.' We went into the library. Miss Tina was not there. I took a seat on a dusty nineteenth-century couch, in the sunlight, and let Miss Eileen do the talking. I had to admire her forthright intellect.

' Well, as we see it, there's no point in trying to stand in the way of this book. As you say, it was bound to get published sooner or later. So the best idea is to try to keep it in your hands. Which university were you at, by the way? ' I said I wasn't, but she brushed this aside. 'Don't suppose it matters. You're obviously a competent, intelligent sort of chap. If you get in first with your book on Esmond, the others'll have to fall in line.' She was taking it for granted that I would write a full biography of Donelly, and I didn't want to disappoint her at this stage, so I nodded and said nothing. Miss Tina came in with tea and cakes, and greeted me like an old friend. And when we all had cups and plates of sandwiches, she said :

'I must say, it came as quite a surprise to hear that Esmond was so notorious. I'd never heard of this book about deflowering virgins.' She said it entirely without embarrassment. I took the opportunity to produce the book out of my briefcase, as well as the typescript of Colonel Donelly's MS. While they looked at them, I said : 'I wonder if you'd mind if I look at Donelly's books again?' I took down the *Observations*, and the four-volume *Travels*, and retired to the window seat, so as not to embarrass them. Periodically, I heard Miss Eileen mutter : 'I *say*!', and she would pass the book to Miss Tina, who would glance quickly at me, then read avidly, making clicking noises with her tongue.

I opened the *Observations* and took out the drawing of the phoenix. I held it up to the light. Yes, there was a watermark, partly obscured by the drawing. And then I had to restrain the impulse to laugh loudly. It was in the shape of a phoenix!

I compared the tinted drawing (or it could have been an etching) with the embossed phoenix on the cover. They were identical in outline, but there were half a dozen differences. Quite definitely, they were not the same bird.

When Miss Eileen looked over at me, I showed her the drawing of the phoenix. She glanced at it, said : 'Umm, rather nice', and handed it back to me. She was clearly not interested.

Miss Tina said : 'Have you showed Mr Sorme the letters, dear?'

'Ah no, I forgot.' She went into the small room next door, and returned with a bundle of papers tied with tape. 'Tina said you wanted to know if there was a wooden phoenix in the attic. So we had a good search. Didn't find your phoenix, but we found a lot of old papers—great boxes full. I don't think most of 'em have got anything to do with Esmond, but these seem to be letters addressed to him.'

I quickly untied the tape. As soon as I began to separate the papers, something fell out of an envelope to the floor. I picked it up. It was an oval miniature, without its frame, and had been painted on a piece of some carved white shell or mother-of-pearl. It was a painting of a very beautiful girl, with her hair in ringlets down to her shoulders. It had nothing written on it.

The letters themselves were not in Esmond Donelly's handwriting; some seemed to be from someone called Thomas Walgrave, some from William Aston, some from Horace Glenney. They seemed to be in no kind of order. Some were in envelopes and some were not. Walgrave was apparently a clergyman of Dublin, and Aston lived in Cork. Glenney, I soon realised, had been a fellow student of Donelly's at Göttingen, and was apparently the son of Lord Glenney of Golspie, in Sutherland.

In the midst of this pile of letters there was a parchment envelope with nothing written on it. Inside, I found a slip of paper cut to the same shape as the miniature; written on it, in Esmond Donelly's handwriting : ' Lady Charlotte Ingestre, 2nd d. Earl of Flaxstead '. Also in the envelope, there was what appeared to be a page of a letter in Donelly's handwriting. As I read this, I knew I had found something else for my book.

Voltaire has argued, in his Philosophical Dictionary, that sect and error are synonymous, since there is no room for sectarian opinion in matters that are known to be true; for example, in geometry or science. Our religious professions, he says, should be confined to matters on which all minds agree. But he goes on to assert that all minds agree upon the worship of God and upon honesty. This is not true, for the Bhoudistes do not accept God, and the Jesuits have reservations about honesty. Is there, then, any common ground for religious agreement?

I would argue, my dear friend, that there is no man of intelligence who does not recognise this world to be a mystery. It takes only a moment's thought to recognise that our certainties are the certainties of habit, obeyed by us like the rules of piquet or whisk [whist], but in no way self-evident.

Religions assert that what lies outside the rules of the games we play is unknowable, or known only to God and the angels. But science has taught us that anything may be understood if the method of inquiry be sufficiently subtle and logical.

I would argue that our certainties are not seen, but felt, as I now feel the warmth of the sun upon my hand as I write. I would argue that our habit of attempting to get at truth by the method of seeing or reasoning has blinded us to its true nature, like a man who tries to tell the difference between Canary sack and cold tea by sight alone. The mystery of the world becomes apparent to us in moments when our spirits are profoundly moved or disturb'd, if the disturbance be harmonious. In these moments of mystery, it is as if we became aware of the vibrations of an underground stream, like the one I heard near Vevey, and may sometimes feel so close to it that we can hear the noise of its rushing.

When I am suffering from ennui, it is like being deaf with a cold in the head; I hear nothing. When I look upon the face of Charlotte Ingestre, the deafness vanishes; I hear the rushing beneath my feet.

And surely if religion is this sense of the mystery of creation, and of the proximity of the mystery, then there are no objects so conducive to holiness as women and mountains? Why should it not be...

The fragment breaks off here, halfway down a page, as if the writer was interrupted. But the words 'my dear friend' seemed to suggest that Donelly had been making a preliminary draft of a letter, and that he suddenly decided that he may as well start copying it into the letter itself. Who was its recipient? The envelope containing the fragment was in the midst of letters from Horace Glenney, and Glenney's own letters to Donelly quoted Voltaire, Fontanelle and d'Alembert; it was a reasonable assumption that Glenney, Donelly's college friend from Göttingen, was the recipient of his confidences and of his religious speculations.

Miss Eileen had put down the typescript, and was looking out of the window in a slightly dazed manner. I asked her:

'Have you ever hear of a Lady Charlotte Ingestre?'

Both she and Miss Tina looked startled. It was the latter who said, after a glance at her sister:

'Why, yes. She was the daughter of the Earl of Flaxstead...'

She paused, as if embarrassed. Miss Eileen finished, in an almost sepulchral voice:

'And the sister of Lady Mary Ingestre, who later became Mary Glenney.'

I needed no reminding about the latter; the name had been in my head ever since last week, when Miss Eileen had first mentioned it over the phone. I said:

'Did you know that Esmond was in love with Lady Charlotte?'

Miss Tina said: 'They say he was in love with all three of them.

'Three?'

'Lady Mary, Lady Charlotte and Lady Maureen.' She glanced nervously at her sister. Miss Eileen shrugged, and said:

'I suppose he'll have to find out about it anyway.'

Miss Tina said: 'They were certainly all very beautiful.'

'Do any pictures exist?'

'Oh yes. Romney's portrait is quite famous.'

'Where is it?'

They looked mildly surprised at my ignorance.

'Here, of course.'

'Could I see?'

The two of them got up without speaking, and led the way out of the room. In the hall, Miss Eileen vanished for a few minutes. She returned with a huge key. We crossed to a pair of great mahogany doors. Miss Tina said:

'The insurance people insist that we keep the gallery locked. Some of the pictures are worth rather a lot.'

Miss Eileen unlocked the door, and a breath of cold, musty air came out. She switched on lights, and we went into the 'long gallery'. It was icy. The windows were covered with shutters,

and the tables and chairs with covers. I could well believe that
no one had been in it for at least a year. She led me to a rather
small picture on the end wall. It needed cleaning, but even that
could not detract from the beauty of the three faces. The girls
were posed conventionally against a background of trees and
part of a fountain. Charlotte, whose portrait I had already seen,
was immediately recognisable. The only thing the sisters had in
common was beauty. Charlotte's face was pink-cheeked and innocent, an arcadian face. The girl sitting next to her, playing with
a poodle, was visibly more intelligent, a fine, delicate face with a
swan's neck, the hair short, almost boyish. Miss Tina identified
her as Mary, who later became Lady Mary Glenney. Maureen,
clearly the youngest, had a face that would become very beautiful, and that was also gentle and generous. She was obviously
impulsive and warm-hearted, the kind who would burst into
tears at a sad story. One of her hands reached out to caress the
dog—a gesture plainly symbolic of a nature that had to give
affection.

Miss Tina said with pride : ' Esmond only paid Romney thirty
guineas for that. We've been offered five thousand pounds for it.'

I could see why Esmond was rumoured to be in love with all
three sisters. After staring at the portrait for five minutes, I was
close to it myself. Each one had qualities in her face that seemed
to emerge as one stared at it; I could have written a novel about
the three of them.'

' Do you have a portrait of Esmond ? '

' Oh yes, two. One by Raeburn and one by someone called
Zoffany.'

The Zoffany portrait told me little; the face was immobile,
lacking any spark of life; it showed Donelly in officer's uniform,
leaning against a tree. He was apparently fairly tall and thin.
The face was long, lantern-jawed, the nose prominent.

The Raeburn was altogether more rewarding. It was unpre-
tentious, with almost no background; it was in some respects little
more than a sketch. But Raeburn had caught a sort of eagerness
in the face, which seemed to lean forward as if listening to an
interesting anecdote. It was not exactly a handsome face; the
bony nose and high cheekbones made me think of Sherlock

90

Holmes, but the mouth was too sensual. Turning back from this to the Zoffany, I now saw other qualities in the latter : the size of the chin, a sort of control about the posture, like a thoroughbred horse standing still at a parade.

As we left the room—all three of us frozen—I said :

'I think that Esmond has all the qualifications for attracting crowds of admirers and commentators.'

'Do you think so? ' They both looked eager.

'This business of being in love with three beautiful girls makes him quite a figure of romance—very Byronic. What a pity the rest of his journals have disappeared. He's a far more interesting character than Boswell.'

Miss Tina said : 'I once saw a film about Chopin. They did it rather well. I cried all the way through.'

'I imagine they might want to make a film about Esmond.'

'Would we make a lot of money? '

'I imagine so.'

'We'd share with you, of course ', said Miss Tina.

'Do you know any details of the romance with the three sisters? '

'Not really. It's just a family story.'

'What about the death of Lord Glenney? '

Miss Eileen said : 'He was shot. I don't know many details, but my father once looked them up in the Dublin National Library, so it shouldn't be too difficult to check. There was talk about Esmond being suspected, but Father said he couldn't possibly be guilty. I hope you'll make that clear.'

'I'll certainly do my best.'

Before I left, they showed me up to the attics. They were very dark, very dusty, and full of lumber that had accumulated for centuries : broken picture frames, baulks of timber with no obvious purpose, broken furniture, porcelain wash-bowls, bundles of paper that might have been anything from farming accounts to the missing diaries. I glanced into some of these and understood what Professor Abbott must have felt in the attic at Forbes House, surrounded by manuscripts. But the memory of Abbott gave me an idea.

'Have you any idea whom Esmond appointed as his literary executor?'

They looked at each other blankly.

'No. We'll try to find out.'

Before I left, I said that I might have to come back again very soon to look at the papers. At which, to my astonishment, Miss Tina said : 'Wouldn't it be simpler if he took them with him, dear?', and Miss Eileen said without hesitation : 'Oh, certainly.' They helped me bundle them into the back seat of the car, and waved aside my offer of a receipt. I drove off feeling rather oppressed by their trust. Then, as I thought about it, I began to understand the reason. They were lonely and rather broke, living alone in magnificent but draughty grandeur, with no expectations except to get older. They probably wondered which one would go first. When they were dead, the house would probably pass to some distant member of the family in Canada or New Zealand. And now the great world was knocking on their door; there was something to dream about—publishers, film rights, scholars visiting them. They wanted to believe in all this, and therefore they wanted to believe in me, to accept me completely, to regard me with a certain affection. What I had regarded as the greatest obstacle—Esmond's reputation as a writer of pornography—turned out to be nothing of the sort, since I declared the pornography spurious, and meant to state this opinion in print. The fragment of Donelly's journal I had obtained from Colonel Donelly was sexually frank, but no more so than Boswell; above all, it was well written.

These considerations made me feel better. I thought there was a very fair chance that there would be a Donelly revival when Fleisher brought out the *Memoirs*. Altogether, it was a satisfactory outlook.

When I examined the new batch of letters, I knew that we now had a book, whether or not any further Donelly MSS turned up. Apart from the Donelly manuscript, this was the most fascinating material yet.

It is difficult to imagine three correspondents more completely different in character than Thomas Walgrave, William Aston and

Horace Glenney, and they revealed the complexity of Donelly's own personality. Walgrave was a Dublin man whose chief interests were astronomy and mathematics, and his letters to Donelly were mainly concerned with these subjects. Aston was studying theology at a Protestant seminary in 1772, the date of the first letter, and later became a clergyman at Ballincollig, near Cork (where his family home was situated). He was greatly troubled by what appeared to be two opposing trends in Donelly's character : towards infidelity and towards ' enthusiasm ' (i.e. fanaticism or mysticism). When Donelly quoted Voltaire, Bayle or Montesquieu, Aston replied with arguments from the sermons of Jortin, Ogden, Tillotson, Smalridge and Sherlock. All this I found unbelievably stuffy and dull—the lengthy hair-splitting on transubstantiation, predestination, the truth of the Scriptures, etc. But it was clear that Esmond did not find it boring, for Aston's replies were long-winded and circumstantial, indicating that his correspondent's were equally so.

It was the Glenney letters that fitted in with what I already knew of Esmond Donelly. When sorted into their correct order (with a certain amount of guesswork—several were undated), they ran from May 1767 to Christmas 1771. Glenney and Esmond were together at Göttingen for most of this time, so the correspondence was not as voluminous as in the case of Aston. Clearly, they exchanged letters when they were apart for any length of time, and this was not often, for they were very close friends.

The story of their relationship, which I was able to piece together from Glenney's letters*, is as follows. When Esmond Donelly had met Rousseau and Boswell at Neuchâtel, he proceeded on to Milan, where he spent the Christmas of 1764. In January, he spent a week in Venice, then spent a further week in Graz en route to Göttingen. Here he made the acquaintance of Georg Christoph Lichtenberg, who later became an eminent philosopher (but who, at this period, was interested chiefly in mathematics and astronomy) and of the Hon. Horace Gordon Glenney. The latter was a handsome, dark-skinned youth with an almost Jewish cast of countenance and a pronounced Scottish

* Which will be published as an appendix to Donelly's *Memoirs*.

accent; slightly older than Donelly, but immensely less sophisticated; the second son of a Scottish laird from one of the wilder regions of that country. Lichtenberg, Glenney and Donelly had one thing in common—a lively interest in the opposite sex. Göttingen was full of healthy young farm girls, 'bouncing creatures from the valleys of the Harz or the Solling', wrote Lichtenberg, 'who have never seen a sum larger than a thaler, and to whom the braided hat of the nobleman is an object of awe, and the requests of such a hat, royal commands'. Göttingen was a town of high academic reputation, unlike Halle, Jena and Giessen, which were full of louts whose chief interest was in duelling. But, like most other towns in Germany, it was a highly ordered, highly regimented place, where the peasants were used to obeying the will of their masters. (It was also, of course, a part of England, since George III was Duke of Hanover as well as King of Great Britain; this was no doubt the reason that Esmond's parents chose it.) Esmond and Horace Glenney were delighted to discover that these delicious creatures did not have to be seduced, like the girls on their estate at home; Glenney mentions in one of his letters that Lichtenberg twitted him with accusation that he aimed at taking every maidenhead in Hanover, in preparation for a lifetime of abstention when he should return to his own puritanical country.

Compared to Esmond, Glenney was a fool; or, if not a fool, at least a man without intellectual breadth. Esmond dominated him completely, and Glenney apparently infuriated a professor called Kästner by telling him that Esmond was one of the greatest minds in Europe after Moses Mendelssohn. (After this, Kästner used to address Esmond ironically as 'Magister Doctissime'.) What fascinated Glenney about Esmond was the combination of intellectuality and physical vitality. Litchenberg was brilliant, but he was also a hump-backed cripple. Esmond was a fine swordsman, a good horseman, a good swimmer, a favourite with ladies, and also something of a poet, a philosopher and a mystic. Glenney had been subjected to heavy parental domination; he was inclined to be dour and repressed. Within a few months, Donelly was describing him as ' an apostle of gallantry, carnality, seduction, ribaldry, stupration and defloration '. Soon they became bored with the serving wenches of the town, and began to pay court to the daughters of professors and other respectable citizens. Both were apparently amazed and delighted with their success, and Esmond came dangerously close to getting married to the youngest daughter of a parson from Nörten-Hardenberg, a Fraulein Ulrica Duessen. But it should not be assumed that Esmond and Glenney were inseparable. Glenney would have been delighted if they had been; but Esmond was also interested in reading Kant, and studying mathematics and astronomy. Glenney makes several references to his feeling of being neglected. But he admired Esmond so whole-heartedly that he accepted whatever attention Esmond could spare.

The letter Glenney wrote to Esmond on December 29, 1766, is fairly typical. He spends a page and a half complaining that Donelly declined his invitation to spend Christmas at the family seat near Golspie, and describing the rigours of the journey north in late November. Glenney's description of the food eaten on Christmas Day has to be read to be believed, beginning at seven thirty in the morning with a breakfast of oat cakes, braised salmon, roast beef, ham, kidneys and porter. But the main item of the letter, inevitably, is the description of his amorous adventures over the holiday. ' I was at first determined that I should obtain the favours of a girl named Maggie McBean, the daughter of one of our tenant farmers who had already shown a tenderness towards me before I left, although she sware then that she would rather die than lose her self respect.' The defloration of Maggie proved easier than he had expected; it was accomplished in a barn after a dance at which the young laird had been the centre of interest to the local girls. (In a district so sparsely populated, the lord and his tenants mixed freely.) Glenney was tempted simply to continue an affair with Maggie, ' which indeed I would have done without further thought than at any time in the past; but I now bethought me of your excellent principle that the basic aim of life is a certain freshness of experience, and I had to confess that my desire for the girl was lukewarm, and that the sight of her linen cap and her check cloth apron no longer produced their old effect. I tried, without success, to devote my mind to study...

'On the 28th, my sister Mary (whom you met in Perth) returned from Kincardine, where she had spent Christmas with Fiona Guthrie, the daughter of an old friend of my mother's. My sister, as you know, is thin and small for her age (fourteen), and I may say without undue pride that she loves me with a warmth that I have done little to deserve. It came as somewhat of a shock to discover that Fiona had changed a great deal in the eighteen months since I last saw her. She is in that charming stage where the manners and thoughts of a child remain, while the body is that of a grown woman. She has a charming, rosy face, and an upper lip that is too short for its companion, giving her mouth an outthrust appearance which might be mistaken for petulance. As a child she had been a tomboy (if that word may be deprived of all connotations of immodesty), and I had often romped with her and swung her by the wrists. And now, since she had grown so pretty, I decided I might do worse than follow Mr Sterne's advice and cultivate a sentimental* relation with her, even though it should be somewhat one-sided...[I have inserted leader dots where there are digressions on his motives, since they serve no real purpose.] This proved to be easier than I expected, for all I had to do was to treat her as I treated Mary, with much attention and brotherly affection. I give you my word that my thoughts up to this stage were as blameless as Pastor Geiss could have wished. Their room had a fire, and I spent hours there drinking dishes of tea and describing the customs of Hanover, feeling for all the world like Othello the Moor. I found the tender regard of these two children more pleasing than the study of Flaccus, and convinced myself at one point that this was what Rousseau had in mind, when he speaks of the bliss of the second state of nature.

'Alas, my elevated feelings suffered their first defeat on the second day of the new year, about half an hour before dinner. The girls were romping when I came into the room, and when I joined in their game, I could not help noticing the bouncing of her bosoms as she jumped upon the bed to escape Mary, nor the fine shape of her calves as she leapt down again. When I paid

* In Sterne's day, this did not mean emotional, but characterised by idealistic or elevated feelings.—Editor.

her a compliment on the change in her shape, she was not embarrassed, but laughed at me, and Mary declared it was through the eating of too much mutton. Then they asked me to read to them from *Grandison*, which I accordingly did, sitting before the fire on the hearthrug, while they sat beside me and sewed the blue muslin dresses they are both to wear for the ball at Strathpeffer in February. After a while, Mary became so absorbed that she laid by her sewing and placed her head on my lap, stretching her legs out to the stool; some minutes later, Fiona did the same; but since Mary had usurped the soft part of my thigh, she had to lay her cheek higher still, upon something that soon ceased to be soft. She also curled up in such a manner that the back of her skirt came high upon her thighs, revealing the shapeliest leg I have seen this Christmas. I soon noticed that the buttons down her back had started to come undone, and allowed my free hand to wander in the gap and stroke her flesh, which she appeared to enjoy…I can assure you, my dear Ned, that the beating of my heart did not improve the quality of my reading. When the bell rang for supper, I was delighted to observe her reluctance in sitting up; she pretended this was because she had fallen asleep, but I, who could see the movements of her eyelids, knew better.

'On the following day, there was no further progress, since the minister returned our sleigh, and father and brother Moray took them out for a drive to show them the view of the towers of Dunrobin Castle. But when I saw Fiona before we supped, she said : " We missed our reading today. You must read twice as much tomorrow." I pulled her close to me, and let my hand wander over her back. She asked what I was doing, and I said : " Seeing how many buttons are done up."

'The next day, the Wednesday, was sunny and cold, and [Lord] Glenney was out all day calling on a retired lady about her sheep. When Jamie told me this news, I told him I would sleep again and take my breakfast and hot water at ten. Shortly thereafter, as I stood in my nightshirt making my ablutions, Mary came in and asked if I would go with them through the empty rooms. Soon Fiona came seeking her, and both admired the material of the shirt, which was one of those I bought in Strasbourg at the linen fair. Then Fiona told a story of a manservant of her aunt, who was running about in his shirtsleeves preparing the table for guests. She told him to put on his coat, but he replied : " Indeed, my lady, there's sae muckle rinnin' here and there, I'm just distrackit, I hae cast off my coat and waistcoat, and faith I dinna ken how lang I can bear my breeks." We all laughed a great deal at this, and I noted with satisfaction that she regarded my state of undress with no more embarrassment than Mary, which indicated that she thought of me as a brother. So before I put them out, that I might dress, I passed an arm around the waist of each of them and squeezed, and remarked that Fiona's plumpness would keep a man warm without his nightshirt.

' I must not describe the morning in full, for this letter would become as long as a sermon by Warburton; so let me say only that we joked and laughed a great deal, and I took every opportunity to chase them both, both to keep warm in the empty wing, and to accustom Fiona to my familiarity. It was, of course, necessary to devote much of my attention to Mary, to stimulate the sense of rivalry between them and make Fiona accept my squeezes as natural. I met no resistance here, for both were full of high spirits...You will take note of the lesson of all this, Ned, and incorporate it in your History. The situation here reveals the truth of Lichtenberg's assertion that the feelings enter into combination like chemicals. Mary was my sister and took every opportunity to remind Fiona of this, as though I were on loan; Fiona accepted the loan and the brotherly attentions that went with it. Since I was now licensed to treat Fiona as I would treat Mary, I had only to treat Mary with the familiarity I would use upon Fiona to make the whole thing appear natural.

' The advantage of this appeared later in the afternoon, when I went to their room to read *Grandison*. I knew they intended to try on the blue muslin dresses before they sewed on the tapes; so I went early. Fiona was still sewing her dress, but Mary stood in her chemise, trying on a whalebone corset. They asked me to give advice from the male point of view, which I did with pleasure, while helping Mary to tie the corset. I told them that in Paris, the women of the court often wore dresses that left their breasts completely exposed. Mary said she would not like that, and I slipped a hand into her chemise, and felt the tiny, hard breast that was barely formed, and said she would have reason to object to such a fashion. At this she pulled the chemise off both shoulders, exposing both bosoms, and asked me if I did not think they would grow a great deal larger. She was not as innocent as she pretended; she wanted me to see them, to prove she was not a child, and she knew I was curious. I pretended to consider the question without prejudice, and told her that the relation of the size of the nipple to the total circumference would give some idea of their future development—upon which, I took one of the nipples between my fingers and began to pinch it. After a few moments, it became stiff; so did another early riser, and I was tempted to bend forward and take the other one between my lips; but I feared it might ruin the professorial air ...After this, I helped her on with the dress, and discoursed like a milliner on the relative virtues of metal or bone as a material for buttons, and of the advantages of loops over buttonholes.

'By now, Fiona had laid down her needle, and I asked her if I could not help to undo her buttons, which this time were between her breasts. She seemed to be shy, but my faithful Mary rallied like a Hessian, and told her she would never again have such an expert lady's maid, upon which, the girl entered into the spirit of the game and allowed me to undo her and pull the dress off her shoulders. This time I took no liberties with the delicious orbs that were now exposed to my sight, for I sensed that Mary would be jealous; instead, I helped her on with her blue dress, and took care to keep my front turned away from them, lest they should note the evidence of my absorption in my new trade.

'The maid came in to make up the fire, and I sat in a chair and pretended to be absorbed in a book. But as soon as we were alone again, I suggested that we might commence our reading before it became too dark (for it was now after four). Mary said they would change first, but I told her it was not worth the trouble, and that in any case, they should learn whether the dresses would crease. This reasoning convinced them, and they sat beside me on the rug. As soon as I began to read, Mary again placed her head on my lap, and Fiona quickly followed her lead. Both had placed themselves so that neither could see the other, and I took double precautions against peeping by resting the book against Mary's head so it would fall down if she moved. You will observe that this manoeuvre left both my hands free, although my position made any sudden moves impossible. I slipped my left hand into the open back of Fiona's dress, and allowed my right one to rest on Mary's breast. I removed it to turn over a page, and replaced it inside the dress, upon her right bosom, and began to gently pinch and tweak the nipple. After the next page, I moved it to her left, and did the same there. From the increased force of her breathing I guessed that she was becoming somewhat less interested in the wearisome virtues of Sir Charles Grandison. When I had finished tweaking the nipples, I gently stroked the breasts, and observed with amusement the involuntary parting of her thighs.

'Absorbed for the moment in the pleasure I was so disinterestedly bestowing upon Mary, I contented myself with a vague caressing of Fiona's back. As it was, I felt like a juggler betwixt Grandison and my two winter flowers. But when Mary had sunk into a trance of contentment, I began to consider the duties of my right hand. Since the dress was low cut, and the back was undone, it was no problem to slip my hand under the armpit, and on to her right bosom. The movements of her skin under my caress told me that this advance would not be rejected. Indeed, she stretched like a cat, and made a single movement with her hips that made me fear that an unbidden guest would burst his flap and peep out to see what was happening. Her breasts were fuller and weightier than Mary's, but the nipples were smaller, and when I began to pinch the right one, I could only judge the result from the increased rate at which her breath came and went. I found this so delightful that after a while, I moved my hand to her mouth, and pinched the lower lip, then played with it between my thumb and forefinger. Then her lips closed around the finger, and she sucked it as if it were a comforter. When I tired of this, I slipped my hand into her bosom again, this time down the front of the dress, and devoted some attention to the neglected breast.

'A log on the fire fell with a shower of sparks, and at the same time, the book fell from off my legs. I was not entirely

100

sorry, for the chair against which I was leaning had slipped, and I was becoming cramped. Fiona sat up and said she would have to leave us for a moment. I was on the point of recommending the pot under the bed, but thought this would place too great a strain on her modesty, and so held my peace. This was something of a feat, for by now I was in such a state of eagerness that I could have driven my ardent Pegasus through a crack in a brick wall.

'When we were alone, I let my hand return within Mary's dress; she covered it with her own. I asked her if she liked me to do that, and she said it gave her a pleasant feeling that was like icy water. The room was now dark except for the light of the fire, and she had moved around to warm her shins. I was in such a state of impatience that I had almost ceased to calculate the consequences. With one hand still pinching her breast, I leaned forward, pulled up her dress, and ran my hand roughly over the inside of her thigh, then up to the source of delight. It was smooth and almost unprotected. I first pressed it with all my fingers; then, discovering it was warm and moist, allowed my middle finger to trace its course upward. She whispered, "Be careful, Fiona won't be long", and I swear she must have read my mind, for I was about to move on her and find whether the inner folds would welcome a larger guest. I knew her admonition was sensible, for the privy was only at the end of the passage. But I needed some further outlet, if I was to preserve my sanity; so I quickly undid the buttons at the top of my flap, seized her hand, and pushed it inside. She knew what to expect, since she had often seen it as a child, but must have been startled at its expansion. She sat up and peered at it by the light of the fire, paying particular attention to the vermilion head, which she squeezed and prodded, and smeared a little smooth moisture around in a circle. At that moment, we heard steps outside, and I could have cursed Fiona and wished her in hell. When she came in, we were both respectable again, and my heart was beating so loud that I was afraid she could hear it across the room.

'She sat down by my side, and said: "It's too dark to read. Tell us about Göttingen." "What would you like to know?" "Tell us again about the time the students fought the journeymen." So with a few deeps breaths to master the racing of my pulse, I told them again the familiar old story. Mary stretched out her feet to the fire, and for a few minutes, I could think of nothing but the pleasant spot I had been exploring, and of how I could find an excuse to get her alone. But a few moments' thought convinced me this was impracticable, so I decided to see what advantage could be drawn from the present situation. Mary was lying as before, with her head against my thigh; Fiona, as before, curled up with her cheek against my breeches, her dress pulled over her knees in front, but free of the back of her thighs. I caressed her breast, as before, then, when I felt her responding, moved my hand down to her buttocks. This alarmed her for a moment, as I could tell, but as my hand rested there without movement, she grew reassured, and I began stroking her side under the dress. Mary glanced across once to see what we were about, but evidently decided it was no business of hers, and from then on, kept her eyes turned to the other corner of the room.

'We all knew the bell would sound soon, and this added to our pleasure. When I said : " It will soon be time to sup ", Mary pressed herself tighter against me, and Fiona muttered impatiently. This decided me that it was time to press forward; I let the hand on Fiona's buttocks move down, and pull aside the cloth of the dress. A moment later, my hand was resting on her bared behind, delighting in its softness and the gentleness of its curve. Indeed, it was such a delight to touch that I could have kept on caressing it until the bell rang. But bethinking myself of my more serious business, I changed my position slightly to extend my reach, and explored further. Her bent position made it impractical to move around to the front of her thighs, but it meant she was accessible from my present position. Here, as in the case of the bosom, she was more developed than Mary, although the hair was soft as down. This new movement alarmed her and she jerked suddenly, so I removed my hand to soothe her. I was certain by now that she must be aware of my state, for she could scarcely believe that the mound against which her cheek rested was a burglar's jemmy. One of the buttons was only half done-up; it took but the slightest movement to release it. I am certain she did not

102

observe this. But I could tell from her stillness that she would not have me believe her offended, so I returned my hand to its former position between her buttocks, and allowed it to rest there, the finger tips pressing in unison. She stirred, then lay still. My voice had become tight, and I had no idea what I was babbling, but I was equally certain that they were also indifferent. I allowed my middle finger to probe. At first, I was disappointed, and believed myself mistaken about her; but after a moment, my finger parted the fold, and I saw that her condition was much as Mary's had been a quarter of an hour earlier. The need for calm had so far reduced the violence of my feelings that I was able to observe the different texture of this moisture; that it was less plentiful, but more slippery, like the feel of a mackerel as you take it off the hook.

'She was moving now, with small movements of her hips, and very cautiously, in case Mary looked round. I moved my lap, as if to ease cramp, and she raised her cheek for a moment. When she replaced it, I felt her hair against the importunate nose of my charger. During this time, I had not forgotten to continue to pinch the tiny nipple under my other hand. Fiona moved again, and I felt her ear, then her bare cheek. She had moved her uppermost thigh to make my access more easy. I longed now for the feeling of her lips, for her head was raised slightly.

'At this moment, the bell rang, and we all started as if it had been a cannonshot. But I kept up my caressing, and the three of us were still, listening to the racket, and wishing the fellow dead. It stopped, and none of us moved; neither did I now bother to speak. Then the tip of my finger found the entrance of the robber's cave, and slipped within; at that moment, my suppressed fluids leapt upwards and bubbled forth. I doubt whether the two of them knew why I tensed; but both of them lay still until it was over, while my spirit leapt up with the sparks of the fire, and the moment of supreme guiltlessness convulsed me like the lightning.

'Mary was the first to sit up. She yawned, and stretched, and made as if she had fallen into a doze. Then Fiona did the same, but cast a quick glance down to see the source of the moisture that had bedewed her hair.

'I hurried down to table, buttoning as I went; and when my

103

father enquired about the two girls, I said I had not seen them, and sent Jamie up to call them. They came down wearing their other dresses, and apologising for falling asleep in front of the fire. Fiona sat next to me, and I looked with satisfaction at the moist place on her hair.

'And now, my dear friend, in closing this Grandisonian epistle, I must once again pay tribute to the inspired teaching that has led to these satisfactory conclusions. The man who can spend two hours upon such a sweet pinnacle of ecstasy has experienced something of the state of the gods, and must become larger of soul thereby...'

Glenney's letter concludes with a page and a half of reflections of this sort—I shall not quote them because their style is bombastic, and by no means up to the standard of what went before —and the assurance that he will press his advantage, and attempt to complete the work he has begun. That he was unsuccessful appears from a letter he wrote the following June, in which he congratulates himself on not having accomplished his design, 'for the thought of the complications that might have ensued makes me sweat and shake with ague'. He was not, I think, referring to the possibility of the girls becoming pregnant, but simply to the personal complications involved in being the lover of totally unsophisticated girls. He eventually became Fiona's lover in 1768, two years later, and Mary's in 1775, as we shall see.

I have quoted the above passage at such length because it makes certain things clear. First, the reference to 'inspired teaching' indicates that in matters such as these, Glenney regarded himself as Esmond's pupil. Can one, in fact, accept everything he has written about that afternoon of January 2, 1767? My own inclination was at first to dismiss much of it as wishful thinking, particularly as the whole development of the passage indicates the influence of Cleland and Crebillon *fils*. But then, Glenney was not a particularly clever man; even some of the felicities of the above letter are borrowed from Esmond. One might say, in fact, that the chief interest of this letter is that it reveals how far Horace Glenney had taken on the stamp of Esmond's personality. In many ways, it might have been written by Esmond. No, I

104

think that what had happened here is altogether more interesting. Like most young noblemen of his time, Glenney was thoroughly licentious from an early age—he mentions elsewhere that he was first seduced by a farmer's wife at the age of eleven, and that at thirteen he had a bad week when another girl's menstrual period was late. But he was licentious in a stolid, unimaginative sort of way, pinching the bottoms of chambermaids, boorish and clumsy with girls of his own class, completely tongue-tied with women he really admired. He was bullied and then patronised by his father, and was in awe of his elder brother (who died in 1770 of bilious fever, after a three-day drinking bout on brandy and madeira). He hardly knew his mother, who had separated from his father ten years earlier because he beat her with a riding crop. Horace Glenney was an emotionally retarded country bumpkin. Then he met the brilliant Esmond, who might have been twenty years his senior as far as maturity went. I do not think that Horace Glenney was homosexual, but I think the only adequate way of expressing what happened at Göttingen is to say that he fell in love with Esmond. He picked up his ideas, his mannerisms, his literary style, his preoccupations. It was as if Esmond was a wizard, and Glenney the sorcerer's apprentice. Women sighed and yielded as if by magic. There was an amazing quality of a daydream-come-true about it all. He returned to Golspie House, and girls treated him like a hero back from the wars. But although he was four hundred miles or so from the beloved, he lived and thought as though they were still in Göttingen together. Instead of sleeping with every girl in sight, he imposes a discipline upon himself, studies his Horace and Aristotle, and then decides upon a ' sentimental '—that is, an elevated and rather detached—relation with his sister's pretty girlfriend—in doing which he is anticipating Novalis, Poe, Dowson, and various other romantics who fell in love with children. Inspired by his ideals, he rises above his normal limitations. And then—proof that the gods are still with him, that the magic is working as infallibly as ever—he realises that these two admire him as much as Maggie McBean and the other farmgirls, and that he can play with fire to his heart's content. The daydream remains unbroken. He has absolutely no sexual interest in his sister; he knows her too well. But like leaves,

105

they fall into the whirlpool of the daydream, and from his god-like eminence, he can choose what to do. How shall the dream finish? Shall he pluck the maidenheads like two blackberries, exercise his *droit de seigneur*? He hesitated; there can be no doubt he would have succeeded if he had really wanted to. It was sensible of his father to put the girls in the same bed; time sped by, and in mid-January he set out on the return journey to Göttingen, taking the long and arduous route via London, in order to travel with Esmond, rather than the much shorter route from Dundee to Cuxhaven. It is also interesting that the only occasion when Glenney again invited Esmond back to Golspie for Christmas was in 1770, when Mary was staying with friends in Brighton. For Mary and Fiona, Horace was still ' the distant beloved ', and he was not going to make the mistake of allowing them to meet the original mould from which he was cast.

As it is, one can gather from the length and detail of this letter the bursting pride that Glenney felt as he made his report to his teacher. He had been alone, with no one to advise him, and he had passed the test with top marks...

Let me admit that my first response to Glenney's letters was unsympathetic, and that my feelings about Donelly experienced another fluctuation downward. But it is necessary to explain that I was not disapproving on moral grounds—as any reader of the *Sex Diary* will know. Like Donelly, I have always been fascinated by the problem of sex because it seems to hold the key to the secrets of a more intense consciousness. I have always been obsessed by the way that sexual experience seems to slip through the fingers like fairy gold. And I must repeat here a number of key experiences that seem to me to hold an important clue to the mystery.

In 1955, I had spent an afternoon in bed with a girl named Caroline, a drama student I had met through Gertrude Quincey. I have never understood why, but Caroline was one of those girls who produce in me a curiously intense level of lust, of purely physical desire. She once told me that when I made love to her, she sometimes pretended she was being raped, and that it increased the pleasure. This made me realise that, almost uncon-sciously, I was pretending that I was raping her, treating her

106

purely as a hungry man would treat a tender steak, absorbing and devouring with a ravenous appetite. On this particular afternoon, I had made love to her a great many times—seven or eight. It was like a game. On one occasion I came back from the bathroom and she was sitting in her panties, trying to hook her bra; I threw her back on her bed, pulled aside the leg of the panties, and entered her with almost a single movement; and again later, when she was fully dressed and ready to go, made love to her against the door. There was always an element of shock, of suddenness, in our coming together.

Afterwards, I felt completely exhausted, blissfully relaxed, as if I had drained off every ounce of sexual desire, and could turn my mind to more important things. Then I went outside to get the milk off the doorstep. I lived in a basement flat, and a girl walked past the area railings, so close that I got a glimpse above the tops of her stockings. It was like a kick in the stomach. I realised with a shock that my sexual desire had *not* been drained; only my immediate curiosity about Caroline. The well was apparently bottomless.

The same realisation came some months later, when I was on my way to spend the night with Caroline—who was by this time sharing a flat with a girlfriend. I called in at a ladies' shop to buy her a pair of stockings. Behind me, as I stood at the counter, there were a number of those cubicles in which women try on dresses. I turned casually, and saw that a woman was in one of the cubicles, her back to me, without a skirt or underskirt. Again, there was the shock of tremendous desire. Yet the woman was middle-aged, as I saw when she turned; under ordinary circumstances, I would not have given her a second glance. Leaving the shop, I was uncomfortably aware that my night with Caroline would not touch this depth of sexual response.

This led me to formulate the notion that sexual perversions are an attempt to escape this oddly unsatisfying element in the normal sexual act. It is the *situation* of the normal sexual act that produces the disappointment. (There is the story of the psychiatrist who advised an impotent man to try self-hypnosis; before he got into bed, he was to close his eyes and repeat over and over again : ' She is not my wife, she is not my wife...') All forms of perversion consist in adding an element of the *forbidden* to the normal situation : the girl has to walk up and down in black stockings, and so on. Colonel Donelly's story about being whipped by the governess makes the same point. This is a rather gloomy view of the nature of the sexual impulse, since anything ceases to be forbidden once you can persuade someone else to participate in the daydream. Sex becomes the pursuit of an ever-receding goal...

In Dublin five years ago, a minor occurrence modified this view. I was walking into the library of Trinity College when I met a girl coming out; she was wearing white stockings, and something about her face produced an intense shock. I had never seen her before, and I tried for ten minutes to place her. Then I remembered : she reminded me of a girl called Hazel who used to nurse me occasionally as a child. She was a pretty girl, who was ten or eleven when I was four or five. I looked upon her as a kind of extra mother; I was never so happy as when she was caressing me or changing my clothes or helping me to put on my shoes. By the time I was ten, she was married. I knew about the physical details of the sexual act, and it seemed horribly exciting and wicked. One day, I saw Hazel in the grocer's, looking as pretty as ever, wearing a black skirt and white stockings. The thought that her husband had the right to raise this skirt and remove her stockings suddenly filled me with an anguished jealousy. I thought of the things they must do in the dark, and I looked hard at her face, thinking that it must have left some sign—of dreamy ecstasy, or perhaps of wickedness. I imagined that their life, when he came home from work, must be one long, gloating orgy. Yet she looked perfectly ordinary, just I had always known her, perhaps a little thinner, without the pink bloom...

And the thought of Hazel—whom I had forgotten for fifteen years or more—brought back memories of other girls I had admired when I was very young : a girl who lived two doors away who seemed to me a saint; a girl in the next street, whose oval face struck me as the most beautiful thing I had seen; a maternal aunt, not much older than Hazel, who sometimes took me to the pictures and then out to tea...It came as a shock to remember how many of these girls—all older than myself—I had regarded as goddesses. It had never struck me before that I spent my childhood in a kind of matriarchal society, surrounded by women whom I worshipped, from whom all I asked was a smile, a caress. For in my teens, I thought of women as desirable creatures who had the whip-hand over man because of the treasure between their thighs, which they could withhold or bestow at will. It was man's job to get the treasure, by persuasion, trickery or violence...And from then on, I devoted myself to the usual male task of ransacking as many treasure chests as possible; they were the prey, I the hunter. Yet the tendency to idealise them remained strong, and seemed to contradict the philosophy of the sex war. Now I understood. The sex war was nonsense. What I wanted from women was still what I had wanted from Hazel—the elder-sisterly compassion and tenderness, the caresses, the attention, producing an immediate sense of security and self-confidence. I had often observed the feeling of peace that comes as the penis passes that ring of muscle at the mouth of the vagina, and slips into the warm, caressing inner folds. Now I saw that this was simply the ultimate caress. In a moment of affection, Hazel might reach out and touch my cheek gently, or rest her hand on my head, and I would experience an immediate flow of satisfaction. The peace of entering a woman's body was an intensified version of this; it is a caress, a gesture of tenderness, but she is caressing the most intimate part of your body with the most intimate part of hers. The aggressiveness that Lawrence called 'the sex war' develops from the starvation of this need, just as criminality may develop from poverty. Even the Casanova obsession can be explained in this way—particularly the type of Casanova who wants to keep his women totally faithful to him, while he is allowed to do as he likes. It is the desire for the total assurance of female love and approval. All the women in the world love him; they are all willing to give him their love; even the knowledge that he is in bed with someone else makes no difference...

All this led me to recognise why I have lost interest in the sex war in the last few years. In Diana and Mopsy, I have a two-woman admiration society; the hunger for security has been fed until it is drowsy. The kind of self-confidence that is the gift of women has been achieved, and I can devote my full attention to more serious matters, to questions of philosophy and human evolution.

All this explains my impatience with Horace Glenney, and with what I supposed to be Esmond Donelly's philosophy of libertinism. I felt that it indicated either unfulfilment or immaturity : the small boy's desire for security. It was not this particular episode—of Fiona and Mary—that irritated me, because I appreciated that it was uncalculated; he wanted a 'sentimental' relation, and it turned into a sexual one. But other letters indicated that he was capable of a coarser approach. For example, in the Christmas of the following year, he returned home via a northern route, sailing from Amsterdam to Grimsby, and decided to spend a few days at Osnabrück, looking at the cathedral and the castle. The inn was crowded, and Glenney was placed in an upstairs room over a washhouse, which he shared with his manservant, a cockney named Doggett. Some time after midnight, he went downstairs to relieve himself, then stood for a while with his back against the wall of the washhouse, which was warm. As he stood there, a girl came out of the inn and went into the washhouse; once in there, she undressed, ladled warm water into a basin, and washed herself, while Glenney peeped in at the window. Then she dressed, and went to bed in another room of the same building. Glenney was about to follow her, when he heard a man's voice, which seemed to come from her room. The next morning, he told Doggett to find out all he could about the girl, and whether she would be available that night. Doggett came back some hours later and told him that she was a respectable girl, a niece of the innkeeper, and that she was engaged to a carpenter's assistant. She could not marry him because his master refused permission. The innkeeper had flatly refused to lend the man enough money to set up in business on his own. Glenney reasoned that it was probably this apprentice's voice he had heard coming from her room the night before; he decided to abandon the idea of sleeping with her.

Later in the day, Doggett told Glenney that he had heard a rumour that the girl was pregnant—she had spells of sickness

during her work. Glenney scented a new approach. He told
Doggett to try to get into her confidence, and find out how much
money her lover would need to set up his own shop. 'I would
have given a thousand guineas for the pleasure of leaving one
lot of life-fluid in that virtuous little womb.' But it turned out
that her lover could set up in business on a far smaller sum than
this, a hundred and seventy-five thalers, the equivalent of about
twenty-five guineas. Doggett told her that his master had a kind
heart and might be worth approaching—these English milords
were extravagant and rash. Accordingly, the girl knocked timidly
on Glenney's door in the late afternoon, and was told to come in.
She made her speech about her lover's need for money, about
how he would repay it, and so on. Glenney opened his purse and
shook out a pile of gold pieces. Then, as the girl's eyes were
riveted on these, he took her round the waist, and whispered
that she could earn the money for her lover very easily. She
tried to break away and leave the room, and he told her that he
knew she was pregnant. This upset her; she hesitated; Glenney
pointed to the money, and whispered that no one would ever
know. It would only take five minutes. And she would live happily
ever after...She allowed him to kiss her, and caress her breast.
She closed her eyes, and had evidently decided that it was worth
it, when they heard someone calling her. She broke away; Glenney
took the money and pressed it into her hand, then kissed her
again. She hurried away.

That evening, she waited at table. He caught her eye twice,
and she blushed. She owed him her body. Glenney knew there
was no danger of her returning his money; Doggett found out
she had been to see her lover early in the evening; she had
undoubtedly taken him the money.

That night, Glenney waited until he heard her cross the yard
and go into the washhouse. This time, she only undressed to her
chemise. Glenney opened the door and slipped in. She looked
terrified, and begged him to leave. She explained in a whisper
that 'he' was waiting in her room. Glenney whispered that this
would not take a moment. He spent a few minutes pacifying her,
persuading her to be quiet. Then he unbuttoned his trousers,
pressed her back against the copper, and possessed her there and

then. After this, he whispered that if she wanted another twenty-five guineas to set up house, she should come to his room the next day. Then he dressed and left her.

He was furious when she did not avail herself of his invitation. He met her once in a corridor and looked at her questioningly; she shook her head and hurried away. Doggett had no success in persuading her either. She had kept her part of the bargain, but to Glenney it seemed the height of unreasonableness that she had given herself to him once, and now withheld herself. ' I would have spent every guinea I possessed for a night in bed with the virtuous little devil.' He told Doggett to try blackmailing her by threatening to tell her lover, and then, when this didn't work, contemplated kidnapping her and carrying her off in a coach. But the girl had had enough; that night, she vanished. Presumably she joined her lover, who was now independent of his master. In a very bad temper, Glenney took coach for Amsterdam, and consoled himself with the thought that ' that five minutes against the copper was worth twenty-five guineas of anybody's money '. The whole episode has a rather nasty flavour. He had seen her undressed and he wanted to have her; the discovery that she was in trouble only added to his determination. He could have waited, and got her to come to his room the next day; she was obviously prepared to keep her side of the bargain. But it would be more piquant to possess her in the circumstances in which he had first decided to have her—particularly as her lover was waiting in her room. It is interesting to note his use of the word ' virtuous '. The girl was not virtuous, for she was pregnant. But it was this vision of her that made him want her : respectable, virtuous, in love with someone else. How appropriate to hoist up her chemise and fuck her against the copper, with his trousers around his ankles! But having done it, he wants to occupy the conquered territory, repeat the whole pleasurable business. He would not normally try blackmailing a girl into bed, or think of abducting her in a carriage; but this ' virtuous ' girl produces a desire to conquer, to degrade; even when he is finally frustrated, he dwells on the thought that she has been had by him; if she remains faihtful for the rest of her life, nothing can take that away. It is the coarsest kind of masculine sadism that informs the whole episode. But Glenney describes it in his letter to Donelly as if certain of his approval. My own feeling was that if Donelly did not find the whole business as unpleasant as I had, then he was as bad as Glenney. They were just a pair of dirty-minded rakes. But since I had none of Donelly's letters, I had no way of knowing his reaction to Horace Glenney's revelations.

For the next ten days, my 'quest' for Donelly marked time. I must confess to an appalling laziness, or, rather, to a perverse disinclination to occupy my energies upon any task for which I am being paid. I felt as if reading the various letters and documents borrowed from the Misses Donelly was a kind of home-work, and I resented it. Instead, I filled page after page of my journals, on topics relating to phenomenology, and studied Wittgenstein, whose *Zettel* had just arrived from Blackwells.

Then several things happened at once. The *Irish Times* published my letter appealing for material about Donelly; two days later, *The Times Literary Supplement* printed the letter I had written from London. Klaus Dunkelman finally wrote me an apologetic letter from Hampstead, explaining that my letter to him had not been forwarded, but had been left lying on the hall table at his old address, where it was accidentally noticed by a friend. A Mr W. S. K. Aldrich of Cork wrote to say that he had been a friend of the late Jane Aston, who died in 1949, and had various letters in Donelly's handwriting. He was not sure what had become of them. Finally, Clive M. Bates, the grandson of Isaac Jenkinson Bates, wrote to me from Dublin to say that his grandfather had been ill, but that if I happened to be in Dublin, he would be happy to see me. He added that his grandfather was delighted that I concurred with his views on the Ireland's Eye murder, and would like to discuss it in person. A postscript added: ' I have seen your letter in today's *Irish Times*. I may be able to offer a few suggestions.' The cautious wording of this last sentence excited me. He could not even bring himself to mention Donelly. It seemed to indicate that he almost certainly knew something : too much even to trust himself to hint at it.

Klaus Dunkelman's letter was very long, and discussed my books at length. But its references to Donelly were brief. He said that he had heard the name mentioned by Otto Körner, the disciple of Wilhelm Reich, who spoke of Donelly as being one of the first writers to note the importance of the orgasm for psychological health. However, said Dunkelman, he was unfortunately unable to offer me more details, since he had now severed connection with Körner. As far as he knew, Körner was now back in Germany.

My inclination was to hurry to Dublin to see Clive Bates; but there was too much else to be done, and besides, haste might spoil everything. So I wrote him a non-committal letter, talking about my project of a biographical introduction to a book of Donelly's journals, and adding that I hoped to see him some time soon. Then I turned to the matter of tracking down the Donelly letters that had belonged to Jane Aston—although without much enthusiasm. No doubt they would be Donelly's letters on the subject of Jortin, Tillotson and other sleep-inducing sermonisers. I drove to Cork and interviewed Mr Aldrich, who was able to tell me that Jane Aston had relatives at Belgooly, near Kinsale. I drove there and discovered that they had gone to Cork for a day's shopping. So I went to Kinsale and booked a room in a hotel, then called back on Mr Philip Aston—a retired coastguard—at seven in the evening. It proved to be a wasted trip : he knew nothing of Donelly letters; but he gave me the address of Fr Bernard Aston of Limerick. I called on him the next day, on my way back to Galway. He had heard of the Donelly papers, but had no idea what had happened to them. He suggested that I contact Jane Aston's doctor, George O'Hefernan, of Cork, who knew her well. (A slight droop of the eyelids hinted that the relationship was closer than he could approve.)
  I was beginning to get a Kafka-ish sensation of being directed from one office to another and never getting any nearer the objective; I was tempted to give up. I wanted to quote half a page of Donelly on the subject of sin and redemption; but it began to seem more trouble than it was worth. When I got home, fortified by a good-size glass of claret, I rang directory enquiries in Cork and asked for the number of Dr O'Hefernan. They said there was only one listed, but he was ex-directory. With a sinking

114

feeling, I asked if I could be put on to the superintendent. Then I took another long drink. A man came on the line, explained the superintendent was away at the moment, and asked if he could help. I knew it would be impossible to persuade them to give me the number, but hoped it might be possible to get the superintendent to ring Dr O'Hefernan and ask if he would speak to me. Ireland is an easygoing, obliging sort of country. So I explained my business—that I was a writer, that I wanted to trace certain documents, and that I thought Dr O'Hefernan might be able to help me. The gentleman on the other end asked me to hang on; ten minutes later, he returned, and told me that the O'Hefernan in question was not listed as a doctor. I thanked him and hung up; that seemed to be the end of the trail.

But a couple of hours later, as I was dozing and listening to *The Pirates of Penzance*, the telephone rang. Diana took the call, and told me the Cork superintendent wanted to speak to me. It was the same man. He had looked through old listings and found Dr O'Hefernan, and then somehow managed to trace him for me. The address was in Killarney. I thanked him effusively, and took his name and address so that I could send him a copy of one of my books. Then, although it was now after ten, I got through to Dr O'Hefernan's number. I told him my name, and explained I was a writer. He immediately became very friendly, and told me he had published a few books himself. He had never heard of me; but when I brought up the subject of Esmond Donelly, he recalled that he *had* seen my letter in the *Irish Times*, and had been meaning to write to me. Yes indeed, he had a large number of Donelly's letters, as well as some other papers, and I would be most welcome to examine them at any time that would be convenient to me. I fixed on the next day.

There is no space here to describe the twenty-four hours I spent with George O'Hefernan, although it certainly deserves description. A short, stockily built man with rosy cheeks, white hair and a white moustache, he was one of those people who seem to have been born happy and full of interest in everything that happens. He presented me with copies of his books, *Clonmacnoise and Other Poems*, *Mangan and his Circle* and *Memoirs of an Irish Rebel*, as well as his volume of translations from the

Gaelic. He had known Yeats well, spent many evenings with Joyce in Paris, and been a drinking companion of Gogarty; I made a note of his stories in my journal, for the versions in *Memoirs of an Irish Rebel* are a great deal tamer and less Rabelaisian than the versions he told me. The doctor was the soul of hospitality; he invited a dozen friends in for dinner, and we consumed several gallons of home-made ale as well as a great deal of Jameson's. In the early hours of the morning, when the last of his guests had wandered unsteadily towards his car, he told me the story of his association with Mrs Aston during the last twenty years of her life—she died at forty-eight of pneumonia. Finally, he took me to a great floor-to-ceiling cupboard in the spare bedroom—where I was to sleep—and showed me piles of rolled manuscripts, letters tied in bundles and heavy black folders. 'You'll find plenty of Donelly's stuff among that lot', he said, and left me to look through it. It was 4 a.m., and the room was chilly in spite of a single-bar electric fire. I had drunk too much, and had a slight headache. But I started pulling papers out of the cupboard on the offchance of seeing Esmond's handwriting. After disturbing a few spiders and a quantity of dust, I found a bundle of letters addressed to William Aston. I had now cleared out most of the bottom shelf of the cupboard. In the corner, at the back, there were two black-bound volumes. I pulled these out and glanced into one of them; the handwriting was Esmond's. I glanced at the front page; it started halfway through a paragraph. I opened the other volume. It consisted of octavo-sized pages that had been bound together; the opening page read : 'October 11, 1764. I have often determined that I should keep a journal in which I would record my everyday doings, but have so far failed to hold to the intention. I have lost recollection of so many interesting events that I have at last determined to carry this resolution into effect, whatever the cost in labour or candles...'

I undressed, pulled on my pyjamas, and clambered into bed, no longer interested in sleep. In 1764, Esmond was just sixteen years of age. This journal was therefore the earliest of his writings that I had seen so far. The handwriting was neater and easier to read than in the later journal. My feeling of triumph was so strong that I was tempted to rush along to Dr O'Hefernan's bedroom and show him. It was only my suspicion that he shared it with the plump young woman who kept house for him that made me restrain myself. What surprised me was that O'Hefernan had not mentioned these journals. He told me that he knew there were letters from Donelly, but that was all. The inference was that he did not know of their existence. And when I asked him the next morning, he confirmed this. The journals of an Anglicised Protestant Irishman of the eighteenth century held no interest for him, for he was a Catholic and a patriot, and his feelings about Cromwell were more violent than most Englishmen's about Hitler.

I read until dawn, slept for about three hours, until the housekeeper woke me with tea, then pulled on my overcoat over my pyjamas and went back to the cupboard. Within half an hour, I had sorted out three more bundles of letters and two more bound journals, as well as the manuscript of his *Travel Diary*. When Dr O'Hefernan came in to tell me breakfast was on the table, he found me surrounded by papers and covered with dust, sitting opposite an empty cupboard. When I showed him the journals, he smiled and said: 'Good. I'm glad you didn't have the trip for nothing.' I took the opportunity to ask the question that had been on my mind all night. 'Do you mean I can make use of all this material?' 'Sure. Why shouldn't you?' 'Would you prefer me to work here, or could I borrow it?' 'Oh, whichever you like. Come on down now and eat something.' And he padded off in his slippers and dressing-gown, while I sat there chortling like a madman.

And I must confess that as I studied the journal, I began to regret that I had accepted Fleisher's contract. Fifteen thousand dollars had seemed a magnificent sum at the time; but with all this material at my disposal, I felt I deserved a great deal more. For the new journal removed the last of my doubts about Donelly's intellectual stature. It showed me why Horace Glenney admired him so much. He was a man who was obsessed by the elusive nature of human experience. But let him speak for himself:

My cousin Frances tells me I have too good a conceit of myself, but I call heaven to witness that this is untrue. I am often the most wretched and self-derogatory creature under the sun, and my dissatisfaction often reaches a pitch where it would be a temptation to blow out my brains. I am writing this journal that I might attempt to introduce some kind of order and continuity into my life, for I am heartily sick of my own disapprobation. Women do often complain that men lack constancy; but why should we have constancy in love when we have none in any other form of thought, feeling or desire? Yesterday, the famous Doctor Gillis preached at our church, and I was greatly moved, and swore that I would in future alter my life according to his recommendations, and live only by the approval of my conscience and sense of virtue. But today it is too windy and cold to venture outdoors, and this morning I read the fables of Gellert in the German for an hour before my usual distemper overcame me, and I became sunk in a monstrous lassitude. Since then, I can see no way in which my conscience or sense of virtue can operate upon this life-consuming weariness. My conscience may tell me how to avoid doing wrong, but it cannot tell me how to escape tedium. And is there anything deadlier for a creature made in God's likeness than this same tedium? For God is God because he can create; so a man crushed by tedium is most un-Godlike.

Dr Gillis made a most ingenious comparison between the body and the mind, saying that the body has its own system for disposing of injurious or pestilent humours, whether natural or the product of sickness, whereas the mind has none. If I have a boil, it will discharge of itself; if I am costive, a green apple will loosen the obstruction; but if I am full of bile or envy, no purgative will serve; either I must give expression to my animus, or withdraw it by an act of contrition. There is no natural channel; it must be, like Macduff, 'from its mother's womb untimely ripped'. And is this not even more true of this *toedium vitae* that stifles me? It is a constipation of the soul, a boil that refuses to discharge.

I know that I cannot be happy without a feeling that my activity is directed to some purpose, but I know not how to imbue my soul with purpose. Half an hour ago I took up Thomson's *Winter* and read:

> Thro' the hush'd air the whitening shower descends,
> At first thin wavering; till at last the flakes
> Fall broad and wide, and fast, dimming the day
> With a continual flow. The cherish'd fields
> Put on their winter robes of purest white.
> 'Tis brightness all, save where the new snow melts
> Along the mazy current...

Why do these words cause a peace like falling snow to descend upon my senses? Is there not within me some appetite for sublimity that is now choked by weariness, as my belly's hunger is blunted and made sickly if I eat too many sweet cakes? And is this appetite not arous'd from its slumber by the memory of winter fields? And also by the sound of the clash of swords in Ossian? And also by the bouncing of a soft bosom when a girl runs upstairs? Why do we not possess a rod to strike the rock of the soul, and make a spring gush forth?

Esmond has here sounded the fundamental theme of the journal: what we would now call the hidden powers of the subconscious. It obsesses him; he returns to it again and again. 'The powers of Nature surround us all the time; the mighty rushing of the torrent, the cannonades of the wind; the very stars dance through the heavens to tell us that nothing in the world stands still except the soul of a wretch who knows only disquiet and self-reproach.' He asks repeatedly why man's intelligence should *exclude* him from the life of the universe, and speculates whether this is the meaning of the story of Adam and Eve: that knowledge itself, the ability to think, was that which separated man from God. Even at sixteen, Donelly shows a remarkably wide acquaintance with the eighteenth-century divines, and even quotes George Herbert. And then, on page 48 of volume one—dated a week before Christmas—the tone changes. I suspect he had re-read his sentence about the 'rod to strike the rock of the soul and make a spring gush forth', for he speaks again of bouncing bosoms. The bosoms he had in mind were those of his cousin Sophia, who was staying with them for the holiday, together with her mother and father. Sophia Montagu, a cousin of Elizabeth Montagu (one of the original 'blue stockings'), became a noted beauty of the period, and even at this time—when she was barely nineteen—she had attracted a great deal of attention when staying at the Mayfair home of the famous hostess. Esmond was a good-looking boy, but she probably thought of him as an unsophisticated country cousin. Esmond was analytical enough to know he was not in love with her, for he wrote : 'S is a fool, but a beautiful fool who has many points of resemblance to a goddess.' And later : 'Sophia told me that she had heard Mr Boswell argue with Dr Johnson in favour of polygamy, and that Mrs Montagu replied that there was no woman alive with so little judgement as to want more than one husband at a time.' Boswell's idea took root; so did Rousseau's *Nouvelle Héloïse*, which he read in French, and Richardson's *Clarissa Harlowe*. In Rousseau's novel, the heroine Julie and her tutor Saint-Preux become lovers, and Rousseau argues that this is right and natural between two people who love one another and are prevented by circumstances from marrying. Richardson's novel is moral by comparison : an account of the abduction and rape of the virtuous Clarissa by the rake Lovelace; Clarissa dies of mortification, and Lovelace is killed in a duel. Esmond heaps mockery on Richardson in the name of Rousseau. Why should a girl go into a decline because a man has done something that is perfectly natural? The presence of his pretty cousin kept the subject of sexual intercourse to the forefront of his mind, and in a short time he is expressing views that made him decide to keep his diary a secret. Like many other critics, he suspected that Richardson's attitude to the rape of Clarissa was not one of horrified disapproval, but of vicarious pleasure. 'For who would not enjoy ravishing a beautiful girl, especially if she were uncon- scious and know nothing of it.' He asks why Richardson allows Clarissa to be ravished when she is drugged, instead of in the manner of Lucrece, and answers : 'If the girl is too virtuous to

120

surrender her body in any other way, then Lovelace is right to adopt this course. The girl's beauty, like that of certain tropical birds, is intended to allure the male sex; why should she complain if she is too successful? She complains because her aim is to get a husband in exchange for her virtue. But supposing the prospective husband finds her a fool and has no wish to devote his life to her support? Is he bound by his honour to foreswear the pursuit? Why should he not try to pluck the flower instead of buying the whole garden?'

It is interesting to observe that he does not actually answer the question of why Richardson preferred to have Clarissa unconscious when she is raped. But it continues to trouble him. He asks: 'Is it not because the man's sense of obligation lessens his pleasure? Would it not destroy my pleasure in a bottle of wine if I knew I had to pay fifty pounds for it tomorrow?' He goes on to discuss Boswell's idea of polygamy, and asserts that this is only another expression of the male's natural desire to pay homage by 'pouring a libation of procreation-juice into its proper orifice'.

The interest in Sophia came to nothing; but at least it served to start Esmond thinking about sex. This leads him to give a full and interesting account of his sexual experiences so far. They had taken place only six months before; the girl was a lady's maid his elder sister, Judith, had brought back from Lyons. He calls her Minou, although apparently her real name was Marie:

When I returned from Dublin, Judith had been home about six weeks. At first, I paid Minou no attention, finding her face somewhat plain; her chin was too large, and she had a nose like a button. But on the second day after my return, as I lay upon the newly scythed grass near the edge of the stream, I heard her laughing and saying: 'No, no, this is not the place', and a man's voice mocking her accent: 'No, thees ees goot place.' It was Shawn Rafferty, who tends the horses and helps with the garden, a great hulking lubber whose right cheek is scarred by the kick of a foaling mare. His trousers and waistcoat never fit him, for they are the cast-offs of his elder brother, who is six inches shorter.

121

I was unable to see either of them, for they were lying in the long grass under an apple tree. After a few minutes of silence, she said again : ' No, not here.' ' Come to the barn then.' ' No, I cannot. I must go back to help with the tea.' (Judith has afternoon tea, a custom she picked up abroad.) But I heard her promise to return to the barn after tea; then she stood up, brushed her dress with her hands, and hurried away. Shawn Rafferty got up, tied his trousers at the waist with a piece of rope, and went off towards the barn.

I knew Shawn's reputation among the village girls, although I had never been able to understand it, for his scar and the wall eye give him a most formidable appearance. My sisters call him the Cyclops. But now I was all agog with curiosity to know what he intended to do with her, although it was not difficult to guess. I had watched him guiding the erect organ of an impatient stallion into a mare, and I had no doubt that he was well versed in the use and control of his own machine. But I knew nothing of the coupling of man and woman; and I now decided that, should the opportunity present itself, I would remedy this defect in my education. I thereupon betook myself to the hay barn—for I guessed this was the one he meant—and climbed up into the loft, among the bean sacks and bales of fodder. All the floor had been covered with the hay, and the smell was most delicious. It was my guess that they purposed to enjoy their union upon this natural carpet; but in case he should take it into his head to look aloft, I hid myself behind the sacks in the corner.

Half an hour later, Shawn came in and began turning the hay with a fork; I could not see him, but I knew him by his voice as he sang ' Molly Malone '. Then he came up to the loft, bringing great armfuls of hay, which he scattered and spread on the floor within a few yards of where I lay. From this I guessed they intended to hold their nuptials up here, and not, as I had supposed, down below.

A few minutes later, Minou came in, and for a while there was no sound. I raised myself to my knees and peeped out over the sacks; they were standing near the door, and she had her arms round his neck. Then they talked in whispers, and he pointed to the ladder; I lay down and closed my eyes, so that they might think me asleep in case they came upon me. He came up first, then turned and helped her off the ladder, which stretched beyond the platform. The light was poor, but I could see them well enough. He stood with his back to the wall, and she flung her arms round his neck, and gave him a long kiss. Then she took one hand away, and reached down to the rope, which she untied with one pull. His trousers fell down to his knees, revealing enormous and hairy buttocks that were turned towards me. Her hand moved around between them and I could only guess what it was doing. Then she suddenly dropped to her knees before him, and her face disappeared behind the curve of his thigh. I saw his hands take hold of her head, and his buttocks begin to move. Then he said : ' Ah, stop it or I shall lose the best of it ', and they stayed like that a moment more, neither of them moving. While she crouched there, he fumbled with the back of her dress; then she stood up, and he raised it from the floor, while she held up her arms as though he were a lady's maid, allowing him to draw it upwards. He took it off, and laid it carefully upon the floor; and as he turned sideways, I saw his instrument of love standing like a maypole, and swaying as he moved. It was not as big as that of the stallion, but it was one of the largest I had ever clapped eyes upon. Meanwhile, as he lifted her chemise, I was able to see her figure, which was so sweetly rounded that I could not believe it belonged to the uninviting face. As she stood there, her arms pinioned above her head by the chemise, he bent his head and brought his mouth down to her breast, which he worried between his lips, while her hands closed over the pole that prodded her belly—its length being ample to accommodate both of them. Then he pulled off the chemise and tossed it on the floor, and they both sank down upon the hay. I raised my face above the sacks, but could see little, for they were sunk into the hay, and the light down there was poor. Suddenly, she

123

gave a sharp cry, and I was afraid she had seen me, and ducked back again; then I heard him hushing her, and she cried out again, but less loud. The hay rustled as though ten thousand rats were in it, and she continued to utter cries and moans, as though she were in pain. Then the rustling became so furious that I peeped up again, and saw him moving his buttocks upon her as though he hoped to make a hole in the floor, while I saw that her knees were now bent, and her feet were in the small of his back, so that had there been more light, I could have viewed the exact site of the operation. Then she tried to cry out again and he placed his hand over her face, while his movements stopped as if frozen. They lay there, quite still, then he gave a great sigh, and seemed to shrink from her. She unwound her legs from his hips, and let them lie straight, while he lay there upon her without moving.

I must confess that all this had me wrought up to a considerable pitch of excitement, which had reached its own moment of release some minutes before their motions had ceased. Now that it was over, I hoped they would dress position. But the silence that ensued convinced me they had themselves and allow me to escape from my cramped fallen asleep, although I dared not move to find whether my guess was correct. After some ten minutes had passed, they began to move again; but the rustling continued so long that I inferred they had only returned to their amorous congress. I peeped over the sack and discovered that my guess was only half correct; for he still lay like a stricken gladiator, while she crouched upon all fours, and seemed to be trying to bring some life to the embers by blowing upon them. After a while, this had its effect...

Esmond's account goes on for so long that it would be pointless to quote more of it here. The girl was a nymphomaniac, although Esmond was too inexperienced to recognise this. She roused her cavalier to further activity three times, and finally left him sleeping so deeply that Esmond was finally able to tiptoe past him without being detected.

But the next development is so typical of Esmond that it must be recorded here. He admits that he was unable to see what went on; but the sounds were so unmistakable that this was unnecessary. And now, having seen the girl naked, his only thought was how he might share her with the stable boy. He repeats several times that the beauty of her shape amazed him; he had always thought that the Greek sculptors exaggerated the beauty of the female form. On the way back to the house, it struck him that the girl could probably be blackmailed into giving herself; he only had to threaten to tell his sister that she and the stable boy were lovers. He went to his own room to wash and brush the dust off his clothes, then went through the servants' quarters to Minou's room. There seemed to be no one about; he opened the latch and peeped in.

Her room was empty, and for a moment I debated whether to wait there or return to my own. Then I heard the sound of water from the annexe—a small closet divided from the rest of the room by a partition—and knew that she was within. I closed the door behind me and tiptoed into the room; but a board creaked, and she called : ' Who is there? ' I said, as quietly as I could : ' Esmond.' She looked out and said : ' Oh, pardonnez moi, I am not dressed.' I stood there, feeling a trifle foolish, and felt myself blushing, which made me angry. She seized her dress, which lay upon a chair, and held it up to her neck, asking : ' You have a message? ' But she was smiling as though she found me pleasing, and this served to dispel my unease. I was staring so hard, trying to determine whether or no she was wearing her chemise, that she remained not long in doubt of my purpose. It was the first time I had known that an exchange of opinions could take place without a word being uttered. Her eyes roved from my feet up to my head, and back again. I said : ' It is cold in here ' or some such foolishness, and then stepped forward, and took her hands, peeping over the top of them. She was wearing the chemise, but it hung low upon her neck, and the sight of the two unsupported orbs so transported me that I hesitated no longer, but took the dress

125

from her and dropped it on the bed. Above the left breast I saw the marks of two rows of teeth, and as she seemed about to protest, I pointed to these. She looked down at them and said something in French which I did not catch, and bent my head to the small nipple that now stood exposed. While she looked, I slipped off the strap of the chemise. I expected her to jerk away, but she stood there quietly and suffered me to take it between my lips; then, after a moment, placed her hands on my head and stroked the hair. Then she unbuttoned my waistband and fore-flap, and reached within to the rod which craved to do her homage. I wasted no more time, but pressed her backward to the truckle bed, and laid my hand upon the nether parts, which were wet, for she had been washing them when I came in. Then, without removing my trousers or hose, I dropped upon her, and entered her without difficulty, the passageway having been already stretched and lubricated by my predecessor. Even in this moment of excitement, I felt surprise to observe how tightly my member was gripped, as though no previous tenant had distended the velvet walls. I was resolved to stay unspent as long as possible, but she undid me by clasping me tight with her thighs and wriggling her buttocks so deliciously that I was unable to hold out longer, and allowed the molten surgings to gush within her, while she wriggled and cried out, though less loudly than in the barn.

The noise of footsteps outside the door gave us cause to fear that someone had come to investigate, but they passed, and I climbed out of bed and slid the bolt, then drew off my trousers and hose, and returned to the bed, which had moved some feet from its original position on its wheels. Though there was scarce room for the two of us turned sideways, we pressed together most comfortably, and after some minutes, she gave me several long kisses, whose manner at first surprised me, since I was unaware that the tongue might usurp the function that is more normally assigned to the lips. After this, she drew back the coverlet, and examined my lower parts with curiosity, praising their whiteness and smoothness, and stroking my thighs and knees...

126

Again, the description is too lengthy to quote. They stayed in her room an hour longer, and the remarkable girl induced him to make love to her three times more. After this, they talked, and Esmond confessed that he had watched her with Shawn Rafferty. Instead of being indignant, she laughed loudly, and then asked him if he was not jealous. ' I was not then. I am now.' She told him that this was absurd, since men and women were intended to give one another pleasure.

It is hard to say whether Esmond was fortunate or unfortunate in his choice of his first mistress. It is true that his own views on promiscuity were already well developed; but a more normal love affair—with an emotional as well as a physical side—would have helped to counterbalance these. He was still unaware that there was anything abnormal in Minou's physical demands, since he found himself able to make love to her as often as she wished. Neither is it entirely true that the strong attraction between them was without its sentimental side; there was even a point where he considered eloping with her. He ceased to think about Clarissa and Lovelace, or Julie and Saint-Preux, and thought of their affaire in terms of Manon and Des Grieux —although he admits that he had previously dismissed Prévost as absurd and unrealistic.

It is a pity that Esmond tells us nothing of Minou's previous history, or even if he questioned her about it. It would be interesting to know whether her perverse sexuality was natural or acquired. She certainly seems to be a textbook case of nymphomania. She liked to be bitten, particularly on the breasts, buttocks and genitals, and liked to be beaten on the behind with a leather strap. She enjoyed sodomy as much as normal sex, preferably standing up or bending over the bed. As soon as she and Esmond were alone in any room of the house, she unbuttoned his trousers and toyed with his penis until he was erect; then, if there was no time for intercourse, she would masturbate him. If she did this orally, she swallowed the sperm; if manually, she licked it from her fingers. On one occasion Esmond's sister Judith entered the room while Minou was on her knees in front of him; she pretended to be cleaning his shoes while Esmond hastily buttoned his trousers.

127

During the two months that this affaire continued, she made no secret about spending as much time as possible with Shawn Rafferty, and Esmond was so far dominated by her that he did not complain. She also tried to persuade him to hide in the barn again and watch her making love with Shawn, but Esmond's pride—or his Protestant snobbery—revolted at this. He also vetoed her suggestion that she should tell Shawn about her affair with Esmond, and that the three of them should join together for romps in the barn.

In August, the affaire took an unexpected turn which leads one to wonder whether Minou (her other name is not recorded) was not one of the most complex and incalculable women of her period. A girl named Delphine Lantier, an acquaintance of Judith's, came to stay at Castle Donelly. One infers from Esmond's description of her that she was not conventionally beautiful, for he says that her face was made beautiful by its gentleness and the large brown eyes. She also had the misfortune to be slightly deformed; she was thrown from a carriage when a child, and broke a hip and shoulder-bone. Neither had been set correctly, so that she carried herself awkwardly. Although her father was French, her mother was Irish, and she spoke English perfectly. (It is significant that Esmond takes the trouble to record the personal details of a girl of his own class, while he ignores those of the far more complex and fascinating Minou.)

Esmond was a romantic sixteen-year-old, and he looked speculatively at every woman he encountered. If Minou was a Manon Lescaut, Delphine was altogether closer to Julie—or perhaps to the docile and sweet-natured Claire in the same novel. Esmond saw she was shy, and took pains to amuse her. He lent her *La Nouvelle Héloïse*, after making her promise to keep it under lock and key. (The reason for this touch of secrecy is not clear, for he mentions elsewhere that neither his father nor his mother could speak French; perhaps he wanted to establish some sort of intimacy.) But he was worried in case Minou should be jealous, and tried not to make his interest in the new arrival too obvious. He underestimated Minou! A few days later, after he had spent an hour with her in his own bed, she told him that she thought

128

Delphine was in love with him, and told him he was stupid not to have noticed. Esmond decided to find out, by the usual methods —allowing his hand to brush against hers as he passed her, touching her arm or waist when they were alone, to find out if she accepted the familiarity. She did. On a picnic in the abbey ruins, he caught her in a corner and kissed her. She burst into tears, and he went away, worried and puzzled, to ask Minou's opinion. Minou told him that Delphine was more serious about him than he about her, and that her tears came from her intuition of this, a remarkable piece of analysis. So on the next occasion when they were alone, Esmond asked Delphine : 'Don't you like me kissing you? ', and assured her that he would never do it again if she objected. She blushed, whispered several disconnected sentences, and then, when pressed, admitted that she had no objection. Esmond invited her for another ramble in the ruins, and spent the afternoon kissing her. On his return, he had to rush to Minou's room and possess her; the self-restraint had been too much for him. Minou told him he was a clumsy lover. What he needed was tenderness and caresses. He should stroke her face, her arm—any part of her that happened to be exposed; accustom her to respond with pleasure to his touch, and then advance cautiously on the forbidden regions. Esmond's description of this campaign lasts for nine closely written pages; he was fascinated by the minutiae of seduction. After a week, he was allowed to expose her breasts and caress them, and to kiss her above the knees—although she held down her dress with both hands to prevent a further advance. They discussed Julie and Saint-Preux, and she agreed in theory that two people in their position should become lovers. In practice, she drew a sharp and clear line between caresses and lovemaking.

And now the inimitable Minou produced a suggestion that dazzled him. She was convinced that Delphine was virtuous ' by theory and inexperience' (as she put it), but that her curiosity was healthy enough. She told Esmond to get Delphine to the barn on the following afternoon, and to make sure that she made no sound when Shawn Rafferty came up to scatter the hay for their usual session of lovemaking. ' If she refuses to look, then she is virtuous, and you had better escape from her before she marries you. If she looks, she is already yours.'

As the hour drew near, Esmond became nervous, and decided several times to abandon the whole preposterous scheme. He suspected that a girl who could draw the line so rigidly would give the game away by revealing the hiding place. His sister announced her intention of calling on a neighbour that afternoon, and Delphine said she would go with her; Esmond heaved a sigh of relief. Then, at the last minute, Delphine said she had a headache, and his mother said she would go instead. Esmond began to play a kind of Russian roulette with Fate. He wanted the project to fail, but he was willing to go through the motions —anxiously looking out for the first excuse to abandon it. He went to Delphine's room at half past three and asked her if she felt like going for a walk. She said she thought it was going to rain. Ten minutes later, the sun came out, and she suddenly declared that the headache had gone and she felt like walking. They took their favourite stroll towards Adare, then walked back along the stream, paddling in the shallows. Esmond talked about his childhood, and the hours he had spent reading forbidden books in the barn. (These seem to have been nothing worse than Mrs Aphra Behn's *The Nun* and Smollett's *Ferdinand, Count Fathom.*) And as they crossed the empty farmyard, Delphine suggested that they look at the barn. It was now half past four; there was a chance that Shawn would already be there. But he was not. Esmond led the way up the ladder to the loft, then went to the place he had already prepared in the corner—placing clean sacks on the floor—and flung himself down. Delphine did the same without hesitation—no doubt this was what she intended.

> We wasted little time in conversation, but fell immediately to kisses and soft caresses, which quickly passed to their usual point of familiarity. She was wearing no stays, so it was less trouble than usual to expose her breasts and commence assault with my lips. I had observed before that I could increase her pleasure by biting the nipples very gently, whereupon she crossed her ankles and pressed her thighs tight with an involuntary motion, from which I drew the inference that the spot thereby compressed was ready for

more delicate attentions. But when my lips moved above her knees, she quickly entangled her fingers in my hair and held me tight. We were in this position when we heard footsteps on the ladder, and she straightaway rearranged her gown, and was about to sit up when I placed my finger on my lips and shook my head. We sat there, scarcely breathing, and then I heard the swish of the hay as Shawn tossed it upon the boards and proceeded to spread it with the fork. Then he went below, and brought up another load, and I whispered to her to remain silent, and all would be well, for it was only the stable boy, a particular friend of mine. But when I tried to kiss her again she shook her head and pushed me away.

We heard Shawn go down and out of the door, and she said : ' Quickly, now is the time to go.' But as we stood up, we heard Minou's voice below, and she quickly sat again without further urgence from me. I had so arranged the bales that we were able to see between two of them without standing up. Delphine was alarmed and whispered : ' What if they should come here? ', but I reassured her, pointing to the hay. It was then, I think, that she began to suspect what Shawn had purposed in spreading it thus, for I could see that she blushed.

Shawn came up first and stood there, and Minou had no sooner joined him than she flung her arms about his neck and gave him a most prolonged kiss, whose nature I could imagine from having experienced it, for she had a marvellous skill in bringing fire to the blood through quick dartings of her tongue. Then she untied the rope at his waist, so that his breeches fell to his ankles, revealing the great crested cock raised in salute. I now observed with delight that Delphine was following every motion with the most avid curiosity, and I recalled Minou's saying that she was already mine. Whereupon I reached out and pulled down the shoulders of her gown, and reached under her arms to place a hand on each breast. She made no attempt to prevent me; I could feel her heart beating with quick, heavy thumps beneath my fingers. Minou, without her skirts, was now on

131

her knees before Shawn, who was turned sideways so that no detail of their actions could escape us. He held her head in his hands, and moved it back and forth to suit his pleasure. I was more interested in wondering how I might take advantage of my present situation than in the progress of their lewd joys. I removed my hand from her breast for long enough to unbutton my flap and allow my own impatient steed to sniff the air, then returned to my caresses. Delphine was kneeling, and from a slight movement of her behind, I guessed the impatience that compressed the lips of her secret place. I therefore raised her skirt above the level of the knee, and allowed my hand to press her thigh. This time, she made no move to hinder me. I raised it higher, and reached the tender mount, scarcely covered with light down; but when I attempted to insinuate a finger tip between the lips, she shook her head and compressed her thighs more tightly. Her breathing was so heavy now that only the rustling of the hay prevented it being overheard. A quick glance through the aperture in the bales showed me that they were still engaged in the preliminaries, although both were now lying down, and his face was hidden between her thighs. I changed my position, without removing my hand from her belly, and began to bite her breast. Her thighs yielded, and my finger slipped in, to find lips that were plentifully lubricated by the tears of the love god. These were so unformed that I had to guess rather than sense the location of the berry that hid within the fold. I moved my finger back and forth, and her body moved to aid its motion, while I continued to bite her nipple—a position of some discomfort. Then her fingers gripped my hair, and her hips moved with a swift oscillatory motion; her thigh closed tight upon my hand, and a long sigh was squeezed from her bosom. Her body drooped, and she would have fallen forward had I not been there to support her. The sounds coming from the hay had now risen to a fury, but she was as indifferent as if it had been a storm outside; she let herself sink upon the sacks, and closed her eyes, tugging and smoothing her gown to re-cover her modesty. I subdued my impatience with some difficulty, observing the regularity of her breathing; but after five minutes or so, fearing that she would sleep, and so lose me my advantage, I laid myself beside her and kissed her. She lay there as though asleep, so I placed my hand on her knee, and slid it up to the mount. She shook her head, and turned her mouth away, but made no other resistance. I now took her lifeless hand and laid it upon my swollen member; she let it rest loosely for a moment, then closed it, but all in a manner so devoid of energy that I wondered if she knew what she clasped. The sounds from the other side of our barrier had ceased, and all was now so silent that a mouse would have been heard. Therefore, I made no attempt to improve my position, but lay there, my hand upon her wet and inert nether mouth, her own hand lightly holding the root of my life, which I moved ever so slightly, being unable to tame its impatience. We lay thus for about a quarter of an hour; then I heard Minou's whisper, and knew that she had renewed her energies, and now intended to arouse her sleeping swain, whose only reply was a grunt. But I knew the power of her arguments well enough to be assured of her success; and it was not long ere the crackling of the straw enabled me to press my own panting suit. I exposed her bosoms, and fell to teasing and biting the nipples, meanwhile pinching the moist berry between my thumb and forefinger. Soon her thighs parted, and I took this as an invitation to rest between them; but when I raised myself upon her, she closed them again, and shook her head. I held it still with a kiss, and moved my weight upon her, letting my balls nestle in the hollow between her thighs, while the head of my charger nuzzled the cold spot I had been caressing. Her knees were pressed too tight to afford any lodgement in the cleft, but when I returned to teasing her nipples, their pressure relaxed, and her ankles uncrossed. Although the head of my steed had now slipped down between her thighs, it had lost its direction, and knew not against what place it battered. Feeling myself so close to the goal, I lost patience and reached down with my hand, which swiftly rearranged the folds so that

133

the entrance lay clear. I gave a sharp push, and felt the head slip within the tight orifice, where it immediately encountered an obstruction. I gave a further push, and she shook her head and moaned. Afraid now of the sound she might make if I persisted, I contented myself with moving the head gently in and out of its new home, which each time closed around it like a garter. Soon, she also began to move under me, and it was too much for my overcharged battering ram, which gushed forth its homage into the mouth that sucked it so shyly. As this happened, I groaned and pushed with all my might; the obstruction gave, her knees parted, and my steed buried itself deep within her as if drinking from a river. Her arms clasped tight around me, and I sealed her mouth with a kiss.

The tone of this whole incident gives the impression that Esmond was already a skilled Casanova who left nothing to chance. The sequel reveals that this is untrue. Casanova would have grown tired of the girl before he withdrew from her. Esmond decided he was in love with her, and that he would marry her. Perhaps he felt ashamed of the stratagem that had overcome her resistance. He was certainly aware of the damage that would follow if he showed any lessening of his tenderness towards her. She was already ashamed of herself for allowing him to see her sexual excitement, and still more for allowing him to take advantage of it. If he had abandoned her completely after her surrender, it would have struck her as no more than she deserved. Esmond determined to prove this was not so. Left alone with her—after Minou and Shawn had left the barn, and the hay had been tossed below again—he told her they were engaged. That night, when Minou raised the catch of his door, she found it bolted on the inside. The next morning, he sought her out and told her he was betrothed, and that from now on they must cease to be lovers. She seems to have taken this philosophically; she was even sympathetic enough to warn him to keep the engagement a secret from his father. He took her advice. But Delphine showed less tact; she confided her secret to Esmond's sister Judith, which proved to be the worst kind of miscalculation. Judith was apparently fond of Delphine, and under different circumstances might have welcomed her as a sister-in-law. But Delphine was a Roman Catholic, and the Donellys were Protestants. It was the most serious obstacle, for in Ireland a Catholic was a pariah. The gentry were Protestants; Catholics were social outcasts. Delphine was the daughter of a French aristocrat, but this made no difference, since they were in Ireland. Judith pointed this out; there were tears and long discussions. Esmond began to feel he had made a mistake. It was a matter of total indifference to him whether Delphine turned Protestant, or he became a Catholic, or they both became Buddhists. He wanted to marry her because he felt he owed her love and protection, and because seducing her had given him so much satisfaction. Now they were 'engaged', and she was not even willing to come to the barn. He remarks ironically in his journal that they would both have been far happier if he had never mentioned marriage.

Judith rather enjoyed her role as matchmaker; she advised Esmond to say nothing to their parents until Delphine could announce that she would become a Protestant. Three days later, she and Delphine set out for Dublin to present the case to her parents. It was the last Esmond saw of her. Judith returned alone, and announced that the Chevalier de Saint-Ange had decided to return to France immediately with his family. Esmond heaved a sigh of relief, and slipped back into Minou's bed. But two months later he also lost Minou, when Squire Donelly caught her in the stable with a new stable boy. The squire was broadminded enough, but he was concerned for the virtue of his son and heir. Minou was packed off back to Lyons, third class, with a month's wages and several of Judith's old dresses. Esmond presented her with twenty guineas that he had been saving for a pony and trap, and told himself that he was glad to be able to call his soul—and certain other vital organs—his own again. But a month after her departure, Esmond began his journal: 'I am often the most wretched and self-derogatory creature under the sun...' He had tasted too many delights to settle down to this tame existence of a gentleman farmer. Between them, Minou and Delphine had been a complete education in the art of love. He had experienced the delight of masculine conquest, the feeling

135

of power over a woman's emotions, as well as the complete abandonment of all his sexual inhibitions. He craved sex as an alcoholic craves his tipple, but there was no one who might provide it. He released his frustration in his journal, re-living the hours with Minou, the seduction of Delphine. He tried to read, but found Rousseau priggish, Voltaire shallow, Sterne irritating. Only Johnson's *Rasselas, Prince of Abyssinia* satisfied the craving for seriousness, and he re-read it until he knew it by heart. Johnson raises the question of the human desire for something *more than* happiness, more than mere contentment. Six months earlier, Esmond might have supposed this was a desire for physical fulfilment, for experience, for pleasure; now he knew better.

And now occurs what is, for me, the most interesting section of the journal. As rainy December dragged into rainy January, Esmond plunged into a crisis of acute nervous depression, accentuated by worry about his father who, in late December, was attacked and severely beaten by a gang of malcontents whose motives seem to have been vaguely political. It happened in the dark, when he was returning from the house of an unpopular local judge; his horse was struck by a stone, and almost immediately afterwards another large flint struck him above the left eye, knocking him unconscious. When he had not returned by midnight, Esmond and a party of grooms went out into a storm to search for him, and found him dragging himself along the road, half naked, still bleeding heavily. The injuries looked more serious than they were; after ten days in bed, Edward Donelly was as well as ever. But no one could find any trace of the attackers, who may have been a party of sailors whose boat was undergoing repairs at Tarbert, on the Shannon.

The whole district was shocked by the violence, although Edward Donelly was not a popular man; there was too much squalor and misery in Ireland for the peasantry to feel any sympathy for a relatively wealthy Protestant farmer. Robbery was common; there were almost as many brigands as in Corsica. But until 1760 the country had been relatively peaceful; then, with George III, the troubles began; there was agrarian unrest; the Catholic gentry began to recover their courage after the

136

Jacobite suppression. Edward Donelly was not a supporter of George III, but as a Protestant he was regarded as an agent of the English usurpers. But Esmond had grown up in an atmosphere of security; the peasantry could not be obsequious enough; he was always a 'fine handsome lad who does yer honour credit' and so on. Now, in his state of nervous depression, it seemed that they were surrounded by hostile neighbours, all waiting a chance to strike a blow in the dark.

Shortly thereafter, Judith heard from Delphine. She was engaged to marry a local lawyer. Esmond was not mentioned in the letter—which was probably written under the supervision of Delphine's mother; but there was a sentence: 'With how much delight I recall our happy hours of conversation in the old barn.' Judith was puzzled by the sentence; she had never been in the old barn with Delphine; Esmond understood. The absurd thing was that he had almost forgotten Delphine; he certainly had no desire to become her husband. Yet the letter filled him with jealousy and misery. He recognised that this was absurd, that he didn't love her, that he had been fortunate to avoid further involvement. It made no difference; every time he thought of their caresses in the ruins of the abbey or the hay barn, he experienced a violent sense of loss, made more unbearable by his recognition that it was the result of having nothing else to think about.

In February, he was ill for three weeks with some gastric germ, and his thoughts dwelt constantly on death, and on the corruption of the grave. He read Johnson's prayers, brooded on Rousseau, and suddenly caught a glimpse of the Truth that had always eluded him. Rousseau said that what is natural is good, that evil springs from man's sophistication, from his interference with Nature. But is not mind itself an interference with Nature, an artificial product? The animal needs only as much mind as is necessary to overcome its everyday problems. Man has developed intellect to serve his laziness, to create a warm, comfortable civilisation; then, having created it (it is interesting to realise that Esmond thought of his own century as the last word in civilised sophistication), he has nothing to do with himself but think. And every thought takes him further from Nature.

But what horrified Esmond was the suspicion that this explained his own nervous exhaustion and boredom. His intelligence had condemned him to a sense of unreality. Doctor Johnson stood before him as an appalling example of what happens when a man is too intelligent: a lifetime of despair and self-torment, with brief flashes of well-being. Esmond began to consider seriously whether he would not be better off dead. 'Everything I looked at reminded me of my misery. Just as any memory of a lost mistress brings a pang of despair, so almost any natural object could remind me of my lost innocence. The ruins of the abbey reminded me of death; the muddy stream made me think of drowning; the bare trees reminded me of a gallows; the baying of a dog put me in mind of funerals. And objects that aroused no specific association—a saucepan, a horseshoe, a book—could bring a stifling despair that was like grief.'

One rainy night in late February, Esmond sat in bed and confronted this sense of hopelessness. If his body felt no gratitude to be in a warm room, when the wind shrieked outside, would it be aroused to some response by the rain itself? He got up and dressed, pulled on a heavy coat, then slipped out of the house. It seemed that his worst fears were realised. The wind made him cold; but he continued to feel indifferent to the discomfort. He walked to the abbey, and sat in the shelter of a wall. Although his feet were wet, the thought of a warm fire failed to bring a spark of pleasure. Cows were taking shelter under the wall; he envied them because they would appreciate the shelter of a warm, dry barn. He wondered how much cold and discomfort it would take to arouse him from his stupor of indifference.

He walked back to the house, now soaked and cold. Passing the barn, he suddenly recalled Minou and Delphine—and experienced a flash of pleasure. He went into the barn to recapture its smell. An old horse snorted and breathed heavily. He climbed up to the loft, and found there was still a pile of hay there. He moved it behind the sacks; then took off his wet clothes, and covered himself with the prickly hay. This was the spot on which he had lain between Delphine's thighs; as he lay there, re-living the experience, drowsiness overcame him, and he fell asleep. The last sound he heard was the snorting and champing of the horse below.

His night in the barn was a turning point. In early March, the weather suddenly became warmer. Esmond went for a walk over the muddy fields, revelling in the sun, suddenly alive to everything. He stood by the muddy River Maigh, and wondered why he had never noticed how fascinating the ripples were. He was healthy and he was nearly seventeen; in a few months he would be setting out on the 'grand tour'. There would be many more Minous and Delphines...In his journal for March 23, 1765, he writes:

> What I find myself utterly unable to comprehend is how human creatures can fail to see the blessedness that is everywhere in Nature? What strange disaster has blinded our eyes to the most plainly observable of all facts? What dark god presides over this labyrinth of our human destiny, watching us in case one of us should by accident find his way out into the supreme simplicity of Nature?

Two weeks before he set out for Dublin, and then Paris (April 17, 1765), he was involved in another brief love affair. On a visit with his father to one of the tenant farmers, he saw the man's thirteen-year-old niece, who was living with him. The girl was extremely pretty. Esmond spent a night dreaming about her, wondering how he could see more of her. But the conquest proved to be easier than he expected. The girl came over the next day to bring eggs. Esmond walked home with her, and arranged an assignation for that evening. She was fascinated by him, and put up a minimum of resistance; although a virgin, she had had some previous sexual experience. On that first evening, Esmond was allowed to explore her breasts and thighs; the following afternoon, he met her in the barn, and took her maidenhead on the same spot on which Delphine had lost hers. During the next two weeks they met as often as possible, spent many more hours on the sacks in the barn, and swore eternal fidelity. But in this case, Esmond knew he was not in love. The ease of the conquest brought almost immediate disappointment. The girl was as pretty as ever, yet when he re-read his journal entry about the first time he saw her, it struck him as another of

Fate's saturnine jokes, another proof that human beings are trapped in a labyrinth, whose god is a supreme confidence trickster.

On the morning of April 17, he took the Limerick–Dublin coach, and experienced keen satisfaction as the hills and fields of Munster receded behind them. This time, at least, the god of the labyrinth was defeated; the love affair had broken off before there was time for the bitter after-taste to creep in. It was then, on the thirty-six-hour journey from Limerick to Dublin (120 miles!), that Esmond formulated one of his central ideas : that life is a battle against the god of the labyrinth. He seemed to think of the god as a cross between an enormous spider and a fat man with pointed ears. And the field he would choose for the encounter would be the field of sex...

Reading of Esmond's journey to Dublin suddenly reminded me of Clive Bates, the grandson of Isaac Jenkinson Bates. It was true that I now had more than enough material to complete Fleisher's edition of *Memoirs of an Irish Rake*. I had earned my $15,000. But this was no longer important. There was too much I wanted to know about Esmond—and when the book was published, a great many other people would be equally curious. The field would be flooded with researchers. I wanted to find all there was to be found before the rush started. Esmond had begun to obsess me. Volume two of the Journal ended as he left London for Boulogne on May 28, 1765, but surely it was impossible that he could have ceased to keep journals after that time? There were many questions I wanted to answer. What about the 'murder' of Horace Glenney, and the rumours about Esmond and Lady Mary? What about the 'affair' with the three sisters? Why did Dr Johnson dislike Donelly? And what of this 'Sect of the Phoenix', of which I had stumbled upon such tantalising hints?

Two days after I arrived back from Dr O'Hefernan's, I received a postcard from Miss Tina. It said : 'Eileen has a bad cold, but she has asked me to tell you that Esmond's literary executors were the Rev. William Aston and Lord Horace Glenney, sincerely, Tina Donelly.' For a moment, I was baffled. Aston, yes; I had already guessed as much. But how on earth could Horace

Glenney be Donelly's literary executor when he predeceased him? I was strongly tempted to jump into the car and drive off to Castle Donelly, for my reading of the journals had made me curious to see it again. But I had already written to Clive Bates to tell him I intended to go to Dublin the following day, and the thought of so much travel depressed me. I picked up the phone and got through to Castle Donelly. Miss Tina answered. The problem about Horace Glenney was cleared up in a moment. This referred to Horace Glenney junior, the son of Esmond's friend. Miss Tina said:

'I suppose it's common sense, really. I mean, if he was in love with Mary Glenney...'

'But are you sure he was?'

'Not quite sure, of course. My father once told Eileen something about it, but she can't talk at the moment.'

'Do you happen to know where Lord Glenney was shot?'

'At his home in Scotland, I believe.'

I thanked her and hung up. As far as I could see, that disposed of the story that Esmond murdered Horace Glenney; if there was even a suspicion of such a thing, would he have asked Glenney's son to be his literary executor?

I was feeling very cheerful as I set off to drive to Dublin the next morning. This was not entirely connected with Donelly. I had intended to travel by train, so that Diana could have the use of the car, but on the previous day she had seen an advertisement for a second-hand Landrover. I felt we could now afford this, so we bought it on the spot. I knew it was absurd—the way that some quite small event like this can start a glow of optimism that turns into a bonfire; but the very absurdity fascinated me, and started my creative instincts flowing. The drive eastward also delighted me, and reminded me of when we first came to live in Ireland and spent our days exploring the country. And now it struck me that all that matters in human existence is a certain intensity of consciousness, of meaning, and that we must discover the trick. When I bought this car, it had an automatic choke, and the damned thing would cut out almost as soon as I began driving, so that the engine would stop on the first hill into town.

So our local garage fixed an ordinary hand-choke instead, and now I keep it out until the engine is warm enough to take the hills comfortably. But if I wake up in the morning with my mind cold and dull, there is no mental choke I can pull out until the engine is heated up. I often spend hours, or even days, trying to cudgel my brains into a state of intensity, trying to work up the inner-pressure to settle down to writing. To some extent, I have discovered the trick : ten minutes of intense, total concentration, involving the whole being—my muscles as well as my brain. As I do this—if no one interrupts me—I can almost watch the pressure of my consciousness rising, until things no longer seem dull and neutral. It is exactly like having your first drink of the evening—that warm glow that is not situated in the stomach, but *in consciousness.*

And now the strange thing happened—a thing I cannot possibly convey to the reader, but which I can at least try to describe. The thought came to me that this was how Esmond had felt as he set out on his *wanderjahre* in 1765. And then two images fused together in my mind. One was of Esmond setting off in the coach from Limerick—something I had dreamed about in the night. The other was the image of the trees on Long Island, suddenly looking as if they were cast out of phosphor bronze, as Beverley bent over me. This latter image was very strong. I could smell Beverley's scent, feel the warmth of her bare breast against my cheek. And with these two images came an explosion of delight. What human beings want is to achieve these moments of freshness and intensity, and not to lose them every time their attention wanders. They want *continuity of consciousness.* And supposing a man said to himself : 'It is obvious that nothing is as important as this : from now on I shall devote my life to the search for this intensity and continuity...'? And I knew, beyond all possible doubt, that something like this had passed through Esmond's mind on that morning drive from Limerick. How? Because I had lived with Esmond for weeks, until I knew how his mind worked.

And now, without any sudden change, any feeling of vision or inspiration, I had a hallucinatory feeling of *being Esmond.* It was absurdly strong. I knew I was driving through a small hamlet called Fardrum, a few miles beyond Athlone, and that I intended to stop at the pub at Moate for a ham sandwich and a draught Guinness. At the same time, I was seated beside the coachman on the box of a jolting coach, smelling the lathery sweat of the horses and the clean air of an April morning, as well as the tang of peat smoke from the clothes of the driver.

There was something very odd about the vividness of this image. It was not 'imaginative' in the ordinary sense: I was not somehow 'intending' it. It was as if something had moved close to me, like a train passing the train in which I happened to be sitting, and giving me a sudden intimate glimpse into a passing carriage. And all this did not surprise me. It seemed a natural part of the upsurge of delight. My mental pressure was high. The sky was a rather cool blue, and I felt as though it were an immense sheet of cool water. It struck me with sudden total certainty: time is an illusion. It is not an absolute state. If you are an insect sitting on a leaf that is swept down a river, you might think that it is inevitable that trees keep passing you and receding behind you, that by their very nature trees only last a few moments, and the only unchanging reality is the ripple and splash of the water. But the bank is real, and if you could get off your leaf on to the bank, you would find that it is quite solid and permanent.

As soon as I had this picture of time as something illusory, and of the reality of the world through which it flows, I saw my own childhood as something I could reach out and touch, just as I can open a book to a page I read an hour ago, or make a tape recorder re-wind to an earlier part of the tape. And it struck me that Esmond's life was no more distant; a mere two centuries ago, two lifetimes. Our trouble is the feebleness of consciousness, which fluctuates like the electric current from a worn-out battery. If we could replace this with a new battery, the mind could stride across centuries...

I stopped at Mike Kelly's for my Guinness; it is a quiet, old-fashioned pub, with low beams, and a turf fire in the hearth. I asked for a ham sandwich, and the landlady's daughter replied that I should have it piping hot from the oven: and in fact, the great chunks of flakey ham were steaming. Having served me,

143

she went out, leaving me alone. I looked around, and reflected that, but for the electric lighting, this place probably looked much the same in the days of Esmond Donelly. And then, even clearer than before, I had the sense of *becoming* Esmond Donelly, or leaning over and looking into his consciousness as he swung past me. This time, with my senses fortified by the smell of ham and the taste of the stout, I made an effort of will to hold the sensation. For a moment it eluded me; then, as I relaxed and did not try to force it, it came back again : a combination of smells, feelings, ideas. And then, quite suddenly, it seemed to *focus*, and everything became clearer. Esmond's consciousness somehow coincided with mine, so that I could look back on his past, on Delphine and Minou, and on the pretty farmgirl called Eillie (short for Eileen). What is more, this last name was new to me; Esmond refers to her in his diary as E——, perhaps afraid of compromising a girl who lived so close. And this excited me. I was not naïve enough simply to accept that I had some-how ' become ' Esmond. I knew too much about the dream-like workings of the mind to make any such assumption. Who has never composed music or poetry in his dreams, or created situa-tions so strange that they seem to be someone else's invention? If I could ever confirm that the girl's name was Eillie—and it was not impossible if I could find more of Esmond's journals— then I would be certain that this strange experience was a form of second-sight, not a waking dream.

I resisted the temptation to drink more Guinness—knowing that it would make me drowsy—and drove on as soon as I had eaten my ham. I did not want to relax. What I wanted was to deepen this feeling of insight, of meaning. Twenty miles outside Dublin it started to rain, and I forgot about my concentration, suddenly enjoying the sweep of the windscreen-wipers and the pattering of the great warm drops. And then once again, without any effort, I ' became ' Esmond. The houses and shops of May-nooth suddenly startled me, as if I had never seen them before. But as I drove past Carton—the great eighteenth-century house that once belonged to the Dukes of Leinster—I realised that I knew the place. I had been inside it. Of course, ' I ' never had; it was Esmond who had been there as a guest of his schoolfriend

Robert Fitzgerald, Marquess of Kildare.

All the time, as I drove into Dublin along the Conygham Road, I experienced this effect of 'double consciousness'. If there had been someone in the car with me, I would have said : 'This used to be the Chapelizod Road in 1765, and here it became Barrack Street.' But before I entered the old Barrack Street, I was driving along Wolfe Tone Quay, and experiencing mild surprise to find myself already beside the Liffey. In 1765, I would have had to proceed from the cobbled Chapelizod Road into Barrack Street, with the river visible over the Long Meadows to my right, and then along Gravel Walk, at which point I could have turned right on to Arran Quay—at that time, the most westerly of the Dublin Quays. I passed on my right the street—whose name Donelly had forgotten—that led down to Bloody Bridge. At Grattan Bridge I was tempted to turn right, forgetting that I could continue to O'Connell Bridge; in Donelly's day, Grattan Bridge (then called Essex Bridge) was the last point at which one could cross the Liffey. I was bound for the Shelbourne in St Stephen's Green; Donelly, when he went to Dublin in 1765, proceeded to the 'Dog and Duck' in Pudding Row (now Wood Quay), the hostelry run by Master Francis Magin. (I knew this from his journal, although I had forgotten it.) There he ate a supper of Boyne salmon and roast lamb, washed down by a large quantity of sweet beer of low alcohol content, and then fell asleep in a comfortable first-floor room to cries of ' Any hare skins or rabbit skins? ' and 'Dublin Bay herrin's '. It was all so vivid that I found myself taking the wrong turn at College Green, and having to make a detour to get to the Shelbourne. In my room there, I opened a bottle of Volnay I had brought with me—although it was only half past four—and found myself less troubled by these odd double-exposure effects. Even so, I only had to close my eyes to see clear pictures of a Dublin that was in many respects like the one I could see out of my window (although in those days Stephen's Green was surrounded by a hedge and a ditch, not railings)—that was certainly just as crowded and noisy—but whose streets were mostly cobbled, and whose houses seemed cleaner and more dignified. It also stank —particularly in midsummer—of sewage and fish. And the masts

145

with furled sails that crowded the Liffey produced an effect that was not unlike Canaletto's Venice. After my third glass of wine, the 'double exposure' faded altogether, and it struck me that Sheridan Le Fanu might have written a powerful and gloomy story about the double-tenancy of a human brain by two men of different centuries. I could even see that, viewed by a temperament like Le Fanu's, it could have been a frightening experience. But then, Le Fanu's basic outlook was defeated and negative. And this is the only fundamental question.

I rang Diana to tell her I had arrived safely; as I hung up, a call came through from Clive Bates. I had written to tell him I would be at the Shelbourne. I asked him if he would like to join me for dinner. He accepted, and suggested that I go to have a drink with him first. He was in Ranelagh Road, opposite the monastery, and I walked over there at about five o'clock. He was a plumpish young man with a drawling Oxford voice. His flat was comfortable, and the drink cupboard well stocked. There were a great many books, some of them on the theatre and ballet. Clive Bates obviously had a private income or a good job, or both. Everything about his room indicated that he was a man who was fond of his comforts. He had great charm and ease of manner; but something about his mouth suggested that he might become very sulky or bad-tempered if he failed to get his own way.

While we drank vodka martinis, the conversation was general; then it turned to my books, and to various writers we had both met. He had worked in the Foreign Office for a while—after Eton and Balliol—and had met a great many literary and theatrical figures in London. For my own part, I always avoid other writers; talking shop bores me, and there are few whose work I really admire. So the conversation soon began to bore me. After half an hour or so, I tried tactfully to direct it into other channels. I asked after the health of his grandfather.

'Oh yes. The old boy wants to see you. I've been telling him about your work.' He looked at his watch. 'He's usually alone at about this time. Would you like to drop over before we eat?' I said yes, trying not to sound as eager as I felt.

We drove over to Baggot Street, although it was close enough. Clive Bates had a Porsche that was so low I had a feeling that my buttocks were within an inch of the road. As we got in, Bates said :

'Of course, you're doing all this for money?'

For a moment I failed to understand him, and looked blank; he said :

'This Donelly chappie. I mean, he's pretty second rate, isn't he? I was looking at his book on deflowering virgins the other day. It's pretty crude stuff.'

I started to say that I thought the book a forgery, and then, for some reason, held my peace. Instead, I explained about Fleisher and his commission.

We parked in Baggot Street. Clive Bates said casually :

'By the way, have you ever heard of the Sect of the Phoenix?'

I stared at him. And then a peculiar thing happened. Suddenly, I was Esmond again, or rather, Esmond was looking out of my eyes. I said :

'Vaguely. Wasn't it some kind of magical cult?'

'More or less. Donelly was a member.'

'How do you know?'

'It's in my grandfather's papers. He's always been interested in this Sect of the Phoenix. He heard about it from a magician called Macgregor Mathers. You may have come across him?'

'Of course. I've got his translation of the Zohar.'

There was no time for more conversation; we were ringing on a doorbell, and a few moments later a young nurse opened the door. Bates called her 'My dear Betty', and pinched her behind. She seemed embarrassed by my presence. We went up to a first-floor bedroom. It was a dark place, although it was still light enough outside; the curtains were half drawn, and a dim bulb burned over the bed.

Isaac Jenkinson Bates was as frail as I had expected from his grandson's description : a little, bald-headed old man with a parchment complexion. When he raised his hands from the counterpane to shake hands with me, they trembled convulsively, and he quickly laid them flat on the bed again. He asked us if we would like a drink. We both refused, but he insisted. 'I know

147

you young people like a drink at about this time.' He told the nurse to pour us sherry. I accepted it out of politeness, but it was awful stuff. The old man talked for a few minutes on the history of sherry, and his own theory of why it was once called sack— because the grapes were strained through sacks. Then, halfway through a sentence, he changed the subject to the Ireland's Eye murder case. I had read up all I could find on it before I left home, but it proved to be unnecessary; he talked in a steady flow for another ten minutes or so.

When he paused for a moment, Clive Bates said :

' Mr Sorme had heard of the Sect of the Phoenix.'

' Oh yes; well, of course, Donelly was a member of that, and a most disgusting and unpleasant sort of thing it was too. Yes, of course, you know it sprang from a belief that if a couple were copulating, they couldn't catch a disease. So at the time of the Black Death it became an excuse for every kind of licence. By Donelly's time it was just a kind of semi-magical sect of ruffians. Do you know de Sade's *Hundred and Twenty Days of Sodom*? I'm pretty certain that de Sade was satirising the Sect of the Phoenix in that—you know, the four filthy old rakes who set up a kind of sexual menagerie in a country house. Old Tom Wise always thought that that was why de Sade spent most of his life in gaol. He knew too much about them.'

Clive Bates interposed : ' Thomas J. Wise. The literary forger, you know.'

' Well, he may or may not have been that. They say he was, but I'm not so sure. But he was always a damned good friend to me. And as I say, he was absolutely convinced that these Phoenix people were after de Sade...'

Clive winked at me.

' But why should they be after him if he was as bad as they were? '

' He wasn't. No. He was satirising them, you see.'

I should explain that the old man's explanations were not as clear as I have made them here. His conversation was distinctly hard to follow, and punctuated with odd rumbles and snorts. I did not try to contradict his amazing statement about de Sade, but my hope of getting any useful information sank lower. I

148

asked him how he had become interested in the Sect of the Phoenix.

'Saw a copy of that rare pamphlet. That was how I got to know Wise, as a matter of fact.'

'Which pamphlet, sir?'

'Oh, the famous one...Henry Martell and George Smithson. Clive, look in the top drawer over there, will you?'

The pamphlet was not in the top drawer; but after ten minutes —during which Bates muttered dark accusations against the world in general, and his nurse in particular—it was found in another cupboard. I snatched at it eagerly. It had been placed in red morocco folders, and was in a rather battered condition. AN EXPOSURE OF THE EVIL CONSPIRACY KNOWN AS THE SOCIETY OF THE PHOENIX, by Henry Martell, M.A., and George Smithson, D.D. Printed for the authors by G. Robinson, the Old Bankside, 1793. Clive was asking, in his smoothest and most insinuating tone :

'I don't understand why you think it genuine when it came from a man like Wise.'

The old man rose to the bait and became very snappy.

'I'll thank you not to speak like that about Wise. He was no more a forger than I am. He was trying to defend the memory of his friend Henry Buxton Forman.'

I said :

'In any case, surely the actual text of the forgeries was always genuine? It was only a matter of spurious dating on pamphlets?'

'Quite', said the old man, and then, to Clive : 'You see, he knows more about it than you do!'

I left them to argue, and read avidly. The whole pamphlet took a high moral tone, and accused the Sect of the Phoenix of being the cause of the downfall of Louis XIV. Since it will be printed complete in the appendix of the Donelly Memoirs, I shall not quote it at length here. If this pamphlet was old Bates's chief source of information on the brotherhood, I could see why he regarded it so unfavourably. I found myself reminded of certain pamphlets and articles published about Rasputin shortly after his murder in 1917—incredible, vague accusations of monstrous conspiracies, wholesale rape and abduction, disgusting

149

ceremonies. According to the authors, it was primarily a magical organisation. The passage which aroused most discussion—after my article about it in the *Atlantic Monthly*—was the one describing the way in which the Grand Master or any of his selected adepts could enslave girls by collecting three of their ' bloddied clouts ' after their menstrual period, cutting a hole in the middle of any stain shaped roughly like the female genitals, and wearing this on the penis for a period of seven days and nights. At the end of this period, the virgin will be impelled to answer the summons of the Grand Master to yield him her maidenhead, and thereafter may be possessed by him at any time, even though they are a thousand miles apart. There follows the strange story of Adele Crispin, who was possessed by the Grand Master on her wedding night, *at the same time* that her husband was possessing her, and whose child had the features of the Grand Master— black hair, dark skin, and so on. (The Grand Master at the time was the Persian Abdallah Yahya, who boasted that he had left his seed in the womb of every pretty woman in Roman high society. The authors cite this as an example of monstrous depravity rather than as imaginative mendacity.) Abdallah Yahya was murdered and dismembered in 1791 by Hendrk van Griss, the monstrous Dutchman. Van Griss is supposed to have weighed over 300 pounds (150 kilos), and to have frequently rendered his victims unconscious, or even killed them, by simply allowing his weight to fall on them. Van Griss was Grand Master for only two years, during which time he was infected with syphilis by the Rumanian courtesan Maria Creanga, which is said to have been of such a deadly nature that by 1794 Van Griss had become a putrefying, featureless mountain of flesh. In the *Journal of Psychoanalysis* for July 1969, Professor Aram Roth interpreted the whole story in Freudian terms—beginning with the fetichistic activities with ' bloddied clouts '—and dismissed it as Gothic fantasy. In the September issue, Miss Marganita Bondeson points out that there was no need for invention, since most of the rituals described can be found in Arabic and Persian grimoires of the eighteenth century, and pointing out that Restif de la Bretonne has described someone who sounds very like van Griss (under the name Cubières-Palmézaux) in his *Nuits de Paris* of 1788, describing him as ' the legendary pervert '. It was I who drew her attention to the Restif passage.

' They were criminals, these people ', the old man said. ' Criminal degenerates. You saw who introduced the sect to France? '

I had indeed. The authors of the pamphlet stated that Gilles de Rais had become a member of the sect in his seventeenth year (1421), initiated by a defrocked priest. Martell and Smithson were in agreement with St Nilus Sorsky that the sect was nothing more than a development of the doctrines of the Brethren of the Free Spirit. Having rejected all moral law, they aimed at the fullest expression of the ' organs of pleasure '. In its earliest days, say the authors, members of the sect dressed as monks, and specialised in rape and necrophily. They would offer to keep vigil over dead bodies of young girls—and boys—and wait until everyone was asleep before ravishing the corpse. The one thing to be said in their favour, apparently, was that they tried to avoid doing actual physical damage to their victims. A young milkmaid who was raped by two of them was left tied and gagged under a heap of leaves, to be found two days later. Another was told that she would find herself pregnant with a monster if she dared to breathe a word, and duly kept the secret until her next menstrual period reassured her. ' Since it was their rule never to kill the victim to avoid later recognition, they were obliged to become masters of disguise, and many of them carried boxes of different coloured dyes that they might change the colour of their habits at will.' Gilles de Rais was their first rich convert, having been received into the sect by one Gilles de Sillé. The talk of alchemy at his trial was a blind alley, according to the pamphlet. The mass murder of children was simply an expression of the ' diabolical licentiousness ' advocated by the Sect of the Phoenix.

Now if Rais was a member of the Sect of the Phoenix, Martell and Smithson would have established their case that it was an evil and horrific organisation. But in fact they offer no evidence for their assertion. I felt inclined to point this out to the old man, but it was difficult to interrupt the meandering flood of reminiscence. I finally managed to ask him if he had anything more on the Sect of the Phoenix.

'Yes. I've a most interesting letter from Tom Wise. I corresponded with him about it—that would be in about 1905. Clive, look in that top drawer again.'

Clive pulled a face, but obediently rummaged among piles of old papers. The nurse came in with a bowl of steaming, aromatic liquid, which she placed in a metal frame on the bed. Old Bates then covered his head with a kind of plastic bag, and breathed in the fumes. I presume it was some cure for asthma. I offered to help Clive Bates search for the papers. He said : ' Oh, I expect you'll find some interesting stuff...', and picked up the pamphlet I had been reading. I glanced through a pile of old letters, but since I had no idea of what I was supposed to be looking for, I felt the whole exercise was futile. I pulled out a black folder from the bottom of the drawer, and glanced into it. What I saw made me look quickly towards the old man, then at his grandson. Neither of them was paying any attention to me. The folder contained a dozen or so pages of manuscript, and I recognised the handwriting. It was James Boswell's. The first sheet was headed ' Saturday 1st February ', and someone had inserted the date 1766 in pencil. Again I glanced at Clive. He was completely absorbed in the pamphlet. The old man was breathing wheezily and complaining to the nurse, who was rearranging the bed. I drew up my chair to the drawer, and settled down to reading the manuscript. At one point, Clive Bates got up and glanced over my shoulder. I wondered if he would ask me what the devil I was doing; but he went and sat down again, and continued reading.

The account described Boswell leaving Paris in the company of Thérèse le Vasseur, Rousseau's mistress (whom Boswell had described in an earlier entry—which I discovered later—as ' a little, lively neat French girl '); the pair were on their way to England, travelling together for convenience. On the second night, they decided to share a bed at the inn. Boswell, to his deep chagrin, failed to perform his manly duties, and he burst into tears, ' whose stains ', he noted, ' can be observed on the previous page '. Thérèse restored his confidence the following night by performing for him the service that Minou did for both her lovers—kneeling in front of him and caressing him with her mouth. ' The sight of her crouched in this humble position made me feel pity, which did so greatly restore my vigour that I laid her down on the carpet there and then, and came at her like a wild bull. I think she was well satisfied by my size, for she gave a gasp of surprise, and then let out her breath in a sigh.' I am quoting from the few sentences that I managed to scrawl in pencil on a scratch pad that I had in my pocket. I knew I was looking at the Boswell manuscript that Isaac Jenkinson Bates had somehow extracted from Malahide. Quite obviously, he had no right to have it. So I knew the chances of his allowing me to borrow it, or even copy it, were minimal.

Clive Bates said : 'Have you come to the bit about Donelly yet?'

'No.' I was startled, and glanced at the old man. His head was completely invisible, and I was certain he had not heard. Clive said :

'Do read it. It's terribly funny.'

I muttered something, hoping that it would not dawn on old Bates to ask me what I was reading, or if I had found Wise's letter. I skipped over two pages of Boswell apostrophising himself as 'you' and reflecting on his qualities of charm and moral seriousness. In the entry for Sunday, February 9, I found the name I was looking for. Boswell and Thérèse arrived at Calais in a rainstorm. They put up at a hostelry that he mentions simply as Mme Duchesne's, where he and Thérèse took a single large room on the ground floor. Boswell changed his clothes and walked around the town. 'Near the docks, someone clapped me upon the shoulder, and I turned to see Esmond Donelly, who had come there by the diligence from Dunquerque.' They went back to Boswell's lodging, where Donelly was able to procure a room. Apparently Boswell and Esmond had met in Dresden. They had 'a collation and a flask of good wine', and talked about Wilkes and Horace Walpole, whom they had both seen in Paris. Thérèse came in—Boswell was unaware that Esmond had met her with Rousseau at Neuchâtel—and Boswell says : 'I had to own I was chagrined at the cordiality of her greeting, and the manner in which she kept on repeating that this was a delightful surprise.' They decided to eat dinner together, and Esmond took them to an eating house. 'At supper, he talked a great deal of bawdy, and since Mademoiselle did not seem to be offended, I joined in, and felt my ill humour disappear.' They returned to their lodgings, and Boswell said jokingly that he hoped Esmond would treat their meeting with discretion if he happened to see Rousseau in London. And then, with the incredible frankness that is so typical of Boswell, he proceeded to tell Esmond of his failure with Thérèse, and of how he had been so alarmed on a later occasion that he drank a whole bottle of wine before going to bed with her. The conversation became more intimate. Thérèse talked about the clumsiness of the English in the art of lovemaking. Esmond thereupon shocked Boswell by offering to demonstrate his own mastery of the subject there and then. And then it struck him that if Esmond possessed Thérèse, he would have good reason for being discreet if he met Rousseau; so he expressed his approval of the idea. It was Thérèse's turn to look shocked, and Esmond twitted her with accusations of prudery. At this, she decided that it would be pointless to conceal her inclination, and agreed to form her own estimate of Esmond's prowess as a lover. 'Come, sir,' said Esmond to Boswell, 'let us show her that the Celts are the life-blood of Europe'. Thérèse giggled; Boswell was determined to show that he was as sophisticated as his young friend (Esmond was eight years his junior), and accompanied them into the bedroom.

What then happened was that Boswell and Esmond helped Thérèse to undress, and while she stood in her shift, both men began to caress her. Each one of them fixed his mouth on one of her breasts, while Thérèse held their two erect members in either hand, and commented that she had never held such fine specimens of lusty manhood. They removed her shift and laid her naked on the bed and Esmond performed an act of cunnilingus. Then Thérèse, groaning with excitement, gasped 'Vite', and both Boswell and Esmond tried to hurl themselves on her simultaneously. Boswell, being slighter, got the worst of the crash, and while he was still picking himself up, Esmond had penetrated her. His description of Esmond and Thérèse making love will undoubtedly rank as a classic of its kind. I had time to jot down only a few lines.

Though small, she was of remarkable strength and vigour, and made him cling to her as though she had been an unbroken stallion impatient of her rider. Donelly clasped her buttocks firmly in both hands, and rammed as though he hoped to drive her head through the wall. As I stood there in my shirt, with my lance upraised as though presenting arms, I was unexpectedly struck by the absurdity of my position, and how it would have appeared to Dr Johnson or General Paoli, had they been able to stand there and observe me. But then, while they were still galloping in mid-career, Donelly of a sudden cries: 'Now it's Bozzie's turn', and unsheathes his weapon, upon which our maid groaned and murmured: 'Unkind.' So as to minimize her inconvenience, I leapt upon her like a brigand and drove my pole into the succulent embrace. But here my headlong fervour undid me, for she had no sooner received my tool than she also received a wombfull of gushing seed, which leapt forth before I could prevent it or admonish myself to practise self-conquest. At this, my own head drooped so low as that of my tool, and my cheeks imitated its colour; but I was scarcely off her before Donelly had replaced me, and was soothing her disappointment with strokes that made their bellies smack together.

The description continues for two more pages, but this was all I had time to copy. The nurse was helping old Bates to remove the plastic bag, so I quickly read on to the end, describing how Boswell, after his first failure, redeemed himself by fucking her vigorously, 'with such style that I regretted that I could not stand by to see it'. He was immensely gratified when Thérèse murmured: 'Ah, it is a sad fate to be an old man's mistress.' He, Esmond and Thérèse spent the night in the same bed—which was big enough for them—and all three found the situation so piquant that they would doze off for a while and then return to lovemaking. Boswell fell into a deep sleep while Esmond was persuading Thérèse to allow him to sodomise her, but he later rolled her on to her back and moved on top of her again. By this time, even Thérèse's long-pent-up desire for a young stallion had been satisfied, and she lay passively, gasping slightly, as Boswell made love for the sixth time. 'I was the last to possess her that night', he records exultantly, 'but in honesty am compelled to admit that Donelly did it seven times to my six'. The following night, Boswell fell sick with a stomach ailment, and spent the night in Esmond's bed. He admits that his heart has gone out of the sport, 'although we saw a young girl of about fourteen in the baker's who could have inspired me for the rest of the week'. The following day, Esmond informed them that business would keep him in Calais a few days longer. As the boat took them from the harbour steps to the ship that would carry them to England, Boswell looked up and saw Esmond standing on the quay—with the pretty fourteen-year-old. Thérèse, luckily, did not notice them. On returning to Dover the following day (February 12), Boswell's published journal resumes: 'Yesterday morning had gone to bed very early, and done it once; thirteen in all. Was really affectionate to her.' He does not record how his score compares with Esmond's.

Clive Bates caught my eye and shook his head warningly. The nurse was removing the plastic tent. I closed the manuscript which I had just finished, and slipped my notes into my pocket. I picked up a pamphlet by Ruskin, and when the old man asked me what I had been reading, declared I found it fascinating. His grandson said we ought to be leaving, and the nurse seemed to agree.

'Has your friend asked me all the questions he had in mind?'

I said hesitantly: 'There's just one, sir. About Esmond Donelly...'

'Donelly? Who's he?'

Clive explained. The old man said:

'Ah yes, I remember now. Now *he* was a member of the Sect of the Phoenix.'

'How do you know?'

'Let me see...how *do* I know? Ah...Yes. Wise told me. It's in that letter I wanted you to find. That pamphlet you've been looking at—it's not by...whatever they're called. It's by another man, a friend of Donelly's. I can't remember his name. He had a title.'

156

' It couldn't have been Horace Glenney, could it? '

' Ah yes, that's the man. Lord Glenney.'

' But how did Wise know this? '

Unfortunately, Bates interpreted this as another attack on Wise, and launched into a long defence of his old friend. I decided to leave it at that. Besides, I was hungry. I thanked him, promised to call again, and left. Outside, Clive Bates said apologetically :

' You see, the old boy's pretty ga-ga.'

' Have you read that piece of Boswell I was reading? '

' Ah, you knew it was Boswell, did you? Yes, of course I've read it. I think it's a superb piece of bawdry. I keep trying to persuade him to send a copy to that chap who's editing the Boswell journals, but he won't.'

' Naturally. It doesn't belong to him.'

' Are you sure? '

I outlined the story of the Boswell papers. He said :

' He always claims he bought it for five pounds. He says Lady Talbot came across it one day and asked her husband to destroy it. He said he would, but he agreed to sell it to Grandfather for a fiver.'

' It *could* be true. Does he have any more Boswell papers? '

' Not as far as I know. That's the only one I've seen.'

It had started to rain as we parked opposite the Shelbourne. I said—conventionally—' Thankyou for taking me. He's a delightful old man.'

' Oh, he's all right. You don't know him.'

I was curious, but decided not to press him. There was no need to. As we sat in the bar, drinking red wine, he said :

' I would imagine that my grandfather is one of the worst compounds of unlikeable qualities that you would find in Dublin at the moment. To begin with, he's a liar. He pretended he couldn't remember Donelly's name. Nonsense, of course. He knows it as well as you do.'

' Then why...'

He interrupted me : ' Second, he's probably the meanest man in Ireland...' For the next five minutes, he offered me examples of his grandfather's meanness that were certainly convincing enough; it may be an Irish type, for Maturin describes another such at the beginning of *Melmoth the Wanderer,* who begs, with his last breath, that he might be buried in a pauper's grave. Then followed stories of his grandfather's petty dishonesty. 'Then there's that poor girl who looks after him. She's only a student nurse, so he pays her next to nothing. But he gets her to sleep with him by promising to leave her money in his will. Of course, he wouldn't dream of it.'

'Are you sure?' I was astounded; he didn't look healthy enough to survive a wet dream.

'Of course. She sleeps with me on her night off.'

I was beginning to feel depressed. Clive Bates was describing his grandfather's faults with a relish that I found rather ghoulish.

'Why don't you tell her he doesn't intend to leave her money?'

He winked. 'She might leave him. That wouldn't benefit him or me.'

I suggested that we should take our wine in with us to the dining room. He said:

'Would you mind if we ate in the long bar downstairs?'

'No. If you prefer it.'

We found a table by the window, looking out on the street. I asked:

'Who is your grandfather's heir?'

'I suppose I am.'

'Then why do you dislike him so much?'

'That's nothing to do with it. He's an old swine. Anyway, I don't need his money. I'm fairly well off. That's why he'll probably make me his heir. His nephew Jim—Jim Hurd—needs it more than I do...'

He broke off and stared out of the window. It was still raining, and a ragged-looking child was looking in at us. They stared at one another, then he grinned. I asked:

'Do you know her?'

'No.' But nevertheless he was beckoning to her with his finger. She shook her head. He got up and went out. I expected to see her vanish before he arrived, but she stood there, looking cold, wet, and rather grubby. He said something to her; she shook her head. Then he took her by the shoulder, and propelled her ahead of him. A moment later, they were back at our table. He said:

'You don't mind her joining us, do you?'

I said no. But I was more concerned about how the management felt. She was older than she looked through the glass—fourteen or fifteen, perhaps. Her hair hung in rats' tails, and her nose was running. She wore a short jacket with puffed shoulders and only one button. The rain had made streaks in the grime on her face. She looked as if she hadn't washed for a fortnight; and to be honest, the rain seemed to bring out smells that confirmed this. Clive asked her:

'What's your name?'

'Florence.'

'Do they call you Flo?'

'Yes.'

The voice was cockney. She sat there, chafing her cold hands together, looking a picture of misery. Our waiter was looking at us disapprovingly, and I thought the manager was about to come over and ask us to leave—he was staring very hard. Clive said:

'Would you like some fish and chips?'

She nodded, but continued to look numb and lifeless. Clive beckoned the waiter over, and gave the order with a sort of bullying flamboyance. My own feelings were mixed. If he had invited her in out of kindness, then I approved, although I would have preferred to take her to somewhere quieter and darker. But he was such an odd and complex character that it was difficult to be sure of his motives. I thought the girl looked uncomfortable and out of place. I finally suggested that we might go up to my room, and have the meal sent up.

'No, no. Why should we? We're all right here.'

I was sitting next to the girl, and would have preferred to be less close. I took her jacket from her to hang it up, and it smelt as if she had found it on a rubbish dump, and as if it had at some point been used for wrapping fish. I have an unusually sensitive nose; but even so, it hardly seemed fair on our neighbours.

The meal was one of the most uncomfortable I have ever had, and I ordered another bottle of wine in an attempt to forget the awkwardness. I could not understand why she had agreed to come in. She answered questions in monosyllables, obviously afraid of raising her voice, and sat in a crouched position, as if still cold. Clive seemed oblivious of the atmosphere. He talked loudly and cheerfully, telling me anecdotes about the Cannes Film Festival, and Bergman's latest film, that failed to arouse the slightest flicker of interest in me. I tried to talk to the girl, but it was clear that she preferred to be left alone. I felt easier when the people at the next table left; and when her fish and chips arrived, she swamped them with vinegar and tomato ketchup, and her own damp, fishy smell was less noticeable. The girl refused a sweet, to my relief. I had intended to put the meal on my hotel bill; instead, I paid cash and left the waiter a large tip. I didn't feel like admitting that I was staying in the hotel.

Clive said, in his loudest and most aristocratic voice:

' Well, if we're not having anything more, we may as well go and have cheese and biscuits back at my place, eh? '

I was so glad the meal was over, I made no objection. Besides, I expected that the girl would now leave us. The sight of her unhappy face was making me gloomy. The waiter's pleasure at the size of the tip was a minor victory.

Outside, Clive said: ' Well, I don't know how we can all pack in my two-seater.' I thought this was intended as a hint to the girl; but she only stood there. He said: ' Oh well, we'll manage it. Come on ', and grabbed her arm firmly. I said:

' Won't your parents be expecting you home? '

She shrugged indifferently and said: ' Naow.'

In the Porsche, she sat on my knee. In the enclosed space— and Clive Bates asked me not to open my window—the fishy smell was stronger. She had to press back against me to get her knees in. Clive patted her on the knee, saying: ' We'll soon be home—oho, you got a hole there '—he was referring to her stocking. Then he winked at me, and said: ' I envy you.' I looked at him with mild amazement. Surely he couldn't find this damp, snuffle-nosed child sexually desirable? Perhaps he had no sense of smell?

Her passivity struck me as odd. When we stopped in front of his flat, I expected her to raise some objection. After all, how did she know we didn't both intend to rape her? But she stood there indifferently, until Clive took her arm and led her to the door.

160

She looked even more out of place in his well-furnished room. She threw off the coat on to the settee, and went and crouched near the fire. She seemed totally uninterested in her surroundings. Clive said :

'Let's play some music, shall we? Do you know James Oswald's Dust Cart Cantata? No? You ought to. It's delightful.' I wondered if this was supposed to be a satirical reference to the girl, but he produced a record of that title, and put it on the turntable. He offered her a drink, but she refused. He brought out cheese, biscuits and stuffed olives; she refused these too. But when he offered her a large tin of assorted biscuits, she took it without a word, and sat munching them, her legs spread apart in front of the fire, dropping crumbs on his modernistic armchair and on the white carpet. I took a chair on the other side of the hearth, but Clive moved close to her. I began to wonder if she was drugged; her small, sharp face remained utterly indifferent. It was not even sullen. When he talked to her, she either answered in monosyllables, or merely nodded or shook her head. When she had crunched her way through an incredible number of biscuits, she asked for a drink. He went to the kitchen and brought her a bottle of Coca-Cola with a straw. When the Dust Cart Cantata was over, she asked, with mild asperity : 'Whyn't you play something decent?' He produced a record of Mantovani and his orchestra, and this seemed to satisfy her, although she said nothing.

I wondered whether he was hoping I would go home and leave him alone with her; but when I suggested that it was late, he immediately contradicted me, and switched on the television news. I sat there, sipping a brandy, knowing I should be feeling drunk, and yet feeling as if I had been drinking water all day.

The news was followed by a programme on the political troubles in Northern Ireland. Clive tapped me on the arm and pointed at the girl. She was asleep. He said softly : 'Rather nice, don't you think?' I found it hard to think of a reply; finally, I said : 'She needs a good bath.' He looked unexpectedly sad, lowering his eyes. 'Yes, poor thing...'

'Don't you think you ought to get her home? Her parents could cause trouble?'

'Oh, I don't think so. She could sleep here if she wanted to.'
I gave up. He knew his own business best.

She had fallen asleep with one leg over the arm of the chair, the other stretched towards the fire; a change of position made her skirt slip back on her knees. Clive grinned at me, leaned forward, and carefully peered up her skirt. I expected her to wake up, but she didn't. He turned to me. 'Look.' I shook my head. 'No thanks.' 'But *look*.' He gave the impression he was trying to show me something important. I changed my position and looked up the skirt. The thick lisle stockings were all holes and ladders. She was wearing aertex cotton knickers, and they were so badly torn at the crotch that nothing was hidden. I looked away quickly—not out of prudishness, but because I would have felt ashamed if she opened her eyes. I said :

'What about it?'

He looked sad and thoughtful again.

'She obviously comes of a poor family. No wonder she's not very clean.' He touched her shoulder. 'Do you want to sleep here?' She stirred, but did not open her eyes, and I suddenly wondered if she was shamming. He felt the cloth of her skirt. 'She'll catch cold if she wears these much longer.' He stood up, placed a hand under her arm and another under her knees, and picked her up. She moved her head and said something. It struck me now that she was either pretending to be asleep, or he had put something in the drink he gave her. If so, it must have been chloral hydrate, to produce such total oblivion.

I followed him to the bedroom—it would have been stupid to ask what he was doing. It was comfortable and warm. He laid her on the quilt of the large double bed, then removed her shoes. After this, he looked around the waist of the skirt and found the zip. I asked : 'Is that wise?' He said : 'I'm not going to put her in my bed with these clothes on. You said yourself they stank.' He found the zip and pulled it clumsily down, then yanked the skirt off her feet. She was wearing no underskirt—only the stockings, held up by suspenders, and the panties, whose waist-elastic was almost completely detached from the body of the garment. 'Pretty little figure', he said. This was an overstatement; she was thin, and the small belly was so flat that the hip bones stood out. He took hold of the bottom of the thin woollen sweater—it was of a muddy green colour—and raised it, then moved her on to her side so he could tug it over her head. She was wearing a bra that had once been white, and the straps at the back had been joined by a piece of black elastic tied roughly to the remains of the cloth. I felt the automatic masculine stirrings as I looked at her. He snapped the elastic with a tug. The small breasts were flat and undeveloped. He looked at me.

' Shall we have her? '

I said positively : ' No. Let her alone.'

He reached down suddenly and placed his hand on the front of my trousers; I started back as though he had hit me. He grinned.

' You can't pretend you're not excited.'

I mastered the impulse to hit him, and said : ' Why don't you put her into bed and let her sleep? '

' No. She'd be disappointed.' He pulled down the panties, and slipped his hand between her thighs. ' Feel.'

' No thanks.'

' Look.' He held out the hand to me. It was moist. He said : ' I think I'll have her.' He unbelted his trousers, and pushed them down. My feelings were mixed. I was fairly certain that she was awake. But if she wasn't, then I was an accessory to her rape. Since she hadn't given consent, I was an accessory anyway. I leaned forward and pinched her shoulder. She did not move. Clive Bates was now chuckling in an insane manner. He prodded her breast with his finger. ' Tell him you're awake, sweety.' He bent over, as if to kiss her, but instead took her lower lip in his mouth and bit it. With his enormous naked behind sticking towards me, he looked obscene. Then he pushed her thighs apart, and moved on to her. He guided his penis with his hand, gave a thrust, and went into her. Then he looked at me, with a blissful expression, and said : ' Aa...ah! ' I turned and walked out of the room. Before I was out of the door, he was after me.

' Now come, my dear Gerard, don't be such a prude. You know you find it exciting. Why don't you come and watch, then I'll watch you? ' He stood there at the door, still in his evening shirt and bow tie, with his penis erect and shiny.

163

'She's not my type. I don't want to sound offensive, but she's not very clean.'

'No, I suppose not.' His face had gone pink and shiny, and his eyes were glittering with a feverish enthusiasm. 'Still, we could bath her if you like?'

'Are you mad?'

'You're just a prude, aren't you, Gerard?'

'I wouldn't say that.'

He came and took my arm—the erection stayed undiminished, and I found it hard to keep my eyes away. He said wheedlingly:

'I've done you a favour today. Listen, when the old man dies, I'll inherit his manuscripts. I'll let you take what you like.'

The situation suddenly reminded me of Colonel Donelly, and it was too much. I said:

'Look, if you want to screw her, go and do it. I won't stop you. But I don't want to. And I don't want to bath her either.' I said this quickly because I could see he had his heart set on a three-part orgy.

'You won't go away?'

'No. I'll wait.'

'I'll leave the door open.' He rushed off into the bedroom, and I saw him fling himself on her again. I thought she raised her knees to receive him. I went and found a bottle of wine in his cupboard, and poured myself a large glass. The sounds from the bedroom left no doubt he was enjoying it. They were interspersed with groans, and comments like: 'Oo...oh, you little bitch...' Finally, the noises stopped. I went on eating cheese and olives, and reading a copy of Waite's *Brotherhood of the Rosy Cross* which I found on his bookshelf. I began to feel sleepy. It would be untrue to say I was not, to some extent, sexually aroused. The girl's extreme passivity had aroused my curiosity, and curiosity about a girl is very close to the desire to take off her clothes. Now as I sat in the armchair, the memory of her torn panties and exposed genitals came back and produced excitement. Under different circumstances, I could have made love to her. What put me off was the personality of Clive Bates, and his attempt to enroll me as a co-rapist.

It was after midnight and I thought of returning to my hotel.

164

There were movements from the bedroom, but I did not look up. Then Clive Bates was standing on the rug, completely naked, holding the girl in his arms again.

' I've brought her for you.'

' That's kind, but I have to go.'

' Oh no, don't go.' He knelt down, and laid her on the white bearskin rug, at my feet. She was also quite naked now. The pubic hairs were a reddish-gold colour, and some of them clung wetly to her skin. Then he went out of the room. I bent over and touched her arm. I said : ' Are you awake? ' She made no movement. There was water running in the bathroom. A few minutes later, Clive Bates came out of the bathroom, carrying a red plastic bucket with steam coming from it.

' What are you doing? '

' I'm going to give her a bath.'

The water was scented. He took a sponge out of it, squeezed it, and then soaped it with a great cake of lemon-coloured bath soap. He parted her thighs, and began carefully to wash her, ignoring the water that ran on to the rug. Then he took a towel and dried her. After this, he carefully washed her breasts, then her belly, thighs and knees. Then he turned her on her face, parted the cheeks of her behind, and repeated the operation. When he had dried her, he bent down and kissed it, then looked up and said : ' There, it couldn't be cleaner.'

' All she needs now are some clean clothes.'

' Oh, I expect we can arrange that.'

He stood up.

' There, she's all yours.'

He turned and walked out of the room, and closed the bedroom door. It was a temptation. Watching him caress her with the sponge had given me an erection. I bent over, and touched her breast. It was cold. I stood up and crossed to the bookcase, then tiptoed to the bedroom door and pushed it open. There was a thump, and Clive Bates was sitting on the carpet, looking bewildered. His erection was back again. I said : ' Excuse me. I just wanted to get something to cover her.' I went to his bed, took off the eiderdown, and went back to the girl on the hearth-

165

rug. As I covered her over, I thought I noticed a smile on her lips.

I heard the bedsprings creak in the other room; I sat down and opened Waite on the Rosicrucians. Then I got sleepy, and must have dozed off; I woke up when the book slipped off my knees. I looked at the clock; it was two thirty. Suddenly, Florence sat up. She looked at the eiderdown.

'That was nice of you.'

'Not at all.' We both spoke in low voices.

She said : 'Well, I s'pose I better go.'

'Like that?'

'No.'

She went across to an antique chest of drawers in the corner, and pulled one open. She began to toss underwear on to the floor. She pulled open the bottom drawer, and took out a pair of shoes. I said :

'You've been here before?'

'Abaht once a week on average.'

Without embarrassment she climbed into a suspender belt— this time, one that looked new and fashionable—and then pulled on stockings. After this, she pulled on panties, and slipped into a bra, which she asked me to hook. I crept over to the bedroom door and looked in, but this time there was no doubt that Clive Bates was fast asleep. Florence had pulled on a nylon waist slip of the same pastel shade as the bra and panties; to my inexperienced eye, it looked expensive. She went to a cupboard near the door and took out a long plastic bag on a hanger, which proved to contain a lime-green two-piece suit. She went to the mirror over the fireplace and brushed her hair with a brush she had taken from the drawer; her hair was now dry, and when brushed, it was the same red-gold I had noticed elsewhere. She made up her face with a few pats of a powder puff and strokes of lipstick. When she turned, I hardly recognised her. She still looked young; but I would now have guessed her age at twenty. She wore the well-cut clothes as if she was used to them.

'Ready?'

'Er...yes.'

Out of the hall cupboard she took an overcoat that matched

the suit, and an umbrella of the same colour. Finally, she settled a small red beret on the side of her head. She switched off the electric fire, then the light, and we went out, closing the door softly behind us.

I asked : 'Where do you live? '

'Oh, I shan't go back. You at the Shelbourne? '

'Yes.'

'I'll come back there and see if they've got a room. I can't be bothered to go out to Malahide.'

Her accent was still recognisably London, but no longer cockney.

It had stopped raining, and we walked back through the empty streets. I asked her if she had ever known Clive Bates's grandfather.

'Oh yes. He used to live out at Malahide. That's where I met Clive. The old boy's just as bad.'

'In what way? '

'He likes 'em young. He used to leer at me when I was only ten.'

She seemed quite willing to talk, and she talked casually, in a business-like way, not as though she was making revelations. Clive had seduced her when she was twelve—that is, he had offered to give her the money for an expensive bicycle if she came to his room half an hour after school for a few days. She was the illegitimate daughter of a bus conductress, and was badly dressed and underfed. Although she did not say so plainly, it was fairly evident that Clive was attracted by the torn clothes and runny nose. The loss of her virginity was a painful shock. Clive had treated her very well, soothed and caressed her, made her feel confident. Then one day, after he had carefully undressed her and smeared her with olive oil, he suddenly drove with all his might and removed her maidenhead with one violent stroke. She screamed and cried for half an hour, until he went downstairs and brought up the bicycle she had wanted for so long. The appointments in Clive's room continued, and the old man soon joined in. They paid her well, and the old man talked to her mother about adopting her. The mother knew what was going on, of course; but the money was too good to reject.

167

Clive's only objection was that she spent too much money on clothes. It was part of his fantasy that she should be a shabby urchin. He used to wander round the second-hand clothes barrows on the quays and buy up grubby clothes. These would arrive in the post, together with a short note telling her where to meet him, and at what time. She had to be picked up, and to behave as if she had never seen him before. Whenever possible, he brought someone else along, and enacted the curious rape scene that I had witnessed. I asked her if his friends ever accepted the invitation to possess her while she was apparently unconscious. She said :

'Oh yes. You're only the second who's refused.'

'What happens then?'

'Oh, you'd be surprised. Sometimes they get so worked up watching one another they carry on all night. If I'm lucky, the two men take a fancy to each other and leave me alone.'

'Is Clive homosexual, then?'

She said : 'Oh, he's everything.'

The desk clerk seemed to know her; she took the key, and we went upstairs together. On the second floor, where our ways parted, she said : 'Shall I come and talk to you?' I knew what she meant. I said : 'I think you ought to get some sleep. You've had a hard night.' She grinned at me. 'You're nice. I wouldn't mind...' She stood on tiptoe and put her arms around my neck. I kissed her, and felt a sudden stirring. She said : 'Goodnight', and walked off down the corridor. I repressed the desire to follow her, and went to my own room. Before going to bed, I took half a dozen vitamin B tablets and drank a pint of water. It made no difference. I woke in the morning with a dry mouth and a head that throbbed like a dynamo.

Two cups of coffee and some hot buttered toast made me feel more human. I sat in bed, reading the morning paper and wondering if a trip to Malahide Castle would be worth the time and energy, but more tempted to put the 'Do not disturb' notice on my door and sleep for the rest of the morning. The telephone rang, and it was like a circular saw cutting into my fragile concentration. I wondered if it was Clive Bates, and was tempted not to answer it. It rang again, and I picked it up. A man's voice said : ' Mr Sorme? '

' Speaking.'

' This is Alastair Glenney. You wrote to me.'

I said : ' Good heavens. How d'you do? It's kind of you to call.'

' Your wife told me you were at the Shelbourne. Look here, what are the chances of your coming to London? '

' It's possible. What had you in mind? '

' It's rather long to explain over the phone. But I'm absolutely fascinated by all this stuff about Esmond. I've got an idea I might be able to help. You know Golspie was sold? '

' No, I didn't.'

' I'm afraid so. Two years ago. They forwarded your letter. My elder brother was killed in Switzerland—drowned in a boating accident. Things turned out to be so complicated—death duties and all that—that we decided to sell Golspie. It's owned by a Canadian called Miller. I know there are great chests full of papers there. And of course, they still belong to me.'

' Do you have access to them? '

' Oh yes. This Miller's quite a decent chap. If you could get to London, we could both go up there.'

I thought quickly.

' When would you be free? '

' Any time at all. I'm not working at the moment.'

' If I took a plane to London today, would you be free? '

' Oh yes, definitely. I'd be delighted to see you.'

I took his telephone number, told him I'd ring him back, and hung up. First, I rang the airport. There was an Aer Lingus flight at twelve thirty-five, and I would have to be at the airport half an hour earlier to pick up my ticket. I confirmed the booking, then rang the desk to ask for my bill. After that, I rang Diana, but could only get on to Mopsy, who had been left in charge of the cleaning woman while Diana went to have her hair done. I told her to tell her Mummy I would be flying to London and would ring later. Then I rang Alastair Glenney back, and said I'd be at Heathrow at 1.45. It was a rush, and my head throbbed warningly, but I made it, scrambling on to the plane five minutes before take-off. I dozed during the trip, and woke up suddenly as the pilot announced our landing.

In the airport building, a voice over the loudspeaker asked if Mr Sorme would go to the Aer Lingus desk. I went there, and found a tall, fair young man waiting for me.

'Mr Sorme? I'm Alaistair Glenney.'

He was younger than I had assumed—hardly out of his teens; his hair was long, and the blue jeans and donkey jacket were not what I would have expected on a peer of the realm. He was extremely good-looking; with shorter hair, he could have made a fortune as a male model.

I said it was kind of him to meet me. He said :

'Not at all. If you hadn't come to London, I'd have come to Ireland.'

We walked about a mile to where his mini-minor was parked. On the way back into London, he amplified what he had told me over the phone. His brother Gordon had died at the age of twenty-eight, a year after getting married. They were the last surviving Glenneys, and Golspie had become the joint property of his brother's wife and Alastair, who was still at St Andrews. Death duties were heavy, and when Gordon's affairs were settled, there was little left but Golspie House (although Alastair had an independent income that came from a grandmother). Golspie was a white elephant, and the agent told them it was hardly worth the trouble of selling—that the price it would fetch would hardly cover the legal costs. Nevertheless, they decided to sell. And within a few weeks they received an incredibly large offer from a Canadian businessman who wanted a 'Scottish castle' to retire to. They closed the deal quickly; Alastair decided this was the time to try to realise his ambition of forming a pop singing group, and moved to London. The group had not materialised, and he was living quietly in Holland Park and studying photography in the hope of becoming a Press photographer.

I asked him how he had become interested in Donelly.

I think I'd better let Angela explain that. That's my sister-in-law—Gordon's wife. She's waiting back at the flat.'

I must admit that I experienced a certain disappointment. Alastair Glenney was obviously a pleasant young man, but he hardly seemed to fit into my search for Donelly. But I thought

170

that it would add a touch of irony to my Introduction to *Memoirs of an Irish Rake* to mention that the present Lord Glenney was an unsuccessful pop singer who hoped to get into journalism. At least he seemed to be interested in his family's history; he outlined what had become of them in the nineteenth century, and how Lord Alexander Glenney—his grandfather— had married an American heiress in 1901 and temporarily restored the family fortunes. His father had reduced them again by living in London and keeping half a dozen mistresses.

We arrived at his flat at about half past three. It was a soft, golden afternoon, and I experienced a sudden sense of well-being as I stood on the pavement in Holland Mews and watched him lock the car. A girl stood at the window watching us, and he waved to her. 'That's Angela.'

Angela Glenney was somehow very Scottish—slim, pretty, lively, with close-cropped hair and a slightly freckled face. She wore a long woollen sweater that came almost to her knees, and jeans.

'Would you like tea? Or a drink?'

I said I'd prefer tea at this hour. They both went into the kitchen, and I glanced at the books on the shelves, and at the pictures. It was clear that Alastair Glenney had brought them from Golspie : there was a fine set of Scott and John Galt in the original editions, and a great many other Scottish writers of whom I had never heard. The bookplates said Horace Glenney, but from the dates this was evidently the son—Esmond's literary executor.

In the corner of the bookshelf I saw a book called *Letters from a Mountain*, by Reginald Smithson. The title page showed no publisher or date, but someone had written '1780' on a flyleaf. There was a design on the title page—of a mountain with a bare tree, and an antelope. Something about it struck me as oddly familiar. I felt suddenly dizzy, and sat down, closing my eyes. It seemed that my hangover was still with me. When I closed my eyes, the dizziness became almost vertiginous, so I opened them and stared again at the book. Then, with sudden clarity, I knew what was happening. I was 'becoming' Esmond again. But this time, I was not seeing the world with his eyes.

171

It was as if we were sharing my head, and seeing things with an effect of double exposure. But I now knew why the book was familiar. I had seen it before. It brought a sense of foreboding. Something unpleasant had been associated with it.

I stared with sudden shock. The door opened, and Horace Glenney came in, carrying a tray. He looked at me, then said :

'Are you all right?'

The double-exposure effect ceased, and I recognised Alastair Glenney. I said : 'Yes, I'm rather hung over, that's all.'

He looked at the book in my lap.

'Oh, you know that?'

'No.'

Angela came in, and he said :

'Isn't that amazing, Angy? He's found the *Letters from a Mountain*. Doesn't that prove something?'

They had made sandwiches, and I realised I was hungry. As I ate, the last traces of the dizziness vanished. I was completely myself again. Three cups of hot tea completed the cure. While I ate, she told me why they were interested in Esmond Donelly. After her husband's death, Angela had decided to complete the university course she had abandoned to get married. She enrolled at Edinburgh; her teacher was Professor David Smellie, the biographer of James Hogg, the Ettrick Shepherd. When Smellie discovered that Angela was Lady Glenney, he was pleased and excited. He was writing a history of the *Edinburgh Review*, and Glenney had been one of the original contributors. He had been recruited by Dr Gilbert Stuart, a man whose chief personal characteristics were envy and rancour. The sharpness of its tone made the *Review* an immediate success when its first issue came out in June 1773 : Glenney contributed an excellent critical article on Lord Momboddo, and a rather harsh review of a history by Dr Henry, one of the most successful Scottish writers of the day. Then, apparently, Glenney—like a great many other people—began to feel that all this bitterness and satire was pointless, and wrote Stuart a long letter—October 1773—explaining his feeling that the *Review* ought to aim at being more constructive; that there was, after all, some merit in Henry, Robertson, Blair and various others whose reputations had been scourged in its pages. Stuart wrote a friendly and reasonable reply, but then seems to have suspected that Glenney had been 'influenced' by Henry or Blair, and wrote a second letter in which he called Glenney 'an ecclesiastical lapdog' (Henry was a 'Reverend').

The remainder of the story can be found in Isaac d'Israeli's *Calamities and Quarrels of Authors.* In November, the *Scots Magazine* (a rival) produced a brilliant defence of Henry and Robertson, which included a skilful and deadly attack on Stuart. D'Israeli quotes this at length. In the pages of the *Review*, Stuart asserted that the author of the attack—signed 'E.D.'—was Horace Glenney. Glenney replied immediately by letter, telling Stuart that while he approved of every word of the attack, its author was actually his friend Esmond Donelly. The result of this letter was a murderous review of Donelly's *Observations upon France and Switzerland* in the February issue of Stuart's magazine. D'Israeli states that Glenney wanted to challenge Stuart to a duel, but was dissuaded by Donelly.

The battle rumbled on, even after Stuart's magazine had collapsed. Stuart went to London, and contributed periodically to *The Gentleman's Magazine.* And it was in that magazine, in June 1881, that there appeared a brief but vicious review of *Letters from a Mountain,* that described it as the 'vapours of a mind unbalanced through lewdness and enthusiasm '. In the next issue of the magazine, it was announced that the author of the *Letters from a Mountain* was actually Horace Glenney.

Stuart died five years later, at the age of forty-four—embittered, seething with hatred, convinced that his enemies had conspired to ruin him.

This was the story told to me by Angela Glenney. It would have excited me more than it actually did if I had not been so tired. Every time she mentioned Horace Glenney, I looked at Alastair Glenney, and wondered if it was true that he resembled his ancestor. If he did, then I had my proof that I was in some kind of psychic contact with Esmond. When she finished, I asked if there was a portrait of Horace Glenney at Golspie.

'Oh yes.'

'What does he look like?'

They looked at one another and laughed. Angela said :

'Terribly like Alastair. That's why he's so interested in him!'

So there could be no possible doubt. Instead of feeling excited, I felt oddly oppressed.

I picked up *Letters from a Mountain*. 'What is it about?'

'Oh, it's a most weird piece of work. Dr Smellie thinks the form is influenced by Goldsmith's *Citizen of the World*. It's really a kind of Gothic novel—rather like Walpole's *Castle of Otranto*. It's really quite amazing for its period—when you consider that Mrs Radcliffe and Maturin hadn't started writing.'

'Could you give me an outline of the plot?'

'It's about two friends called Rodolpho and Conrad. They're a sort of David and Jonathan. When they fall in love with the same girl, each tries to persuade her to accept the other. They go to university together, and swear eternal friendship and blood-brotherhood—you know the kind of thing. Then one day, when he's standing in a bookshop, Rodolpho gets approached by a mysterious Moor named Abdallah Saba, who offers to tell his fortune. He tells him that he's destined to be one of the rulers of the world, and invites him back to his home. Rodolpho goes —in spite of the warnings of Conrad—and falls in love with a girl called Nouri, who's supposed to be Abdallah's daughter...'

At this point, Alastair interrupted: 'Surely he doesn't want to hear every blessed word of the stuff.'

I assured him that I did. Angela went on. The Moor gets Rodolpho involved in magic ceremonies involving a great crystal globe. They stand on top of a tower in the light of the full moon, and Rodolpho looks into the globe. He sees a vulture that looks at him with yellow eyes, then suddenly seems to hurl itself towards him. Rodolpho is saved from falling off the tower by Nouri. She then becomes his mistress and promises to marry him if his family will give their consent. She confesses that Abdallah is not her father, and that it is all a plot to involve Rodolpho in a terrible secret society that plans to destroy Europe.

The next day, he finds that Nouri and her 'father' have left. He is in despair, and searches everywhere for them. One day, in an old church, he sees the figure of a vulture cast in bronze, and buys it for a few crowns. Then he writes a travel book, describing the places he has visited in his search for Nouri, and has the cover embossed with the symbol of the vulture. A few weeks later, Rodolpho receives an envelope containing the symbol of a vulture, and a note ordering him to destroy every copy of his travel book. He does this by setting fire to the London warehouse of his publisher, and several people die in the fire, which spreads to adjoining houses. When this is done, the Moor contacts him again, and he is able to rejoin his lady love. Now he becomes a full member of the evil secret society known as the Order of the Vulture. They feel that Nouri is a bad—or rather, a good —influence on him, and she is ordered to renounce him. She refuses, and is murdered. Rodolpho, now completely in the power of the Order, accepts a mistress called Fatima, who is also a witch...

It would be tiresome to summarise the rest of the novel, which is confused and melodramatic. There can be no doubt that it owes a great deal to *The Castle of Otranto*, and that, in turn, it influenced Mrs Radcliffe and Maturin. Rodolpho is tempted to do more and more evil deeds, in spite of Conrad's attempts to save his soul. Finally, he is ordered to murder Conrad. But this is too much. The David-and-Jonathan bond is too strong, in spite of the years. At the last moment, Rodolpho throws down the dagger, and he and Conrad embrace. Rodolpho is in despair at his evil deeds, and they decide to go to Mount Athos to ask for penances. On the last stage of their journey, Rodolpho is awakened in the night by the voice of the dead Nouri. He gets up to follow it, and falls over a cliff. When the body is found, the face is so horribly contorted that the monks refuse to have it buried in holy ground, declaring that the corpse is obviously that of a demon. Conrad himself buries it in the middle of a barren steppe, then goes on to Mount Athos, where he writes his story—in the form of a series of letters to a father confessor.

As Angela Glenney summarised the plot, my fatigue vanished. I knew now that my investigation had taken a crucial turn. The most important piece of the jigsaw puzzle had fallen into place. I knew that Esmond had, in fact, received the sketch of a phoenix soon after publishing the *Observations* in 1771. I knew that the complete edition had been destroyed in a fire at the

London warehouse of his publisher. Now it was impossible to doubt that Esmond had been approached by some envoy of the Sect of the Phoenix in 1771. At the same time, the rest of the story could not be taken seriously. Esmond was not plunged into evil ways after that date. He and Glenney remained on close terms for years after, and the *Scots Magazine* article of 1774 revealed that he was still an avid reader of sermons. It was not until nearly ten years later that Glenney wrote the *Letters from a Mountain*.

I owed this vital clue to Alastair and Angela Glenney. There-fore, it was clear that I owed them the full story of my own researches. So when Angela said: 'Now, what have you dis-covered about Esmond Donelly?', I suggested we have a whisky; then I told them the full story, as I have written it here. It took three hours, and I finished it in a restaurant in Notting Hill Gate over dinner. I had Esmond's journals with me, as well as Glenney's letters; I was glad of them, for there were times when the whole thing sounded so absurd to me that it was a relief to convince myself it was not an involved dream. Angela listened without saying much, her eyes never leaving my face. Alastair kept saying: 'My God', and walking up and down the room. As we walked to the restaurant, he said: 'You realise this is the biggest literary discovery since the Dead Sea Scrolls?', and it sounded so funny that Angela and I both started to laugh.

But it was when I told them that Esmond had appointed Horace Glenney's son as his literary executor that they became really excited. They had been hoping to find some of Glenney's material at Golspie; now it seemed possible that they might find some of Esmond's papers there too. Angela pointed out that Alastair could be regarded as Esmond's literary executor, since he was a direct descendant of Horace Glenney, and there were no Astons left alive. That meant that if more Donelly papers were published, Alastair and Angela could share the profits. I already had more than enough material for my own edition of *Memoirs of an Irish Rake*.

We sat up until two in the morning talking about Esmond and Horace Glenney. The chief regret, naturally, was that neither of them had taken any interest in Glenney before selling Golspie

House. Angela remembered that her husband had showed her a room at Golspie where a murder had taken place—a man had been found dead under mysterious circumstances. Alastair thought he recalled something of the sort too; but when she described the room, it was not the one he remembered as the ' murder room '.

I slept the night on a bed-settee in the sitting room; Angela was occupying the bed in the guest room. Alastair wanted to leave for Scotland the next morning, but Angela said she had some research to do at the Museum. I decided that I might as well go with her. I spent the morning there, and found the ' Martell and Smithson ' pamphlet on the Sect of the Phoenix. Tim Morrison was embarrassed when I pointed it out to him, and said that he had overlooked it because its title refers to the ' Society of the Phoenix '. To make up for the oversight, he had the pamphlet photostatted for me, so I was able to take a copy away.

Angela and I ate lunch in a Greek restaurant near Cambridge Circus. I remarked at one point that it was kind of them to trust me in this way. After all, we were technically rivals. Sooner or later—probably sooner—they would have searched Golspie House for the Glenney papers, and then the discovery—assuming they made one—would be entirely theirs. She said :

' No. I'm glad you joined us. We both trust you.'

I said thankyou. She said :

' In fact, I'm delighted you came along. You know, Alastair used to adore his brother Gordon. It was Alastair who persuaded me to marry Gordon, in fact. He went on about his virtues at such length that I had to meet him. I was Alastair's girlfriend first, you know.'

' Didn't he feel hurt when you married Gordon? '

' Oh no. He was delighted. You see, it brought him closer to Gordon—it meant he'd really given Gordon something important. Anyway, what I started to say was—I think he's inclined to look up to you as he did to Gordon.'

' But he's only known me twenty-four hours.'

' That makes no difference. The odd thing is, you're rather like Gordon, physically.'

177

She stopped, and I thought she reddened. She drank a gulp of lager to cover it up. I saw what she was thinking : that if Alastair had presented her to Gordon, then I might be regarded as the next in the line of succession. We changed the subject and talked about Donelly. Then I remembered something I had forgotten to mention : the letter from Klaus Dunkelman. I had his address and telephone number in my address book. She said :

'Why not ring him? He might be interesting.'

'I suppose I ought to.'

I went to the restaurant phone. A woman with a foreign accent answered, and sounded hostile until I mentioned my name. Then she became very friendly, introduced herself as Annaliese Dunkelman, and began to talk at length about my books. Finally, her husband came on the phone; he asked me if I could join them for supper. I said I might be engaged then, but asked if I could go around later that afternoon. We made a date for four o'clock.

I was not entirely happy about this development. It sounded as if it might be a dead-end. But Angela said : 'Good, he sounds interesting. Do you mind if I come too?'

We spent another hour in the Museum; then, since the afternoon was so pleasant, decided to walk up towards Hampstead. We strolled up through Bloomsbury as far as Camden Town, then took a bus to Belsize Park. The Dunkelmans' address was in Keats Grove.

The door was opened by a tall, thin man with very thick glasses that made his eyes seem distant and strange, like an octopus looking out of an aquarium. He looked a little surprised to see Angela, but invited us in cordially. We followed him along a corridor into a large sunlit studio. The floor was covered with stone dust, and there were huge Amazonian statues of women with massive breasts and buttocks. A big, grey-haired woman put down her hammer and chisel to come and greet us. She shook my hand enthusiastically, with a grip like a lobster, and nodded perfunctorily at Angela. She was less tall than her husband, but built like a wrestler, and her arms—with the sleeves rolled up above the elbow—gave the impression that she could have felled any one of us with a stroke. Her German accent was thicker than her husband's, and I shall not try to reproduce it here, or its curious syntax. She placed a hand on my shoulder.

'Good, I have been waiting very impatiently. Ever since I read your *Sex Diary* I have wanted to meet you. Come along to my den.' She turned to Angela and smiled. 'Do you mind? I want to talk to him alone. Klaus will show you the garden.' Angela was too surprised to object. And Frau Dunkelman grabbed my arm in a grip of iron, and steered me up a flight of stairs. I caught Angela's eye for a moment, and she raised her eyebrows and bit her lower lip.

Anna—as she insisted I call her immediately—led me into a small, comfortable room that smelt of tobacco. On the sideboard there were three gallon bottles containing, respectively, gin, whisky and brandy. She offered me a drink, but I said it was too early. She poured herself an enormous gin, and filled it to the top with tonic. Then she lit a cigarette in a holder that must have been a foot long, and flung herself into a deep armchair, crossing her knees. I have to admit that her legs were not bad. At the same time, it made me uncomfortable to be able to see so much of her at such short notice, for the short tweed skirt she was wearing hardly reached the tops of her stockings when she was standing up. She indicated that I should sit in the chair opposite, which left me no alternative to contemplating her.

'Yes, you have great penetration for such a young man. How old are you? Really? You look much younger. When I read your book I said to Klaus: "Ah, what a pity he does not live in London. There is so much we could teach him." And now you are only here for one day! How preposterous! What can you do in one day?'

She told me that my books all showed considerable intelligence, and great intuition, but that what I lacked was experience. 'You must not be offended if I tell you that in many ways you are immature.' I said I wasn't offended. Then, without explaining the transition, she began to speak about her own qualifications for teaching the young. 'I should be a schoolteacher like my mother. But I have no patience with large groups of students. What I would like is two or three brilliant ones. I am creative, you see. My hands have to shape stone and clay, my mind has

179

to shape souls.' She stared at me penetratingly. 'Now I want to ask you a frank question. When you make love to a woman, can you hold back your climax until you have given her all the pleasure she needs?' I thought of Diana, and said I thought so. 'No, no, that is not what I want to hear. I want a truthful answer. You must think of me as a doctor—as if I was your psychoanalyst...' She took a long swallow of gin, reached out for a fresh cigarette, and uncrossed her legs. It was hard to keep my eyes on her face. She glanced away for a moment, then looked back quickly, evidently hoping to catch me peeping. Then she leaned her head back against the cushion, her face to the ceiling, and closed her eyes. I wondered whether this was some kind of test. She was wearing panties that might have been made of pink cellophane, and she was facing me with her feet on a leather pouffe, her knees spread apart, so that without any effort I could see the open lips of the vulva, and the entrance to the vagina. She had no pubic hairs—she had obviously shaved them off. Her legs and her bottom were shapely. But the powerful arms, the big shoulders, the grey hair, made it seem as if she was some mythological monster, with a top half that didn't belong to the bottom. I deliberately looked away towards the empty fireplace, and kept my eyes there. She was saying:

'I sense that you are an extremely shy person who tries to cover it up. In this, you are rather like Klaus. Klaus is my son, of course.'

'Your son?' I was astonished.

'Not literally. I mean that our relationship is mother and son. I am the creative one, the earth mother, like Erda in Wagner. Our relationship is very close. I am his teacher. If you ask him, he will tell you that he has become a different person since he has known me—more profound, more sensitive. I have this power to communicate my own talents to those I love. And when I say love, I mean, of course, the love of teacher and student, for there is none deeper than this...'

Periodically, I glanced at her, to discover that she had sunk even lower in the chair, so that she was lying in the coital position. But she talked on without a sign of embarrassment, as if she was standing in front of a class of students and discussing

180

a diagram on the blackboard. What she seemed to be asking—in a complicated and discursive way—was whether I would like to join Klaus as one of her students, to absorb the benefit of her knowledge and creative talent. She was explaining to me the difference between the male and female intellect, when there was a gentle knock at the door. She ignored it and went on talking. I expected her to close her legs, or at least sit more upright, but she remained completely unmoved. Klaus looked into the room.

'Are you coming downstairs, schatz?'

'In a moment.' From where he was standing, his view of her genitalia was less intimate than mine—I could have leaned forward and inserted a finger—but still comprehensive. He showed no surprise. 'The young lady would probably like a drink too, and this room is too small.' Then the footsteps of 'the young lady' sounded on the stairs. I had to admire her timing. For a moment, I thought she meant to lie there and allow Angela to join the spectators; but a few seconds before the steps reached the door, she yawned, closed her legs, and sat up. 'Come, then.' She went to the door, and gave Klaus a playful but hard smack on the rear. Then she beckoned to me, and we all trooped downstairs. When her eyes fell on Angela, she frowned slightly, as if she was having difficulty remembering who she was, and then as if she had remembered and thought 'How tiresome'.

We went into a larger room, furnished more formally. I accepted a small sherry; so did Angela. To my surprise, Frau Dunkelman now became very affable towards Angela. Perhaps this was because Angela mentioned she had only met me the day before. She asked her how many of my books she had read; when she discovered the answer was: 'Hardly any at all', she wagged her finger at her and told her that she should begin immediately. Now Angela was accepted into the flock as a 'student', and lectured about creativity. Klaus sat in a corner, sipping tonic water ('He is not allowed to drink—it makes him sentimental'), and making no attempt to interpose. When Anna paused to take another drink, I asked him to tell me something about Körner. He said quickly:

181

' I would not advise you to bother about him. He is a complete charlatan.'

'That is not quite fair', said his wife. 'I agree that he has become a charlatan. But he was not always so.' She addressed me. 'Do you know about Reich?'

' Not very much.'

' He was a great psychologist—as great as Freud. He believed that the only way to create a healthy society is to have people without sexual repressions.'

' That sounds like Freud.'

' Certainly. His basic ideas are very similar to Freud. His great contribution was in the treatment of neurosis. He believed that repressions form a kind of shell over the personality, like a tortoise, you know?' She pulled a forbidding face and made a motion with her hands to indicate armour plating. She pointed to her husband. 'When I first met him, his face was like a mask —all the muscles were tense. It was necessary to teach him to relax completely—to love his genitals.'

Angela looked startled. I asked cautiously :

' In what way?'

' To be frank and open about his sexual functions. We used to hold therapy groups in Stockholm. We would sit without any trousers or skirts, having a discussion, drinking coffee, and the men would be encouraged to play with their genitals, just like children. It was wonderful.'

Klaus said solemnly :

' She used to come and sit beside me, and masturbate me while we discussed our problems. It was a great release—to learn not to be ashamed of genital play. When I was small, my nurse often beat me for touching my penis. Reich taught me that the penis is as much an instrument of social intercourse as the tongue or the hands.'

Anna, impatient of the interruption, thumped the arm of the chair with her fist, and said :

' If Reich's theories had been properly understood, the last war would have been impossible. Hitler used sexual repression as a political weapon. The Germans are the most repressed nation in the world. That is why they are so aggressive.'

I asked: 'And what about Körner? Where did he come in?'

'The groups in Stockholm were organised by Körner. He invented the notion of group sexual expression, not Reich. Reich was still a little prudish, you know, and at this time he was already brooding on these mad ideas about orgone energy—you know, he thought he had discovered pure life-energy, and that it was blue—he said it is orgone energy that makes the sky blue.'

Klaus said gloomily:

'At this time, we believed that only Körner preserved the doctrine in its purity. So when he came to London, we came with him.'

'And did you continue with your sexual self-expression groups?'

'Ach, yes, more than before. And that was the trouble. Reich warned us that if we were not careful, they would cease to have therapeutic value, and become sexual orgies. Körner would not listen. He had a great obsessive idea—to disinfect the sexual impulse. That is how he put it. He said that sex must be rid of all shame. After all, most sensitive people are socially shy. If they have to stand up on a stage and address an audience, they get stage fright. But they can get over this, and when they get over it, they express themselves freely, without fear. Körner wanted people to get over their sexual stage fright.'

This was Klaus. His English was a great deal more fluent than his wife's. Angela was frowning. She said:

'But wouldn't too much sexual freedom destroy all the fun?'

'No!' They both shouted at once; Anna quelled her husband with a glance, and went on determinedly:

'On the contrary, people are too ashamed to learn to enjoy sex. Why do you think there are so many rapes and sex murders? Because there is a thick wall between the sexes. A man gets on a bus, and sees a pretty girl, and he is like a fox with a chicken. He does not rape her because there is no opportunity, and perhaps he is afraid of the law. This is not a natural relation between the sexes. All society is sex-starved. In a healthy society, he might sit beside her on the bus, and persuade her to masturbate him, without anyone paying any attention. Why not? You'—her finger suddenly darted out at Angela, who was leaning forward, her forearms on her knees. 'Why do you sit in that position? You think it is natural. But it isn't. You are wearing a mini-skirt because you think it attractive. Why do you not open your knees boldly?'

Angela, a little taken aback, tried to make a joke of it. 'I might get raped.'

'No! That is not logical! Why do women wear short skirts? To interest the men. You play a game to see how high you can wear them. Do you not see what this means? You want to display your genitals, but you are afraid. You want to make men stare, but you are afraid of being raped. Is that not proof that there is something wrong?' Angela involuntarily tugged at the bottom of her mini-skirt. 'You see! Why do you wear it if you want to keep it down? Why do you not sit like this?' She leaned back in her chair and opened her knees, so that Angela got the same view that I had had in the 'den' upstairs. Angela dropped her eyes. Anna, without closing her legs again, went on: 'No! We must develop a society without sexual fears and inhibitions. If the young man on the bus wants to know whether you are wearing tights or panties, he should be allowed to look!'

I interrupted, to divert attention from Angela:

'Why do you say Körner became a charlatan?'

'Because with a theory like that, it is possible to attract all the wrong people for all the wrong reasons. That is what he has done. He says that his aim is to try to teach people to achieve mystical ecstasy through sex. But all he does is to organise petting parties.'

It was difficult to stop the flow, which went on like this for half an hour more. What she said struck me as good sense, to some extent. It is true that most people are obsessed with sex in a negative way. But when I thought of Diana and Mopsy, and my study lined with books, it struck me that there are more important things than sex. The ideal way to cure a man who is obsessed by sex is not to tell him to masturbate on buses, but to get him to learn to enjoy music and poetry and ideas. When I suggested this to the Dunkelmans, there was an outburst of scorn. 'That is merely what Freud called sublimation. It is a refusal to face the real problem. You suppress it and pretend to be interested in something else.'

I began to feel impatient. In any case, it was nearly seven, and Alastair would be wondering where we were. I said we had to go. They tried to persuade us to stay to supper, but we excused ourselves. Anna said she would write me a long letter, and that perhaps I might help her with the writing of her book on sexual freedom for all.

As we stood up to go, Angela asked :

'By the way, do you know anything about the Sect of the Phoenix? '

Anna shrugged.

'What is that? Some new fad of the young people? '

It was obvious that the name meant nothing to her. Angela did not pursue the subject. At the door, Dunkelman asked :

'You are leaving London tonight, yes? '

'Tomorrow.'

'I hope we shall meet next time you are here.' He bowed stiffly. I said :

'I must also write to Professor Körner.'

Anna said : 'That would be no good. The police have ordered him to leave England. He is back in Germany.'

'Oh, I'm sorry. Why? '

Klaus said : 'He was nothing more than a professional brothel-keeper.'

In the taxi, on the way back to Holland Park, Angela said :
'You certainly seem to come across some astounding people. It's really a pity we can't meet Dr Körner.'

'But it would probably be a dead-end. Admittedly, Dunkelman told me it was Körner who first mentioned Esmond Donelly, but I presume he'd simply read the book on deflowering virgins.'

We talked about the Dunkelmans. Angela said :

'I don't think you're right that Klaus is just a henpecked husband. I got a very queer feeling as he looked at me.'

'In what way? '

'I got a funny feeling that he was willing me to open my legs. You saw the way I was sitting—even his wife noticed it.'

'I suspect she's half Lesbian, anyway.'

'I wouldn't be surprised. I got a most unpleasant feeling

185

talking with them. Did you notice?'

'What kind?'

'Well—they're so ugly, they're really rather repellent when they go on about sex. And yet in another way, it has an odd fascination.'

I knew what she meant. Until we went to the Dunkelmans, I had looked on Angela simply as a rather pleasant, intelligent girl, but with no more sexual interest than if she had been my sister. Now, sitting beside her, I found myself looking at the curve of her breast under the black sweater, and having to repress a desire to fondle it. Anna Dunkelman had done this somehow, by directing attention to Angela as a sexual object.

She said suddenly: 'I'm glad you were there', and shivered, moving closer to me. It was natural to put my arm round her shoulder. A moment later, her face was upturned to mine, and I was kissing her with a passion that startled me. It was like taking a mouthful of food, and suddenly realising you are ravenously hungry. We clung tightly together, my tongue in her mouth, my hand crushing the breast I had been looking at a moment earlier. There was not simply a desire to caress her, but to hurt her, to squeeze her, to absorb her. She was clinging against me with complete abandonment, and when my hand moved downward, pressing hard against her ribs, then her stomach, her legs opened. My hand slid between them, on top of the skirt, and pressed hard against her crotch; she gasped, and her mouth opened wider. Then my hand found its way under the mini-skirt, and inside her pants. I was in a state of acute discomfort, having got so far; the natural thing would have been to remove the rest of her clothes and penetrate her. Since this was impossible, my body had become an iron bar of lust.

The taxi hooted and swerved to avoid a car rushing the lights; we broke apart guiltily. She said: 'I'm sorry.'

'Why?'

'That was my fault. I've been wanting you to do it ever since we left the Dunkelmans.'

We were still clinging together, and my heart was still pounding so hard that I could hardly speak. She said:

'I've never done that before—not like that. I don't know if

you'll believe me, but I'm quite a puritan inside.'

I said, half-jokingly : ' They've hypnotised us.'

She looked at me seriously. ' I think that might be it. I'm sure they have some odd power. I'll tell you something that will shock you. If I'd been there alone, I'd have ended by giving myself to that awful Klaus.'

I said, laughing : ' If I'd been alone in that den for another ten minutes, I'd have ended by making love to Anna.'

' But she's so ghastly ! '

I told her about how she had sat with her legs open. It was true that after another five minutes, I would have obeyed the impulse to lean across and touch her, and then it would have been very easy to take out my erect penis and plunge it home. It would have seemed silly to refrain.

The taxi stopped outside the house. She said :

' I'd better tidy myself up.'

I knew what she meant. I also had the illusion that I was as dishevelled as if I had just crawled out of bed. I paid the taxi while she quickly added a touch of lipstick to her mouth and ran a comb through her hair.

Angela opened the door with her key, and we went into the flat. Everything was still as we had left it that morning. She called : ' Alastair.' There was no reply. She shook her head and said : ' No ', and I knew she was not commenting on Alastair's absence. I put my hand on her breast. She said : ' There's not time.' But I knew she was not serious. I was still glowing with the curiously violent lust, which was almost feverish. I tugged the bottom of the sweater out of the skirt, and slid my hand underneath. She was wearing a cup-bra, and a slight tug exposed the breast. I took the nipple between my forefinger and thumb and pinched it. She moved into my arms, and her mouth opened again. I reached down for the zip of her skirt and fumbled it undone. It dropped to the floor. I slipped my hands inside the elastic of the panties, and pushed them down as far as her thighs. Then I raised the black sweater; she lifted her arms, and let me pull it over her head. I undid the bra and it dropped to the floor. She stood there wearing a black suspender belt, the black panties around her knees. Her hand fumbled at the waist of my trousers, and I helped her undo it, and pushed them down. We stood there, in the middle of her room, clinging together, both half-naked. Then I stepped out of my trousers and underpants, and led her to the bedroom. As soon as I slipped into her, she groaned, and seemed to writhe against me. I held her very close, and worked up and down with a steady, machine-like drive, one hand still on her breast. I had seldom known sex to be so vertiginous. I think that if a battery of photographers had appeared in the doorway with flashlight cameras, we would have kept on making love, totally unable to pull our bodies apart. The feverish sensation was still there, making the room unreal. We seemed to be all moisture. Our bodies perspired; the moisture from us ran down between her buttocks and on to the bed; our tongues ran in and out of each other's mouths, so that our faces were wet; her breasts made a squelching noise against my chest. It occurred to me that Alastair might come in at any moment, but there was a certain pleasure in the thought of someone watching us. Then the pleasure was too exquisite to hold back; her body seemed to be begging me to pour the seed into her. We clung together, gasping, as the climax burst over us like a wave, and I felt the hot moisture gushing along my member and into her. It seemed to go on for minutes. Then we relaxed, and I lay there, still inside her. A few minutes later, we lay side by side, and the sweat felt cool. I opened my eyes and looked at her; and realised with a shock that this was Angela, the demure Scots girl who had struck me as 'nice' but not my type. She opened her eyes, and looked startled to see me. Suddenly, we both remembered that half our clothes were lying in the other room, and that the door was open. I got up and went in to collect them. When I came back, she was standing up, pulling on her panties. I went over to her and kissed her. She gave me her mouth primly, as if it was a formal goodnight kiss. Then, as if repenting, she put her arms round my neck. She said :

' Whatever came over us? '

I knew what she meant. It had not been 'normal' sex, the sex of two people who decide they like one another and want to explore one another's bodies. It had been a kind of frenzy, as if we were two animals. And now I was 'Mr Sorme' again, and she was Lady Angela Glenney, and we were two people who liked one another, but were not lovers. Except, of course, that it was impossible for us not to be aware that we had just abandoned ourselves to one another.

She said suddenly : 'My God, I forgot. It's the worst time of the month.'

I placed my hand gently on her stomach. 'Then there's probably a little Sorme in there.'

'Probably.'

'Do you mind?'

She laughed suddenly.

'No. I don't think so.'

The telephone rang. It was Alastair, saying he was having a drink with some old schoolfriends, and would not be back for another hour.

Angela and I took a shower together. I felt oddly cool and fresh, totally relaxed. Every time I looked at Angela, I experienced a faint shock, as if what had happened had been a sexual fantasy inside my own head.

Half an hour later, as we sat on either side of the fire, sipping vodka martinis, she said :

'I think they put something in the drinks.'

'An aphrodisiac, you mean? I don't think so. Spanish fly has an irritating effect on the lining of the stomach—I once tasted some in Algiers.'

'But surely you don't believe it was something psychic, do you?'

I said : 'I'll tell you what I believe. I believe that Klaus wanted to make love to you, and she wanted me to make love to her. If we'd stayed for supper, we'd have finished up in bed with them. As it was, whatever they did to us made us want one another.' When I thought back on the fury of our lovemaking, I knew there was something odd about it.

She said : 'It makes you wonder whether there's really something in these stories about love potions—Tristan and Isolde, and all that.'

'I knew a man who could tell you—a man called Caradoc Cunningham.'

189

'Yes, I know about him. I read your book. I don't think I'd like to meet him.'

When Alastair came in half an hour later, she was cooking a meal, and the flat was full of the fragrance of garlic and mint. He said : 'I hope you didn't get too bored without me.' Angela said : 'No, we found plenty to do.' 'To do?' 'I mean to talk about.' He was joking, of course; he knew that neither Angela nor I were the type to become lovers within a few hours of meeting one another.

In the night, I had disturbing dreams that I could not remember; but when I woke up, I was Esmond again. This was the strangest sensation so far. I had drunk a little too much Pommard after supper, and although I was not drunk, I had that feeling of slight separation from reality, of meaninglessness. On the other hand, Esmond was wide awake. For him, this high-ceilinged room seemed familiar enough; the only slightly puzzling element was the occasional sound of a passing car or lorry on the Holland Park Road. My sense of being back in the eighteenth century was stronger than it had been in Dublin, perhaps because there were no distractions in the dark. I fell asleep again, and had confused dreams of Horace Walpole, Lichtenberg, Boswell and Johnson. When I woke up in the morning, I had a very clear memory of Johnson saying emphatically—and spluttering with his large, pendulous lower lip : 'The man is a lecherous rogue, sir, and you would do better to avoid him utterly.'

We took a plane at 11.30, and were in Edinburgh an hour and a half later. We ate lunch in the back room of a pub with Dr David Smellie, Angela's professor, a small man with a face like a terrier. He had once given one of my books a particularly vicious review, so he smiled sheepishly when he was introduced to me; but when he made an oblique reference to the subject over lunch, I pretended I had not seen it, and we got on well enough. There was no need for me to do a great deal of talking —Alastair and Angela wanted to tell him all about Esmond Donelly, and my discoveries. He listened politely for a while, then said :

'I'm afraid I don't see why you find him so interesting. It

sounds to me as if he was a typical eighteenth-century rake. Did he ever think about anything but sex? '

Angela looked at me; I think she was inclined to agree. I said :

' In a sense no. And in another sense, sex didn't interest him at all.'

He said snappily : ' Isn't that what is called casuistry? '

' No.' He was unsympathetic, but I decided to try to explain. ' I see Esmond as a man obsessed with the problem of meaning.'

' The meaning of what? Human existence? ' I recalled that he had made a number of jeering comments in his review on what he called my ' crypto-religious obsession '. But I wanted to explain to the other two. I said :

' It's a matter that either you understand or you don't. To me, it's a self-evident problem. Sometimes life is intensely interesting and meaningful, and this meaning seems to be an objective fact, like sunlight. At other times it's as meaningless and futile as the wind. We accept this eclipse of meaning as we accept changes in the weather. If I wake up with a bad cold or a headache, I seem to be deaf to meaning. Now if I woke up physically deaf or half-blind, I'd feel there was something wrong and consult a doctor. But when I'm deaf to meaning, I accept it as something natural. Esmond didn't accept it as natural. And he also noticed that every time we're sexually stimulated, meaning returns. We can hear again. So he pursued sex as a way of recovering meaning.'

Angela asked : ' How about Horace Glenney? '

' No, he wasn't interested in Esmond's search for meaning. He admired Esmond, but he didn't understand him.'

' Having read *Of the Deflowering of Maids*, I doubt whether there was anything to understand." Smellie remained unconvinced. I said :

' I don't believe Esmond wrote that book.'

' No? Then who did? '

' I don't know. But the style isn't Esmond's.'

He shrugged as if to say I could indulge in any fancies I liked, but it was none of his business. I said :

' Do you happen to remember the date on the edition you saw? '

' Of course. 1790.'

191

This excited me. The edition I had seen in Galway was printed in Leipzig in the 1830s.

'Who printed it, and where?'

'There is no printer, but the university catalogue says it was printed privately in Edinburgh.'

'Are you sure?'

'I am not in the habit of confusing my facts.' I recalled that this was another of his jibes, so I dropped the subject. But my cordiality as I shook his hand half an hour later was not entirely feigned. Another piece of the puzzle had fallen into place. And a suspicion I had already entertained began to seem less absurd. For assuming that the *Deflowering of Maids* was a forgery, who could have written it? Obviously, someone who was interested in making Esmond out to be a rake and a writer of pornography. This might easily be Gilbert Stuart, who had been friendly with Horace Glenney, and who had a motive for blackening Donelly's reputation. But he was dead by 1786. That left only one obvious candidate : Glenney himself. And if the 'Deflowering' book was printed in Edinburgh, it became a distinct possibility.

It was after four o'clock that we finally left Edinburgh in a hired car, and started on the long drive north—almost as far as from London to Edinburgh. We broke the journey at Pitlochrie, and left early the next morning. By four that afternoon we were on the last stage of the journey, from Dornoch to Golspie. The wild, open moors and the sudden views of the sea were impressive; but what really occupied my thoughts was the sheer effort involved in making this same journey in 1770—in a bumpy coach, over roads that were little better than dirt tracks. Most of the people of Golspie had probably travelled no farther than Dornoch or Inverness. No wonder Horace Glenney was an object of such admiration when he returned from his European travels. We stopped in the village to ring Franklin Miller—the new owner of Golspie House—then drove on to the north-east. Golspie House stands on the slopes of Ben Horn, overlooking Loch Brora. As we drove this last lap of the journey, I tried hard to relax, to see it with Esmond's eyes; but it was no good. It was all too strange. The sight of the square, grey house brought a flash of recognition; but I could have been deceiving myself.

There was a great deal of scaffolding up at the front of the building; evidently its new owner was improving it. The drive had been tarmacked, and the lawns looked well kept. It might have been an expensive hotel.

Franklin Miller was a big, friendly man who looked as if he had been born to be a country squire. He seemed genuinely delighted to have us as guests. He led us into the great library, where there was a huge log fire burning. We accepted whiskies, and met Mrs Miller, who begged us to stay for as long as we could. After walking around the grounds and down to the side of the loch, I asked if we might spend an hour before dinner looking through the attic, where Alastair had seen bundles of old papers. Our host told us to treat the house as if it had never changed owners, and went off to find out what his workmen were doing.

'I know where we can begin', Alastair said. 'The family Bible. It lists the births and deaths of all the Glenneys of Golspie.'

This was in the library, on a top shelf—a magnificent, shiny-leather thing that weighed half a hundredweight. It was a 'Great Bible'—the Cranmer version of 1539. It struck me that it was probably worth nearly as much as Golspie House, but I didn't like to say so. The half-dozen pages at the back were covered with writing—page after page in illegible scrawl, written in faded ink, beginning with an Alexander Gleinnie, who died in 1579 (before Shakespeare had left Stratford upon Avon), and who was apparently knighted by Henry VIII. The Glenneys were raised to the peerage by James I. Sometimes, the dates were followed by the cause of death, 'fever', 'cholick', 'of a twisted middle' (whatever that meant). There were several entries in the hand-writing I recognised as Horace Glenney's. His own name was followed by two dates: 1747, and 1796; but there was no mention of cause of death. His father died in 1778, upon which his brother Moray became Lord Glenney; Moray was killed 'by a fall from a misen' (mizzen mast?) in 1781, upon which his younger brother assumed the title.

This at least was helpful; I now knew Horace Glenney's dates. But not the cause of his death. I asked Alastair if he could remember which room had been showed to him as the 'murder room'.

'Oh yes, of course.' He led me out of the library, up the main staircase, and along a corridor. He knocked on the door, then opened it. The room was now apparently a guest bedroom; it overlooked the loch, and a workman was whistling on the scaffold outside.

Angela said: 'This was definitely not the room Gordon showed me. That was in the other wing.'

After some hesitation, we found this. It overlooked the back part of the house; there was a sheer drop outside the window to a small courtyard. It was a plain, cold room, and one wall was not panelled; the granite had been smoothed to form a flat surface. Angela pointed to a brown stain that ran down this to the floor. 'Gordon said that was a bloodstain—that he was lying in bed when someone shot him from the doorway.'

This was possible; it looked like a bloodstain. On the other hand, it seemed to me unlikely that the master of the house would sleep in a room like this. What was more probable was that the bloodstain had led to the story of a murder.

Three more flights of stairs took us to the attic, which proved so dark and dusty that Alastair went off to borrow a torch. Angela and I sat down on an old chest, after I had brushed off the dust with my handkerchief. We were both tired; it had been a long journey and we needed a good night's rest. I put my arm round her shoulders, and she leaned her head against me. I let my cheek rest against her hair, and closed my eyes. It was very quiet. There was no sound but the hiss of the wind against the gables, and the distant chirruping of a bird. The feeling of her warmth against me was pleasant. And suddenly, without transition, I remembered. Or rather, Esmond remembered. The smell of dust was familiar, and so was the smell of Angela's hair. I realised what had been wrong. When we see new places, the mind finds them strange, and makes an *effort* to grasp them to adjust to them. It is this effort that destroys the instinctive familiarity of memory. I was so anxious to enter into the spirit of this house, to remember it, that I was forcing my own impressions upon it. Now, for a moment, I stopped seeing it as a strange place; I relaxed; and it was as if an old picture had superimposed itself on my new impressions of the house, and then blended with them. I knew this place; I knew the loch and the hills and the glimpse of the sea down the valley. I also knew that Angela had been right. The room we had just seen was the one in which Horace Glenney was murdered. But Angela was wrong in one respect; he had not been shot. He had been stabbed. I felt a curious certainty about this.

Alastair came back with an enormous length of electric wire, and one of those metal cages with a bulb inside that car mechanics use. We attached the bayonet plug to a socket on the floor below, and hung the bulb over a low beam in the attic. Then we surveyed the place. Nothing was more obvious than that it had not been looked at for years. Alastair could not remember ever investigating it in his childhood. Everything was inches deep in dust and a kind of fluffy moss, and one half of the attic was closed off by a series of enormous spider webs that were so thick with dust that they made an opaque curtain. (I have often wondered how spiders make a living in closed attics.) There was obviously plenty to investigate, including a pile of broken bagpipes. As soon as we moved anything the dust choked us. I broke the spider's web with an old metal poker, and looked into the other part. There were all kinds of crates and boxes here, and piles of account books and bundles of paper. I tried undoing one of these, and it began to crumble away, just as if it was paper that had been made brittle by a fire. Other bundles were soaked through with a brown stain that made them illegible.

After half an hour of this, we were all very thirsty, and had been sneezing steadily about once a minute. Franklin Miller came up to investigate, looked around for a minute or two, then went away, after remarking: 'Rather you than me.' Alastair said finally: 'I think I'll go down and have a beer. Anybody coming?' Angela said she was. I decided to stay on for a while, but five minutes was enough. I began to think longingly of a long, cool pint in the local pub. My eyes were smarting, and I was getting impatient, so that every time I moved I disturbed more dust than was necessary. I felt as if I needed a good bath, and as if my hair was full of baby spiders. After pulling a huge

195

chest out of its corner, and struggling to undo a great leather strap that had hardened until it was like steel, I moved over to the trapdoor to get a little fresh air. I sat there, yawning, thinking that if Esmond intended to help me, now was the time to get on with it. A spider walked over my neck, and I stood up so suddenly that I hit my head on a beam, and sat down on the floor, with brilliant lights flashing on and off. I sat there, staring up irritably at the spider that swung on a length of thread, suspended from a tattered diagram of an electrical circuit that was pinned to the beam. It was the last straw. I climbed down the ladder, and spent five minutes in front of an open window, brushing myself down and looking with envy at a man fishing from a boat in the loch.

I reached up to unplug the attic light, when the thought suddenly struck me. Since there was no light in the attic, why was there a circuit diagram there? I went back up the ladder. I picked up a duster, and brushed away the spider's web that covered the sheet of paper. Now I looked closer, I saw why I had mistaken it for a circuit diagram. It was neatly drawn, with various small boxes connected by lines. The boxes had letters written on them; and at the side of the sheet there was another list of letters, with writing beside each one. I suspected what it was as I took it down; my intuition was working again. It was so dusty that I could not read it in the dim light. I went down to the floor below, brushed it carefully with a clean handkerchief, and took it over to the window. It *was* a diagram—a diagram of the attic. If I had thought about it more carefully, I would have noticed that the various chests and bundles in the attic were laid out in a neat and orderly manner that suggested they had been arranged by someone. And whoever had carefully arranged them had made this sketch to act as a key.

Alastair called : 'Are you coming down, Gerard? It's dinner in half an hour.'

I said : 'Who was G. Rullion?'

'George Rullion? He was a sort of steward here in my grandfather's time. He lived to be ninety-one in the gate lodge. Why?'

I showed him the back of the diagram. The neat signature at the bottom read 'G. Rullion'. I ran my finger down the list, and stopped opposite 'K': 'Papers r. to 9th Lord Glenney'. That was Horace Glenney. I turned the paper over. 'K' was a space in a far corner of the attic.

It proved to be an enormous tin chest, and the catch had rusted. We forced it open with the poker. It was jammed with account books, letters, loose papers. Either it had been disturbed since 'G. Rullion' had filled it, or its contents had been thrown in without much attempt at order. I opened a letter. It began 'My dear Mary', and the contents seemed to be about some family problem relating to the sale of a house in Guildford. I dipped into the chest, and opened several others at random. One was addressed to Miss Fiona Guthrie, and began 'My dear Miss Guthrie' and ended: 'yours respectfully'. This was dated from Göttingen in August 1766—that is, a few months before the events he described in his letter to Esmond.

Alastair and I tried to lift the chest down the ladder, but it was too heavy. We decided to leave it. We marched triumphantly down to the drawing room to announce the discovery, and caused a gratifying amount of excitement. I left them to troop off to examine the chest, while I drank a glass of iced lager, then went and had a shower. When I rejoined them, they had piled bundles of papers and ledgers on the hearthrug, and were looking through them. I glanced through their finds, but could see nothing of importance.

Dinner was half an hour late. We ate large amounts of pheasant and woodcock and drank Beaujolais; after which we all became sleepy and retired to the lounge to drink coffee and watch the television news. At nine thirty, I asked if I might use the telephone; I had not contacted Diana since we left London.

The line was a good one; I could hear her as clearly as if she was a mile away. I told her the news—that I had found some of Glenney's papers, but nothing that looked promising. I asked her if she had any news.

'Not much. There's a letter from a girl who wants you to go and live with her in Miami. And a man who wants you to write a book denouncing computers. And there's a note from a man called Corner who says he'd like to meet you next time you're in London.'

' How do you spell it? '

' K—O—R—N—E—R.'

I shouted : ' What ! What's his first name? '

' I can't remember. Shall I find the letter? '

' Yes, please.'

A few minutes later she was back, and reading it to me. It was Otto Körner, the man the Dunkelmans said had been deported. He was living in West Hampstead. He said that he had read my letter about Esmond Donelly in *The Times Literary Supplement* and that he would like to talk to me about him. He gave his telephone number.

When she rang off, I rushed into the drawing room, chortling and waving the paper with Körner's address. I felt this was a major breakthrough—not so much because I expected Körner to know anything about Esmond that I didn't already know; but because I felt the gods were on our side. Miller was almost as pleased as we were about it; he was beginning to get caught up in the ' quest for Esmond Donelly '. He said : ' Why don't you call him right away? ' I needed no urging. Five minutes later, a voice that sounded like a comic German professor was saying heartily :

' It iss very goot that you reeng, Mr Zorme. We haf much to discuss.'

I said : ' I saw the Dunkelmans in London two days ago. They told me you'd returned to Germany? '

' What ! They know that is not true ! You must not trust them...' He went on for ten minutes about the Dunkelmans, frequently relapsing into German. He ended by strongly advising me never to see them again. I wanted to find out what he had against them, so I said mildly that they seemed a harmless couple. He shouted :

' What? Harmless? Why, that man is a murderer.'

' Are you sure? '

' Sure. He is a murderer. He marries a rich girl in Switzerland and boils her body in a glue machine. At this time he is owner of a glue factory. He marries this girl—although he is already married—and after a few weeks, she disappears. Then a doctor analyses a sample of his glue and says it is made of human bones.

But they cannot prove anything. He gets three years in prison for bigamy.'

The story sounded so revolting as to be unbelievable. (In fact, I later discovered that Körner had kept back the most horrible detail—that Klaus had cut off her flesh with a razor in small slivers, and fed it to his pet piranha fish.) I talked to Körner for a few minutes longer, and promised to call on him on my way back to Ireland. He said : 'Good. I hope you stay in London for a few days. I have much to tell you.'

That sounded promising. I went back to give Angela the astonishing information about Klaus Dunkelman, and we ended by describing our visit in detail to our host and hostess. We omitted what happened after.

I was so tired that I went to bed early. But I was awake at seven the next morning. Wearing my overcoat, I sat on a low stool in the attic, and carefully removed every bundle and ledger from the chest, placing loose sheets in a neat pile. I had been searching for half an hour when I came across the first promising find : a bundle of letters tied with a ribbon, and addressed in a round, girlish hand to ' Horace Glenney Esquire, Ferdinandstrasse 9 (der haus von Herr Jülich), Göttingen '. These were letters written by Fiona Guthrie to Horace Glenney, beginning in February 1767 —a month after he had come close to seducing her. They were the letters of a girl in love; moreover, a girl who felt herself to be engaged. The letters are full of gossip about her home, his sister Mary, a dog he had given her. I found them pathetic to read because they made her real—a schoolgirl in love for the first time, a girl who has allowed her lover certain liberties because she can refuse him nothing, and who believes that he thinks about her as continually as she thinks of him. One of them has a note from Mary : ' I hope the girls there are as ugly as donkeys.' Horace seems to have replied at length, and mentioned Esmond with too much enthusiasm, for Fiona writes : ' I am sure your friend Esmond Donelly is a good and [illegible] student, but [I] really cannot admire him without having met him...I would rather hear details of your own doings.' Apparently Horace spent too much time praising Edmond.

The following Christmas (1767) they seem to have had a quarrel about a maidservant: 'I wish I could understand why you should want to touch so greasy a creature': which no doubt explains why Fiona retained her virginity for another year. It must have been a frustrating Christmas for Glenney after the failure of his attempted abduction at Osnabrück.

I laid Fiona's letters by for more careful study, and went on emptying the chest. Nearer the bottom, it seemed to be less disordered, and account books were piled up in one corner. I took all these out and, when the last one had been removed, saw a black metal box buried under bundles of paper. I tugged it out, and found it to be about eighteen inches long and nine inches deep. It was unlocked. I opened it and found myself looking at a handwritten title page: 'Letters from a Mountain', by George Smithson, D.D. I found the notebook I had been using for my Donelly material. As I thought, the published edition of *Letters from a Mountain* was by Reginald Smithson. But the pamphlet on the 'evil Society of the Phoenix' was by Henry Martell and George Smithson, D.D. This was published ten years after the novel. Yet Glenney had changed the author's Christian name. The inference was that Glenney had written the pamphlet before the novel, and had altered the name on the novel so as not to duplicate that already on the pamphlet.

I picked up a handful of sheets at random and glanced through them. And almost immediately, my eye caught the words 'society of the phoenix'. I read the context. There could be no possible doubt; in the original manuscript—and the elisions and alterations made it clear that this *was* the original —Glenney had referred to the 'Society of the Phoenix', *not*, as in the published version, the Order of the Vulture. Obviously, he had decided to change it—or been persuaded to change it. I took out the whole manuscript from the tin. The sheets on which it was written were not regular in size; but the ones at the bottom were notably smaller than the rest. Then I saw they were not part of the manuscript. They were in Esmond Donelly's handwriting. The first one began:

My dear Glenney,

I beg you to believe me when I assure you, upon my most solemn word of honour, that you are wrong to fear for my safety. I can also assure you that you are completely mistaken about the nature of our society. It is not 'secret' in the ordinary signification of that term. Would you call the Royal Society 'secret'? Yet a beggar who found his way into one of its meetings might believe they were talking in some strange language to cloak their true purposes.

I had discovered something that I had often daydreamed about in the past week or so : definite evidence of Esmond's association with the Sect of the Phoenix.

Trembling with excitement—and the damp cold of the attic —I made my way back to my bedroom, clutching the tin box. I used the bedside phone—which our host had thoughtfully installed—to ask the kitchen if I could have a light breakfast sent to my room. No one disturbed me, although I heard Alastair pass my door on his way up to the attic. And during the next hour I learned more of Esmond Donelly than I had learned in all my weeks of research.

I shall not quote these letters in full, for obvious reasons of space : they would occupy some fifty pages. The story I pieced together from them was briefly this. Esmond had learned of the existence of the Sect of the Phoenix from two sources : Rousseau, and Restif de la Bretonne. The latter was himself a member, as Esmond discovered later. Esmond had already evolved ideas that were close to theirs, as we have seen—and as these letters make very clear. He knew the Sect existed, but he had no idea where to seek it. So he brought out the *Observations upon France and Switzerland,* with the device of the phoenix on the cover, and the brief account of their history attributed to a Lutheran pastor (who never existed). We know what happened then. He received the device of the phoenix in the mail. And who was his first actual contact with the Sect? Absurdly and amusingly enough, it was the girl who first initiated him into the delights of love : his sister's maid Marie, or Minou. Minou had continued her career of ardent nymphomania in Paris, and had become the mistress of a member of the Sect, who saw in her disinterested worship of

201

the male genitals the true spirit of a devotee.

Glenney and Esmond were close friends. But Glenney lacked the essential quality of a member of the Sect : the disinterested pursuit of sex as a supra-personal experience. Esmond suggested him as a member; anl Glenney spent two days in Paris with Esmond and Abdallah Mumin (who appears in *Letters from a Mountain* as Abdallah Saba—Glenney chooses as a surname that of the Grand Master of the Order of Assassins). What happened is not clear, except that Glenney quarrelled with Esmond and left in a rage. Two months later, he and Esmond met again in London, and made up their quarrel—largely, apparently, at Glenney's instigation. It was on this visit that they met Mary and Charlotte Ingestre, the daughters of the Earl of Flaxstead, who were staying with Esmond's second cousin, Elizabeth Montagu, and they made a joking compact to wed the two girls, and to share their favours between them. At some point, Glenney induced Esmond to tell him something about the Sect of the Phoenix. In London, they also met Restif again—and the result was another quarrel, or rather, another outburst of fury from Horace Glenney. (All this confirmed my earlier guess that there was, on Glenney's side, a strong homosexual element in the relationship.) Glenney hired a Grub Street hack to do his research, and wrote the pamphlet 'On the Evil Society of the Phoenix'. Esmond got wind of this, and persuaded Glenney not to publish. Glenney agreed, and devoted the autumn of 1772 to the seduction of Mary Ingestre, while Esmond laid successful siege to Charlotte. But in November there was a further quarrel; Glenney returned to Scotland, and wrote the *Letters from a Mountain* between December and the following February. He wrote to Esmond to tell him that, while his promise bound him not to publish the pamphlet, he felt that fiction was a different matter altogether. (And what was all this but an attempt to claim Esmond's attention at any cost?) The result was the long letter from Esmond that I found in the back of the manuscript.

For many years, you and I have been friends—nay, brothers. Many's the bottle we have emptied together, and many's the wench whose virtue we have loosened by a

202

judicial mutuality of shakes and caresses. Why, then, do you choose this time to doubt me and accuse me of double dealing? What has happened to the brotherhood we swore in the inn at Heidelberg, when I had run a loutish fellow through the arm, and you had slashed t'other above the eyes and so blinded him?

These reminders of past friendship, of meals eaten together and women seduced together, sound false coming from Esmond. Horace Glenney was of coarser stuff, and he knew it. What he was now doing was tantamount to blackmailing Esmond, and both of them knew it. Their relation had been that of master and disciple. They came together when the brilliant Esmond had just discovered the delights of the female body, and he preached his gospel of seduction with the fervour of a revolutionary. We have seen how Glenney responded—in the episode of Fiona and Mary. From the list of names Esmond mentions, we can infer that the two of them shared a great many mistresses at Göttingen. But Esmond was not fundamentally interested in sex *as such*. For him, sex was the key to a mystery, and it was the mystery that interested him. Temperamentally, Horace Glenney bore many resemblances to Casanova—whom he met once in Utrecht. He liked the good things of life, and he loved women. He could not understand why Esmond, his master in the art of seduction, should not live in England's capital and take up the Hell Fire Club where Sir Francis Dashwood had left off. For Glenney, this London—of Sheridan, Wilkes, Dashwood—was the most fascinating place in the world : cockfights, horse racing, bare-fist boxing (a fairly new sport), nights at Drury Lane, the company of beautiful women. What more did Esmond want? Why had he become such a spoilsport? Their joint seduction of the Ingestre sisters revealed that their partnership was as irresistible as ever. And who was this formidable Arab who spoke perfect French and who seemed inseparable from Esmond? When Esmond finally confessed that the man belonged to the Sect of the Phoenix, Glenney was appalled. Esmond had often spoken to him about this brotherhood; it had fascinated him ever since Rousseau had mentioned it. Glenney had never really believed in its existence.

203

And now Esmond was a member! *That* explained everything. Esmond was no longer a carefree seducer because he had fallen into the hands of a secret society run by sinister foreigners, of whom this giant and scarred Arab was an example. Glenney's reaction was a mixture of fear, anxiety, and jealousy—with the last predominating. He talked openly around London about the Sect of the Phoenix—this must be where Johnson picked up the gossip about Esmond—and wrote his pamphlet. If Esmond had been less loyal, he would have returned to Ireland and broken with Glenney. Instead, he tried to placate him. Or perhaps it would be truer to say that he tried to make Glenney understand the changes that had taken place in him since their Göttingen days.

I have always been of the opinion that this world is at bottom magical, and that if we are not magicians, the fault lies in ourselves. Diderot makes d'Alembert say: 'Why am I what I am? Because it is inevitable that I should be.' I have always asked myself: 'Why am I what I am? For it seems to me the most arbitrary thing in the world.' I might be anything or anywhere. My form is no more fixed than is that of a wisp of smoke rising from a fire. On a still morning, the smoke may seem as stable as a column of marble; but we know that the slightest breath of wind will change its form and disperse it into the atmosphere. I sat one morning on a bridge and watched the cataract that descends near Mont Blanc; and was struck suddenly by the reflection that men are surrounded by forces they fail to understand, yet have the vanity to suppose themselves as enduring as the rocks. In the days when men were hunters and fighters, they had no time to stagnate; they understood their own nature; they did not mistake smoke for marble. And in that respect, they understood the world better than M. Diderot or M. Voltaire understands it. Only a fool would wish to return to the state of Numidian savages; and as to myself, I am neither a hunter nor a fighter. But I had long observed that when my battering ram sinks into its predestined home, -whether it be between the thighs of a titled lady or a stable-maid, it becomes self-evident that this world is rich, warm and infinite. The blindness falls from my eyes, the heaviness from my senses, and I see at once that man has allowed himself to be robbed of his birthright. But if this magic vision is my birthright, why should I be content to accept it in disjoined fragments, as a dog snaps up scraps of meat tossed upon the floor by its master? It is mine; shall I not seize it and hold it?

This I have always believed. And I know enough of theology to know that this birthright is that which was lost to men through Adam's sin. But how may we hope to find that which was lost unless the search be systematic? I have always believed there must be a *way* to recover this lost power. Now I have discovered that there are men who have devoted their lives to the search for this way, and can teach me something of their methods. Can you truly believe that such men are evil, that their intention is to ensnare my immortal soul? And what would it signify even if this were true? For neither you nor I believe that the soul can be ensnared, except by dullness and too much concern with the unimportant.

No, I am after more important quarry than the maiden-heads of infatuated girls.

But what exactly did the Sect of the Phoenix *do*? Esmond expresses its basic aim in one sentence : ' Our purpose is not to degrade and pollute religious feelings with venery, but to raise venery to the level of a religious feeling.' But how was this to be done? Esmond is deliberately obscure; he had reason to distrust Glenney. But it is clear that when he came to Golspie— in April 1773—he told Glenney a great deal more than he was willing to set down in writing; and Glenney, in turn, wrote down some of this material with the intention of using it eventually in his book. I think it is impossible to doubt that Glenney always intended to publish the book. I personally am reluctant to condemn him. The novel is a remarkable achievement, in spite of its absurdities; one might almost say that it constitutes Horace Glenney's chief claim upon the interest of posterity. Can a writer be blamed for deciding not to destroy his best work?

From Glenney's notes—which I shall summarise rather than quote at length—it seems clear that the Sect of the Phoenix had much in common with the Rosicrucians or Freemasons. There was a Grand Master, who was a kind of pope, and who was elected by a committee known as 'the dominoes', presumably because they wore hoods with a short cloak, of the kind worn at masquerades. Each country had only one domino—in France, it was the writer Choderlos de Laclos, author of *Liaisons Dangereuses*. Esmond later became the domino for Ireland.

What is quite clear, both from Glenney's notes and from *Letters from a Mountain*, is that there was always a certain basic difference of opinion within the Sect upon a fundamental point of doctrine. The Sect believed that man approaches the sense of the world as a 'magical mystery' more frequently through the sexual act than through religion or art. (The important word here is *frequently*. No one ever denied that the ecstasies of mystics may reach greater intensity than anything to be achieved through sex. But they are rare. On the other hand, man can approach the sexual mysteries every day.)

All members of the Sect seemed to be agreed that mere uncontrolled promiscuity leads to boredom. But there was a considerable difference of opinion about the remedy. The tradition of the Sect—dating back four centuries—insisted that women should be treated as vessels of a religious mystery. The Hegumenos of Southern Russia brought this idea to its fullest development in the late sixteenth century. On the other hand, the Huldeians, a nomadic German sect (whose name derives from the Teutonic goddess of marriage), were closer to those early 'monks' who committed rape as often as possible. They believed that sex is most intoxicating when it is violent and abrupt. In the eighteenth century, to be a Huldeian meant simply that one aimed at penetrating as many vaginas as possible, preferably virgins. It amounted basically to a cult of seduction. Horace Glenney was a Huldeian without knowing it, and so was Esmond in his early days. Laclos was a Huldeian; so were the Grand Master, Abdallah Yahya, and his successor Hendrik van Griss. The man who was responsible for Esmond's initiation, Abdallah

Mumin, belonged to the tradition of the Hegumenos. The original Hegumenos (named after their first leader, the renegade 'hegumenos' or abbot of an order of Basilian monks) chose a beautiful young girl as a kind of pythoness, and another dozen girls as her handmaidens; these latter were also priestesses. The women were worshipped as divinities; but the males of the sect were allowed a certain amount of contact with the divinities, which could even culminate in sexual intercourse. In order to qualify for this, the male had to fast for three days out of every week for many months beforehand, and go through a number of well-defined stages of approach to the mystery. If he could lie on the steps of the 'temple' naked on a winter night—from dusk until dawn—he was allowed to act as a servant to three of the priestesses for an hour every day, bringing their food and cleaning their rooms. He was allowed to eat the left-over scraps of food. After more tests, involving sticking slivers of wood under his nails and burning himself on the tender part of his forearm, he was allowed to become a 'body servant' to another three, laundering and sewing their clothes and washing their hair. Their physical waste products were regarded as sacred, and it was his job to take them into the depth of the forest and bury them in a place where no other males of the tribe could find them. He was allowed to smear himself with excrement and wash it off with their urine—a privilege envied by all the other males of the tribe. The mingling of the worshipper's semen with the waste products of the 'holy ones' was regarded as the first degree of union with the divinity. If he could pass increasingly difficult and painful tasks, he was allowed an increasing number of privileges, until he might be one of the eight men who were the body servants of the Holy One herself. In that case, he might be the one who was chosen by lot to participate with her in the ceremonies that took place on the night of the full moon following the harvest, and to have intercourse with her, dressed in the robe of a bull. The loins of the priestess, and the phallus of her worshipper, were carefully dried on a sacred napkin after this ceremony, and the napkin was divided into eight parts and given to the eight servants, who then wore it attached to the head of the penis for the remainder of their term of office.

It can be seen, I think, that the basic idea of the hegumenos was to try to build up a state of sexual frenzy combined with religious adoration, and that each painful and difficult stage was designed to prevent the aspirant from becoming in any way relaxed or casual about his task. If he lost his erection at any time in the presence of the priestesses, he would be flogged and sent back to the tribe in disgrace. This meant that he came to rely a great deal upon his imagination. It will also be noted that his position was really that of a maidservant; he was treated as a woman, so that he would feel humiliated, and his sexuality would become furtive. The whole idea was that sex should never be treated as something ' above board ', normal, to be taken for granted. Every object associated with the ceremonies became sacred and fearful—and also sexually exciting. The vagina of the priestess became an ultimate sacred goal, and the eight servants were envied by all the males for their possession of the fragment of napkin stained with her moisture.

Esmond preferred the Hegumenos doctrine to that of the Hudeians. And much of the long letter to Glenney is taken up with argument against the kind of seduction that Esmond had once advocated. He keeps repeating that it has no lasting effect; it leads to satiety.

The next episode is one of the most interesting—and worst documented—in the Esmond–Glenney relationship. It can be pieced together from several sources, including letters from Esmond—those we found in the trunk in the attic—letters and diaries belonging to Horace Glenney, and letters written by Mary and Maureen Ingestre. These will all be quoted at length in the forthcoming volume. The story that emerges is as follows :

When Esmond and Horace Glenney had their reconciliation in London in October 1772, Esmond was staying at the house of his cousin Sophia, in St James's. She was now Sophie Blackwood, having married Sir Edmund Blackwood, a wealthy brewer, whose father had been one of Handel's backers. Lady Mary and Charlotte Ingestre were staying with Elizabeth Montagu, the bluestocking, who was instructing them in astronomy. Esmond was fascinated by the delicious and innocent Charlotte, then $19\frac{1}{2}$. Glenney was impressed by Lady Mary, brilliant, beautiful and more self-possessed than her sister, although she was a year her junior. (This is typical of the different characters of the two men; Esmond, clever and dominant, preferred innocence and sweetness; Glenney, not entirely sure of himself, was dazzled by the more intellectual of the two.)

It seems likely that Glenney would never have aimed so high without Esmond's encouragement; he felt more comfortable seducing his social inferiors. What impressed Esmond was that most eligible men were shy of the Ingestre girls because of their reputation for brilliance and wealth. The sporting set made crude jests about them, and were secretly overawed by them, and the respectable young men—who probably sounded and behaved rather like Jane Austen's Darcy or Mr Bingley—paid them grave compliments and tried to start intellectual conversations. Esmond's response was simpler. He thought them both delicious, and remarked to Glenney that a man could spend an exquisite night between the two of them.

Glenney knew that when Esmond said a thing like this, it was not mere wishful thinking. If there was any man in London who could seduce the Ingestre sisters, it was Esmond. He had the ideal qualification for seducing intellectual girls—a good mind. He and Lichtenberg had been the two best mathematicians of their generation at Göttingen. The Ingestre sisters actually knew Lichtenberg—they had been introduced to him by no less a person than the King, at Hampton Court, and had examined the King's great telescope under Lichtenberg's supervision. Obviously, Esmond would have no trouble seeing a great deal of the Ingestre sisters, since they were staying with Sophia's cousin Elizabeth. Esmond's own telescope—made by Schwarmz of Leyden—was an exceptionally powerful one. He set it up in an attic room in Sophia Blackwood's house, pinned his diagrams on the walls, and invited Elizabeth Montagu and her two charming guests to come and study the stars with himself and Lichtenberg. Elizabeth Montagu had not met Lichtenberg; she was anxious to do so. Esmond had the foresight to have a small meal prepared in his ' observatory '—pheasant, woodcock, capon, an Irish ham, and various other delicacies. The ladies asked many questions, and peered through the telescope for over an hour. Then the conversation shifted to philosophy, and Esmond and Lichtenberg discussed Leibniz, Voltaire, Hume and the inaugural dissertation of the brilliant German, Immanuel Kant, in which he argued that reality is unknowable, and that the senses dictate the form of all our knowledge of phenomena. (The *Critique*, which developed these doctrines, would not be published for another nine years.) Elizabeth Montagu was deeply impressed; she said she had never heard such profound and disturbing discourse—no, not even from Burke, Garrick or Dr Johnson himself. It was heady stuff, this German critical philosophy. The effect was achieved. Elizabeth Montagu later remarked that Esmond was one of the most eligible bachelors in London. And Esmond was already convinced that he had made a favourable impression on Charlotte. He took her hand for a moment on the pretext of helping her on a dark corner of the stairway, and she allowed him to retain it several seconds longer than necessary.

Horace Glenney was not present on this occasion. We know exactly why, for Esmond explains in one of the letters included in the manuscript of *Letters from a Mountain*. Esmond knew that Glenney would not make an immediate impact on the ladies, being rather shy. (What Esmond obviously means is that Glenney would hardly be noticed in company that included Lichtenberg, Elizabeth Montagu and himself.) His entrance had to be prepared. Esmond found out what Mary Ingestre had been reading, and Glenney spent twenty-four hours skipping through it and preparing brilliant remarks. Esmond rode in the park with the sisters two days after their evening with the telescope, and told them about the delicate, shy, noble character of his friend Glenney. He told Mary that Glenney had been brought up in a strictly religious manner, and that his acquaintance with German philosophy was undermining his faith; he invented a particularly moving anecdote about Glenney in Chartres cathedral, asking with tears in his eyes: ' Is all this beauty a monument to man's ability to deceive himself? ' So when he took Glenney to call on Elizabeth Montagu a few days later, there was no need to encourage Mary to take an interest in him. She took the first opportunity to get him into a quiet corner, where she could question him earnestly about his doubts. The meeting was more successful than either of them could have hoped; she agreed to ride in the park with Glenney the next day, and spent the night storing up arguments from Butler and Tillotson on the evidence for divine workmanship in Nature. Glenney, in turn, did a certain amount of spadework for Esmond, hinting at secret sorrows and lost love. There can be no doubt that they made an impressive team.

Esmond was ideally placed for spending a great deal of time with Charlotte. Elizabeth Montagu was his second cousin, and the girls had become friendly with Sophia Blackwood. No one thought it unusual if Charlotte walked from Mayfair to St James's to call on Sophia and discuss what they should wear at Lady Sandwich's autumn ball. And if Sophia was not at home, why should she not spend an hour discussing astronomy and metaphysics with Sophia's cousin?

By mid-October, Charlotte was admitting to Mary that she would be inclined to accept if Esmond proposed to her. Mary passed this on to Glenney, who told Esmond. He was surprised when Esmond did not seem particularly pleased at the news. But Esmond was clear-sighted enough to see that the situation was developing too fast, and was beginning to look dangerous. If Sophia and Elizabeth and Mary had all set their minds on matchmaking, he would probably find himself engaged before the end of the season. It was time for a temporary retreat.

It was at this point that Horace Glenney decided to elaborate his story of the 'lost love'. He confided to Mary that Esmond had been engaged to the daughter of a Swiss pastor. Esmond's father had objected to the idea of an alliance with the daughter of a Calvinist parson and threatened to disinherit him. Like Gibbon, Esmond 'sighed as a lover, but obeyed as a son'. They had been separated now for over a year, and she had written to tell Esmond that she was engaged to a wine merchant of Geneva. But Esmond had recently heard that this was untrue. She was still unmarried and unbetrothed, perhaps waiting for Esmond...

Esmond was furious when Glenney told him what he'd done. He had no wish to make Charlotte miserable and jealous; he only wanted to disappear for long enough to discourage the matchmakers. Now they all believed he meant to return to Switzerland

211

to take another look at his lost love. It was no good denying she existed; no one would believe him.

Riding with him in Marylebone Fields, Charlotte asked him to stay long enough to partner her at Lady Sandwich's ball. Esmond knew this would be fatal; he explained that this would be impossible. Charlotte returned home in tears. The next day, Mary Ingestre called on Sophia, and the two of them asked him to stay; Sophia said it was absurd to leave London at the height of the season, and that his business in Ireland could wait. Esmond tried to put them off by saying that he would return to London as soon as his business was completed, but it was no good. Charlotte was convinced that if he left London now he would never come back to her.

She called the following afternoon—when Sophia was out—and tried coaxing him. Esmond explained apologetically that he had to leave on boring family business, connected with the estate. She asked him pointblank what the business was, and why it could not wait. Then she tried tears, and Esmond found himself petting her and comforting her. He was twenty-four and very susceptible; she was very beautiful. Some years later, in a letter to Laclos, he wrote:

I have always been of the opinion that the most innocent and virtuous girls are those whom Nature has schooled best in the art of seduction; and if they are in love, they are almost irresistible. The only time I was ever seduced was by such a virgin, a foolish friend had made her believe I intended to rush to marry another woman to whom I had given proofs of my esteem. She came to persuade me one day when I was alone in the house. Until this time I had not so much as kissed her. First I tried honesty; I told her that my friend was a fool and that I had no intention of going to Switzerland. She asked why, in that case, I could not stay a few weeks longer. Then she cried, and I took her in my arms. When I kissed her, she stopped crying; then began to kiss me with such passion that I began to wonder if she was as virtuous as I had supposed. My common sense told me it was time to stop, but when I tried to calm her,

212

she stopped my mouth with kisses and clung the harder. Then she said she felt she was going to faint, and sat down on a sofa; I said I would go to fetch water, but she begged me to stay and sit by her. Now would you not consider it reasonable, under these circumstances, to make the assumption that she was innocent of the effect she was having upon the organ of my adoration? My logic told me that if I pressed the discovery upon her, she might be shocked into modesty and prudence. Therefore, as I knelt with my head upon her breast, I slipped my hand into the open bosom of her dress and loosened one of her breasts from its corsage. When she made no protest, I understood that she permitted it because she felt she was winning me from the maid in Geneva. I became curious to see how far this reasoning would carry her. I transferred my lips to her feet; she was wearing no stockings and her legs were smooth and soft. When my head reached her knees, she twined her fingers in my hair, and I thought this was to prevent further advances, so I moved on with determination. But she made no attempt to hinder me, even when I pushed up her skirts to her waist and uncovered a downy mount and lips that were still undeveloped. I pressed my lips to this nether mouth, although she wriggled, and kept them there until I had moistened it with my spittle. Then I moved up, upon her, and began to loosen my trousers. She now said 'No, no' and moved her hips sideways, but otherwise made no determined attempt to hinder me. I unsheathed my weapon, pressed its head against the lips I had prepared for it, and began to move it up and down. When I felt the narrow orifice below me, I thrust gently, felt the mouth open slightly, and then felt myself tightly gripped by her. At this point, it was impossible to go further, and she lay there and gasped whenever I moved. I felt my climax come upon me, and withdrew in time to shed my dew upon the soft down at the base of her belly. Now she lay there, holding me tight, knowing now that she need fear no desertion, and might reasonably expect a proposal. I felt her victory had been gained too easily; therefore after I had recovered my vital powers, I went to the door and locked it, threw more logs on the fire; then went back to her—she was standing looking at a telescope that stood on a tripod—and began undoing the strings of her dress. She protested, but I ignored her, for I felt that if she intended to become my wife, she should begin upon her duties immediately. The protests were not seriously meant, for she allowed me to remove every article of clothing. I then made her lie in front of the fire, and went to work upon her breasts with a will. When I tried to introduce my tongue into the temple of love, she seemed shocked by such strange attentions; but soon grew accustomed to them. Thereupon, I tried again, and again had no more success than a child trying to push down a wall. After spending again, this time inside the cramped chamber, I allowed her to dress. We went downstairs and rang for tea, and spent half an hour talking of marriage. After this, since we were still left alone, I told her to come back to my room for one more try. She came unwillingly, being sore. This time I laid her down with her skirts above her waist, anointed the gates of the temple with a little butter that I had brought up with me, and pressed in upon her. She made it more difficult by wincing from me whenever I thrust, so half the force was lost. Then I whispered to her to open her knees wide and press them against my hips. And as I drove forward, so also did she, throwing herself upon me like a warrior falling on his sword. Then I felt myself tightly gripped, so I almost wondered if I should ever withdraw; she cried out, and two more hard thrusts had me buried deep in her, my whole member gripped tight from the head to the root.

And so we know how the apparently impossible came about, and Lady Charlotte Ingrestre yielded her maidenhood to a man who was determined to reject it. Esmond's letters to Laclos seldom enter into so much physical detail; both men were more interested in discussing the psychological peculiarities of women. At twenty-four, Esmond was not experienced enough to divine that there was a distinctly masochistic element about Charlotte Ingestre; she wanted to be mastered and taken by a man who

214

ordered her to lie down and open her legs. She became Esmond's mistress, and followed him around in much the same manner that Lady Caroline Lamb later followed Lord Byron. It is equally indicative of her yielding temperament that, having become his mistress, she ceased to talk about marriage; again, her masochism revelled in her anomalous position.

What happened next must be summarised briefly. Gossip about Esmond and his daughter may have reached the ears of the Earl of Flaxstead; he told her one day that he had selected a husband for her—a respectable Scottish baronet who spent his days hunting on his moors. She said she wanted to marry Esmond; her father told her to forget any such ambition; Esmond was a nobody, the son of an Irish landowner without enough money to maintain a London house. There were scenes and hysteria; she was taken back to the family home at Weston upon Trent, where she fell ill for a few weeks. Mary Ingrestre wrote to Sophia, asking her to advise Esmond to return to Ireland, because while he was in London, her father was determined to keep Charlotte away from it. Esmond went. Oddly enough, Mary became hostile to her sister after this crisis; perhaps she resented the ease with which this gentle, sweet-tempered girl had captured Esmond, who would have been altogether better suited by Lady Mary.

And what was the scandal about Lady Mary that the Misses Donelly had mentioned to me? It was that Mary preferred Esmond to Horace Glenney, whom she married in August 1773. This was largely Glenney's own fault. Having installed his wife in the west wing of Golspie House, and invited Charlotte to come and stay, he lost no time in asking Esmond. Esmond accepted promptly, and his relations with Charlotte resumed immediately; she spent every night in his room, returning to her own at dawn.

The sequel is also described in a letter to Laclos, in which Esmond criticises an episode from Prévost's *Memoirs and Adventures of a Man of Quality* describing how a virtuous lady got her maid to sleep with her lover, so she could preserve her chastity. Esmond says this is absurd, unless the lover was drunk.

Some years ago, a friend and I were drinking port in front

of the fire, long after his wife and her sister had retired for the night. We fell to discussing the different temperaments of the two women, and he remarked that he believed he would have been happier if he had married the sister. We discussed the way in which their temperaments were reflected in their lovemaking, and soon discovered that the sisters had one thing in common : if asleep, they would allow themselves to be made love to without fully awaking. This suggested to us the idea that we might try what would happen if I were to get into bed with his wife, and he with her sister, my mistress. The idea seemed to us amusing, and we tried it. I went along to his room, which was in darkness, and very cold; I undressed and slipped into bed. He had told me that if he desired to take her, he gently pulled her on to her back by her shoulder, pulled open her thighs by laying his hand upon her knee, and then mounted her without further caresses. This I did. Her back was turned to me; when I was warm, I took hold of her shoulder and turned her over. She gave a low moan of protest, but lay still. I raised her night gown, which was of silk, caressed between her thighs for a moment, then moved on to her. She was soft and warm, and I scarcely moved, afraid to wake her, enjoying the contrast of her with her sister. Then she moved her buttocks slightly and raised her belly; this undid me, and I gushed inside her. When I withdrew, she turned over again, and seemed to sleep peacefully. Half an hour later, I did the same again, but this time determined to get the most of the pleasure, and so moved up and down on her. This time she responded, moving with me, until we achieved our ecstasy together. We said nothing, and she slept again. An hour later I woke and felt her hand on me, caressing my priapus with skilful fingered delicacy; we came together quickly, and went at it for a long time. When it was over, she whispered : ' I wonder if Charlotte is enjoying her change as much as I am? ' They were the first words either had spoken. Before dawn, I went back to my own bed, and the next day learned that Charlotte had also detected my friend after their first coming-together, although she had been asleep while he possessed her.

What Esmond does not mention in this letter is that as a result of their night together, Mary began to treat Esmond openly as a second husband—to Charlotte's indignation. Now they had spent a night together, Mary no longer felt the need to hide her feelings for Esmond. She had always been fascinated by him—ever since that first meeting when Esmond and Lichtenberg had explained Kant's critical philosophy. Her relation with her husband was entirely different; she was fond of him but could not admire him. And she was aware that his mind—such as it was—had been almost entirely formed by Esmond and, to a lesser extent, by Lichtenberg. When Esmond returned to London—he had by this time bought the tall, narrow house in Fleet Street, close to Dr Johnson's—Mary followed him, staying with Sophia Blackwood; and soon it was common gossip that Esmond slept with Charlotte and Mary in the same bed. There is no evidence for this, although it is likely that Esmond continued to be the lover of both women. We know that on November 23, 1773, Esmond wrote to the Earl of Flaxstead, making a formal proposal for the hand of his daughter, and that on the 28th he received a cold and brief note declaring that Charlotte was already betrothed to 'a gentleman of Kent'. It is not known what pressure the Earl brought to bear on his daughter—who was still under age; Charlotte later told Mary that he had threatened to have her head shaved and send her to a Belgian convent. Two days after Christmas, Charlotte was quietly married to Sir Russell Frazer, of Sevenoaks, a gentleman whom Walpole refers to as 'imbecilic'. The Earl is said to have remarked to the father of Thomas Creevey, the diarist: 'Now she is off my hands, I don't care how she compromises herself.' Creevey's story of a duel between Esmond and Charlotte's father seems to be one of those inventions whose source cannot be traced. If the 'imbecilic' Frazer knew the story of his wife's infatuation for Esmond, he had the sense not to be jealous; for Esmond and Glenney were frequent guests at Blades House, Sevenoaks, during the 1780s. Charlotte came to him with a handsome dowry, and it was said that Frazer kept a French mistress in Dover; so it may have been one of those typically civilised arrangements of the eighteenth century. Sophia Blackwood described Charlotte a year after her marriage as 'blooming and very happy'.

The story of Maureen Ingestre, the youngest of the sisters, is probably the most interesting of the three, and is unfortunately the worst documented. Boswell quotes Horace Walpole as saying that it must be a delightful experience to have had the love of three such beautiful sisters, and that it is an experience that every man should have once in a lifetime. When Mary married Horace Glenney, Maureen was only thirteen,and her father refused to allow her to go to London to stay with Elizabeth Montagu, no doubt having heard what had happened to his other daughters there. But once Mary was married, it was impossible to forbid Maureen to stay at Golspie. Besides, oddly enough, the Earl held Horace Glenney in high esteem, and in 1881, when Glenney succeeded to the title, described him as 'the kindest and most delightful man in England'. This is an aspect of Glenney that should be borne in mind. As Esmond's Leporello, he appears in an unfortunate light; but when not wracked by jealousy, or trying to emulate Esmond, he seems to have been a charming and kindly man, who became increasingly a typical member of the sporting aristocracy. (Another side of his nature is his interest in Scottish folk-tales. His conviction that Ossian was a forgery led him to seek out the genuine folk-tales of the highlands, which he combined together, rather in the manner of Lönnrot's Kalevala collection, into a narrative called *Reliques of the North* [1793].)

In the letters at the back of Glenney's manuscript, there is only one hint of what took place between Esmond and Maureen Ingestre. In the second letter, Esmond writes : 'A German tribe of the Upper Danube holds that certain virgins are sacred, and should be regarded as the holy receptacle of the mysteries of creation...Such women may be known by a certain dreaminess in the eyes, a softness of expression combined with the natural grace of a goddess. When men encounter such women, they have only one duty : to worship; and in worshipping, to confirm the goddess in her divinity.' And by this, in the margin, there is a scrawl in Glenney's hand : ' He cd have [illegible] Maureen Ing.'

And this, for the moment, was the sum of my knowledge of Maureen Ingestre. Later that day, Alastair, Angela and myself went through every item in the chest from the attic; but we found nothing more to our purpose. I shall write elsewhere of the manuscript of Esmond's early novel *Allardyce and Leontia*, written when he was nineteen, at Göttingen, and the long poem *In Memory of Charles Churchill*, written at about the same time. Both these were found in the library at Golspie House, and they were no doubt passed on to Horace Glenney junior in accordance with Esmond's will. The latter is by no means without merit. Charles Churchill was one of the best-known poets of his period; a clergyman, satirist, bruiser (he had a tremendous physique), member of the Hell Fire Club, he died at the age of thirty-three of a fever contracted when visiting Wilkes in France. Esmond met him, and apparently admired him, and in the manuscript of *Letters from a Mountain*, ' Churchill ' [*sic*] is mentioned as ' one of the most notorious of the Society of the Phoenix '. If this is true—and from all accounts of Churchill, it is very likely —then it raises the interesting possibility that Churchill was the first person to tell Esmond of the Sect.

I was so excited by the discovery of these further materials that I wrote a long letter to Fleisher from Golspie House, out-lining my discoveries so far—including the information about the Sect of the Phoenix—and suggesting that I might write this present book as an introductory volume to Esmond's *Memoirs*. There were still many unanswered questions : how had Horace Glenney died? what became of Maureen Ingestre? above all, what happened to Esmond in his later years? But these could be left for later researchers.

Before I left Golspie House, two days later, I had discovered partial answers to two of these questions. We decided to leave at about ten o'clock in the morning, to try to get to Edinburgh late at night. We had breakfast early; and then, while Angela did some last-minute packing, I looked around the library. Many of the books had been spoiled by damp at some time, and someone had made a pile of these in one corner of the room, perhaps with the intention of having them re-bound. I was aware that this room must have looked much the same when Esmond and Horace Glenney did their late-night drinking here—and decided to exchange beds. I tried several times to place my mind in a passive state, to try to ' receive ' Esmond, but the house was too busy and I could not concentrate. Then, very suddenly, it came; the library became familiar in an unfamiliar manner—this is the only way I can describe it. Our feeling for places is made up mostly of memories and associations. Esmond's memories of this library were very different from mine. So, in a sense, it became a different place. And I found myself looking at a high shelf in the corner, close to the window. I went across to this. Already, ' Esmond ' had faded. The shelf was empty, and the woodwork behind it was warped and stained with damp. It struck me that if there had been books on this shelf, they might now be among the piles in the corner of the room. I went over to them and arranged them in a row on the floor, with the spines turned upwards. None of the titles seemed at all interesting : sermons, a few travel books, Cowper's poems, some Scott; even a Tauchnitz edition of Henry James. I began opening them at random, glancing at title pages. I picked up *An Account of the Sandwich Islands* that was badly mildewed, the pages corrugated with damp. And as I looked at the title page, I knew I had found what I was looking for. It was by Maureen Ingestre. It was printed by Murray, Byron's publisher, in London in 1812, by which time Maureen would have been fifty-two. The book was dedicated ' To the memory of Horace, Lord Glenney '. Underneath this, someone had written : ' was stabbed in the right eye by unknown assassin, July 28, 1796 '. The words, badly stained, were hardly legible.

So when we left Golspie House that morning, I knew two more things about the Glenney family : that Horace *had* been stabbed, and not shot; and that Maureen Ingestre travelled in the East in her later years, visiting Japan, Australia and the Sandwich Islands. I later ascertained that the words written under the dedication were in the handwriting of Glenney's son.

I was well pleased with myself; the visit had not yielded as much as I might have hoped; but everything it *had* yielded was valuable. Alastair and Angela were also happy. They had not found the rest of the Donelly journals; but they had found a Bible worth twenty thousand pounds.

The knowledge that Glenney had been stabbed provided material for speculation, particularly in view of the postscript to Esmond's first letter : ' I beg you to destroy, or at least suppress this work, not only in the name of our old friendship, but of your safety, and mine.' Could Esmond have been in any danger from the Sect? Could it be that Glenney's death was the result of his decision to ignore Esmond's warning? There was at least one odd feature of the murder : that it took place in a small room on the second floor. If Glenney was killed in bed, why was he not in one of the large bedrooms overlooking the loch? I found myself wishing that I could contact Esmond and ask him; but no amount of concentration gave me the clue I needed.

We arrived back at Alastair's London flat at two o'clock on a Friday afternoon. It was a superb day; in fact, slightly too warm for comfort; I found myself wishing I'd brought summer clothes. I was thinking of Esmond—whose body had been mouldering in the family vault for more than a hundred years—and wishing I could somehow share the day with him.

Alastair had business in the City; Angela and I ate a late lunch together. It is impossible for two people to become suddenly and violently intimate, and not continue to think of one another, in some sense, as lovers; and the kind of warmth that had grown up between us was not unlike that of husband and wife. I found myself telling her about these odd experiences of ' being ' Esmond, and how the last one had led me to the finding of the book by Maureen Ingestre. I expected her to find it interesting, perhaps amusing, but not really credible; after all, I *had* been soaking myself rather intensely in Esmond, so it was natural that I should feel like him sometimes. Her reaction surprised me; she was perplexed and worried. I said :

' It's nothing to get excited about. I find it rather interesting.'

I found myself arguing the rationalist point of view I had expected her to take. She said that Alastair had talked about ' feeling strange ' at Golspie, and wondered if his bedroom was haunted.

Half an hour after lunch, when I was examining the manuscript of Glenney's novel, she said:

'Do you think he's trying to tell you something?'

'Who?'

'Esmond.'

I tried to explain that I didn't have a feeling of Esmond's *presence*; I simply saw things through his eyes, as if I *were* Esmond. You don't try to tell yourself something.

She said: 'I think we ought to ring that Dr Körner.'

I had intended to, but I meant to leave it another twenty-four hours. I wanted to spend a quiet evening going through the various papers we had brought with us. Angela said:

'Let me ring him.'

'All right. If you want to.'

Ten minutes later, she said:

'I've invited him over for a drink at six o'clock.'

At about half past five, the phone rang; Angela took the call. She put her hand over the receiver and said:

'It's Anna Dunkelman...'

I shook my head heavily, to indicate that I didn't want to speak to her. Angela told her I was out and wouldn't be back until late. I went out to the bathroom while they talked, and had a shower. When I came back in, ten minutes later, she was still talking. She hung up while I was changing in the bedroom.

'That woman's quite dreadful. I wish I hadn't given her this number.'

'What did she want?'

'She must have second sight. She said she'd just heard that Körner was in London, and wanted to advise you not to see him. Then she went on with long, rambling stories about how wicked he is.'

'What did she say he'd done?'

'Oh...quarrels about what Reich meant, and so on. But she said he'd been spreading false rumours about them, and that she intended to sue him for slander. What it all amounts to is that she wants you to avoid Körner, and if you happen to meet him, don't believe a single word he says.'

I was sitting on the bed, tying my tie; Angela came over, and placed her hand on my damp hair. I was mildly surprised, but assumed she was a little shaken and wanted comforting. I put my arm round her waist and gave her a squeeze. She took my hand in both her hands and pressed it against her breasts. I stood up, bent my head to give her a reassuring kiss, and found myself holding her very closely, her body pressed tightly to mine. After we had kissed for a moment, she said in a strained voice :

' It's dreadful, but I want you to make love to me.'

' There's hardly time.'

But she could feel me hardening against her. She slipped her hand into the top of my trousers, which were still unbelted, and gripped my erect member. I slid my hand up her mini-skirt, and inside the crotch of her panties; she was more than ready to be made love to. Then suddenly, she twisted away from me. I said : 'What is it?' She burst into tears and said : 'I hate myself.'

'Why?'

' It's that foul woman. I think she uses hypnotism. As she talked to me...'

She couldn't go on. I held her close again, but this time without desire. I pointed out that it was hardly shameful to be susceptible to suggestion. A little more questioning revealed that Frau Dunkelman had talked about sexual ceremonies. Angela said :

' I know, but it felt so awful. I wanted to rape you.'

'Don't let me dissuade you.'

But we both knew the fever had passed. To prove it, I pressed her on to the bed, and kissed her gently, then stroked her breasts and thighs with my hand. She relaxed like a child. We could have made love then, but it would have been the gentle love-making of a married couple, an extension of our kisses, not an erotic frenzy. Ten minutes later, when there was a ring at the doorbell, I was having a badly needed martini, and Angela was in the shower.

Körner was a strange-looking man; tall, with stooped shoulders, and an almost completely bald head; he reminded me immediately of the conductor Fürtwangler. The chin seemed weak, and the face somehow indeterminate; yet the overall effect was

223

of a strange, introverted intelligence. His voice was rather high-pitched, but gentle, and almost hypnotic after he had been speaking for a few minutes. The German accent was strong. His grey suit looked expensive, but well worn and slightly baggy.

He refused a drink—'I take only a little fruit juice '—and then sat on the edge of a deep armchair with his bony hands loosely between his knees, managing to look at the same time uncomfortable and relaxed. When Angela came in, he leapt to his feet, and bowed over her hand with a natural courtliness and grace that seemed an expression of his inner character. Angela suggested he sit on the settee; this time, he flung himself back into a corner with exaggerated casualness and crossed his legs, revealing silk socks with a bright check pattern. Then he began :

' Well, my dear Mr Sorme, this is really a great honour for me. I know your books well, of course. [This later turned out to be true; in his pedantic German manner, he quoted from them extensively.] And let me say at once that I hope you will find a few of my ideas as interesting as I find yours...'

I could see that Angela was dying to ask him about the Dunkelmans, but it was difficult to interrupt the flow of conversation about ideas; besides, one got the feeling that he would find it trivial in comparison to discussing Hölderlin and Jaspers.

I shall not try to report his conversation fully. It went on, fairly steadily, until he left at midnight. It ranged from German romanticism and metaphysics to the ideas of Reich and his own development of them. I can only try to offer a sketch of his central ideas.

The Dunkelmans had outlined the position of Wilhelm Reich. Körner described it much more fully : the three periods, beginning with his work as a Freudian, then his breakaway from Freud into ' character analysis '—which most psychologists would consider his major contribution—and finally, his ' crank ' period as a ' physicist ', when he believed he had discovered a mysterious energy called ' orgone ' that could be concentrated in various strange ways. What surprised me was that Körner approved of Reich's more or less materialistic theories about neurosis (Reich was a member of the Communist party until he was expelled for his heterodox views on the causes of fascism).

224

I began to understand Körner better when he talked about Reich's concept of 'character armour': how people develop various rigidities of character to cover up their inadequacies and insecurities, and how these rigidities may eventually become a suit of armour that suffocates the person inside. Körner had obviously taken this to heart. It seemed to be his aim to have absolutely no character armour; he seemed utterly fluid and unprotected. He told us frankly how Reich had cured him of a muscular stiffness that had caused him agonies of cramp. This stiffness was basically due to the embarrassment of an over-sensitive man—as when a schoolboy's writing hand begins to feel stiff when the teacher looks over his shoulder.

After all this, it was difficult to understand how Körner made his transition to his theory of the subconscious—although he himself professed to see no inconsistency. His notion, basically, is that civilisation and reason have forced man into an artificial mould. He saw man's ability to think logically as a fall from grace, a form of original sin. He called consciousness 'artificial daylight', and compared it to electric lighting that has enabled man to see in the dark, but which has the effect of sharply cutting him off from the night outside his windows. Animals, he said, are somehow identified with Nature; man is trapped inside his electric-lighted room of consciousness.

This shows particularly in the sexual sphere, for sex belongs essentially to that 'night' outside the windows. Animals slide into sex like a crocodile sliding off a sandbank into the water (Körner's image); man has to dive in from a high bank. He gets there all right; but unless he is a good diver, the impact may destroy him. It is true, he said, that sex depends upon the separateness of male and female, as a dynamo depends upon the polarity of magnets. But we have exaggerated this separateness until it has become another lock on the prison door. Frustrations built up; we become alienated from society and from one another, as well as from Nature. The sickness shows in the increase in crime, and in the sickeningly barbarous nature of certain crimes—he cited a number of examples mentioned in my own books.

The answer, according to Körner, is beautifully simple. Sex

must be 'disinfected', until the sexual relation between human beings is as natural as between animals. If the great sexual barrier can be removed from between people, the old link between the conscious and the subconscious will be re-established; man will have the advantage of his civilisation—which will cease to be a Frankenstein's monster—and the simplicity of a healthy animal. The Book of Genesis is right in declaring that 'sin' came with man's consciousness of sexual shame. *All* shame must vanish.

Alastair returned home while Körner was expounding Reich; he was so fascinated that he forgot to pour himself a drink. An hour later, I suggested that we all go out for supper, and continue the 'discussion' (which was really almost a lecture, although delivered with the most charming informality). We had Chablis with the meal, and Körner drank two glasses, with water in. Then we walked around the block for a while—Körner said he needed constant physical exercise if his mind was working well—and then went back to the flat. I had certain reservations about Körner's ideas, but I could see that the other two found them revelatory. Without prompting, Angela described the sexual repressions of her childhood, and Alastair told us how he had never lost the feeling of shame at being discovered masturbating in the lavatory of his public school by someone who looked over the partition. I saw Angela looked startled at this; I suppose it had never struck her that boys are that highly sexed. And then, to my amazement, Angela proceeded to describe what had happened to us last time we had been to the Dunkelmans. I thought at first that she only meant to tell him how Anna Dunkelman insisted on exposing herself; but after blushing, and glancing at me, she plunged on to talk about what had happened in the taxi. It was Alastair's turn to look startled, if not shocked. She ended : ' How would you explain that? '

Körner looked interested and concerned; he kept nodding his head slowly.

'They are cunning, very cunning. I had to expel them from our group because what they really wanted was to organise a society for sexual orgies. [When Angela said : 'That's what *they* said about you ', he nodded even more gravely.] You see, they are not truly civilised human beings. They belong to a more

226

primitive stage of society—the stage of taboo and human sacrifice. I will tell you what led to our final break. I had to go to Germany to arrange some legal affairs. I knew Reich trusted them, so I left them in charge of our group. She came along to a meeting one day with a great wooden phallus—what you would call a dildo. She claimed it had been used by an African tribe for the ceremonial deflowering of captured virgins before they were sacrificed. You know that it is one of our basic principles that our exercises in intimacy should stop short of sexual intercourse. This is not because we regard it as bad, you understand, but because it releases the tension too quickly, and the tension should be built up until it can be used to transform the mind. [I thought of the Huldeians and their ceremonies with sacred virgins.] These two—these Dunkelmans—did not try to contradict this idea directly. But they insisted that some of our intimacy exercises should culminate in a sort of priest making love to a woman with the dildo, and squirting warm milk into her at the moment of orgasm. Of course, they all enjoyed this, and the girls used to get so excited that they all screamed as the woman had an orgasm. Of course, the "priest" was usually Klaus Dunkelman. He used to insist on being fully dressed, in an evening suit, but with his penis sticking out of his trousers, and painted with bright colours like a snake. (Reich said that the Dunkelmans had every perversion described by Freud.) Fortunately, I came back after this had been going on only a short time. The Dunkelmans asked for a democratic vote of the members to decide who wanted to continue the practice. [Here Körner went red, and the veins stood out on his forehead.] I told them there would be no vote. It was contrary to *my* ideas, and if they disagreed, they could go and form their own group. I offered to resign completely and form another group elsewhere. But of course, nobody wanted that—I had become the father figure. Only the Dunkelmans thought it would be a good idea. I had to expel them. After this, they tried to start their own groups, without success. But you see [here he raised his finger like a prophet summoning heavenly fire] they possess no intellectual foundations. In short, they are brainless.' He pointed his finger at me. ' And that is why they are so anxious to gain your support. Your ideas would win them disciples. You would become Frau Dunkelman's lover...'

'God forbid', I said.

'But you would. She knows how to gain power over men, as you saw. When she was a member of our group, she always wore the most beautiful underwear, as if she was a ravishing young girl instead of an old harridan of fifty. And I know she found many lovers.'

Angela asked: 'Do you think she possesses some hypnotic powers, then?'

'No! Of course not. What you have just told me is simply a proof of what I have been explaining to you. The sexual gulf between human beings is not natural. Even the healthiest people are full of repressions. You are a rather puritanical girl—I would be prepared to guess that you have only had one lover? [She nodded.] So then. This woman not only speaks frankly about sex and the need to abandon repressions; she demonstrates what she means. The balance between your reason and your sexual energies is disturbed. The energies burst out like lava from a volcano, and you think she has bewitched you. You are doing it yourself.' He smiled happily at the completeness of his demonstration. Angela said:

'And when she rang this evening...'

'It happened again! You were reminded!' He suddenly understood what she had said. 'She rang you? What for?' Angela told him, and he shook his head. 'Ah, the cunning devils. I told you he was a murderer? In any country but Switzerland, he would have been executed. The Swiss are too tolerant.'

As midnight struck, he looked at his watch, and sprang to his feet like a Hussar leaping to attention. 'I must leave you. Tomorrow is a difficult time for me.' He looked at us thoughtfully. 'I must be frank with you. My group is closely integrated because we have worked together for years, so new members are kept on a long probation. But in this case, I feel that haste is justified. I had already decided to ask friend Gerard to an intimacy group. If you two would also like to come along...' Six hours before, both would have refused promptly; now they were so under his spell that they accepted with enthusiastic gratitude. I asked when.

'Tomorrow afternoon. You have a car?'

Alastair nodded.

'Good. I shall send someone to fetch you at midday tomorrow. You will realise why I cannot give you the address.'

He clicked his heels, bowed slightly, and left. I expected Alastair and Angela to hurry off to bed—I was ready to sleep —but I had forgotten they were both more than fifteen years my junior. They began discussing what he had said, and kept appealing to me for my opinion. I was too tired to speak about my reservations. Then Angela asked him if he had been shocked about the episode of the taxi. He flinched, then rose to it. 'Not exactly shocked. Rather jealous. I suppose I kind of think of you as part of the family.'

She asked: 'And what do you think of jealousy if we all followed Otto's ideas?' (We were all on first-name terms.)

'I don't know. Animals get jealous, don't they?'

'That's not the same. Otto said we're not trying to get back to the animal. We're trying to combine the animal's naturalness with human intelligence.'

I could see she would make an admirable disciple; she already had all the answers at her fingertips.

He said pacifically: 'I suppose you're right.'

'Of course I am. I love Gerard. [I blinked.] I love you too. Gerard likes you and you like Gerard. Why shouldn't we treat one another as if we belonged to the same family?'

I felt that her logic was getting slightly mixed, but I said nothing. Finally, I yawned, and intimated that I wanted to sleep. The bed-settee was in the room we were sitting in. At this, she proposed that they should let me alone, and go and continue their discussion in his room. I opened up the settee, changed into my pyjamas, and was asleep within minutes. I woke at one point when the door clicked; in the light from the window, I saw a naked figure—I could not tell if it was Alastair or Angela—go to the bathroom. Then it re-emerged, and went back into the bedroom. I sank back into a heavy sleep. The sunlight woke me at about five o'clock. I opened my eyes, and was mildly surprised to find Angela's head on the pillow beside me. When I stirred, I was even more surprised to find that Alastair was lying on the other side of her. I went to the bathroom, then climbed into Angela's empty bed, and slept for another four hours. I am not opposed to 'intimacy', but for sleeping purposes I prefer a bed to myself.

The telephone rang five times that morning. We assumed it to be Anna Dunkelman, and left it unanswered. The sixth time, Alastair answered it; it *was* Anna Dunkelman. Alastair said we were both out for the day, and rang off before further complications could develop.

At a quarter to midday, there was a ring at the doorbell. A powerfully-built, bullet-headed youth stood there. We invited him in, and he sat on the settee, looking shy. He refused tea and coffee, explaining that he did not drink either. We asked him what we should take with us for the weekend; he shook his head vaguely and said: 'Er...nothing.' His name was Chris Ramsay, and he hardly seemed the type to be a disciple of Körner's; there was something innocent and very likeable about him, but he hardly seemed to be a man of ideas. He talked about wrestling, water-skiing and parachute jumping. We threw a few clothes into one case, and went out of the house with Chris. He was driving a small sports car. He suggested that I drive with him, and that the other two should follow in Angela's Cortina. We drove off up the Edgware Road, then cut across to Barnet and Potters Bar. We drove through Welwyn Garden City, then turned off the main road. A mile or so farther on, we came to a long red-brick wall, with trees behind it. Two peeling gateposts in whitewashed cement led to a drive full of potholes. The house was a fairly large but dilapidated Regency structure. The lawns and flower beds were, on the whole, better tended than the house.

The afternoon was mild and delicious. There was a smell of cut grass in the air, and the sound of water from a small weir behind the house. Chris told me the place had belonged to one of Gurdjieff's groups, and had been taken over by them. Since the people in the nearby village were used to the oddities of Gurdjieff's disciples, they were incurious about this new group. This, as I already realised, was just as well; it would have provided a sensational scoop for the *News of the World*. And this was brought home immediately. Since Körner had apparently not yet arrived, I strolled around the house, through the wet grass (there had been a shower as we came through Welwyn). Around the back of the house, under the shade of the trees, two naked figures were wallowing in the grass. They sat up, smiled at me, then went on with their rolling. One was a pretty but plump girl who looked about sixteen; the other was a stringy middle-aged man. I said: 'Excuse me.' As I started to go away, the girl called: 'Come and join us.' 'Join you in what?' 'It's an intimacy-with-Nature session. The wet grass feels delicious.' I explained that I was new here. She asked: 'Are you shy?' 'No.' It was a challenge. 'Then come on.' The man seemed to be as welcoming as the girl—in his place, I would have resented the intrusion of a third party. I stripped off my clothes—there was no embarrassment in this, for I usually wander around the house naked when I first get out of bed—and went over to sit down. 'Try it', the man said. I laid down on the grass and rolled, feeling rather foolish. But he was right; it was a delicious sensation on the naked skin. When I'd rolled until I felt a little chilly, I went and lay in the sun, which soon dried me. The man was now lying on his back, and the girl was pulling up handfuls of the grass and rubbing it into him, caressing him with it. After a few minutes of this, she lay down on her back, with her thighs open, and he did the same, pulling up large bunches, with earth still adhering to some of them, and rubbing the grass quite gently over her breasts and belly. He said to me: 'Come and help.' I preferred a sitting position, to hide my rising interest in the girl, whose open legs aroused Pavlovian responses; but when, after a moment of effort, this vanished, I went over to them, pulled up some grass—they had moved because the previous spot was denuded—and tried to rub her as the man had; I soon gave this up and followed my own instinct, lowering the wet ends of the grass until it touched her sunlit breasts, then letting it descend and caress gently. I was successful; she gave a gasp of pleasure, and moved her hips sensuously. She said to the man: 'He has a marvellous touch.' I used the grass as I might have used my tongue if I had been trying to arouse her.

231

When I reached her navel, she opened her thighs wider.

At this point, the man turned away and said: 'I think I'll go and bathe in the stream.' He walked away quickly with his back to us. I said: 'I'm afraid he's not dead to the sins of the flesh', and she burst into a gurgle of laughter that broke off in a gasp as I applied a fresh and cold bundle of grass. She said dreamily: 'I wish we were in a bedroom.' 'I didn't think you were allowed that kind of thing.' 'We're not, strictly. But we haven't all got your control.'

Sighing, she moved on to her elbows, then buried her head against my thighs. The warmth of her mouth around me was delicious, but I was nervous in case anyone should come; we were completely exposed, with the house on one side—and anyone who might be looking out of the windows—and the man who might return from the stream at any moment. I put my hands in her hair and gently pressed her away. 'Later. Not now.' She said: 'Promise?' I said yes, and she moved back on to the grass. It cost an effort to cause my flesh to subside, but I succeeded.

I heard a car arrive on the other side of the house. The man was returning from the stream. I said: 'I think I ought to go and look for Dr Körner.' As I pulled my clothes on again, I noticed that my loss of control had lowered the level of the intensity I had felt earlier. The girl lay there in the sun, her eyes closed, a smile on her parted lips, looking as if she was having a slow-burning orgasm.

It was not Körner, but a car containing four bespectacled young woman, looking like schoolteachers or computer operators, and a thin young man wearing thick glasses. But I found Körner inside, in the large, bleak hall that seemed to be full of battered statuettes of Greek discus-throwers and goddesses with bunches of grapes. Körner looked busy, directing where these should be placed; but when he saw me, he came over with a warm smile, shook my hand heartily, then held up his hand for silence. The others came and gathered round, and Körner introduced me as the well-known author and philosopher. They all looked impressed. I found the build-up embarrassing; they were looking at me as if they expected me to rise slowly from the ground.

Körner took me by the arm. 'One of our group is an antique dealer, and he has presented us with these. Some of them are not very artistic, but we shall allot them as symbols to individual members.'

'Symbols?'

'For them to meditate on.' He evidently felt that this was self-explanatory, for he said : 'Let me show you the rest of the house.'

It was large and rather draughty, the kind of place that could only be made comfortable by a millionaire. Körner and his students were trying to do it themselves; and certainly a few of the rooms were impressively comfortable, indicating that at least some of the students could afford to present good furniture.

Körner showed me to a sunlit bedroom. 'This is where you will sleep. Unless, of course, you prefer to join the intimacy group below.'

'They sleep together?'

'Yes, but with perfect chastity, of course. It is no hardship for them to restrain their desires. They know they are gaining a new intensity by doing so.' He went off into his lecturing manner, picking up a chunk of electric wire that some electrician had left on the window-seat. 'You see, the reason that sex is so disappointing to most people is that they are like a thin wire that can hardly carry any current. You will agree that sexual ecstasy is like an electric current? If you are healthy and you have been restraining your desires for a long time, it becomes a high-voltage current. That is our whole aim—to turn us into a heavy wire, like this one.' He waved the thick copper wire under my nose. 'Once the wire can carry the current, the current will not be lacking. I think you would agree with this?'

I said I did; I knew that intense self-discipline increases one's capacity for ecstasy. But before I could express certain reservations, Körner laid his hand on my arm.

'And now, I wish to speak to you. You will gather that I have a purpose in bringing you here. Come and sit down.' He evidently felt that this was serious. We sat in the sunlight in the window-seat. 'It is not simply that I want you to become a member of our group—that is self-evident. You are completely qualified for it. I would like you to become my second-in-command, my lieutenant—and eventually, my successor.' He held up his hand to stop me interrupting. 'You do not have to make a decision now, or even next week or next month. I want you to see how we work, see whether you feel we could help you, or you could help us. You see, you have integrity. Most of the people around me are good students, but so far I do not see the qualities necessary for a leader. The Dunkelmans wanted to be leaders—but they would simply have turned our group into a kind of brothel, a personal harem for the two of them. Work like this requires pure dedication, the scientific spirit. You have this.'

I made apologetic noises, and said I would need time to make up my mind. Deep inside me, I knew this was out of the question; I am a loner, not simply by inclination, but by nature. I didn't want to mix with all these people.

He patted my shoulder. 'Of course. Take as long as you like. But there is one thing I had better tell you frankly. So far, we have tried to keep our activities fairly quiet, because they could be misunderstood. But now the time has come to go out and show ourselves openly, to make converts, to tell the world of our aims. Because our aim is to prove that civilisation will never be stable until everyone thinks as we do.'

He had become very serious, and I was not entirely unsympathetic; but suddenly I thought of Anna Dunkelman's picture of strangers masturbating one another on buses, and found it necessary to stare out of the window to control my face. As we went downstairs, I said:

'I think this is a great idea. Angela and Alastair were completely bowled over last night. You've made two enthusiastic converts there.'

'Good. But we shall not be satisfied until I can say the same of you.' As we approached the group, still busily arranging statues, he gripped my arm. 'For the moment, treat what I have told you in strict confidence.'

At two o'clock, lunch was announced. In the dining room, looking out on the lawn, a simple meal had been laid out on trestle tables—two huge tureens of soup, plates piled with cubes of

cheese, whole-wheat rolls and biscuits. Körner introduced me to
a bearded young man named Paul, who seemed to be his assistant. Paul had horn-rimmed glasses, a northern accent, and an
intensely serious manner. He explained :

'We try to eat light meals. Otherwise, the body has too much
trouble digesting food, and the discipline does no good. This is
actually a pretty large meal. Our other group—the over-forties
—eat much less.' I gathered that Körner kept the two groups
separate, and had meetings on alternate weekends. Paul said :

'We have to be practical about this. Theoretically, there's no
age limit, of course. But it's our experience that older people are
more interested in sex than young ones. And if we allowed too
many of them to join, the young ones would leave. A lot of
young girls don't seem to mind older men, but young boys don't
often take to women over forty. Of course, the groups can inter-
mingle, to some extent—but only by special invitation.' This,
apparently, explained the presence of a number of men and
women who were obviously over forty—even over fifty.

There were about sixty people present in the hall, with a
slight predominance of women. They struck me as a fairly
average group of people. I noticed that there seemed to be a
fashion among the women for long-sleeved dresses and spectacles
with rather heavy frames, giving them a studious appearance.
There were no teenagers present; the girl I had seen in the
garden seemed to be one of the youngest there. I observed that
a large proportion of the men seemed strongly built, or wore
bulky polo-neck sweaters to give an impression of size. Very few
of those present were strikingly good-looking, but I saw no one
who was downright unattractive. The women, on the whole,
were more intelligent-looking than the men. I saw very few men
whom I would describe as ectomorphic types. For all their
appearance of being an ' average ' group, I got the feeling that
these might have been more carefully selected than at first
appeared.

They seemed to know one another very well; there was a great
deal of laughter, of pushing and jostling, of hand-shaking and
kissing between acquaintances, and offering of plates and bowls
of soup to one another. I found the friendly atmosphere impres-

235

sive, although I seemed to feel a certain tension behind it, a lack of casualness and relaxation.

Paul went off to speak to someone; a voice in front of me said: 'Hello', and I found myself looking down into the brown eyes of the girl I had met on the lawn. We were pressed together in the crowd, and as she smiled up, her hand reached behind her and gave my genitals a friendly squeeze. She said: 'My name's Tessa', and beckoned me to bend my head. She whispered: 'I don't want lunch. Let's go to bed.' 'I'm hungry.' 'Spoilsport.' 'Besides, they'd notice. I'm being given special treatment.' Paul came back, and frowned at her disapprovingly; I got the feeling she was regarded as a disruptive influence.

I ate my bread and cheese, and drank my soup. Then we went out of the french windows and on to the lawn. A group of people were standing in a circle, and seemed to be doing some kind of exercises. They placed their hands on each other's shoulders, then moved forward, then leaned forward and drew together in a sharp knot like a Rugby fifteen. Paul said:

'This is a warm-up intimacy group. They're trying to get rid of the constraint of urban life—touching one another, doing things together, trying to get rid of the feeling of separateness.' A young man in a white polo-neck sweater was calling out instructions to the group, occasionally moving in among them and slapping someone on the shoulders or back. As I stood there, he went up to a woman of about forty, and did something to her breasts—apparently rearranging her bra through her sweater—and ending by sharply slapping her buttock as if she was a cow being driven into a field. Paul said:

'You see, they like being given orders. It helps them to throw off the feeling of responsibility—civilisation neurosis. The aim is to make them feel like innocent children again.'

I noticed that the people in this 'intimacy group' were all dressed rather heavily, in view of the heat. Paul explained that this was part of the procedure; as they got rid of their sense of oppression, they could dress in lighter clothes. 'You'll see what I mean this evening.'

I mentioned my chief misgiving: that since sex comes so naturally to human beings, all the high-minded aims of a group

236

like this would tend to blur into mutual sexual excitement. He nodded in agreement.

'In a group of this size, it's bound to happen to some extent, of course. We try to take precautions. But you'd be surprised how little it happens. There are no taboos here, no repressions, and that makes a great difference.'

We went back in the house. I asked him what he meant by 'precautions'. 'I'll show you.' We went up to a room on the first floor which I knew to be a women's dormitory. Paul walked in without knocking. Half a dozen women were lying on beds powdering their noses, and one was sitting in a bra and panties, taking off her stockings. They smiled at us, and seemed unconcerned. Paul went over to a bed that had an open case lying on it, and tipped it upside down on the bed. He scattered its contents over the surface of the bed—a grey woollen mini-dress, tights, underwear, some cosmetics—and glanced into a pink washing-case. No one seemed to pay any attention. 'I'm looking for contraceptives. It's the surest way of telling if anyone intends to break the rules.' He picked up the case belonging to the woman who was still dressing. She said : 'Oh, for heaven's sake don't mess everything up. Let me show you.' She took the garments out one by one, opened them out and gave them a brief shake. Paul pointed to a pair of pink French knickers. 'They're not much good.' 'I know. I left in a hurry and threw in the first thing I saw.'

Outside, he explained : 'We have spot checks every weekend, to see if they've brought contraceptives. Of course, we've no way of knowing if they've taken the Pill.'

'Doesn't that rather invalidate it?'

'Oh no. Otto advises against the Pill for health reasons anyway.'

'How about the men?'

'They're checked by women. Anyone's allowed to check anyone else. We try to be a single family.'

'Why did you object to that girl's knickers?'

'Wide legs. There's no rule about it, of course, but if people intend to have sex, those panties are ideal—if the lights go on suddenly, the girl's fully dressed.'

'The women are supposed to keep their panties on, then?' I asked, thinking about Tessa on the lawn.

'Oh no.' He looked almost shocked. 'That would miss the whole point of our group—intimacy. But if they're going to be caressed, they have to pull them down, at least around their thighs.' He went on earnestly: 'You don't seem to understand. We're not trying to regiment people. But you know yourself that the more obstacles there are, the more interesting it becomes. So we try to prescribe silk panties with fairly tight legs, so that if they're tempted to have intercourse, the girl would have to take them right off. We don't much like crêpe nylon or French knickers because you can pull the leg aside too easily. Some of these things are no protection at all.'

There was the sound of a gong from the hall. 'What happens now?'

'We have lectures until five. I have to lecture myself, so I shall have to leave you. Attendance at lectures is compulsory, by the way. Anyone who skips lectures is not really serious. We don't tell newcomers that—it helps us to weed out people who come for the wrong motives.' He advised me to wander around the various lectures, and to ask questions if I felt so inclined.

I took his advice. The 'students' divided into four groups. Körner spoke to one; Paul to another; Chris to a third; and an attractive but slightly schoolmistressy woman called Gwyneth to the fourth. I was glad to see that Angela and Alastair were sitting eagerly in the front row of Körner's group, which was out on the lawn. I sat at the back of this for twenty minutes or so, and heard him explaining why he was a materialist. 'Idealists', he explained, believe that such things as life, thought, ideas, can exist *apart from* matter, in some sense. His arguments against this view were devastating and, for me, completely convincing. As far as I was concerned, of course, they missed the point. I agree that minds and mental processes are inseparably linked with matter; but I still believe that life has somehow entered matter from *outside*, not that it is an emanation of matter, as fire is an emanation of coal.

I had a feeling that Körner would not welcome questions, so I moved on to the next group, the lady named Gwyneth. She

238

was giving an enthusiastic but, I thought, rather muddled summary of Reich's ideas, and her talk about 'vital fluid' that accumulates in the loins in sexual excitement seemed to me dangerously close to Reich's orgone energy. I wondered how Körner would feel about all this. Gwyneth tried to draw me actively into the discussion, which soon became lively. Her group struck me as intelligent, and more independent-minded than I had expected—they disagreed with her on a great many points. I made some attempts to explain my own theories of the origin of the sexual impulse, and my theory of symbolic response, but I could see they found this very strange and, as one lady said, 'unnecessarily abstract'. The discussion became so warm that we were all surprised when members of other groups strolled on to the lawn and told us it was time for tea.

In fact, we did not drink tea—which Körner disliked—but sanka—caffeinless coffee. We also ate wheaten biscuits spread thinly with butter. Gwyneth took charge of me, and told me she found my ideas fascinating. I found her very likeable. About forty years of age, with a fresh, pink complexion, and rather large, white teeth that made her smile amiable and dazzling, she tended to exaggerate the school-marmish style that seemed to be the prescribed fashion, wearing a long-sleeved black dress, and a necklace of gold leaves with a cross on it. I gathered she was on her local parish council, and held a good job in a public relations firm. She had an enthusiastic and slightly woolly way of discussing ideas that had its own charm; but I could not imagine how she had got into Körner's group.

After tea, we all went into the main room. This had little furniture, but good carpets that looked as if they had cost as much as all the rest of the furniture put together. (Gwyneth explained that they were 'donations' from older members; I had my suspicions that some of the older members bought their way into the group with expensive gifts over and above the fees.) Although it was now growing chilly outside, this room was warmed by a log fire that burned in the huge fireplace. Now the people broke up in small intimacy groups, and I moved from one to another, watching their activities with interest. And it soon became clear that the earlier part of the day had been a mere prelude; this was the beginning of the serious part. They joined into tight knots, pressing very close together, running their hands over one another's bodies, starting at the ankles, moving up to the head. Many of the groups split into pairs, and repeated the pressing and fondling operation. There was nothing specifically sexual about this; I noticed that hands lingered only briefly in the erogenous zones, but seemed much more interested in heads and in arms. A tall, thin girl drew me into a group as I stood watching, and began to stroke me, pressing her hands together on my belly or chest, and then drawing them apart, pressing hard. After this, I did the same to her, standing behind her, pressing my hands tight against her belly, then massaging her as far as the hips. I repeated this operation on her breasts and thighs; then, in accordance with her instructions, began to stroke the outsides of her legs, beginning at the waist and running my hands over her dress, down to her feet. I noticed she was wearing a suspender belt and stockings. After this, she caressed my shoulders, arms and head, running her fingers through my hair, along my cheeks, opening my mouth and putting her finger-tips in, inserting her little finger into my ears. What she was doing was caressing me as if we were lovers; but since we remained fully clothed, it had a strange quality of excitement, of the forbidden. If we had been alone, partly undressed, it would have ended in coitus within minutes; this lingering massage in a room with fifty or so other people had the effect of creating a new set of responses, breaking old habits.

I observed that some other couples had fetched bowls of water and were washing one another's hair; they did this near the open french windows, where there was no carpet. The couples frequently split up and changed partners; after ten minutes of caressing the thin girl, I got a more heavily-built middle-aged woman. At first I felt that the change was no benefit; but after five minutes of caressing, I noticed that we had achieved the effect of intimacy, of knowing and liking one another. After this, I got Tessa, who smiled and whispered in a mock-seductive voice : ' I'm afraid this is bound to be an anticlimax.' To some extent she was right. My trousers concealed no secrets from her; neither did her dress from me. But the feeling of her softness through the dress was exciting. She made something of a joke of it, slipping her hand under my sweater and pinching my nipples hard. When I massaged her, and pushed her dress between her thighs, she said : ' I hope no one examines me now. I'm soaked.' ' Is that forbidden? ' ' Of course. But I can't help it. If people feel me down there, I just have an orgasm. I've had two already.' After a few more minutes, she said : ' I'm bloody hungry. I've got a lot of chocolate in my room, if you want some.' ' Is that allowed? ' ' Not really. But all this intimacy makes me ravenous.'

At half past seven, the gong sounded, and Tessa said : ' Thank God for that.' We all streamed into the dining room. I needed food. All the excitement made me feel as if I'd walked twenty miles. The supper was slightly less sparse than the earlier meals : huge plates of cold beef and ham, tureens of tomato soup, hot vegetables (no potatoes), and wheat biscuits. To my surprise, I observed that there was also a bar, and Gwyneth—who took charge of me—told me I could have beer or wine. She explained that there was no heavy drinking, but that a little alcohol helped most people to relax and enjoy their meal. I observed with interest that the 'intimacy' went on in the dining hall. Men and women, jostling together, took the opportunity to caress one another, and even to kiss. There had been a certain amount of kissing in the previous session—of the arms and neck, mostly; now, I saw, they often greeted one another with kisses on the mouth. Although some of these kisses were lingering, none could be described as passionate, in the sense of indicating a desire to get into bed.

I ate well, and a glass of beer greatly refreshed me. After the meal, I made my way across the hall to the toilet, but it proved to be occupied. I made my way upstairs to a place where I recalled seeing a sign—a rather demure sign showing a man's top hat and a lady's handbag, with an arrow underneath pointing down the corridor. I followed its direction, and found myself in what was obviously a newly built toilet, with a number of booths as in public lavatories. But there was no indication on the door as to whether this was a ladies or gents. As I stood there, footsteps sounded along the corridor; to my relief, I saw it was Tessa.

'I'm glad to see you. Which is the gents?'

'Oh, either. We don't have two. Intimacy, see? Are you coming?'

'I suppose so.' I had to admit to feeling shy, but could see that this was illogical. I went into the end cubicle—and realised, with a shock, that the wall that divided it from the next was made of glass. Tessa went into the next one and grinned at me. Then, without self-consciousness, she hitched up her dress, pushed her panties down to her knees, and sat down. I said:

'Good God, this is a bit much, isn't it?'

'I thought so when I came. But you soon get used to it.'

'But I don't like farting where I can be heard.'

'Why worry? Dr Körner says it's a natural voice of the body, like your speaking voice.'

I felt silly standing there, and so lowered my trousers and sat down. I had never felt less like relieving myself. Then more voices sounded outside, and two more women came in. They moved to the cubicles at the other end, bared their behinds, and sat down—the glass was exceptionally clear. They did not even glance at us, but went on talking about what Körner had said that afternoon. Their voices relaxed me, and the spring inside me unwound. Watching Tessa clean herself with paper made me reflect that we are all more inhibited creatures than we recognise, and that once again Körner was probably right. But I made a note to use the ground-floor toilet in future; that had ordinary walls. I went downstairs with Tessa.

When I went back into the main hall, I found that most of the students were sitting on the floor on cushions. As I came in, Körner, who was standing near the fire, beckoned to me. I went over to him. He banged a bottle on a table for silence, then said:

'And now I want to introduce you all to the noted novelist and philosopher, Gerard Sorme, who has been described as the most interesting British writer since Aldous Huxley and D. H. Lawrence. [I think he invented this on the spur of the moment.] Mr Sorme's views on sex differ from ours in many respects, and I am now going to ask him to say a few words about them. I should tell you that I have not warned him about this, so it will be completely impromptu.'

I had no time to be surprised or nervous. I stood up and sketched my theory of the sexual impulse, its intentional nature, and the way that it illustrates my phenomenological theory of all human interaction with the world. When I felt that I was losing them in Husserl, I talked of my feeling of the sexual impulse as a 'key to the keepers of the keys of being', and the relation between sex and the mystical experience. I ended by trying to explain my most fundamental point: that sex gives us a glimpse of a concentration of the mind that would make us god-like if we could command it in other spheres. I mentioned my idea that human beings are like grandfather clocks driven by watch-springs; that the body is too heavy for the tiny spring of will-power. Only in sex do we seem to develop a spring powerful enough for a grandfather clock. I ended by saying that my own central interest was in the question of how to learn to tap the immense springs of the will.

The discussion that followed was interesting, but not entirely to the point. Several people raised the objection that to allow such importance to the will was dangerous. They were arguing a view similar to Lawrence's—and Körner's. I could see that this was where I differed from them all; I did not distrust the will or the intellect.

It had been a long day, and I was feeling tired. It was now nearly ten o'clock—time had passed very quickly—and I was beginning to feel like sleeping. It had all been very interesting and promising, and I felt Körner was on to something important; but it would take a great deal of thinking to clarify my attitude towards it all. I hoped that the evening would now break up into something more purely social, and that I could slip off to bed. And it was all a long way from Esmond and Horace Glenney.

Körner thanked me, and said he hoped that they would be seeing a great deal more of me; then he introduced them to Angela and Alastair, who had to stand up, looking embarrassed. Everyone clapped politely, and began to stand up and move out of the room. I asked Körner: 'What now?'

'Ah, now the most interesting part begins. We have another intimacy session.'

I was not entirely pleased. The previous one had been pleasant but tiring; I didn't feel like stretching my faculties again. He beckoned to me, and I followed him out of the room, wondering if he would resent it if I suggested skipping this final session. I started to speak, then changed my mind. Instead, I asked:

'I'd like to ask you about Esmond Donelly some time.'

He looked at me and smiled.

'I think I may be able to tell you some interesting things. But we can discuss that later. Now we have other things to do.' I followed him, rather wearily, up the stairs. We turned right, and I thought we were going to the girls' dormitory. But he unlocked a door next to it, and went in. I followed him. It was a small room that had probably been a store-room, but was now empty except for a few high stools. One wall contained a large window. To my surprise, Gwyneth was standing in front of it, rearranging her hair and staring in at us.

'This is a two-way mirror, of course.'

It was the first one I had ever seen. 'Are you sure she can't see us?'

'Not unless I do this.' He reached up and pressed a switch. Immediately, the window became a mirror in which I could see my face. 'Now she can see us. I have reversed the polarity.' He flicked the switch again, and Gwyneth smiled at us and waved through the window. I waved back, forgetting she could no longer see us.

'What is it for?'

'For observation. You will see that the women are now changing.' This was true. In the crowded dormitory, women were stripping off dresses, underskirts and suspender belts. Gwyneth, without self-consciousness, reached back behind her neck and undid a button, then pulled down her zip. She carefully peeled off the dress, and folded it on the bed. She was wearing a black underslip with a lacy hem that looked very fetching. She seemed to have forgotten us. She slipped off the shoulder straps, and let it fall round her feet. She was apparently not entirely in favour of black underwear; she was wearing a white bra, a black suspender belt that held up black stockings, and small white panties of lacy crêpe nylon. Evidently she was exempt from the rule that

244

women should wear panties that could not be stretched too far. Most of the other women I could see had adhered to it. None were wearing bikini briefs. Most of them wore the pink or blue satin things that completely encase the stomach, with elastic at the waist, although in my own experience the elastic in the leg of these has a great deal of yield, and, pulled down an inch or two, they present no problem.

A few other men joined us as we stood there. I saw that the women were all putting on grey woollen mini-skirts of the kind I had noticed earlier in the day in the cases we had inspected.

Körner said : 'Come, it is time to change.'

I had noticed that most of the men were now wearing a similar uniform of grey flannels and white T-shirt. We went towards the men's dormitory on the next floor. The question I was about to ask was answered when a door next to it opened, and I saw several women standing in there, evidently watching the men undressing through a similar two-way mirror. Körner called in sharply : 'Come along, ladies. No more voyeurism. Time to change.' They all hurried out; I noticed Tessa was amongst them. And as we went into the dormitory, I turned and saw that she slipped back into the observation room.

In the dormitory, most of the men seemed to be nearly naked, and the one standing near the mirror actually was. I asked Körner :

'What is the exact point of the mirrors?'

'Most people have a touch of the exhibitionist in them, even the most stable. And most people have a touch of the Peeping Tom. Here they can gratify it without feeling guilty. There is almost no sexual urge that has to be concealed in this place. We try to bring it all into the open, to make it straightforward and above-board. Now, I think those trousers you are wearing will be suitable. You only need a shirt.' He called to Paul, who was fully dressed, to find me a shirt. A few minutes later, Paul came back with a thin cotton T-shirt. I observed that this was exceptionally long, and tucked it into my trousers. I noticed that most of the men were putting on underpants—of the brief variety advertised in health-and-strength magazines—and white tennis shoes. Many of them were taking showers in the next room. Körner clapped his hands and called: 'Come, gentlemen, time to get dressed. There are no ladies next door now.' I remembered with a start that Tessa was still in there, and that I was undressing within a few feet of the mirror. I hoped she enjoyed it. Or perhaps she was watching the other men.

In the main room, a huge screen had been placed in front of the fire, which was low. I saw Angela, looking very sweet in her grey mini-skirt. I noticed that, like many other women, she was wearing stockings. This part, apparently, was optional. She came over to me and took my hand. I said: 'How do you feel?'

'Fine. It's a bit shattering losing so many inhibitions all in one weekend, but it's a marvellous experience. I can't tell you how grateful I am for meeting Körner.'

'I wonder what happens now?'

'Don't you know? More intimacy. The girl on the next bed has been describing it. This is the big moment. I hope I get you. I can't bear some of those other men. I hate hairy males.'

'But what...?' Before I could go on, Chris called: 'Are we all here?' Various voices answered: 'Yes.' 'All right. Form the circle. Paul, will you take the light?' I wondered where Paul was intended to take it to; as we moved into a circle, hands on shoulders, the lights went slowly down. Men scurried to arrange themselves next to women, but since there were slightly more women than men, a few women were bound to pair. Then there was total darkness. I asked Angela: 'What do we do now?', but a strange voice answered: 'We all walk into the centre, mingle together, then take the first person of the opposite sex.' We began to move forward. There were a few moments of confusion. I wondered how to distinguish women from men, and ended by touching breasts. (I discovered later that this was normal procedure.) I found a girl and took her hand tightly. Paul's voice called: 'All ready?' There were shouts of 'Yes', 'No'. Slowly, the lights went up. I discovered I was holding the hand of a small, blonde girl I had noticed earlier. She was not pretty, and her blue eyes seemed short-sighted; but she had a charming, pert face. I asked her: 'What now?'

'We can either join with other couples, or stay on our own. Which would you prefer?'

'Let's stay on our own for the moment.'

'All right.'

I looked at my next-door neighbour—the thin girl I had been with earlier in the day—and was startled to see that she was just in the process of stepping out of her panties. The man she was facing—a rather good-looking, nervous man in his mid-thirties —was doing the same, blushing. She handed him her panties and took his underpants; she donned his underpants while he climbed into her panties.

'What's all this for?'

'The beginning of the intimacy—we can change clothes ad lib. This is the bit designed for the fetichists, I think. Do panties do things to you?'

'They have a definite sexual connotation.'

'In that case, we'd better change.' Without embarrassment, she slipped off a pair of pink knickers, and handed them to me. I took more time to get my trousers off and step out of my underpants. She said : How about your shirt?' 'Do we change those too?' 'If you'd like to.' The crotch of her panties was damp, and its contact with my scrotum produced a twinge of sexual excitement that dissipated the last vestige of tiredness. Obviously, such a contact is basically a contact between the male and female genitals at one remove. I began to understand what Körner meant by 'suspended orgasm'. What he had done was to fill a room with men and women, and in actual or potential sexual contact with one another, where the sexual stimulus was maximal, but group discipline held everything in check. Körner stood by the fire, watching us with a benevolent eye, and I found myself wondering what he was experiencing.

I gave my partner—whose name was Norma—my T-shirt, and accepted her mini-skirt, which was approximately the same length. I noticed, as she removed her dress, that her bra was the low cut type that almost allows the breasts to escape.

I pulled my trousers back up, and fastened the catch. I said : 'I don't know why we bother to put them back on. These mini-skirts are long enough for modesty.'

'I know. But Dr Körner thinks that the act of actually taking off his trousers destroys inhibitions in the male. In the girl, it's taking off her knickers.'

I saw her point. Some of the others seemed to want to go on changing clothes. The good-looking young man next to us had no sooner finished dressing than another girl approached him. This time, I saw, he did not exchange clothes with the girl, but with her male partner, who was already, presumably, wearing her panties and singlet.

Norma said: 'This part bores me. Let's move away from them.' We moved to the edge of the group. 'Shall I do you first, or will you do me?' I said: 'You'd better do me. I'm not sure how to go about it.' 'Would you rather stand up or lie down?' 'I don't mind.' I saw that some of the couples were taking folded tables, that seemed to have retractable metal legs, from a pile in the corner, and setting them up in empty spaces. They were made of aluminium, and seemed to be about six feet long. The man or woman would lie down, as if about to receive massage treatment, and the 'intimacy' would begin as before. Norma proved more expert than any of my previous partners; or perhaps I was more excited. She stood in front of me, and ran her hands over my chest, stomach, thighs, then down to my feet. When she stood up, she unzipped me, and for a moment I wondered if we were going too far. But she only reached inside and plunged her hands down my legs, pinching gently and stroking as far as my knees. She made me sit down, and stood behind me, running her hands through my hair, inside my shirt —or, rather, dress—over my cheeks, inside my lips. I reached to my zip, to close it, but she pushed my hand away. 'More inhibitions.' 'Sorry.' She leaned forward, reached inside, and stroked my thighs, letting her hand wander freely. I had given up all attempts to suppress my normal reactions; now she slipped her hand inside the waistband, and let her fingertips run lightly up and down my stomach, then farther down. I controlled my voice to ask: 'Is that allowed?' 'Oh, yes. It's completely up to us now. Shall I stop?' 'I think you'd better.' There was a burst of laughter from next to us. Two women and the man were laughing at the shy man, who was blushing. Others began to laugh as he blushed; but Körner, standing by the fireplace, looked stern and shook his head slowly. The man turned and hurried out of the room. Norma said : ' Poor Mr McCann. He can never restrain himself. I'm afraid the women take it in turns to make him lose control.'

The strange thing was that I was no longer feeling fatigued. A strange glow had started inside me.

We were interrupted by a group of six : four women and two men; they wanted to change clothes again. Norma looked resentful, but slipped off my underpants resignedly. She was handed a pair of black briefs in exchange. I was given the French knickers that I recognised from that afternoon. I exchanged the mini-skirt for a longer one, worn by a pale, intense-looking girl. When this was over, Norma said : ' Come on, my turn now.' And then, with a shock, I realised that I had been Esmond for the past five minutes, and that this explained why I had been feeling slightly puzzled by these odd garments. It was as if Esmond had emerged from some depth of my consciousness to find out what was going on. As soon as I became aware of him, the effect of double exposure increased, so that for a moment I felt almost sick, and the sexual excitement vanished.

We had found a quiet place on the edge of the crowd. Gwyneth, no longer looking in the least school-marmish, was leaning back against the wall, her eyes closed in an expression of almost agonised ecstasy. A man was kneeling in front of her, his cheek against her thigh. When he turned his head I saw it was Alastair. Esmond said to him : ' Greetings, comrade ', and Alastair looked suddenly startled. Gwyneth had sunk gently to the floor, and was half-sitting, half-lying, her eyes closed, her knees apart. Then Alastair winked at me. ' You should try her. She's marvellous.' The faun-like expression on his face was new to me—but not to Esmond. I realised that this was a lineal descendant of Horace Glenney.

The effect of double exposure ceased to be unpleasant, as if Esmond and I had made a bargain to inhabit the same body without argument. The feeling was clearer now than it had ever been, and I could no longer believe it was some odd quirk of my subconscious.

I put my arms around Norma from behind, caressed her breasts, and then, with a twist of either hand, freed them from the brassiere that held them. She sank back gently against me, and I felt her dress rough against my bare flesh. She leaned her head back on my shoulder, her face raised, and I bent down and touched her lips; as I did so, she reached behind her and gripped me tightly with her hand. She said: 'You're getting over-excited.' I continued to stroke her, enjoying her response; she was like a cat that arched its back against me and purred. I realised, with sudden awe, that she had achieved the 'suspended orgasm', and then realised, a moment later, that it was not I who knew it, but Esmond. He was infinitely more experienced in such things than I.

Norma suddenly said: 'Look, there's a table free. Let's go over. I can't stand up any longer.' In fact, her knees seemed to be buckling. I helped her over to a table near the fire, where Körner was standing, looking benevolently at the room, nodding and smiling. He patted me on the shoulder. Esmond said to him: 'Greetings, dark one.' Körner's hand dropped, and his face went very pale. He leaned forward and stared into my face. 'You knew all the time?' 'I'm not a fool, domine', Esmond said. Körner said quietly: 'So you've been playing with me.' It was not a question. 'But why?' I was touched by his expression of sad dignity; I wanted to explain to him, but it was too ridiculous. Then Körner seemed to pull himself together. He pursed his lips, gave a wry smile, and shrugged. Then he went towards the door, and out of the room. I said: 'What the devil do you mean?' But Esmond ignored me.

Norma was lying on the table, her eyes closed, apparently asleep. I went over to her, and slipped off her shoes. Her small feet looked very white. I bent down and kissed the sole of her foot, and then took the toes in my mouth. She stirred and sighed. I moved my head up and kissed her thighs, at the same time slipping my hand into the waist of the panties. This time she gasped and made no attempt to stop my explorations. In spite of the people around us, it was hard to resist the temptation to move on to her.

Glancing around the room, I saw that Esmond and I were among the last on our feet. I now understood why the carpet was so thick. Prostrate bodies were lying everywhere. I could see

Angela, lying on her back, her legs open, without panties, apparently fast asleep; Paul was lying beside her, one hand on her thigh, his eyes also closed. Gwyneth, who seemed indefatigable, was now naked, lying on the carpet, a man sucking her breasts. Another was stroking her legs and stomach, as her hips rose and fell gently. Other figures were entangled in absurd configurations that looked as if they had been dreamed up by a pornographer with a sense of the grotesque.

Norma was holding my hand tightly, to prevent it escaping, and moving her thighs up and down with it trapped between them. As I looked down at her, a memory stirred; I tried to fix it, but it evaded me. I made another effort, staring hard at the rounded golden flesh of her thighs. It came to me that Esmond had seldom made love to sunburned women. Although there was as little prudery in his day as in our own, clothes were regarded as a part of the essential humanity of men and women; naked sunbathing would have been regarded as a curious eccentricity. So the thighs of Esmond's mistresses were always white and soft.

And then, in some way that I fail to understand, Esmond and I ceased to be two men inhabiting the same body, and were suddenly identified. To explain this would be of far more interest than to describe the mere physical events of the next few hours; but I cannot do it. Language was not made to express the subtleties of the human psyche. I can only say this : it is almost impossible for human beings genuinely to forget themselves, to escape their obsessive self-preoccupation, and to realise that there is a world outside them. Blake understood that every bird that cuts the airy way is ' an immense world of delight, closed to your senses five '. But here, suddenly, in a flash, I was inside somebody else's consciousness, a human being whose life and experience had been in every way different from my own. It brought a feeling of tremendous delight and freedom. It was like being let out of a coalmine. What had suddenly vanished permanently was that basic fear that enters the mind of all intelligent people at some time in their lives : that they are really the only person in the universe, that life is an elaborate joke, a film show created by a bored god who knows he is alone, and who has given himself amnesia to forget his loneliness. For here was Esmond's conscious-

251

ness, as undeniably real and elaborate as my own, mingled with my own.

And in a flash I understood the meaning of sex. It is a craving for the mingling of consciousness, whose symbol is the mingling of bodies. Every time a man and a woman slake their thirst in the strange waters of the other's identity, they glimpse the immensity of their freedom.

Esmond's memory was far more powerful than my own. Because of the powers he had developed, he could recall past epochs of his life with incredible vividness. And this, I now saw, was why he had chosen me. I have always been aware that human life is dream-like because most human beings exist passively. Their consciousness is little more than a reflection of their environment. In the sexual orgasm, the voltage power of their minds surges, and they become momentarily aware that they are not forty-watt bulbs, but two hundred and fifty, five hundred, a thousand...Then the voltage drops, *and they sink back to forty watts without a protest.* They are like empty-headed fools who cannot remember anything for more than a few seconds. Human beings are so mediocre that they can scarcely be said to possess minds in any real sense. In a flash, I understood the absurd and obvious truth : nothing is worth possessing except intensity of consciousness. This is the truth we glimpse in the orgasm. If human beings understood it—if their minds were not so incapable of understanding even the simplest things—they would abandon all other pursuits for this one. What does it matter where you are, what you are doing, how much you possess, if your mind is limp and feeble?—just as the most beautiful surroundings mean nothing to a man suffering from a fever. On the other hand, because Esmond had understood this, and pursued the secret, he had solved the problem that occupied Proust throughout the twelve volumes of the *Recherche de Temps Perdu,* the problem of how to tap our enormous and unimpaired stores of memory. If I try to recall my childhood, my memories are a dim carbon copy of the real thing. Yet some accident, like Proust's biscuit dipped in tea, can momentarily revive some distant time as vividly as if it happened yesterday. Why is the memory so feeble? Because consciousness is contented to run at forty watts, when it has all the power of the universe available to it.

In this moment, I recalled suddenly an event that should have taught me what Esmond knew. A few years ago, a schoolgirl had written me a letter about one of my books. She sounded intelligent, so I met her in Cork—where she was at a convent school. She was a dazzling girl—one of those lovely, healthy, self-confident products of a wealthy home with riding stables and great lawns. She fascinated me—not because she had any power over my emotions—which were fully committed to Diana—but because perfection always fascinates, in a landscape, a race-horse or a symphony. Apparently I fascinated her too, for she declared her intention of marrying me, although she was a Catholic and she knew I was married. She expected her family to use their influence to get a Papal dispensation.

During the holidays, her family sent her to Dublin to stay with an aunt, and I was able to find opportunities to see her about once a week. The whole thing was fairly innocent, physically. At sixteen, she was a romantic virgin; she was infatuated with me, but afraid of sex. And then one day, just before she was due to return to school, she apparently decided that it was time to allow the affair to progress a stage further. It was a rainy August afternoon. We had parked in some woods at the edge of a great estate. And ten minutes or so after we had begun to pet in the back of the car, I realised that she had decided to allow me as many liberties as possible, without actually yielding her virginity. But her own temerity frightened her. She allowed me to unhook her bra and remove her pants, then suddenly began to worry in case anyone looked in through the windows of the car—which were too steamed-up for anything to be visible. Aching with frustration, I locked the doors of the car to reassure her. Then I set out to make her forget her guilt in physical excitement. It took a long time—a very long time. It struck me that part of her trouble was that she felt like a harlot without her pants, so I put them on again. This made her confident enough to allow me to lie across her, with her skirt around her waist; but when I tried to move into a position where friction would satisfy my own excitement as well as hers, she became frightened again, and I had to start from the beginning. I found her so delicious that

253

I would have happily started a hundred times over; she aroused in me the appetite of a starving man. To be in this situation, caressing the most beautiful girl I had ever kissed, seemed more like a sexual daydream than reality. The final act of lovemaking was unimportant; absorbing her femininity was enough to slake my thirst. An hour later, when I realised that she had reached a pitch of excitement that dissolved all barriers, I deliberately kept my word, and allowed my accumulated excitement to explode harmlessly against her. It was enough that she had withdrawn all prohibitions.

But as I drove home, after dropping her back in College Green, I was aware that my consciousness had not relapsed to its old level of fatigue. My two hours of intense concentration had implanted in it a *habit* of intensity, of refusal to allow the energies to sink back to their source in the subconscious. And as I drove back slowly through the dark, I was aware that my mind had achieved a new level of power; the heartbeat of my vitality was deeper, stronger; my memory functioned better than usual; my capacity for intuition was deepened...And the long drive home failed to lessen the intensity; I arrived at dawn, feeling as fresh as when I set out from Dublin.

And yet I had allowed myself to relapse back to the old level. My discovery was wasted : the knowledge that two hours of concentrated effort can intensify the mind until it approaches the vision of mystics. And now, in this room, surrounded by prostrate men and women, I rediscovered that insight. They looked strange to me, as if I had never seen them before. This room was not familiar. Familiarity is a function of the fatigue of consciousness; to a fully awake mind, everything seems new.

I was free of sexual excitement. My chief feeling towards these people was one of amused contempt. As Norma moved convulsively against my hand, I felt that she was caught up in a reflex over which she had no control. At the same time, it struck me with great force that I was completely the master of my own sexual desire. Whether or not these women attracted me, I could perform my male function. It was an interesting idea, although not particularly attractive. It was far more interesting to recall the exact intonation of Doctor Johnson's voice and the aggressive outward thrust of his lower lip as he said : ' Sir...', the malicious twitch that convulsed the left corner of Voltaire's mouth before he delivered himself of a witticism, the high, strained note of Shelley's voice as he read his *Adonais* aloud to me. But Esmond had a point he wanted to make, and since he was my mentor, I was willing to wait. At the moment, he wanted to demonstrate to me that sexual desire is entirely a matter of imagination—or of intentionality, as I would say. My attitude towards Norma could be altered according to my own will. I could see her as a rather stupid, oversexed girl who was incapable of thinking beyond the pleasure of her loins, or as an incarnation of the earth goddess. And if I chose to regard her in this way, then I should make a formal act of obeisance, like a priest before the altar. Accordingly, I removed her pants, then my own, and climbed on to her. She opened her eyes in surprise for a moment, then gasped sharply as I entered her, and began to move under me. Since this was an act of ritual worship, not of desire, I concentrated on giving her the maximum of pleasure, adjusting my forward drive to her movements.

In spite of my detachment, it was like having sex for the first time in my life. Most of us are aware that sex is sometimes better than at other times. Entering a girl can generate an electric shock like accidentally putting your finger into a light socket, or it can seem dull and ordinary, a physical act like any other. This is because of the human capacity to go into a hypnotic state of blankness, of taking-for-granted. I was not only not taking Norma for granted; I was aware that she was simultaneously every girl in the world. I felt like an eagle poised in the air, looking down into an immense gulf.

The power being generated by Esmond was affecting the others in the room. They felt it as an obscure excitement, 'a certain odour on the wind'. Some were watching us; others were following my example and ignoring Körner's rule against actual copulation. I felt a hand running gently down my back, over my buttocks, then between my legs; it was Tessa, leaning over me, an oddly dreamy expression on her face. Suddenly, I remembered whom she reminded me of; it was Minou Bauer, Esmond's first mistress; I had not known her surname before, but now I remembered it. I increased my speed, feeling Norma's mounting excitement; then, as her stomach curved and pressed tightly against my own, I simulated a climax, feeling at the same time Tessa's fingers squeezing and kneading me. Norma relaxed slowly; I withdrew. Someone said: 'My God.' It was Gwyneth, who was standing on the other side of us and staring with admiration at the member that, even to my own eyes, seemed unusually swollen. Alastair, who had just risen to his knees from a girl I at first mistook for Angela, said with amazement: 'Incredible!' Tessa seized my elbow and said: 'Now me.' Gwyneth pushed her aside, seizing me lower still, and said firmly: 'No, me.' As far as I was concerned, it made no difference. Esmond, for reasons of his own, was determined to complete the demonstration. And although his memory was accessible to me, my own consciousness could not embrace the full extent of his intentions. I only knew that he intended to use my body to satisfy as many of the women who should choose to call upon his services. And so, when Gwyneth leaned back against the wall, pressing the instrument of pleasure against her moist outer lips, I reached my hand behind her, and guided it to the orifice; then, with an upward thrust, penetrated and drove until she was pressed tightly against the wall. The position was not entirely comfortable, since I was taller than she. There was a table close behind me; I moved backwards and rested on its corner, drawing her astride me. She groaned, pressing down, then raised herself and plunged down quickly; I pulled her close to me, holding her tightly against me, somehow conscious of her as though she were a familiar musical instrument. It was her intention to remain there as long as possible; her capacity for sexual stimulation was almost limitless, and the present situation appealed to an element of exhibitionism in her nymphomania. Esmond had other plans; he was skilled in the principle of the conditioned reflex; a few delicately sensual thrusts undermined her control; then a surge of what I can only describe as sexual electricity made her contact points—the points of the nipples and the distended anus—spark with an intolerable pleasure that approached pain. She gave a wailing scream, writhing and twisting, and I had to prevent her from falling off me. As I kept her pressed against me, the convulsions subsided; the moan changed into a deep sigh. I pushed her gently off my lap, and supported her as she sank to the carpet. The unfatigued godhead sprang upright like a jack-in-the-box, and I was startled by a burst of applause. Seated with my back to the rest of the room, I was unaware of the audience that had gathered to watch. Paul and Angela were leading the clapping and cheering. Paul said : 'You are a Master ', and I realised with a shock that he knew more of the Sect of the Phoenix than I had supposed. I restrained the immodest comment that Esmond started to make. Angela pushed towards me, but Tessa was there first, saying : 'No, it's me ', and pressed me back against the table, trying to move on to me. I helped her—since she was even smaller than Gwyneth—and lifted her slightly before allowing her to sink down upon me. Her head collapsed on my shoulder, and she gave a long sigh, then began to move slowly, as if tired, giving small cries as she did so, like some tiny animal being beaten. I put one hand up the T-shirt and pinched her nipple; she convulsed gently, her small tongue thrust deep into my mouth, and went slack against me. As I eased her gently off me, a man with a Scottish accent said loudly : ' The man's a freak.'

It was Angela's turn next; she pulled me over to the rug, in front of the fire, and flung herself down, her knees bent. With her, I made a new discovery. It was as exciting as after the visit to the Dunkelmans. Obviously, there was something about her, or about the psychic-chemical combination of the two of us, that made us curiously well adapted for producing the maximum pleasure in one another. This is a factor that has seldom been observed by writers on sex, who seem to feel that the difference between one act of intercourse and another is purely a matter of the meanings one chooses to project into it. It was so delightful with Angela that I was tempted to relax my control and cease to withhold my tribute, if only as a matter of common politeness. Five minutes would have been enough for recovery. But this was not part of Esmond's purpose; he seemed to be determined to continue the exhibition, for reasons of his own. I began to feel like the engine of a powerful car that reaches the temperature of perfect performance. There was no fatigue; my body seemed to hurtle forward at eighty miles an hour, the movements of my hips taking on a strangely weighted quality, almost resembling a pendulum. I increased speed to bring Angela to her climax, crushed her against me until her violence had spent itself, then moved on to the woman who was already waiting on the other side of me. Something was happening to me, a sense of dissociation from my body, almost as if my mind had separated from it, and hung above us. When I thought back on my ordinary sex life, it seemed an undisciplined waste. Each time a man moves into a girl, a god awakens in him, a god who is dissatisfied with the dreary, beetle existence we lead; who knows that man was made for vast horizons, for infinite conquest, for a superb purity of will. And as flesh encounters alien flesh, his brain is gripped by a sharp clarity of purpose that refuses to tolerate the normal fuzziness and heaviness of the flesh. Like a superb officer, it can make this squad of sloppy recruits we call the body drill like a crack regiment. Then the orgasm passes; the officer is forgotten, the sloppiness is back.

Esmond was not doing this for fun. On one level, this was a demonstration. Without words, he was telling us that the real objection to Casanova, Don Juan, Frank Harris and the rest, is that their seductions were oases of purpose in a desert of undiscipline; they soared for a second like eagles, then plunged back into the swamp. Esmond was telling me that the aim is *to stay in the air.* What would we say of a general who drove out a horde of invaders, then retreated from the captured territory and allowed them to return immediately? But this is what has happened to human beings; and they take it so much for granted that the invaders plod in directly behind the retreating rearguard, with no attempt at concealment. Esmond wanted to demonstrate that sexual intensity offers an insight as valid as mystical vision, and far easier to induce; but if it is to be effective, it must be disciplined with a passion equal to that of the yoga or ascetic.

After the fifth woman, the sex ceased to interest me; I was dazzled by the truth that had stared me in the face all my life. Every time we are deeply happy we know that there is only one good : strength of will; and only one evil : to abnegate the will. If life is as good as we know it to be in our moments of delight, then all obstacles should be regarded as molehills; man should be undefeatable. As I looked around this room of naked goddesses, a deep joy rose in me. These were the mothers, the procreators of the race, whom men have always enslaved and degraded. I worshipped them as divinities. Their loins are man's entrance to the world of dreams, of greatness, of the primeval purpose that lies behind matter. I saw no distinction between them, between the young and pretty and the tense middle-aged. The desire to serve them all was impersonal and free of lust. I stood up, and took the hand of a thin, neurotic-looking girl who had been waiting; we moved over to the corner of the room. A part of my being stood behind an altar draped in red velvet, in a temple of carved sandstone; I wore a mask in the shape of the head of a great bird. Forty naked women stood in a row before the congregation; their bodies shone with oil, and each held in her hand a phial in which glowed a green, effervescent liquid whose nature I suddenly understood.

I woke up with the sunlight on my face, and with a surprising feeling of well-being. My muscles ached, but my body tingled with suppressed energy. I looked at the girl beside me—a girl whose name was unknown to me—and felt a surge of pity. Oddly enough, she had been a virgin. She had accepted me as a husband; but I was Diana's husband and Mopsy's father. I have not mentioned Diana much in the course of this narrative; but I had phoned her every day, and thought about her whenever I had time to relax and think. Unlike Esmond, I am a home lover; now I wanted to get back to it.

I slipped gently out of bed, and made my way back to my own room. I took a cotton dressing-gown out of my case and a towel from the rack, and went downstairs. The morning was delicious, full of the smells of April grass. I made my way to the stream, which was on the other side of a row of fuchsia bushes at the edge of the lawn. A surprised rabbit hurried off into the undergrowth, without haste. The stream was shallow, but near the weir it was waist deep. It was so cold that I had to take my feet out after a few moments, and allow the ache to subside. Then I lowered myself in, and squeezed water over my chest and back with a sponge. I stayed in until I began to feel cold, then spread the towel on the dewy lawn, and stretched out in the sun. In ten minutes, I was dry.

I knew I had to leave here before the others were awake. If I stayed, there would be personal involvements with too many people. Every woman I had made love to would feel that it was her right to take away a small part of my life. My only objection to this was that there were too many. I would have enjoyed getting involved with every one of them; but there was only one of me.

Back in the house, I woke up Angela—and told her I wanted to leave. She was asleep in her own room, and she yawned, smiled, and opened her arms. I kissed her and shook my head. 'Not now.' 'You must be tired.' She reached down, and slid her hand into my dressing-gown. 'Good heavens.' Her tongue went into my mouth. I tossed the clothes off the bed, and moved on top of her. She was still sleepy. It was warm and pleasant, but not explosive. I tried to withdraw for my orgasm, but she shook her head, and held me tight. After this, I covered her up again. 'Can I take your car?' 'Of course, but you don't have to go.' I took her car key from her handbag, and the front-door key of the flat. I said : 'Apologise to Körner, and tell him he can reach me at the flat any time today. He'll understand.'

Ten minutes later I was driving towards London, suddenly intensely happy, my brain seething with insights and ideas.

What interested me most, of course, was the question of Esmond. My studies in psychology and occultism (of which I have written a history) had convinced me that two personalities may exist in the same body. The strange case of 'the three faces of Eve' is a classic of psychology that no one has tried to explain: the quiet, well-behaved housewife who would suddenly turn into a fun-loving tart. The strangest feature of this case, reported by Thigpen and Cleckley*, is that while the housewife was completely ignorant of what happened when the good-time girl took over her body, the good-time girl was conversant with all her alter-ego's activities. And Diana told me of a case that she

* *The Three Faces of Eve*, by Corbett H. Thigpen and Hervey M. Cleckley. London, Secker and Warburg, 1957. The 'third face' was the cured and integrated Eve.

actually witnessed as a teenager. One of her uncles went mountain climbing in Switzerland; one day, his sister-in-law—with whom Diana was staying—began talking in her uncle's voice, using his vocal inflections and tone of voice (although, of course, her voice remained feminine). This continued for three days until her uncle's body was found in a crevasse, then stopped.

We have no explanation for such things, and it would not matter greatly if we had; it would probably be the wrong one. All that interested me was that, in some sense, Esmond was not dead. This was the only outstanding and important fact.

There were other problems. What had Esmond said that produced such a startling effect on Körner? What did Körner know about Esmond, and how did he find out?

But this was only a small part of what occupied my mind as I drove back to London. What was really important was what I had learned last night. Esmond had found some way of sustaining the orgasm, keeping it burning for hours. This meant that he had taken a step beyond any human being who had so far existed. What fascinated me was the thought of the vistas of will and consciousness that had been opened up. Already, my will felt stronger, my consciousness somehow broader, deeper. All my life, I have obscurely felt myself in the grip of powers beyond myself, that are somehow manipulating me by remote control. If I am tired, and my brain feels dull, I am easily discouraged, and become a bad instrument of these powers. On the other hand, if I keep faith, and drive myself hard, and keep up a high level of optimism by sheer will and imagination, I have a sense of being used for a purpose that goes beyond my own, and seems to endow me with new powers. There is a sense of inevitability and ease, and I feel mildly surprised, like a sparrow that suddenly finds itself flying at the speed of a jet aeroplane.

In *Fifine at the Fair*, Browning argues that man is like a swimmer, floating on his back in a calm sea. He cannot fly like a butterfly; if he tries to raise his shoulders too far out of the water, the rest of his body sinks. And if his head goes under the water, he drowns. That, says Browning, is the position of the artist; only his head can emerge from life, and discover freedom in a world of imagination; the rest of him is doomed to remain in the water, subject to the law of floating bodies. As an evolutionary existentialist, I have never accepted this stoical view. I am certain that these powers of imagination and ecstasy developed by the romantics presage a new stage in human development. In *Fifine* (which is about Don Juan), Browning accepts that man is inconstant, that his sexual desires give him glimpses of some alluring reality, which vanishes and leaves him bewildered and empty-handed. What I had always suspected is that this need not be so. We possess powers we are hardly aware of in the dull round of everyday life, to make the spirit rage like a tempest or sink into a breathless calm verging on ecstasy. In order to discover these, we must push ourselves to new limits. The man who sticks to everyday habit catches no startling glimpses of self-discovery. But exploration of the physical universe offers no possibility of new revelations. We have to master the strange trick of allowing the body to remain quiescent, while pushing the mind to explore interior savannahs and mountain ranges.

And quite clearly, Esmond, with the aid of sex, had taken a huge step in that direction. No wonder he was able to make use of my body and brain. We had both devoted our life to the pursuit of the same idea. Across two centuries, our minds reached like outstretched hands, and clasped. There were many respects in which I had advanced further than had been possible for Esmond, for I had experienced another hundred and fifty years of European culture. But his will had reached further and deeper than mine. What might not be possible for our minds in combination?

It was shortly after ten when I got back to the flat. I was ravenously hungry. I found some good gammon in the refrigerator, and cooked half a dozen slices of it with three eggs. After eating that, with toast, marmalade, apple juice and coffee, I felt better. The feeling of well-being, of expanded awareness, continued. It struck me that the chief problem with human consciousness is that it is focused upon the present most of the time. Only in moments of relaxation—holiday moments—do we achieve a state where it is at once *fully awake* and yet *unfocused*. It is a trick; to overcome the old habit of allowing consciousness to become

262

relaxed when it is unfocused. Here was I, full of a sense of strange potentiality, my mind completely alert, and yet not focused on anything in particular. The consequence was that almost anything I looked at or thought about filled me with excitement and elusive insights.

Alastair had a rather fine edition of the poems of Chatterton on his shelf. I had never read the Rowley forgeries; yet as I looked at them, I had a sense of knowledge, of familiarity. I took them off the shelf and looked at Chatterton's dates : 1752–1770. He was four years Esmond's junior, and apparently in London for the last four months of his life—before he took a dose of arsenic. Esmond could have met him. I sat in the chair by the window, the book open on my knee, and emptied my mind. Instantly, I was Esmond; he appeared like an old friend, behind my eyes, looking at the book. I knew the answer to my question. He had never met Chatterton—he had been in Göttingen when Chatterton was in London; but he had spoken to Walpole about Chatterton the previous Christmas. Walpole had been furious because the boy had sent him verses that purported to be by a certain Abbot John; Walpole had been taken in until the poet Gray declared them forgeries. He wrote to Chatterton, gently hinting that he should use his talents to better purpose, and received in reply what he described as 'an abusive screed'. In telling Esmond this story, Walpole had omitted to mention that Gray had discovered the forgery; he took the credit himself.

The telephone rang; I assumed it would be Körner or Angela. But when the heavy German voice asked 'Is Mr Sorme there? ', I knew I had made a mistake to answer. I said 'Speaking' with forced briskness.

'Ah, thank heavens. This is Annaleise Dunkelman. I have been trying to contact you all weekend. How are you? '

We exchanged polite courtesies for a moment; then she said : 'Listen, it is important that I see you. Can you come over here? '

'I'm awfully sorry, but that's impossible. I'm leaving for Ireland this afternoon...'

While I talked to her, I felt a curious tingling of the loins, and the thought of her open thighs and the genitals under rose-coloured silk suddenly came back to me with great clarity. It struck me that Esmond would understand this, but it was too difficult to try to make my mind a blank as she talked. Suddenly, the line went dead. I assumed we had been cut off, and hung up. It struck me this might be a good moment to ring Diana in Maycullen—so that if Anna Dunkelman rang back she'd find the line engaged. I dialled the operator, and a few minutes later was talking to Mopsy, who told me that Mummy was in the greenhouse. A few minutes later Diana came on the line, and told me she had been trying to get me since yesterday; Fleisher had managed to get a film offer for his Donelly materials, and wanted an immediate reply. The sum was very large indeed. But Fleisher proposed to take fifty per cent, which struck me as excessive. We talked for nearly twenty minutes; I told her I hoped to be back within a couple of days, and to do nothing about the telegram. Then the doorbell rang. I said goodbye quickly, and went to glance out of the window. Anna Dunkelman stood on the front step.

I was tempted not to answer it, but this seemed cowardly; besides, she had probably heard my voice on the telephone—I had opened the window. I went and let her in.

She smiled at me in an exuberant, possessive manner.

' Ah, my dear Gerard, it is good to see you again.' She seized both my hands, and pressed against me affectionately for a moment. I found myself wondering if she was wearing the gauze panties, and felt a twinge in my loins.

The astonishing thing was that she was the sort of person I would normally have found downright repellent. She wasn't bad-looking and her figure was good—if hefty—but I found her basically masculine. In some odd way, this seemed to increase her attraction by dissolving the normal male–female barrier, and substituting a comradely frankness. I had to admit, she had the charm and plausibility of the devil.

She even had the subtlety not to refer to her attempts to contact me; that would have implied reproach. She was all warmth; we were old friends who had come together, and were delighted to see one another.

She asked me where my friends were. I said they were out for the day. I thought I detected a flicker of self-congratulation. She

264

said: 'A pity. I wanted to meet this young man. He sounds intelligent.'

She unbuttoned her coat and I helped her off with it. She was wearing a dress of soft brown material, and her large breasts made it strain outwards. It was very short.

She sat down on the settee—rather demurely, with her knees together, turned sideways; but the shortness of her dress made it inevitable that she showed the tops of her stockings, and an area of thigh. I offered her coffee. She said:

'No thankyou. I want to talk to you about many things. To begin with, if you are in Ireland, you need a literary helper, yes?'

I said perhaps, very cautiously; but I must admit that I was beginning to wonder whether Körner had not been exaggerating about the Dunkelmans. She radiated warmth, and a kindly vitality.

'Good. I have just the person. There is a young girl called Clara Viebig, a Swiss. When I told her I have met you, she can hardly believe it. She has all your books, and a great scrapbook full of Press cuttings of you.' She smiled confidentially. 'Of course, this is the kind of infatuation that happens to young girls —she has only just left college. She says she has written to you twice but had no reply.' (This could have been true; I reply to letters only when I have no other writing to do.) 'Now this girl has a lot of free time—her father makes her a good allowance and she does some studies at London University. As soon as I told her about your work on Donelly, she has offered to be your literary correspondent in London. She wants nothing for this. She only wants to work with you...'

I found it all flattering. No writer ever gets so blasé that he doesn't enjoy female admiration. I found myself charmed with Frau Dunkelman's disinterestedness; obviously, she was not the jealous type.

'Good. I told Clara we would try to go to see her some time today. She lives in Notting Hill Gate, so it is close. I have a picture of her.' She opened her handbag and took out a wallet. I stood up to fetch it; she also stood up, and began searching in the wallet. She was wearing some faint but very pleasant perfume, and the soft material of the dress moulded the curve of her breasts and hips. 'Ah, here it is.' She moved closer to me, and her buttock pressed lightly against my loins. I experienced a tingle of desire that almost made me jump. The picture she was showing me was of a girl in ski-costume, standing at the top of a ski-jump. The girl seemed to be pretty and slim, but it was hard to tell.

What surprised me was the pleasure I was deriving from leaning against Anna Dunkelman. She was lightly pressed against me, leafing through pages of the photograph wallet, and the warmth that came through the thin dress seemed to communicate itself directly to my penis. She seemed to have several photographs of Clara Viebig. A close-up showed a pretty but slightly masculine girl with high cheekbones and a great deal of dark hair. She reminded me vaguely of Anna Dunkelman.

Standing here behind her, looking over her shoulder, I was puzzled at the violence of my desire. Our sexual responses are so complex that it is hard to tell why a certain person exercises attraction; in this case, I was reluctant to place the entire blame on my subconscious. I stared blankly at the picture of the girl, trying to remember something. Suddenly, Anna Dunkelman said: 'You feel warm.' And without self-consciousness, she reached back and slipped her hand between her buttock and my loins. She left it there, flat, for a moment, then ran a fingertip lightly along the length of my now throbbing penis. I did what I had been thinking about since she came in: reached down to the bottom of her skirt, and slipped my hand above the top of her stockings.

'That is good. We are friends. There is no reason why we should not treat one another with frankness. I am too old to be your lover, of course, and neither of us want this. But there is still a vestigial male–female attraction between us. We can be frank about this.'

It was the right approach. The thought of carrying Anna Dunkelman to bed would have worried me. But she expected nothing. She said:

'You will find that Clara is much more your type. She is a sweet girl. We should go and see her.'

266

I thought this might be a good idea. I was beginning to experience the same unhealthy lust as in the taxi with Angela, the kind of thing an exhibitionist probably feels : the desire to do something indecent with my penis. Anna Dunkelman's wet cleft seemed an ideal receptacle for it. On the other hand, caution told me it would be better to skip it. I said :

'Yes. Why don't we go over there now?'

'Good. But first, I want to tell you a little about our plans...' She took my hand quite naturally, and drew me to the settee. I sat down beside her. From her handbag she took several typed sheets. 'This is in German. Do you read German? Then I will translate.' She was sitting in the familiar position, leaning back, her thighs apart, the dress over the tops of her stockings. Her thigh was touching me, and I felt something like a faint trickle of electricity running from it direct to my loins.

And then, abruptly, Esmond was there, and everything changed. It felt as if I had suddenly stepped out of my body, and was looking at myself from some other part of the room. The fever passed away. At the same time, with no definable mental process, I understood. Anna Dunkelman had power, a curious, primeval power that all women possess instinctively. But in most women it is buried under layers of personality, of inhibition. Anna Dunkelman had learned to free this power, and direct it. It would not be inaccurate to speak of it as a form of magic; the actual powers possessed by witches are basically of the same nature. And this, I saw in a flash, is why Witches' Sabbaths are traditionally licentious, with the stripping off of clothes, intercourse with goats, and so on. She throws off inhibition and learns to concentrate her natural sexual power.

Esmond understood Anna Dunkelman; he had known many of her type, and most of them were even more gifted. I found myself looking into Anna Dunkelman's mind, and feeling a gruesome fascination. Unlike her husband, this one was not a pervert. Perversion springs from some deep psychological block. Klaus was hypnotised by the forbidden; the thought that anything was forbidden was enough to give him an erection. Like de Sade, he wanted to be wicked, to spend his life in a search for new and shocking things to do. Anna Dunkelman's sexuality complemented this perfectly. The maternal instinct in her had been distorted into a kind of voracity. I saw clearly that she was bisexual, and that Clara Viebig was her lover. Her attitude to sex was oddly masculine : she would have liked to be possessed by every healthy male in the world, and to possess every pretty female. And she was insatiably curious; she wanted to be ' in ' on everything. This, I saw, was her motive in grasping at me. I could add an air of intellectual solvency to her ' group ' and attract disciples. Her plan was that I should possess her and Clara Viebig before the day was out; then it would be Clara's task to keep a hold on me, with the airs of an infatuated disciple.

I am not pretending that I could read Anna Dunkelman's mind. All this was, in a sense, speculation : but speculation based upon Esmond's enormous experience. It seemed obvious. And now I understood, it even seemed a little pathetic. She had too much energy and not enough opportunity to use it. Why should she not grasp at any possibility? It was understandable.

She was unaware that she had ' lost ' me; my insight came in a flash, while she was still unfolding the typed sheets. She held these open in one hand; the other moved between us, increasing the contact. And it was at this point that Esmond began to amuse himself. What he did was simply to draw upon my own sexual forces, and direct them against her. In fact, this was not entirely strange to me. I had always done it unconsciously, when in contact with any girl who attracted me. If a woman wishes to attract, she may flutter her eyelids or flaunt her charms; but if she is subtle, she keeps the surface demure, and uses the inner-telepathic charm that Anna Dunkelman was now using. The male seldom flaunts his attractions openly; from the beginning, his method is to appear disinterested. In a sense, therefore, I had an advantage over Anna Dunkelman in this matter. But I would not have known it without Esmond's experience.

I felt guilty about it; I didn't really want to attract her. But I had to admit that there was poetic justice in it. It had become a game, a duel with wooden swords.

She started to translate; and then the hand holding the paper trembled. She was resisting. She was used to being the witch, not the bewitched; she found the sensation unpleasant and bewilder-

268

ing. I said politely: 'Go on', and increased the flow. She started to read: 'The rules for a freely co-operative group of students of Reich...', then stopped. 'We ought to find another name for them', I said. 'Yes...we must think of a name...' She regained confidence and went on reading.

I had observed that her dress was zipped at the back, and held at the top with an enormous button. Now I understood its significance. Her loins were a weapon of aggression, a fly-trap for males; but her breasts were part of her femininity, the maternal part of her. I pointed at a sentence on the paper, saying: 'What does that mean?' The bone of my wrist touched the point of her breast. She winced and drew away. I placed my hand firmly on the breast and held it; for a moment, she lost control and tried to push it away with as little calculation as a frightened girl. Then she gained control again, and said in a remarkably steady voice: 'That is a quotation from Reich...' and began to translate it. I reached behind her, and carefully undid the large button. She repressed the temptation to stop me; after all, it was she who had talked about 'treating one another with frankness'. I pulled down the zip, and saw that her back was bare, except for the strap of her bra. I untied a bow at her waist, and drew the zip down to its limit, below the top of her panties. She said: You are distracting me!' 'You're distracting me.' She tried to press back against the settee, but she was too late; I had already unclipped the bra. She sat back hard, and for the first time her control slipped; she was suddenly unsure of herself, tempted to fight me. Without looking at her face, I took hold of the shoulders of the dress, and drew it forward. It came away from her shoulders, which were white and statuesque. She would have looked excellent in a shoulderless dress in a Second Empire ballroom. Her breasts were large, and still good. I was struck by their whiteness, and the contrasting red of the nipples. I placed a hand over each of them and felt warmth flowing into her. There was something admirable in the way she tried to regain control, and partly succeeded. I knew what was happening to her, from the way her legs opened. She was experiencing the same feverish tingling I had felt earlier. She reached over and laid her hand on my trousers, then pulled down the zip of my

269

fly. Before she could reach inside, I said : ' Stand up.' She hesitated, then did as I ordered. The dress fell on to the floor; she
stood there in the pink panties, with a suspender belt over them,
and sheer stockings. I drew her close to me, and took a nipple in
my mouth. She began to tremble, and her hand strayed between
her thighs and pressed tight. Then she saw that my own excitement was rising to meet her, and reached her hand down. I
transferred to the other nipple. She suddenly raised her hands
to her waist and started to push her panties down. The suspender
belt prevented this, so she had to push the belt down too. I
reached up one hand, and slid it between her thighs. Her genitals,
which had obviously been recently shaved, were very firm, and
the faint smell of animal excitement that came from them was
pleasant. I felt her increasing tension, and her unwillingness to
go any further; she wanted me to take the lead now. But as my
finger pressed into the warm cleft, she suddenly said : ' Please! '
It came out like an explosion.

I laid her on the settee, and bared myself fully. As I moved
on to her, she tried to reach down to guide me; I pushed her
hand away. The panties and suspender belt formed a tangle in
the area of her loins. I brought the head of my penis against the
material of the panties and pushed. It entered the cleft and was
caressed by warmth. She made another attempt to push the
gauzy material aside, but as she did so, I pushed forward hard,
at the same time pressing her breast with one hand. Her resistance vanished; I felt her dissolve, gasping, as the tide of the
orgasm swept from her breasts to her loins, then back again. At
the last moment, she sank into a solipsist universe in which there
was only a pleasure that came close to pain. Her eyes were closed
tightly, her loins tensed, her body arched upwards. Slowly, the
frenzy passed, and she relaxed. She kept her eyes closed. I understood why; she did not want to look at me.

The sound of the telephone startled us both. I zipped my
trousers as I crossed the room to it.

A man's voice said : ' Mr Sorme? '

' Speaking.'

' You don't know me. My name's Nigel St Leger. I wonder if
I could come and see you? '

270

' *The* Nigel St Leger? '

He gave an embarrassed laugh. ' I suppose you could say so. Could I come and talk to you about the death of Horace Glenney? '

' Well, yes, of course. When? '

' I'm quite close to you at the moment. Could I come over now? '

' Of course. Do you know the address? '

' Oh yes. Be with you in a few minutes.'

When I looked around, Anna Dunkelman was already clasping her bra. She said nothing. She stood up, and I helped her to pull up her panties. I felt her resistance, but she made no attempt to prevent me. I picked up her dress and helped her on with it. Then she said :

' I suppose you think I am very stupid? '

' No.' I didn't know what else to say.

I could feel her getting angry. I held out her coat. She said :

' Why did you not tell me? '

I said the first thing that came into my head.

' Perhaps I wasn't allowed to.'

She stared at me, suddenly interested. For a long moment her eyes stared into mine. She said :

' I think I understand.'

That was more than I could say.

She went towards the door.

' Well, we remain friends.' She said it in her bluff, hearty manner. She was back in control again. She stood there, her coat open, her hand held out, her legs planted firmly apart. But it seemed absurd. I looked at the upstanding breasts, and down to her thighs; she was a woman pretending to be a man.

And then, suddenly, she blushed. I had not realised the look had been so obvious. She dropped the hand, turned without a word, and wrenched open the door. I made no attempt to follow her. To begin with, I was glad to see her go. Secondly, I suddenly felt sorry. Esmond's game may have been amusing; but it had left her exposed and vulnerable. What could she do now? Try to cultivate her feminine aspect? It would only lead to frustration. It struck me suddenly that there was one fundamental difference between Esmond and myself. He belonged to the eighteenth century, before the age of sensibility. For him, Anna Dunkelman's discomfiture was funny; and beyond that, unimportant.

I went to the window as I heard the car draw up outside; I recognised Nigel St Leger before he stepped out on to the pavement. I had never seen him in the television series that made him known to so many people; but I had a book about his cases, with a great many photographs. He was smaller than I had expected; but his walk had a determined forward drive that indicated something about his character.

I met him at the door. 'Mr Sorme?' He shook my hand, but the smile struck me as bleak. I led him into the flat. He was a good-looking man, powerfully built, in his early fifties. I could imagine that his penetrating, rather cold stare had worried a great many prisoners in the dock.

I said: 'Who told you I was here?'

He looked at me sharply, as if tempted to say 'I'm asking the questions'; then said: 'Dr Körner, naturally.'

He took a cigar case out of his pocket, and offered it to me; I shook my head. He came over to me as I stood by the window, and stared into my face. He said: 'I've never read any of your books, but I shall take care to do so now.'

I said nothing. He crossed to a chess table near the window, and absent-mindedly moved one of the chess-men.

'Do you play dominoes, Mr Sorme?'

I said nothing. I was trying to make my mind a blank. St Leger stood looking at me, fixing me with his best prosecuting stare. Esmond said:

'Greetings, domino.'

St Leger was startled, and showed it. He recovered by going to the settee and sitting down. He said:

'I gather you know a great deal, Mr Sorme. But you don't belong to our house. And the Grand Master has never heard of you.'

I knew I had better leave this to Esmond. There was no time to take my bearings. Esmond said:

'Then you should have, shouldn't you?'

St Leger lit his cigar.

'Apparently so. If all I hear is true.' He tried to relax. 'Let me make myself clear. I am not denying your right to belong. Your qualifications are obviously great. Incidentally, where do you live?'

'In Ireland.'

'Ah.' I thought he seemed to expand. 'Of course, there hasn't been anything in Ireland for seventy years. Perhaps we might do something there.'

He stared at the tip of his cigar; I had a feeling that he wasn't certain how to handle this. Then he looked across at me.

'How *did* you find out, Mr Sorme?'

Esmond offered me no lead. I decided to tell the truth.

'An American publisher asked me to write about Esmond Donelly. For the past few months I've been trying to track down his journals and papers.'

'And you knew nothing before this?'

'No.'

'I see.' He seemed relieved. There was a ring at the doorbell, and we both started. He said: 'Are you expecting someone?'

'No.'

'I see. Then I think I know who it is. Would you mind?'

But it was Angela. She said: 'Chris gave me a lift. He's had a terrible row with Otto...' She came into the room, and saw St Leger, who stood up politely to greet her. She obviously recognised him. I introduced them, and they shook hands. He displayed a great deal more cordiality towards Angela than he had showed so far.

'You're a member of Dr Körner's group? Charming! I presume it was you who introduced Mr Sorme?'

'You know about them?' she asked.

'Oh yes, I know about them.' Angela looked at me, hoping for information. I said:

'Sir Nigel is the domino of the English house of the Sect of the Phoenix.'

St Leger went pale; for a moment, I thought he was going to lose his temper. Angela said:

'Is he joking?'

St Leger was obviously put out.

' He certainly has an unfortunate sense of humour.'

Angela said to me : ' Körner thinks you're in the Sect of the Phoenix. What did you say to him? '

St Leger cut in : ' If you'll excuse me, I think this is a subject that should be dropped. It could be dangerous.'

Angela said : ' Dangerous? '

St Leger stared at her for several seconds, then stood up and went over to the window. I got the impression he felt more comfortable on his feet. He looked out of the window, then said :

' You asked me about the assassination of Lord Glenney. It is not a subject about which I know a great deal, but I can tell you one thing. Glenney was not the intended victim. Esmond Donelly was.'

As he said this, I experienced a momentary feeling of dizziness, as if something had blurred in my brain. In some way I cannot explain, it was the sound of St Leger's voice saying ' Esmond Donelly ' that did it. I have said that during the past week I had frequently felt as if Esmond and myself were inhabiting the same brain. But we were like strangers, and his memory was not available to me. And now, it was as if everything became clear, like a microscope suddenly becoming focused; as if Esmond's mind and mine clicked together and blended. I knew that this *could* have happened a week ago; but the final adjustment was wanting. Now there were no more questions; Esmond's memory and mine had intermingled. And now, when Angela asked St Leger how he knew it was true, I found myself saying :

' I can tell you that.'

St Leger said : ' You can't possibly know.'

I said : ' Glenney's great mistake was to name names. In the original version of *Letters from a Mountain* he names Abdallah Yahya as the Grand Master, and mentions that Hendrik van Griss was the domino of Holland. Esmond persuaded him to change the names in the printed version, but it still caused an upheaval in the movement. Van Griss wanted to have Esmond assassinated; Yahya refused. In 1791, van Griss poisoned Yahya. From then on, Esmond knew he might be killed any time. He woke up one morning in Paris, and found a dagger driven into his pillow. This was one of their favourite tricks—to demoralise

a man with fear before they killed him. It was used by tne
original Assassins—the Ismailis—by way of a threat. They once
made Saladin raise a siege of the Assassin Grand Master by
leaving a dagger stuck in his pillow. Esmond took the warning,
and went to Russia, then to Greece. When he got back, he discovered that Glenney had committed the ultimate folly: he'd
published his pamphlet denouncing the Sect, and naming van
Griss as the new Grand Master. That was the last straw as far
as van Griss was concerned. He had a little French assassin
who'd trained in Turkey—a man called Jacques Crevea—and
he sent him after Esmond. It was Crevea who killed Horace
Glenney—in Esmond's bed.'

'But what was Glenney doing in Esmond's bed?'

'He'd told Esmond some silly story about seeing a ghost in his
own room. Esmond agreed to sleep in it for a week—he didn't
believe in ghosts. Of course, Glenney didn't really believe he was
in danger—the room was seventy feet above the ground, and he
kept the door locked. He didn't know that Crevea was known as
The Fly.

St Leger was looking astounded. He said:

'All this could be true, but I doubt it. No one knows the
details. It became one of the most closely guarded secrets of
the Sect. There is probably only one person in the world at the
moment who knows the details.'

Angela waited for him to go on; then, when he was silent,
asked:

'Who is that?'

I said: 'The present Grand Master.'

She said: 'Then it *does* still exist?' She looked at St Leger.
'And he wasn't joking?'

St Leger turned around angrily.

'My dear young lady, my advice to you is to ask as few
questions as possible. I am extremely sorry that you returned
when you did, and even more sorry that Mr Sorme has been so
indiscreet.'

I was beginning to feel angry with St Leger; the pompous
manner was getting on my nerves. I now understood a great deal
about him. He had the basic requirement for a domino of the

275

Sect : the sexual obsession. It was present in his manner towards Angela; she was potential bed-fodder; he was already imagining her spread underneath him, her eyes closed. He was an attractive man, sexually and personally. And he was a long way from being a fool. But he was an actor. It showed in the way he had walked across the room before his announcement about Glenney's assassination. And I represented a serious threat to him; this explained why his manner towards me was so edgy. I felt disappointed that my first contact with the Sect should be through a man like this.

I heard a car draw up outside. St Leger said :

' And now, I think I must leave you.'

I went over and stood beside him. It was a London Airport taxi. He was already moving to the door. I said :

' I don't think there's any point in leaving. Since you were expecting him, we may as well see him.'

He said quietly : ' Will you excuse me.' He turned to Angela. ' I hope we shall meet again.'

I slipped past him, and went to the door. He came after me, saying angrily : ' Really, Mr Sorme, this is...'

A man had got out of the taxi, and was looking at the numbers of the houses. He was very big, and his face was brown and scarred. His eyes met mine; then he saw St Leger behind me, and smiled. St Leger said, with sudden authority : ' I would be grateful if you would wait here a moment.' He went past me and down the steps. I saw no point in pushing him further, so I went back into the house. Angela was standing by the window.

' What on earth's happening? Who's that man? '

' I assume he's something to do with the Sect of the Phoenix. Beyond that, I don't know.'

From behind the curtains, I watched St Leger talking to the dark man. I said :

' He's worried about you being here.'

' Would you like me to go out? '

' It might be the simplest solution.'

The two men now came towards the house. I went out to meet them.

' The young lady is going out now, if you'd like to come in.'

The big man stared at me inscrutably. I thought he was going to ignore me. Then St Leger said: 'This is Mr Sorme. Mr Xalide Nuri.' At this, he held out his hand, and said how do you do. His silence, I realised, had been Eastern punctiliousness. Then Nuri said:

'I think there is no need to trouble your friend. Mr St Leger has a car. He could take us to my home.'

'I'd be happy to.' St Leger was showing his nervousness. It was not his day.

I said: 'Would you excuse me a moment?' I went back into the house and told Angela I was going with them. Then I asked her if she'd ever heard of a man called Xalide Nuri. She looked startled. 'Of course.' 'Who is he?' 'Some sort of millionaire—oil, I think. His name's always being mentioned with Onassis and Paul Getty. You must have seen it.' I explained that the world of high finance was the least of my interests.

'Watch him. He's the sort of person who has real power.'

I went out again, closing the door behind me. A grey, chauffeur-driven Daimler had moved in front of the house. The chauffeur opened the door for us. As we sat down, Nuri said disapprovingly: 'Too conspicuous.'

St Leger reddened. 'I always use it.'

I saw Angela's shape behind the lace curtain as we pulled away. She was probably wondering whether the Sect still maintained a staff of assassins.

Neither of them spoke until we were turning down Park Lane. Then St Leger said: 'It was kind of you to come so far.' Nuri acknowledged it with a bow of his head, as if it were a compliment. Then he said:

'It may, as you say, be important.' There was no rebuke in his tone, but St Leger reddened again.

My sense of Esmond's presence had vanished. These events were too unusual not to create a tension in me, and tension made my own personality too dominant. I relaxed by thinking about Anna Dunkelman. It had been a satisfying experience—and one of which I would have been incapable without Esmond. His personality had a confidence, a forward-drive, that I found liberating.

We had stopped in front of a house in Brook Street. Nuri

said : 'We are here.' Then he looked at St Leger. 'Thankyou for driving us here.' His meaning was clear. St Leger said : 'It's a pleasure...', and opened the door for us. I stood there, blinking in the bright sunlight, looking at the gay summer dresses of women in Grsovenor Square, feeling that what was happening was somehow irrelevant.

Before we reached the front door, it opened. I somehow expected an Eastern manservant, but it was an ordinary English butler who let us in. Without St Leger, Nuri seemed more relaxed. He said :

'I do not live here, but I keep this place for my weekends in London. It is convenient.'

It was a typical rich man's house; comfortable, discreetly furnished. Only the balustrade of the stairs suggested the East; it was of a fine, wrought ironwork that might have come from a sultan's harem.

We went up the stairs, through a drawing room with a grand piano and Matisses on the wall, into a library. He waved me to a deep armchair.

'Can I offer you a drink? Tea or coffee, perhaps? I drink coffee all the time.' He pressed a bell.

Now I looked more closely at Nuri, I seemed to recognise him. Perhaps I had seen pictures of him. He was over six feet tall, and the face and bearing were somehow those of a soldier. He wore a light, double-breasted grey suit. His hair was short-cropped and going grey. The face was scarred, but handsome with the cold attraction of a bird of prey. His movements were economical, brief, as if he felt grace to be effeminate.

He sat down opposite me and offered me a cigarette; I refused. He took out a black and gold Russian cigarette and tapped it against the case.

'I have come from Paris to see you, Mr Sorme. Because if half of what St Leger tells me is true, we have much to say to one another. Do you know who I am?'

'Yes. You're the present Grand Master.'

'You guessed that, of course.'

'It was a fair inference. You're not a domino, or St Leger wouldn't have been so nervous of you.'

278

He laughed, showing excellent white teeth.

'That man is a fool. He should not be a domino.'

'Then why is he? You have the authority to remove him.'

'Alas, no longer. Our organisation is more democratic than in the days of Esmond Donelly.'

The butler came in, pushing a trolley, and left immediately. As he poured coffee, Nuri said:

'We must not waste time, Mr Sorme. We have much to say, and I have to be back in Paris tonight. There is much about you that puzzles me. You seem to have access to a great deal of information. That means either that someone has been indiscreet, or that you have found documents of whose existence we were unaware.' I said nothing. He went on: 'So far, you might be anyone. But now I discover that you are something of a prodigy. Our friend Körner tells me you have undone two years of patient work with what sounds like an impossible feat. I presume he was not exaggerating?' I said nothing. 'I take your silence to mean he was not.' He placed the small cup of Turkish coffee in front of me. 'Who are you? Where do you come from? How do you know so much?'

'My name is Gerard Sorme, and I'm a writer. As to how I know so much, the answer is that I don't.'

Nuri offered me a plate of small, round biscuits with the coffee. They were flavoured with cinnamon, and I found the taste agreeable. He said:

'That is a strange statement. I wonder if you would mind if I investigate it?'

I did not understand what he meant, but I said no, of course not. He reached out and pressed a button. Neither of us spoke for the next few minutes. It was a comfortable feeling, sitting in silence; there was something in Nuri's personality that made it seem natural. The door opened very quietly, and a man came into the room. I had to look carefully to decide that it was a man. The tow-coloured hair was fluffy and long, and the face looked as if someone had drained every drop of blood from his body, allowing the veins to collapse. His eyes were so pale that they seemed colourless. Although he was wearing Arab dress— a dirty yellowish robe—he was unmistakably a Westerner. Nuri

279

paid no attention to him. He sat down on a low stool, roughly between the two of us. I saw that his toes were long and knobbly, like something out of a horror film, and the nails were yellow, grainy and curved.

Nuri said: 'This is Boris Kahn.' The man ignored us, staring into space. 'He used to make a living as a mind reader in the theatre. Then his powers developed to an extent that frightened him, and he became an addict of heroin. I found him crawling one night in the gutter with a broken neck—he had fallen from a second-floor window. Now he travels with me when I have important business. He is completely mindless, but he knows when people are telling the truth.' He took another cigarette out of the case, then said: 'Did St Leger tell you I was the Grand Master?'

'No.'

'I didn't think so. But I wanted to be sure.'

I was looking at 'Boris' curiously. He was eyeing the cinnamon cakes in my lap with avidity.

'How does he indicate if someone isn't telling the truth?'

'It would be easy enough to arrange a demonstration.' He pointed towards the window, and snapped his fingers. Boris quickly hurried across to the window, bent almost double, like a frightened dog, and slipped behind a heavy velvet curtain. Nuri pressed another button on the table. About thirty seconds later, there was a sound of feet pattering across the carpet of the room next door. The door opened, and a girl ran in. She stopped at the door, glanced at me in an odd, suspicious way, then ran across to Nuri and flung her arms round his neck, making absurd chirruping noises. She was wearing long Arabic trousers and a blouse, but they were so transparent that she might as well have been naked. I would have judged her to be about sixteen. Her figure was well developed, her hair long and dark. She was kissing Nuri repeatedly, like a small child welcoming a favourite uncle. He smiled indulgently, and let her continue for a moment. Then he said to me:

'This is Kristy, the baby of our household.' He sat her on his knee. 'And how is our baby?' His hand slipped inside the transparent trousers. She obediently opened her legs, and his hand slipped between them and felt her crotch. 'Has she been good?' The girl nodded her head enthusiastically, her face as vacant as a doll's. It struck me that Nuri had a taste for mindless people. 'Has she had any lovers since I was here last?' She looked virtuous, and shook her head emphatically. From behind the curtain there came an odd noise, a kind of 'chuk-chuk-chuk', like an animal coughing. The girl rushed over to the curtain, tore it aside, and dragged out Boris by his hair. She screamed : 'Liar.' He lay quiescent on the floor, his cheek against the carpet, his buttocks raised in the air. When she drew back her slippered foot and kicked him in the ribs, he did not even move. She rushed back to Nuri and flung her arms round him. 'Baby's not a liar. *He's* a liar.'

Nuri caressed her back affectionately. 'How many?'

'None.' The completely virtuous expression came back and she shook her head. The odd chuk-ing noise came from Boris's throat. She was about to leap up and rush across to him again, but Nuri held her by the wrist, and repeated : 'How many?' She pouted.

'Three.'

The chuk-ing noise sounded again. She screamed at Boris : 'I'll kill you.'

Nuri said indulgently : 'Baby's a bad little nymphomaniac, isn't she?'

'Not', said the girl, looking like a Quakeress.

'Baby deserves a spanking, doesn't she?'

'No.' She was pleading. 'He's a liar.'

'How many?'

She scowled across at Boris. 'Seven.'

No sound came from him. Nuri said : 'Men, or times?'

'Men.'

'Seven smacks, then.'

She stood up, pushed down the trousers to her knees, and then lay across his knees. He took a leather slipper from under the chair, raised it, and gave the round, pink bottom a resounding smack. She yowled half-heartedly. The howls became louder and more genuine as he smacked her six more times. At the seventh smack, she leapt off his knee. He shook his head, and said :

'One more.'

She bent over, and Nuri gave her one more hard smack. Then he said. 'Now run along.'

When she had gone, Nuri said :

'Now, Mr Sorme, you say that you know nothing about the Sect of the Phoenix? '

'I didn't say that. I know far less than you suppose.'

'I don't see how that can be true.' He looked across at Boris. I also looked at Boris, who was now sitting on the carpet, hugging his knees. Boris was looking puzzled.

Nuri was looking at Boris. He said : 'What does he mean, Boris? '

Boris stared at him blankly out of his pale eyes, as if trying to avoid the question by pretending not to understand; but as Nuri's hard stare remained fixed, he said in a slow, stuttering voice :

'He...he...he...mm-m-means he...he's...m-m-more than one p-p-person...'

Nuri said : 'Is that what you mean, Mr Sorme? '

I said : 'I'm afraid it would be pointless to try to explain. You'd doubt my sanity.'

Nuri looked at Boris, and said like a whip-crack :

'What does he mean? '

Boris, startled, said in his weak, throaty voice :

'He's someone called Esmond.'

Nuri's eyes swept on to me; I could see that his face could be very menacing.

'You are not Gerard Sorme? '

'Yes.'

'Who is Esmond? '

'You know. Esmond Donelly.'

He stared very hard at me, as if wondering if he had understood correctly. Then, to my surprise, the blood drained from his face, and the stare became fixed. He said : 'That is impossible ', but his voice was suddenly thick.

And then Esmond was looking at him with my eyes, peering hard into his eyes. Nuri's face changed. I would have liked to

282

look into a mirror to see what he saw. Whatever it was, it convinced him. It took him several seconds to control himself. His lips had gone white, and the red scars stood out on his grey face. He said :

'You were right, then. You learned how to come back.'

Esmond only nodded. Boris was staring at Nuri in a frightened manner, like an animal which cannot understand what is wrong with its master. Nuri stood up, and crossed to the sideboard. He picked up a decanter, and his hand shook as he poured into the tumbler. Then he gulped it down. Whatever it was—it was clear, like arrack—it made his eyes water, and constricted his breathing for a moment. He wiped the sweat from his face, then came and sat down, glancing up at Esmond as if hoping it had all been a mistake. He said :

'Forgive me. You cannot expect me to accept this easily.' He leaned back in the chair and closed his eyes. Staring out through Esmond's eyes, I found myself puzzled at why Nuri had been convinced so quickly. Esmond waited. It was his moment. Nuri sat up, and gestured at Boris. 'Get out.' Boris hurried out of the door. Nuri said :

'What do you want me to do? Resign the mastership? '

Esmond said patiently :

'No. I couldn't become Master if I wanted to. Mr Sorme has other things to do. But there must be a return to the agreement of 1830.'

Nuri made for the sideboard, and poured himself another drink without apology. He said :

'I don't see how that's possible. It would mean breaking our oath.'

'It's the only way, believe me.' He was being patient and reassuring. 'Listen, Xalide, I don't blame you. You've been an excellent Master. But important things are happening. Even this fool Körner is a portent of the future. New men are developing. The human mind is reaching out for powers that I only glimpsed. In many respects, this Sorme knows far more than I do. You've got to be ready to play an important part. You can't do this as a secret society.'

Nuri said : 'The other dominoes would never agree.'

'They won't have a choice. This man Sorme knows all about us. He will publish everything that he knows. And it will be up to you to protect him.'

Nuri sat down again. He was beginning to take a grip on himself, but I thought he looked ten years older. Esmond said kindly :

'Listen, Xalide, let me explain. When I joined the Sect, two hundred years ago, it was a society of lechers. Their basic idea was that a small élite should possess complete sexual freedom. It was a good idea as far as it went, and I accepted it. I did what all the others did—rhapsodised about the magic, the poetry, the mystical ecstasy of sticking the prick in a strange cunt. I possessed inner-power, and it developed until no woman could resist me for more than a day or so. You know some of the things I did. I persuaded frightened convent girls to surrender their virginity in the course of an evening. I slept with three queens and eight princesses. I've possessed women I'd met only ten minutes before —inhibited women who thought afterwards that they'd been bewitched. By the time I was thirty-five, I'd probably had a more complete sex life than any man who ever lived. And then I began to outgrow it. I got tired of being a mere instrument of a force I didn't understand. When I felt like a god in the moment of supreme achievement, I asked myself the question : Is this the real Esmond Donelly? Or am I the fashionable rake who uses his intellect and sincerity to seduce clever women? One day in Moscow, I watched a brutal cabman beating his horse, and before I knocked out his teeth, I felt sickened by his gloating sadism. Later the same day, I got the youngest daughter of the Tsar into a summer-house, and persuaded her to let me take her maidenhead. And as my penis forced its way inside her, I had a sudden vision of the cabman's face, and knew I was doing the same thing—deriving pleasure from *imposing my will* on something weaker, enjoying the sensation of power. And I realised that I'd been doing this for twenty years, repeating the same stupid act as if to reassure myself that I wasn't a boring fool like the rest of the young bloods. Suddenly, I felt miserable and ashamed. My revulsion took the form of feeling sorry for the girl, so I even contemplated the folly of asking her to elope with

284

me. Then I saw this would be another cul-de-sac. This is the end of most repentant rakes; they try to make themselves feel moral by treating the girl like a human being instead of a city under siege. In fact, it's no more moral than dropping a shilling in the poorbox to salve your conscience. The answer was not to substitute one form of stupidity for another, but to try to understand the nature of the will-o'-the-wisp I kept pursuing through the undergrowth of petticoats.

'When I got back to Ireland, I saw a girl I had known many years before—a girl I'd seduced when I was fifteen. It brought back the memory of that summer in the barn behind our house. I stood in the barn and remembered everything. And then I saw what had gone wrong. When I first possessed Minou and Delphine, I expected a future of infinite potentiality. I expected life to treat me like a favourite child. And indeed, it did. But I allowed myself to become too passive. I accepted the pleasure, but I failed to make any real effort. The first time I entered Minou, I felt god-like. But a hundred more seductions did nothing to redeem that promise of divinity. On the contrary, they destroyed it, for it became a matter of habit.'

He stopped. His voice—I can hardly call it mine, for even to me it sounded different—had had a soothing effect on Nuri, as he intended it to. It must also be remembered that Esmond was using my brain, my vocabulary, my memory associations, and that since these could express his thoughts more concisely than his own natural language, the words came tumbling out at a speed that was sometimes hard to follow. The effort of concentration had calmed Nuri, restored the self-possession. Esmond said :

'Are you following my train of thought? '

'What you say is not strange to me. I have often been struck by similar thoughts, but I could see no answer.'

'The answer is closer than you think. Mr Sorme has almost found it himself. I had one great natural advantage—I had always thought of myself as a favoured child. That is important —the optimism, the forward-drive. I had the audacity to ask whether the god-like states did not represent the truth of my inner being. When I decided that the answer was yes, only one simple question remained : why does the mind sink back into a state of dullness when the orgasm is over? '

'Surely because we cannot sustain such intensity? A kettle that stays on the fire is soon empty.'

'No. That is muddled thinking. The ecstasy of the orgasm is not the result of the release of energy, but of the vision that accompanies it. You can have the orgasm without the vision, if your mind is tired. Or you can have the vision without the orgasm, if the mind becomes absorbed in poetry or music. Do you get more tired than a blind man because you can see things that are invisible to him? No, the contrary is true, for the blind man is more likely to be bored, and boredom leads to tiredness. The question at issue is vision, and I quickly saw that we lose the vision because we stop trying to see it. We relax, we turn away from it, like a man yawning and closing his eyes.

'I had known holy men, men who had walked over mountains and deserts seeking the same vision, the constant awareness of the world as a mystery. Now I knew why they were obsessed by open spaces. Man has developed the power to concentrate on small things, like a Swiss watchmaker. And, like the watchmaker, he has grown short-sighted until he can no longer stare into the distance. The holy men were trying to correct their myopia by seeking out distances. I now saw why they were wasting their time; they were trying to exchange one faculty for another, and pursuing mountains in the same muddled, repetitive way that I had been pursuing women.

'Do you understand me? As soon as I became fully conscious of the possibility of a broader vision, I recognised that it depended upon the development of new faculties and new powers of will. At first, I did the most obvious thing. As the power of the orgasm flooded my brain, I tried to seize it, to refuse to allow it to recede. I soon found that I was developing a remarkable power of concentration. It is true that I could not cling on to the intensity of the orgasm. But once my mind was turned outward, like a young eagle that stares at the sky and tries to launch itself into the air, I could concentrate on widening my vision. Man's chief trouble is that he is timid. Every time he loses his sense of purpose, he stands still, and then retreats. Boredom makes him

286

wander in circles, and he wastes most of his life in this state. The pursuit of love gives him a momentary contact with his hidden springs of purpose, and this has been the deepest justification of our Sect. But the real need is plainly to turn these springs into fountains that never dry up. Boredom should be impossible. It is the emotional equivalent of losing your way in a desert. But as soon as the compass was invented, this ceased to be a problem. I saw that my task was to concentrate until I had developed a compass; a clear knowledge of my purpose. I saw that boredom is the enemy of the god-like, and that all my powers had to be directed to the overthrow of this enemy.'

Nuri said : 'And you did it. You succeeded.'

'Yes. And you will succeed too, now you have seen that it can be done. And Sorme will succeed. And when a dozen men have succeeded, the rest of the human race will follow. The springs of purpose are not buried very deeply. Even that little girl who was in here has the power, if she knew how to direct it. It is a mental trick, like jumping on to a galloping horse.'

The image I put into Esmond's mind was of a man using a wave to carry his surf-board, but he failed to understand it. Esmond lacked the concepts for explaining himself fully, the notion of the 'promotion' from one level of the being to another, the recognition that the human personality is a series of platforms. But I had them.

Nuri said : 'May I ask some questions? Where are you now? Is there literally another world beyond this one?'

Esmond laughed.

'What you call "this world" is what you can see through a crack in a door. It is like calling this room we are sitting in a world. Mr Sorme can explain this to you better than I can. He talks about life-worlds. As to where I am now, I cannot explain this easily. As I developed the power of my will, I began to understand things that ought to be self-evident. When you are tired, the spirit is held close in the embrace of the body. The more you become healthy and alive, the more you have a sense of controlling your body from a distance, as the falconer controls his bird. And at a certain point in the mental cycle, it becomes possible to achieve a degree of control over this body that you cannot even envisage. When this happens, all kinds of strange things can be done—for example, I can project what you call my astral body to great distances.'

'And this is what happened when you appeared at the Berlin meeting of 1830?'

'Quite. But do not overestimate the importance of this power; it is a mere by-product. What matters is the new degree of control over the body. For once this is established, it is almost impossible to die.'

Nuri said: 'But you died.'

'As you see.'

'But your body died in 1832. You were buried in the family vault in Ireland.'

Esmond said nothing; his memory was closed even from me. Then he said:

'Let us not waste time on irrelevancies. Let us say only that Mr Sorme has been an invaluable instrument, and that you should treat him with the same confidence that you would treat me. In return, he will be able to help you a great deal. Like myself, Mr Sorme is not basically interested in sex. He is something of a puritan. But I think he has seen some interesting possibilities in Körner's group. You can show him far more interesting things. I am relying on you.'

'What about you? Will you go away now?'

'No. But I really cannot keep imposing on Mr Sorme. He has his own work to do.'

I said aloud—for Nuri's benefit: 'You're welcome to drop in whenever you want to.'

'Thankyou. You are most hospitable.'

Nuri said: 'What do you want me to do immediately?'

'Nothing. Concentrate on the trick of leaping on the galloping horse. And remember one thing. Pessimism is a leaden weight around the feet. Defeat is always self-chosen. Mr Sorme can explain these things better than I can—he has his own system of philosophy based upon a man called Husserl. And now, my dear Xalide, I shall leave you. I would be grateful if you would also extend your protection to the present Lord Glenney, the great-great-great-great-great-great-great-grandson of my friend

Horace. He contains a large number of Horace's elements, so in a sense you might regard him as a reincarnation. Say nothing of what has taken place to that fool St Leger. He is not to be trusted.'

Then he was gone, and Nuri and I were alone. Nuri was not sure of this until I said : 'He's gone.'

He stood up. 'Well, Mr Sorme, I think we deserve a drink. Whisky?'

'A small one, thanks.'

As he poured, I said : 'How did you know that Esmond intended to come back?'

'There is a tradition, Mr Sorme, that he never died, and that the body buried in his family vault was that of an old mendicant. He also said as much in his diaries, which are now at my house on the island of Hendorabi. You and your family would be welcome guests there if you would like to examine them. They cease after the year 1800, which has always puzzled me. Now I understand.'

'There's one thing I'd like to ask him. Did he give up sex after this insight of his?'

'I think I can answer that. You are aware that he chose the youngest of the Ingestre sisters as a sort of divinity, and she later became a priestess at the headquarters of the Sect in Constantinople? You can read about this in the diaries. I believe he chose her because he said she had some secret quality of grace that made her more purely feminine than any woman he had ever known. The Sect treated her as a kind of divinity after Esmond became Master in 1810. After that, her daughter and then her granddaughter took her place. It is generally assumed that Esmond was the father of her daughter.'

'Who wrote the books attributed to Esmond—*The Deflowering of Maids* and so on?'

'That was written by Glenney himself, at a time when he wanted to discredit Esmond with the Sect. But there were many later forgeries. As Grand Master, Esmond was likely to have works attributed to him as minor Elizabethans foisted their plays on Shakespeare.'

'What did Esmond die of?'

He said : 'That is something that puzzles me. The story told by his biographer, Ismat al-Istakri, is that he suffered a brain haemorrhage after a ceremony in which he penetrated fifteen young women. This, of course, is possible; as Grand Master, it was sometimes his task to take part in such ceremonies. Yet I have never been able to accept this story completely. Now I am less sure than ever.'

' Is this biography in English? '

' Unfortunately, it is in Arabic. But I can have it translated for you.'

Glancing at my watch, I was surprised to see that it was after six. It struck me that Angela would be worrying about me. So I asked if I might make a phone call. I was right; Angela and Alastair were just debating whether they ought to call up the police. St Leger's dark hints about Glenney's murder had them worried. While I was still on the phone, the discreet butler sidled up to me. ' Excuse me, sir, but Mr Nuri suggested that you might like to ask your friends to come here for supper.' I passed the suggestion on to them, and they accepted immediately.

When I got back to the library, Nuri was wearing a beautifully brocaded dressing-gown, and four girls in transparent clothes were standing behind his chair. He said :

' Ah, Mr Sorme, I hope your friends have accepted my invitation? We have another hour to dinner. Have you ever tried the relaxing properties of an Imrali bath? It was invented by a Turkish Grand Master of the seventeenth century. These young ladies have learned the art to perfection. I suggest we have one now, before dinner, and perhaps you could explain how you came to hear about Esmond Donelly? '

It was the prelude to one of the most interesting evenings I have ever spent; but this is no place to describe it in detail. The history of the Sect of the Phoenix is a subject of such complexity and richness that it would be unfair to speak of it here. When the editing of the Donelly papers is complete, I shall hope to undertake the writing of it myself. Nuri also told us something of his own history, and ended by demonstrating some of those remarkable powers that led to his appointment as Grand Master. (This had occurred after a spectacular struggle with Ludwig Bindig, the German domino who was also an ex-Nazi. Bindig ran the famous 'sex camp', whose existence has been denied by recent German historians.)

We retired to bed, utterly exhausted, in the early hours of the morning. When we woke up, Nuri had left for Paris. Later the same day I flew back to Shannon, where Diana met me. When we returned home, we found a telegram from Nuri, asking if we could join him at his home on Hendorabi the following weekend. His private plane collected us at Shannon. In the four months since that date, we have basked in the sun, and I have written this account of my quest for Esmond.

My researches into Xalide Nuri's archives—aided by his excellent librarian, Dr Fa'iq Khassa—have answered most of the remaining questions about Esmond, and about the history of the Sect in the late eighteenth and early nineteenth centuries. These results will be published in due course. Angela—who is also working here—has already accumulated the basic materials for a biography of Esmond, on which we shall probably collaborate.

The chief problem that faced me in writing about my 'quest' was how far I could be frank about certain episodes. I have accepted Howard Fleisher's suggestion that I write everything as it occurred, and leave it to him to decide how much alteration is necessary.* I must also confess that I have not, so far, allowed Diana to read the manuscript; luckily, she is an understanding girl, and I can lay most of the blame on Esmond.

And what of Esmond? Since that afternoon in Brook Street, I have occasionally sensed his presence; but I cannot be certain that this is not my imagination. I often find myself thinking about a curious incident that took place late that night in Nuri's home. Boris had been demonstrating his powers of second sight for the benefit of Angela and Alastair. Nuri had put him into a

---

* When this book was in the proof stage, I heard that the remains of Colonel Donelly had been found in his burnt-out farmhouse; foul play is not suspected. I have accordingly restored the passage on Colonel Donelly to the form in which I wrote it.

hypnotic trance; and his answers to questions about our private lives were frighteningly accurate. Before he woke him, Nuri asked us if we had any questions we would like to put to the sleeper. Angela said :

' Yes. Can he tell us where Esmond is at the moment? '

Boris's sightless face turned to me.

' He is Esmond.'

Note to The God of the Labyrinth

Some time in 1968, the *Daily Telegraph* published a leading article deploring the increasing amount of pornography that is being printed, and citing myself and Miss Brigid Brophy as two ' serious ' writers who aim at larger sales by spicing their books with episodes that would have led to prosecution in less liberal times. I took no exception to this article, for it is true that I have written about sex in some of my books in a way that would not have been legally permissible fifty years ago. I do not think of myself as a writer of pornography; but if someone else wishes to do so, it is surely a matter of the point of view? A few weeks later, the *Telegraph* article was syndicated in a New Zealand newspaper, and a reader wrote a letter indignantly defending me; he pointed out that more than half my books are about such subjects as philosophy, art, music and literature, and that of my seven novels, four have little or no sex. When I read this letter I was convinced; I was not a pornographer. It is true that a New England bookseller had to appear in court for displaying *The Sex Diary of Gerard Sorme*, but nothing came of this. The judge's opinion was that although I was totally devoid of literary talent, the book was not technically obscene.

A few weeks after the *Telegraph* article, I was asked by a firm of solicitors if I would appear in court to give evidence in favour of a Bradford bookseller who was being prosecuted for selling *My Secret Life*, the sexual autobiography of an anonymous Victorian. I replied that I was too busy to travel to Yorkshire—a two-day journey from Cornwall—but that they were welcome to quote my opinion that the book was not pornography, and ought to be published openly in England. I offered to write a letter to this effect. And when I began thinking it out, I saw the difficulty

293

of the task facing the defence. *My Secret Life* has no literary merit. When Grove Press published it in America, they argued that it was a valuable social document of the Victorian era; but this is not true either. A sociologist could learn more from ten pages of Charles Booth or Henry Mayhew than from the three thousand pages of *My Secret Life*. Its author was the male version of a nymphomaniac. Sex was a vocation. He tried every possible kind of sexual experience over forty years or so, and then decided that it had all been so fascinating that he ought to write about it. Who can deny that he was right? It is true that not everybody would want to read it; but then, not everybody wants to read autobiographies of soldiers, politicians and travellers; that is no argument against them.

One cannot even say that *My Secret Life* was written ' without obscene intent ', or whatever the phrase is. He had enjoyed the sex, and he enjoyed writing about it. The man is a dirty-minded bore; to write at such length about sex argues complete empty-headedness. All the same, the book is real; it is a man's life; it is ' fact ', just as the massive volumes of White Papers the Webbs studied for their history of trade unionism were ' fact '. Now I agree that there is a case against the publication of certain kinds of unpleasant fact—for example, the details of sexual assault that emerge at murder trials; these could lead to imitative crimes. But anyone who imitates the author of *My Secret Life* will do no particular harm, or come to any; so this does not apply. I can think of no valid ground for suppressing the book—and certainly not for sentencing people who sell it to two years in gaol—as happened to the Bradford bookseller.

But the ' fact ' argument can hardly be applied to de Sade and *Fanny Hill* (whose publication I would also defend), particularly if they are kept fairly expensive, so that the cost acts as a ' filter ' where minors are concerned. I do not like de Sade; I do not think him ' significant ' in the way that Jean Paulhan and Mlle de Beauvoir apparently do. The basic spirit of his books is one of schoolboy revolt—like writing dirty words on walls. But I would not be in favour of suppressing his books. As to *Fanny Hill*, Cleland admits he wrote it for money; it is a prime example of what Sainte-Beuve called ' books that one reads with one hand '.

It is amusing, well written, and there is nothing in it that every adult reader does not already know.

It must be borne in mind that to suppress a book—to declare that it is unfit for public consumption—is the literary equivalent of executing a criminal, or burning a witch, or having a political opponent thrown in gaol. It is difficult to defend it impartially —with detachment. Like the Index of the Catholic Church or the Nazi burning of the books, it can only be defended on sectarian grounds : from the basis of accepted dogmas. We can argue against the open sale of drugs, or of intoxicating liquor to minors, on pragmatic grounds : it can cause physical damage. We know about the limits of the body; we know nothing about those of the mind. This kind of argument cannot be transferred to books.

I agree that all this sounds like special pleading—like a cunning lawyer who knows he has an indefensible case, and decides to try to blur the lines and confuse the issues. I get this feeling reading a great many liberal opponents of censorship. But when I look inside myself, I find I have a very definite intuition of what constitutes pornography and what doesn't. Let me try to explain the nature of this intuition.

I might take as a starting point a paragraph from my autobiography, *Voyage to a Beginning* :

> The hero [of *Ritual in the Dark*] is obsessed by the feeling that there *is* meaning in human existence, and that it is accessible to the mind—if only the mind knew the right way to go about finding it. One of the commonest 'meaning experiences' comes through sex, and therefore sex makes a valuable *starting point* for the search for meaning. (I italicize 'starting point' because it seems to me that nothing can be more futile than sex carried on as a kind of vocation —as by Casanova or Frank Harris.)

Sex *can* be the starting point of the 'search for meaning', the denial of Sartre's assertion that 'it is meaningless that we live and meaningless that we die'. This argument obviously applies to D. H. Lawrence, as well as to those books of mine that the

Telegraph had in mind. De Sade is defensible because he also saw sex as somehow containing the meaning of human existence. It is true that there are basic errors in his thinking—the failure to reckon with the ' law of diminishing returns '—that invalidate his work in the last analysis; it is a curious monument of error, like the geocentric theory of the universe or the phlogiston theory of combustion, and it remains a useful symbol of an interesting fallacy. It also makes an excellent starting point for existential philosophy. Dostoevsky's Kirilov argues that if there is no God, then man is god, and must prove it, and he carries this logic to the point of suicide. De Sade carries it into an ultimate defence of amorality. In either case, one can begin to argue fruitfully.

I get a feeling of real pornography when I read certain books that no one has ever thought of suppressing—books like *No Orchids for Miss Blandish,* or *The Carpetbaggers,* or even some of the James Bond novels. Forster accused Joyce of trying to cover the universe with mud; he was mistaken; the dirt and violence of *Ulysses* is intended to act in reverse, as an emetic. Joyce himself recognised his kinship with Swift. James Hadley Chase and Harold Robbins are out to please—and to make money by pleasing. The sex and violence—particularly the violence—are intended to make the meal more palatable. They are like brothel-keepers in that they are willing to cater for anyone who is willing to pay. And if one drags their premises into the light of day, one finds another version of the de Sade argument : that what gives pleasure is, by definition, good. But de Sade, like Voltaire or some modern logical positivist, was arguing against ' metaphysical ' notions of goodness. He says, in effect : ' People say that virtue, self-denial, self-sacrifice, public spirit, honour and bravery are good. I say this is just confused thinking. To the level-headed realist, only pleasure is good.' What he then proceeds to do is to refute himself by trying to demonstrate his thesis at exhaustive length. The only thing that surprises us is that he himself was not bored sick long before the end of *Juliette.* But at least he was clearly aware of the values he was trying to erode.

Now no one criticises Conan Doyle or Rider Haggard for not being as intelligent as Thomas Mann or Aldous Huxley. They set up as entertainers, and the 'values' they advocate—honour, bravery and so on—are in no way controversial. Since their time, the popular entertainer has become more realistic, more sophisticated. Unfortunately, not more intelligent. He rejects the older values—but not in the name of a questing intellect; only in the name of entertainment, of 'giving people what they want'. But the rejection of values—if it is to be a useful activity—must be fully conscious of its own nature. When we come across people who hold opinions they are not willing to think about, we rightly call them fools or bigots. And the objection to this kind of stupidity or bigotry is that it is somehow *life-denying*. I have a digestive and an excretory system to deal with the food I need to keep me alive. I have a mental digestive and excretory system to deal with my experience, and my growth as a human being depends upon this as my bodily growth depends on the physical system. If either system gets blocked, I shall be slowly poisoned. Ian Fleming and Harold Robbins do not possess a digestive and excretory system to deal with the values they reject. The result is a smell of decay, of a system blocked with its own waste products. If one reads them for too long, the result is that feeling of headache, of dyspepsia, of futility, that is the outcome of severe constipation.

This law also applies, of course, to much greater works of literature. One gets the same feeling of futility if one reads too much of Rolland's *Jean Christophe,* or Powys's *Wolf Solent,* or even *War and Peace.* These books possess a digestive system, but it is not big enough to deal with so much 'experience'. It is worth observing that a digestive system is not simply a capacity for abstract thought. Huxley or Mann are intelligent enough; yet their books are curiously static. What is important is a writer's capacity to *attack* his experience; not simply to 'suffer' it, but to get beyond it. Dostoevsky is never boring, in spite of his clumsy style and meandering length, because of this feeling of smouldering fires trying to *consume* his material, as a furnace smelts ore.

This defines my intuition of the nature of pornography. It is bound up with the question of the digestive system. We do not give rice to ducks, or suet pudding to small babies, because we know their digestive systems cannot cope; if I did so, knowing the result, I would be guilty of criminal negligence. The same applies to a writer who produces a sticky, undercooked mixture of sex and violence, aimed at the 'lowest common denominator' of reader.

This also explains why I would not consider *My Secret Life*, *Fanny Hill* or de Sade truly pornographic. The test is whether it contains this element of poison, of life-denial. *My Secret Life* becomes very dull and repetitious after the first few hundred pages, but it is no more 'poisonous' than *Hansard* or the *Congressional Record*. The narrator is coarse and stupid, but he is not cruel or mean. One might object to his basic values : to his feeling that sex is the most important human experience. But one can take it or leave it. There is nothing to prevent the reader putting a Beethoven quartet on the gramophone after reading a dozen pages or so. The same is true of *Fanny Hill*. As to de Sade, reading him provokes a reaction that would actually enhance the Beethoven quartet. The trouble with Hadley Chase or Harold Robbins is that after reading a few pages, one would no longer be capable of enjoying Beethoven. He would seem to be irrelevant to this vicious, dangerous, violent world in which we live, a 'beautiful ineffectual angel' living in his absurd musical dream-world.

In short, pornography involves a sense of the debasement of values. If art is a battle between man's mind and the material world, then the pornographer is on the side of the world. It is interesting to note that Fleming, Harold Robbins and Hadley Chase all exploit crime as well as sex, and often seem to equate the two as a kind of destructive activity. Shaw pointed out that we judge the artist by his highest moments, the criminal by his lowest. This means that art may be seen as an advocate of man's highest moments as against his lowest. The writer who exploits crime and violence purely to titillate the reader has become an advocate of the lowest. But if he goes on to treat sex in such a way as to bracket it with crime as one of man's lowest moments, the offence is compounded.

But now to the next stage of the argument. It will be noted that Thomas Mann and Aldous Huxley are also concerned about the

298

battle between the material world and the mind, and that both of them tend to be defeatists. I personally find Huxley almost as depressing as Graham Greene because the material world always seems to win by a short head. He talks about life-affirmation, but somehow, none of it ever seems to get through in his books. His ' affirmative ' people are always unpleasant and stupid; his sensitive people are always weak. The same is true of Thomas Mann, but his ' objectivity ' makes it less oppressive.

Life-denial, then, while it is an essential element of pornography, is not restricted to pornography. This raises the question of how far the converse is true. Is pornography possible if the spirit of life-denial *is not* present?

This is a more important question than it sounds. This question of morality and immorality, health and decadence, has been concerning us for nearly a century, ever since the great Zola and Ibsen controversies of the 1880s. The arguments on both sides have always been roughly the same. As early as 1782, Thomas Jefferson wrote : ' Those who labour in the earth are the chosen people of God…Corruption of morals in the mass of cultivators is a phenomenon of which no age nor nation has furnished an example.' These simple, primitive societies are like a healthy body; the rejection of ' corruption ' is an automatic function of the health. When the ' dubious ', the unhealthy, the corrupt, begin to find a foothold, it means, *ipso facto*, that decadence has set in. If my physical body became more susceptible to germs, I would take steps to cure it, to reject the germs; I would certainly not accept them as an interesting variation of the boring routine of being healthy. This is the line Max Nordau pursued in his *Degeneration* (1893); decadence should be recognised for what it is, not tolerated and encouraged. Shaw's counterblast, *The Sanity of Art*, was sub-titled : ' An exposure of the current nonsense about artists being degenerate ', and its argument could be summarised in the words : ' Not degeneration, but *development*.' Thomas Mann, who was writing his first stories at this time, took a less positive position (which he maintained all his life) : that as art becomes more sensitive and subtle, it develops *and* degenerates; evolution *means* degeneration, beyond a certain point. Spengler said the same thing in *The Decline of the West*.

Shaw disagreed fundamentally. He would have said : 'Of course, evolution *can* mean degeneration, if sensitivity outruns vitality. But it does not necessarily follow.' And this is obviously another form of the question we have already raised. Mann and Huxley were writers in whom sensitivity outran vitality. One might have thought that if sensitivity outruns vitality, it ought —in theory—to be possible to increase the vitality to match it. Neither of them believed this possible. But is this true? Let us suppose I have a crude and oversimplified view of something. The result is a head-on collision with reality which leaves me wiser—more sensitive—but, for the moment, less confident and assertive. Must I remain like this for the rest of my life? Obviously not. I make a mental effort, I *digest* the experience, contemplate it until I have absorbed all its implications : that is, until I have mastered it. Then the confidence returns; the vital springs flow again. That is to say, it depends upon the same 'digestive' act that I have already discussed in connection with pornography.

This view presents an alternative to the Jeffersonian position : that simplicity and health and stability all go together. If you upset the stability, you will upset the simplicity and health; but with a certain effort and a certain optimism, they can be re-established on a higher level, and the result will be a genuine evolution. The alternatives are not a stick-in-the-mud conservatism or galloping decadence.

All of which, then, would seem to argue not only that pornography cannot exist unless life-denial is present, but that what would be pornographic in the presence of life-denial would cease to be so in the presence of life-affirmation.

The conclusion may sound abstract; but for me, it was of immediate practical interest. When I started writing my first novel, in my late teens, I was obsessed by the problem that led Joyce to choose the Odyssey to provide the structure for his own chaotic novel of modern Dublin. The problem was expressed by Yeats in the three lines :

> Shakespearian fish swam the sea, far away from land;
> Romantic fish swam in nets coming to the hand;

But what are all those fish that lie gasping on the strand?

That is to say, Shakespearian art held a mirror up to Nature : or perhaps one should say, a magnifying glass. Its basic unit was the event, the story. Character is important, but only *within* the story; after all, it would not really matter if it was Hamlet who got jealous and murdered his wife, or Lear who became Thane of Cawdor. In romantic art, character *became* the story. Goethe's Werther, Senancour's Obermann, Hölderlin's Hyperion, are not interchangeable because they *are* the story. The magnifying glass moved closer, so that the basic unit ceased to be the event, and became the character.

A story will tell itself if you let it. But a character has to be lived by the author. Goethe had to *become* Werther and Wilhelm Meister in a way that Shakespeare never had to identify with Hamlet or Lear. But still, if the novelist got 'into' the character, the events then developed naturally; Wilhelm becomes the manager of a theatrical troupe, and Faust becomes a public benefactor.

That is, provided the character was clear-cut. But the essence of romanticism was its self-division, its sense of a lack of definite identity. And slowly, Werther gives way to Stephen Dedalus, Rilke's Malte Laurids Brigge, Sartre's Roquentin, Camus's Meursault—the last being the completely static hero—Kafka's K. The fish no longer has strength to swim, or even thrash around; in Beckett, it only gasps and flutters its tail. There is a gain in detail—the magnifying glass is now within an inch of the fish's nose—but no story is possible. And without a story, how can the novel be possible?

Joyce's solution was not generally applicable; in fact, as far as I know, he is the only person ever to attempt the 'mythological method'. The novel has stopped trying to solve the problem; it has regressed to an earlier stage, and come to terms with its loss of status.

The drama passed through a similar crisis in the twentieth century. It also drifted into subjectivism, symbolism, expressionism, even a kind of deliberate nightmare in Artaud's theatre of cruelty. It was Brecht who attempted to re-establish contact with the beginnings, with the source of the stream. Drama began as spectacle, as a story told to an audience who knew it was not reality. So why try to compete with the cinema? Why not make the best of the limitation; in fact, *affirm* the gap between the audience and the players? Yeats had been toying with the same idea—the theatre of ritual—but Brecht had the genius to combine the theatre of ritual with the lecture platform, the music hall and the soapbox.

I had written several novels before it struck me that what I was doing was to bring the Brechtian alienation effect to the novel. My first novel, *Ritual in the Dark*, began with a mythological structure based on the Egyptian *Book of the Dead*, until it struck me that if I intended to use a 'framework' that did not spring naturally from the inner-meanings of the story, I might as well choose a framework that could be accepted by ordinary readers. I chose the story of the Ripper murders and the structure of the psychological thriller. But it was still basically a realistic novel in the Dostoevsky tradition. In later novels, I aimed at the 'alienation effect' more consciously by choosing conventional forms, and aiming at an effect approximating to parody. In *Adrift in Soho*, it was the picaresque novel; in *Necessary Doubt*, the *roman policier*; in *The World of Violence*, the German *bildungsroman* with comic overtones; in *The Mind Parasites* and *The Philosopher's Stone*, science fiction; in *The Black Room**, the spy novel; in *The Glass Cage*, the detective novel again.

Now the letter that defended me against the charge of writing pornography raised a question in my mind. Could one use the form of the conventional pornographic novel, *à la* Cleland or Apollinaire, as the basic framework of a novel, and achieve this same alienation effect? I had tried something similar in *The Man Without a Shadow* (whose title was later changed—without consulting me—to *The Sex Diary of Gerard Sorme*) and I had observed then that writing about sex tends to destroy the alienation effect because the reader becomes involved. But the *Sex Diary* did not use the *form* of the pornographic novel, but of

* Still unpublished at the time of writing.

the confessional journal; it was a novel of ideas taking sex only as its starting point. It is an interesting challenge, for the pornographic novel is more rigidly formalised than any other type I can call to mind; it has something of the symbolic rigidity of a ballet. So much the better for the alienation effect. The challenge is, of course, to endow this structure with life. The trouble with the conventional pornographic novel—*Justine* may be taken as an example—is that one is aware that it is a series of 'set pieces' connected by an arbitrary thread of narrative, like a Monteverdi opera. I am far more interested in the story and the ideas than in the set pieces. I must also admit that, formally speaking, this book does not obey the rules of the pornographic novel so much as those of the detective story—particularly the literary detective story of the sort popularised in Russia by Irakly Andronnikov. The 'sect of the phoenix' is developed from a hint by Jorge Luis Borges. In fact, if *The Mind Parasites* and *The Philosopher's Stone* borrowed the mythology of H. P. Lovecraft, the present book may be said to be based on the mythologising of Borges.

The success or failure of this novel as an exercise in the alienation approach should not be taken as a measure of the value of the approach. I am convinced that the answer to the problem of the 'Shakespearian fish' and the stranded fish lies in applying the alienation effect to the novel, whether or not it works in this particular case. But I would argue that if it *can* work in this case, it can work anywhere.

There is a final point, which I raise with some hesitation, since it seems obvious. As we grow from childhood into adulthood, we enter new ranges of experience that would have been impractical or undesirable for a child, from drinking alcohol and smoking to climbing mountains and listening to string quartets. Sex stands out from all the other experiences as being one that must be treated as a kind of secret, as if it were some strange tribal initiation involving a name that may not be spoken. Now this may be essential for certain primitive tribes, or patriarchal societies; but how far is it desirable for a civilisation like ours whose basic aim (whatever gloomy historians say) *is* 'sweetness and light'? The evolution of Western civilisation has been an evolution of reason;

the rejection of the dogmatic and authoritarian element in religion, and also (hopefully) in politics. This evolution did not come to a halt when England rejected the pope, or Voltaire rejected Christianity; even Newman and the Oxford apostles must be seen as a development of the same trend, an insistence on the claims of a deeper, subtler reason related to man's metaphysical needs. Freud had to fight the same battle; to overrule social taboos and reticences with the demand for frankness and openmindedness; so did D. H. Lawrence. The extermination camps of the Nazis may be seen as an attempt to return to a more primitive—and uncomplicated—form of society, in which problems are solved by force and dogma, not by reason.

It seems to me that this development presupposes an important humanistic premise : that 'forbidden-ness' is bad in itself, although it may sometimes operate for the good on a limited scale. For example, sex murders are not committed by people who think and talk about sex without inhibition, but by people in whom frustration has built it up into something forbidden and darkly alluring. 'Forbidden-ness' should not be confused with discipline, which is basically a liberating factor. A good army is like a well-oiled machine; its discipline is the factor that allows it to run without friction.

If all this is true—and I find it hard to conceive any reasonable person denying it—then it follows that mature adults should be able to think of sexual experience as they think of any other form of experience—in art, science, sport, adventure. When I read Rider Haggard as a child, I experienced both detachment and involvement. The detachment came from sitting in an armchair reading a book, the excitement from marching through snake-infested jungles with Alan Quatermain. This is the essential quality of civilised experience—detachment *and* involvement. But where sex is concerned, this notion is still not accepted. We are supposed to be either directly involved—in bed with a partner —or totally detached, as when I read a case in Havelock Ellis and murmur 'How interesting'. There seems to be an element of absurdity about this. Most adult readers have had the basic experience that is described by Cleland or D. H. Lawrence; and, unlike cruelty or crime, this experience is not regarded as socially undesirable. Is there really such a gulf between the subject of sex and subjects like history, adventure, sport? Is there any reason why civilised adults should not, if they are so minded, read about sex with feelings of detachment, or humour, or even a certain involvement? If we can say that a thing is 'shocking', without meaning that it is ugly or wicked, then it seems to me an excellent idea to use it to shock as many people as possible, until it has lost its shock-effect, and can be seen calmly and without distortion. In a really civilised society—and we are still some distance from it—there will be no forbidden books, or forbidden ideas.